THE Daphne PROJECT

JACQUI LENTS

To my mom, Roni.
My biggest fan.

Playlist for The Daphne Project

1 Growing Pains – Alessia Cara

2 Gotta Get Up – Harry Nilsson

3 No More Tears (Enough is Enough) – Donna Summer and Barbra Streisand

4 I Am...I Said – Neil Diamond

5 The Pretender – Foo Fighters

6 Cake by The Ocean – DNCE

7 You Can't Make Old Friends – Kenny Rogers and Dolly Parton

8 Look What You Made Me Do – Taylor Swift

9 I've Been Waiting for You – ABBA

10 SOS – ABBA

11 Better Together – JJ Heller

12 Secret – The Pierces

13 Don't Stop – Fleetwood Mac

14 Bad Reputation – Joan Jett & the Blackhearts

15 I Am Woman – Helen Reddy

16 Slow Hands – Niall Horan

17 Who Knows Where the Time Goes – Nina Simone

18 If We're Honest – Francesca Battistelli

19 Time Waits For No One – Freddie Mercury

20 I'll Be There – Jess Glynne

Find the list on Spotify – The Daphne Project Book Playlist.

Chapter One

DAPHNE'S FOREHEAD CREASED AS she scrunched and squished her clothes as tightly as possible, wishing they would shrink in size. Her first attempt at packing involved an armful of beat-up duffle bags. Mrs. Sarah Patterson, her mother and the world's most capable woman, took one look at them, frowned, and returned with "proper" luggage. With great focus, Daphne continued transferring the wrinkled pile on her bed into a compact suitcase and an even smaller Louis Vuitton carry-on bag. Would it all fit?

Four physical books were all the space would allow, and that was only if she left her jacket behind. She shivered with horror. Only four? Which four? And she didn't have long to decide. Her phone held plenty of ebooks, but something about holding a paper copy in her hands brought her comfort.

Her mother frowned. "I don't see why you need more than a carry-on. You're making a quick trip to that godforsaken place, selling the house, and returning home. How many clothes do you think you'll need?"

Daphne sighed at the start of yet another fraught conversation. Daphne had inherited her mother's blonde hair but little beyond that. Sarah's straight, controlled tresses, taller stature, slim body, and blue eyes contrasted against Daphne's wild curls, five-foot-five curvy frame, and brown eyes that matched her father's.

She took a deep breath and screamed inside her head. *Home? This place is a prison, and I'm jailbreaking. Not even the Great Sarah Patterson can keep me here forever. I'm thirty years old. I can pack for myself. It's just two pieces of luggage. You can afford the extra bag, Mom.*

Oblivious to Daphne's barely controlled breathing and strained silence, her mother continued. "Make sure you leave room for your makeup bag." She looked at the lotions and powders scattered atop the dresser disapprovingly. "Some women can pull off that natural look, but we both know you are not one of them."

Have you forgotten that you purchased most of that makeup for me? I will be in Maine tomorrow, and you won't even know if I have any on. Do the women in the small town of Cobb even wear the stuff?

She tried to recall her aunt's face. Had she worn eyeshadow or blush? But she only saw a fuzzy image. It had been twenty years, and most of her memories of the woman had faded.

Daphne chose her next words carefully. A direct attack would never land. However, shamefully, exploiting her mom's sense of pride was not beneath her.

"Mother, I don't know what kind of outfits I will need. I want to look nice. I wouldn't want to embarrass the family or anything." She planned to bring comfortable but cute clothes, ready for warm or cool weather—both of which could be expected at the beginning of June in Maine.

"Fine. Whatever." Stepping into the hall, she shouted down to her husband. "Edgar! Go down and get the big blue suitcase!"

The rare victory in an argument with her mother ignited a spark of confidence in Daphne's soul.

But then her mother asked, "Did you see the printouts I left for you on the table?"

The spark fizzled out. *Shit. She gave in on the suitcase because she had been aiming for a bigger prize.*

She turned away from her mother and started counting out pairs of socks. "Yes, I saw the printouts. That was kind of you to think of me."

"It's time to get a job. We love having you home again. Of course, you can stay in your room as long as you need. It reminds me of when you were in high school." Her mom began searching through the closet and went on. "But you're not working yet. The ladies at the club ask about you, and I don't know what to say. It's embarrassing. You've been back for months, and nothing has changed. If you were dating someone, at least I could mention that."

"Mom, those jobs were not even with a library. One was for a receptionist at the funeral parlor in town. I have a master's degree, for heaven's sake."

She hated hearing the whiny tone of her voice, but she couldn't control it. She noticed it appeared more frequently when talking with her mother.

"Yes, dear, but what good is your fancy education? You lost your job and couldn't find another. Thank goodness your father and I were there to pick up the pieces and bring you back home. You need to start accepting responsibility for yourself and your choices, especially at your age. Real life isn't like your books. Without Wallace looking out for you all these years, I shudder to think what would have happened to you."

Daphne stared at the floor. She wanted to ask her mother if being with Wallace, the liar, was better than life as a spinster. She didn't. She never would. Hearing a yes might crush the little spirit she had left.

Her father appeared in the doorway to her room with a suitcase held out in one hand. His eyes looked tired. Daphne took the bag and felt sorry for him. With her gone, he would again be the sole focus of her mother's attention—this journey meant liberty for her, but more stress for him. They exchanged knowing glances. Then he returned to the den.

Sarah held out a sleek, black silk jacket and matching pencil skirt that shimmered on the hanger. "Ah, here it is."

"I'm going to a small town in Maine. What will I need that for?"

"When you talk to the Realtor. I want them to know they are not dealing with a local half-wit. I wish I were going with you."

Daphne's heart pounded so hard she could hear it in her ears. This trip offered her a bit of blessed independence. Her mother's presence would ruin everything. *Think fast, Daphne, or this will be over before it begins.*

"Mom, you are the co-president of the country club summer bazaar and cookout. They need you. It would be a disaster if you weren't there. Face it, Mrs. Bantry would make a mess of everything. I can handle this."

"You have a point. Mrs. Bantry was discussing some rather wild ideas for this year. I don't understand what she means by it. We have traditions for a reason. Make sure you pack the suit, Daphne. With two bags, you'll have plenty of room. I always knew a second bigger bag would be required."

Daphne accepted the neatly hung clothes, and her mother left the room. Closing the door, she fought the urge to cry out in frustration. Instead, she focused on her packing in an attempt to improve her mood. Tomorrow, a plane would whisk her away from her mother. With the money from the house sale, she'd be able to escape this nightmare. Her mom was right. Being in this house felt like high school all over—not her best years.

After moving home, she had turned to her books instead of hunting for a job. Life had knocked her down with a swift kick, and she felt entitled to lick her wounds for a bit. Comfort came from imagining herself as the heroine in Eva Gates's *Lighthouse Library Mystery* books and Jenny Colgan's *The Bookshop on the Corner*. The novels featured a woman living a fantastic life with the perfect bookish job. Daphne knew, just like the women in those books, she'd find her dream job again. Why shouldn't she?

Her freedom on the horizon, Daphne could see it unfold: a new library job, far from her parents. A cozy place of her own with enough shelves for her books. Maybe a return to Chicago or maybe a fun new destination full of friends and excitement. It would be a dream come true. And if a romance came along, that would be alright. She could see it in her head: a meet-cute with a handsome neighbor in her new apartment's elevator.

But she needed money to get her second chance. Her plan to fly into Cobb, sell the house, and get out from under her parents' roof had to work. Unbidden, a second, scarier vision flashed before her: If she didn't leave her parents' house soon, she would give in and apply to one of those unfulfilling jobs, like at the funeral home. Her mom would trick, guilt, or bribe some man into dating her. Under the constant browbeating, a white flag of surrender would wave, and Daphne would agree to a flavorless marriage. The Gothic image of her standing stony at the altar for her country club wedding was vivid in her mind. *Maybe it's time to cut back on the Brontes.*

Snapping out of her reverie and turning back to the bed, she found several more outfits that her mother had laid on her floral quilt. Daphne put them into the suitcase. She could leave them behind, but her mother would know. Looking for the silver lining, Daphne reminded herself she could bring more books with her thanks to the larger blue bag. But what did one read when settling an estranged relative's affairs?

Chapter Two

DAPHNE SAT AT HER deceased great-aunt's home, looking at an image of the older woman in a photograph. Adorned in a worn fishing hat, Florence Winkler returned Daphne's gaze. The cheap plastic frame encircled a face more wrinkled and tired than Daphne remembered. But shining from the steely blue eyes was the same assured, penetrating gaze that generated respect in Daphne years ago. She turned away from the intense stare. She bet that woman had never lost an argument in her life.

She knew, if Auntie Flo, instead of herself, had walked in to find Wallace, her fiancé, screwing the cleaning lady on their couch, the response wouldn't have been to squeak like a mouse, turn around, and flee the room. Hell no. She would have grabbed that good-for-nothing's baseball bat and started swinging.

She smirked at the image. What kind of jerk keeps his high school "game bat" around in his adult apartment? He had a glorious moment when he won the regional championship at age eighteen. The egomaniac was thirty-two.

A year had passed since the incident, but Daphne was still mortified at the memory.

The photo brought back the distant voice of Auntie Flo, who, in her gruff timbre, would have instructed her, "Get over him already. He wasn't a prize anyway. Two years and no wedding date? Get some gumption, girl."

She had thought she hardly remembered her great-aunt, but being here in her home, Flo felt closer.

No, no, she wasn't going to think about Wallace. She could only handle so many negative thoughts at once before spiraling out, and she had too much to do.

Carefully, she placed the picture on the coffee table, relieved to be in Maine, miles away from her parents and out of her mother's reach. She'd always harbored the suspicion that her Auntie Flo was a lesbian. As an adult, she now wondered why. Probably the idea had been put there by her mother's indelicate description of Flo as "butch." However, not only had Flo never lived with a man, but there had never even been a mention of any romantic partner at all. No utterance of "the one that got away" or "my heart still belongs to him."

Though now, as Daphne sat on the practical hunter-green, maroon, and yellow plaid couch, she could never imagine those soft, mushy words coming out of her aunt's mouth. Auntie Flo's speech tended more toward biting sarcasm, with quips like, "An apple a day keeps anyone away if you throw it hard enough."

Given the lack of evidence of a relationship with a man, she guessed it was easy to assume that Flo wasn't interested in men. She doubted the truth about her aunt's romantic preferences would come out now. Not that it made a difference in her opinion of Flo.

Glancing at her watch, Daphne figured she had enough time to shower and change before meeting Noah Tippett, the lawyer. Papers needed to be signed now that she was in town. Mr. Tippett offered to come in on Saturday for her, though he made it clear he usually didn't work weekends.

With a deep sigh, she rose and headed to the guest bedroom, where she had placed her bags. While the primary held the larger bed, her aunt's room felt out of bounds. Out of respect for the dead, Daphne would sleep down the hall.

Blinded by the bright sunshine, she stepped out of Mr. Tippett's office and back onto Main Street. Her head spun. She had quickly lost track of the papers she signed and their purposes. From behind, she vaguely heard the lawyer saying something about giving him a call if she needed anything else. Absently, she nodded and hugged the thick manilla envelope full of documents to her chest.

She stumbled across the pavement towards Flo's pickup truck. Two thoughts penetrated the brain fog as she unlocked the vehicle and climbed inside. First, the welfare of Flo's well-cared-for truck now belonged to her. The second, Auntie Flo, was well and truly dead.

Safely tucked miles away in Michigan, everything felt distant. Sure, there had been a clipped statement from her mother about a police call and the words "heart troubles" six weeks previously. A follow-up call from the lawyer soon after announced the surprising news: Daphne was Flo's sole beneficiary. The keys to the house and car were sent in the mail. A trip out east needed to be organized. But somehow, the fact that Flo was actually gone hadn't seemed real until this moment. Any secret childish wishes for a reunion evaporated. Being back in Cobb, the loss for the past and what could have been became acute.

The first tears dripped down her cheeks. She didn't bother to wipe them away. She attempted to comfort herself by gently rocking back and forth. The thick packet in her hands suddenly felt hot, and she tossed it on the passenger seat.

Why had Auntie Flo left all her worldly possessions to her? She suspected it was due to their summer together all those years ago, or more likely the tension in Flo's relationship with Sarah. A geyser of guilt built up and erupted from deep within. Tearing her eyes away from the papers, she put the key in the ignition and started the truck.

Barely checking for oncoming traffic, she shifted into Reverse and pressed the gas. She probably should have walked, given that her destination was a mere mile away. But she needed the privacy and security the vehicle provided. It was a quiet place to try and collect herself.

She headed down Main Street toward the local park, known locally as The Green. The Green's large grassy rectangle, complete with a white gazebo, acted as the town's focal point. It divided the downtown, with Main Street split in two and stretching out on either side.

Hanging a left, she drove past the expansive lawn and lines of parking spots. On the opposite side was a row of charming buildings covered in cedar shakes intermixed with ones of white clapboard. Making a right, she found herself at the park's north end, with a view right down to the Androscoggin River. A classic, white New England church, with tall windows and a steeple stretching toward the sky, stood vigil overall. It looked like the cover of a book about picture-perfect small towns in Maine.

With a last right turn, she arrived at her destination. The imposing three-story, federal-style brick building served as Cobb's city hall. Attached to the side furthest from the river was the small police station. Relieved to find an open parking spot, she steadied herself.

As the reality of the situation began to seep in, she wondered what exactly had happened to Flo six weeks prior. She needed some answers; she owed that to her aunt. Mr. Tippett's response had left her uneasy and unsatisfied.

"It was sudden. A surprise to us all." Mr. Tippet shifted in his seat. "Seems she had heart trouble. No one in town knew about it. She kept to herself, of course." He cleared his throat. "On the certificate, it lists heart failure as the cause of death. You can read it for yourself. It is all perfectly legal."

Why *wouldn't* it be legal?

"Yes, but what about her final days and moments?" Guilt coiled around Daphne's throat, making it hard to speak. "What specifically happened, Mr. Tippett?"

"If you want more details, I suggest you talk to Sheriff Allett." He cleared his throat even louder, shoved the papers across the table, and marched her out before she could ask another question.

So that's exactly what she decided to do.

Reaching for the door handle, Daphne read the Cobb Sheriff's Department sign. A smiling, matronly, redheaded woman glanced up as Daphne strode to the front desk.

"I'm looking for Sheriff Allett. I'm Daphne Patterson."

The smile disappeared, leaving a blank expression.

Taking a gulp, she tried again. "I'm Florence Winkler's great-niece. Mr. Tippett sent me over here."

"Ahh." The woman gave a sympathetic nod. "I'm sorry for your loss, hon." She stretched back in her chair and yelled, "Tad, someone here to see you."

A middle-aged man wearing a tan sheriff's uniform a size too small came from an office in the back. His furrowed brows accentuated the lines around his eyes. He ran a hand through his salt-and-pepper hair, leaving a few errant locks pointing upward. He gave her a quick appraisal, then turned a questioning gaze at the redheaded woman.

"This is Flo Winkler's niece." The woman and the sheriff shared a furtive look. "Seems Tippett sent her over."

"I see. Well, I'm Sheriff Thaddeus Allett." He offered his hand. "You can call me Tad. Everyone else does."

Daphne stood as straight as possible. "Nice to meet you," she said, shaking his rough, meaty hands. "I'm Daphne Patterson. I have some questions about Auntie Flo's life and death. Mr. Tippett suggested you could help me."

"Of course, why don't you come back to my office?" Tad gestured for her to follow him. "Ruby, could you hold any calls for me?"

Ruby, for a redhead? That was awfully on the nose.

He settled into a beat-up chair behind the worn metal desk. She sat on the edge of a smooth wooden seat across from him. Tad bent over, his elbows on the desk, his fingers interlaced below his chin.

Electricity sizzled in the air. She suspected there was something with her aunt's death people didn't want to talk about.

"Sheriff Allett..." she started, using the voice she generally reserved for controlling a room full of children at the library. The success rate was 50/50. Maybe she should have worn the black suit after all.

"Tad," he interrupted her.

"Tad." She switched to her normal, unassuming tone. "I just want to know what happened to my Auntie Flo. I get the impression that something strange occurred. As her heir, I feel it is my right to know."

He looked her over. Daphne shrank back a bit, hunching her shoulders, uncomfortable being studied.

"Honestly, I feel a duty to her to find out." Daphne squirmed. "I hope you can understand that."

"I do. May I call you Daphne?"

She nodded.

"Daphne, what I'm going to share is for your ears only. As her family, I agree you should know the truth. Six weeks ago, a call came in that your aunt was found on her front porch, slumped over. She was dead. At first, it looked like a heart attack."

"*Looked* like a heart attack?"

"Upon entering the house, in the kitchen, we found dried foxglove flowers and roots on the counter. They had been ground up. Next to Flo's body, we also found an empty mug."

"I'm sorry, Sher... Tad. I'm not following."

"It was pretty clear that your aunt had put a quantity of dried foxglove into her drink." It was his turn to shift uncomfortably. "Foxglove's Latin name is digitalis. Maybe you've heard of it?"

"Yes, I have." She swallowed hard as the information started to process in her brain. "Digitalis is very poisonous. It causes heart attacks."

"Correct. Your aunt was steady as a lighthouse. I'm afraid she knew what she was doing."

"But the death certificate says heart attack, and not... you know."

"Did you know that Flo was a dispatcher for the police department?" She nodded.

He continued. "It was a long time ago now, but she worked for the force for thirty-five years."

"Yeah, she retired just before I came to stay with her for a summer." Daphne blinked back tears. Tad's voice sounded as if it were coming from the end of a long tunnel.

"She was one of us, law enforcement. We're a family. We may not all get along, but we watch out for each other. I know your aunt wasn't... well, universally liked in town. And in small places like this, there can still be prejudice about suicide."

Daphne winced.

"After the autopsy, the coroner agreed to list the official cause of death as a heart attack." His fingers repeatedly pulled apart and entwined once more. "Technically, that is what killed her. The discovery of the digitalis was left out. You can understand why I ask you to keep this under your hat. I really am sorry for your loss."

Standing up from his chair, he glanced at the door.

Mindlessly, she followed his lead and got up from her chair. Internally, Daphne reeled at the news. She allowed him to take her elbow and direct her to the front of the building. Absently, she said a rote thank you and heard him say some platitudes back, but she wasn't listening. Ruby's "poor thing" penetrated the fog as she stumbled out the door.

This escape from her mother was not going as she had planned. Hopefully, after a good cry, she could focus on the business at hand and restart her life. But could she forget Flo that easily?

Chapter Three

Twenty Years Ago - Daphne

A SCARED AND NERVOUS ten-year-old Daphne pleaded with her father. "Why am I going to this person's house for the summer? Why can't I stay home?"

"You're going to see your mother's Aunt Florence in Maine. You'll have a great time. Please stop asking questions, sweetie. Do this for Daddy, okay? A nice flight attendant will watch over you on the flight."

Satisfied she would behave, her father handed her off at the airport gate, and she watched him walk away. A kind woman led Daphne to her seat, where she pulled out her copy of Brian Jacques's *Redwall*. Gripping the paperback as if her life depended on it, she focused her attention on the words. Soon, she was far away, living among the animals.

Great-Aunt Florence waited for her on the other side of the airplane ride. Her face, framed by a close haircut, was not mean; it wasn't exactly warm and fuzzy either.

Daphne introduced herself and whispered as her mother had drilled into her, "It is nice of you to have me, Aunt Florence."

Florence chortled as she guided her young charge to baggage claim. "It's Flo. But if you must, you can call me Auntie Flo," she barked.

Daphne stared at her brusque relation, terrified. On the verge of shaking, she overheard Flo mumble to herself, "Sarah will choke when her kid comes home calling me Auntie Flo."

Why would her mom choke over Auntie Flo? Was it a bad thing? The older woman's eyes were sparkling with delight. Why did this crusty woman dislike her mom? Had Mom been mean to Auntie Flo? Her fear transformed into curiosity.

Maybe she'd unearth a dark family secret while in Maine. Had her mom done something unforgivable and been banished from Maine forever? In Daphne's eyes, Auntie Flo transformed into a haunted and mysterious heroine, and she no longer viewed her as rude.

"It's still kind of you, Auntie Flo." Daphne tried out the new name as she put her arms around to hug the startled woman.

"It's no big deal, child." She rigidly took a step back. "Family helps out. No need to make a fuss about it."

Daphne's face fell at the rejection. Flo frowned. They walked in silence until they reached the luggage carousel.

"You flew here on your own?"

"Yes."

"Had you ever been on a plane before?"

"No."

"Well, you didn't come out bawling your eyes. So, you're no whimpering weakling. Winkler women are strong. You did a brave thing." Flo cleared her throat and stepped back, watching warily for signs of another hug.

"Thanks. It's no big deal. No need to make a fuss about it," she mimicked her aunt's earlier words.

Flo gave an encouraging nod, and Daphne beamed.

It took several days for the two to become accustomed to each other's ways. Daphne quickly learned that following her aunt's routines and rules allowed her plenty of freedom to read or run around in the wooded area surrounding the house.

On their fourth morning together, Daphne found Flo in the kitchen, finishing her coffee in a trout-shaped mug.

Over breakfast, Flo pulled out her to-do list. "They help you focus. What do you need to achieve? But keep it manageable. It makes for an orderly day. By the end, you feel accomplished because you know you did what you set your mind to. Now, what shall we put on today's list?"

Daphne understood that her participation was expected. However, her fear of making a bad suggestion kept her mute. Holding her breath, she waited for the moment to end.

"Hmm. Nothing to add, huh? Well, maybe tomorrow."

After the breakfast items were cleared away, Daphne went upstairs to dress for the day. Upon her return, Flo gathered the young girl's long, curly, blonde hair in a ponytail. Pulling out a red-print handkerchief from a drawer, she folded it in half and covered Daphne's head and hair, tying the scarf under her tail in a peasant style.

"You are fit for duty. What's the first thing on the list?" Flo inquired.

"Umm. You wrote down 'clean pantry,'" Daphne stammered.

"Right. I hate this job. It can be sticky, and lots of moving cans and jars. So, it's not very nice. What kind of music do you think we need for this?"

"I don't understand."

Please don't yell, please don't yell. I'm sorry, I don't know the answer.

"If we are doing a chore we don't like, what sort of music should we listen to that will help us?" Flo urged her on.

"Happy music? Something fun, maybe?"

"Yes. Exactly. Happy and fun." She gave a wry grin. "Let's see what I've got."

Flo searched under the staircase and through the shelves lining her living room wall opposite the front door. Except for the vintage record player sitting on the edge of one of the shelves, every inch of space was taken up with vinyl records, clearly collected over decades.

With an "Aha," Flo held an album over her head. "Donna Summer. Disco has a wonderful beat to get your blood pumping, and the music is fun and happy. Do you know her?"

Daphne shook her head.

"Then you're in for a pleasant surprise."

Chapter Four

As the morning sun poured in through the windows, Daphne kept her eyes closed for a moment. The warmth of the mug cradled in her hands tingled pleasantly. Dipping her nose, she breathed deep and inhaled the rich scent of strong coffee, dark and plain the way Auntie Flo liked it. Sadly, Flo's old trout mug was nowhere to be found.

When Daphne returned home two decades earlier, at the end of August, she peppered her mother with stories and questions about Auntie Flo. Then school started up, and she had slipped back into her old life. Months without a word between her and Flo turned into years. The memories they built became harder to hold on to. She missed the gruff woman, but felt like the relationship was out of her control. The lack of contact convinced her that the fondness had gone only one way. The less she thought of Flo, the less painful the rejection.

Now, years later, every minute in the house loosened long-buried memories, triggered by any small item. Flo had filled every room with her presence. The feeling of checking off chores side by side as they sang overwhelmed her. That summer, Daphne had come to grow very fond of her aunt, and the feeling was reciprocated. She was sure of that now. Why hadn't she tried harder to stay connected to her aunt?

The guilt from her casual acceptance of Flo's disappearance from her life gave the coffee a bitter taste as she swallowed the warm liquid. A smell assaulted her senses, overpowering the contents of her mug. She let out a series of sneezes. The unpleasant mix of stale air and dust that came with a closed-up space could not be ignored. The house needed proper airing and scrubbing down. None of its surfaces had been cleaned in at least six weeks. There was a grimy feel. Auntie Flo would never have allowed her home to get into such a state.

Daphne walked through the empty house to the dusty record player. She crossed her fingers and was pleased to see the power light kick on when she flicked the switch. Her fingers caressed the tops of the albums as she walked along the shelf. She stopped when she came to the well-worn cover of Harry Nilsson's *Nilsson Schmilsson*, a favorite of Flo's.

At the start of that long ago summer, her aunt selected stacks of albums and introduced her niece to artists that she had never heard of, from the '50s through the '70s. Before long, Daphne requested specific albums to serenade them in their chores. Fleetwood Mac's *Rumours* became her favorite by far.

She slid out the vinyl disk of *Nilsson Schmilsson*, placed it on the player's waiting deck, and lowered the lever. A hiss came from the speakers. A smile crossed her face as "Gotta Get Up" began its up-tempo beat, perfect for cleaning the house.

Sweaty and sore, but satisfied, Daphne surveyed her progress. She had completed dusting, scrubbing, vacuuming, and what felt like endless surface wiping. Her out-of-practice arms ached. However, the first floor of the compact house was, at last, clean and presentable.

Sunlight streamed in through the windows, illuminating the effect of her efforts. How long had she been working? The only measure of time she had was changing albums, and she'd lost count of how many she'd listened to. The clock informed her that it was two in the afternoon. She was so focused on her task that she had forgotten a lunch break. It did explain the grumbling that was going on in her stomach.

She sighed, looking down at the bucket of filthy brown water at her feet. She hefted it outside with a grunt and dumped it on the bushes edging the porch, which were dogwood shrubs intermixed with patches of black-eyed Susans and coneflowers. Most of the yard was filled with oaks, sugar maples, and tall pine trees, with limbs ending in long, soft needles that carpeted the ground beneath them. She wondered if the old blackberry bush was still hidden at the edge of the property.

Over her shoulder, the cushioned glider tempted her to sit and rest. How many hours had she sat there as a kid with a book in hand?

Flo's house was an old Victorian-influenced, one-and-a-half-story farmhouse. It was covered in faded yellow paint. The roof peaked in an A design, and a beam descended on two diagonal sides along the length of the house. Two charming dormer windows peeked out in the front. Below the dormers, the green metal roof ran downward, covering the porch, making it the perfect spot to listen to the rain ping above.

Not wanting to stop moving until she was finished, Daphne turned to head back inside. She stopped halfway across the threshold when she heard a thrashing sound from the trees and bushes separating the yard from the neighbors. Next came several barks, and a yellow Labrador Retriever burst through the undergrowth. The dog bolted toward her. She put the bucket in front of herself, unsure if it was a friendly animal or a rabid beast.

"Bella!" a deep voice called, and Daphne looked up to see a man running toward her up the long driveway.

Daphne tried to get a better look at the stranger. His tall, lean body, dressed in a blue t-shirt and jeans, clomped up the driveway in well-worn boots. His dark, scraggly hair looked like he had missed a few haircuts.

"Bella, you naughty dog," he said. "You know you shouldn't run over here. Sorry about that..." He paused, looking uncomfortable.

"Daphne," she offered. "I'm Florence's niece. Well, great-niece. But she always just called me her niece, so that's what I call myself. I just got into town yesterday. Don't worry about the dog."

Stop rambling at the super cute man. Gosh, he is handsome and looks my age, too.

"I'm Philip Nolan. You can call me Phil. This is Bella. She's my dad's dog." He laughed. "But I seem to be doing more of the looking after her at the moment."

"Oh, good you found her." Another voice called from down the driveway. The approaching man looked similar to Phil, but shorter and a good thirty years older. When he reached the porch, he puffed out, "Chester Nolan, your next-door neighbor."

"How do you do, Mr. Nolan? I'm Daphne."

"Ha! Is everyone so formal where you come from? Call me Chet. I know who you are. Your aunt told me about you." He gave a wink and then turned to make sure his dog was no worse the wear for her adventure. "Sorry about Bella coming over like this. But she's likely to do it again. Your aunt used to sneak her treats. Those two were good friends."

"I'm sorry, I don't have any treats. I don't know where Auntie Flo kept them." She'd probably know the answer if she and her aunt had kept in contact. "Wait, she told you about me?"

"Sure did. We often talked about her missing niece, and that summer you stayed with her. Sounds like the two of you had a lot of fun." He shook his head as he petted the dog. "Shame your momma wouldn't let you come again."

Her mouth hung open.

Phil looked at her and his father nervously. "*Dad.*"

"Wouldn't let?" Daphne repeated the words, looking from Chet to Phil and back again. It was as if someone had ripped off a Band-Aid to expose an unhealed wound.

"That isn't our business." Phil grabbed his father's arm. "You seem to be in the middle of something," he told Daphne. "We should leave you to it."

"We'll have you over for supper sometime soon," Chet said over his shoulder, as Phil ushered him and Bella back down the drive.

Daphne shuffled back into the house, closing the door behind her. Her mom wouldn't *let* her return? That must have meant Auntie Flo had offered, and her mom refused. Her mom never asked if she wanted to return; Daphne would have remembered. Another visit would have been pure joy. She always assumed that her aunt had forgotten about her, as Flo slowly faded from her life. What had really happened? Only her mother could explain.

Daphne headed to the kitchen. No longer basking in the glow of her morning's hard work, she hardly noticed the gleaming Formica counter-tops. In the fridge, she found the tuna sandwich she had purchased at the airport.

Closing the refrigerator door, she noticed a slip of paper held to the sur-face by a pumpkin-shaped magnet. A note was written in Flo's neat script. It read, "Remember get limes!" Daphne's fingers instinctively touched it—a physical connection to her aunt.

She sat at the kitchen table in the adjoining nook and ate her sandwich like a zombie. Glancing over the note again, she couldn't help but wonder what Flo wanted the limes for. Maybe she was making a pie. Or margaritas. She thought about throwing the note in the bin. Auntie Flo never left an old list lying around. Once that day's or week's list was accomplished, she would crumple it up with ceremony and throw it out. Lists were not meant to be kept for sentimental purposes. However, Daphne thought she'd make an exception in this case. It was Flo's last list, after all.

That night, Daphne tossed and turned in bed. Sleeping in the guest room felt as unfamiliar now as it did at the start of her visit twenty years ago. What had started as scary had become comforting by the end, though. She recalled how Auntie Flo would knock on her door after bedtime, the lamp still on for late-night reading. Flo warned her not to stay up too late, or she'd be tired the next day. Flo's gentle tone was so different from her mother's barking to turn off the *dang* light and go to bed.

Now, something nagged at Daphne, a feeling that things were wrong and out of place. It wasn't the memories, but she couldn't put her finger on it. She flipped her pillow over, felt the cool side against her cheek, and began to do some deep, meditative breathing. After five minutes of deliberately pushing and pulling air in and out of her lungs, her mind and body relaxed. In the quiet, a thought whispered from the corner of her mind.

The list. The limes. That meant it was something Auntie Flo still needed to get done. People who commit suicide don't make to-do lists. They don't plan to get limes.

Her eyes flew open, even though they saw nothing but darkness. Her hand covered her mouth as she gasped. When she'd arrived, there were no rotting limes in the fridge waiting. She knew what this meant. The note, a message from beyond the grave, was telling her that Auntie Flo hadn't killed herself at all. *She had been murdered!*

Chapter Five

EARLY THE NEXT MORNING, Daphne paced back and forth on the clean kitchen floors. While tired from the sleepless night, she couldn't sit still. Murder. Murder? Yes, Murder! Okay, maybe she was jumping the gun, but it was weird, right? Yes! It was weird! And what if someone *had* killed her aunt? She couldn't let that go. Could she?

Daphne had planned to come to Cobb, sell the house, and go off and start her life over. A life with a librarian job, a relationship with a guy who wouldn't cheat on her, friends who had her back, and most importantly, a life free from her mother's control.

Getting involved with the possible murder investigation of an estranged relative was not on her to-do list. Neither was reawakening dormant feelings about Flo. A wave of hurt, guilt, loss, and anger threatened to crash down on her. It was too much. She needed a distraction from those paralyzing feelings.

So, Daphne reasoned that trying to find out what really happened to Flo would give her a good excuse to stay longer in Maine and give her more time to refine her escape plan. At least she should bring her suspicions to the attention of the police. Yes, they were the professionals. They could take it from here. She didn't have to get more involved than that. Before she could talk herself out of it, she grabbed the keys and headed back to the sheriff's department.

The hard plastic chair made it impossible for Daphne to get comfortable. She assumed that was on purpose. She doubted the police wanted people to get cozy and settle in for an extended stay. Shifting again, she glanced at her watch. Ruby assured her that the sheriff would be free soon, though her tone was not as friendly as it had been forty-eight hours ago.

After seven years at a public library as a trained librarian, however, Daphne knew how to get information. She enjoyed a good mystery novel, and if those books had taught her anything, it was the importance of finding little clues. The crime was always solved by little bits of evidence that a lazy reader might skim over. Unless it was a mystery that pulled out some new information in the last few pages, and in those, it didn't matter how meticulously you cataloged all the suspects, their motives, means, and opportunities; you couldn't guess the ending without random luck. But she was talking about the good mysteries. The ones that laid out all the evidence for the clever reader to piece together. The limes were just such a clue.

She shook her head to bring herself back to reality. While she was well-versed in the cozy mystery formula, Daphne was no amateur sleuth. She knew it was best to let the police handle this.

Ruby cleared her throat, getting Daphne's attention. Tad was finally free, and she could go back to his office. Ruby's face displayed a painted-on smile, but there was a hint of suspicion around the corner of her eyes.

"Hello, Tad," Daphne began, taking the hard chair she had previously used.

"Hi there." He leaned back into his chair. "What brings you back in?"

"It's about Auntie Flo. I found something when I was cleaning up yesterday." She withdrew the note from her pocket and handed it to him. "It isn't something you would have noticed or understood."

"Limes?"

"I know. It seems like nothing. But hear me out." Daphne outlined Auntie Flo's penchant for lists and how she didn't keep them lying around once finished. Using her educator's voice, the one for explaining the online catalog system to a patron, she pointed out that making plans for the future seemed very unlikely behavior for someone planning suicide. "I know it seems a bit of a leap, but I think Auntie Flo may have been murdered."

"Murdered?" He stared at her and crossed his arms. "Daphne. I know it can be hard to process that someone would choose to take their own life. But, given the evidence, suicide makes a lot more sense than murder. That's quite a leap."

"But if she was murdered, then the killer planted all the foxglove stuff in the kitchen to make it look like suicide. Trying to throw us off the scent. They didn't understand the importance of the list, or they would have thrown that out." Her tone was on the verge of slipping into a whine.

"Look. I'm sorry, but I don't see it. A slip of paper is barely *circumstantial* evidence. There isn't enough to open a case. Daphne, just let sleeping dogs lie." He began to stand up.

This was starting to feel like he was mansplaining or, like her mother always did, ignoring her thoughts and desires.

"You are not going to investigate this?" She remained stubbornly in her chair, looking at him in shock.

"There is no need. This isn't murder. This is just a sad old lady who ended her own life. I'm sorry." He came around his desk.

Daphne stood up and spoke to the floor. "But you can't stop me from investigating, right?"

"No, I can't. Not unless you break a law doing it." His voice deepened, and his body tensed. "But I strongly recommend you trust us professionals on this."

"Well then," she muttered. "Thank you for your time."

She turned on her heel and slunk out of the office. Without saying a word to Ruby, she hurried out of the building.

Wow, you sure showed him who's boss, she reprimanded herself. *Thank you for your time? You let him walk all over you.*

Her heart raced, pumping blood through her veins like water rushing over Niagara Falls in spring. She dashed across the street and cut a path through The Green. Had she just said she was going to conduct a murder investigation?

Shit. I'm totally in over my head. I wanted to be out of this town in, like, two weeks, four tops. I don't think I can solve a murder that fast. Then, Daphne thought of Jessica Fletcher, who could catch a killer in under an hour. *Get serious. This is real-life Cobb, not Cabot Cove.*

Tad was the sheriff. He probably knew best. This was his job, after all.

So, I potentially let a murderer walk free? Auntie Flo deserves better. I let her down as a kid. I'm an adult now. Could I? There are books about this. Do I want to? Daphne needed a drink.

She looked at her watch. It was three in the afternoon. Society frowned on drinking before five p.m. She'd followed the rules and been a good girl her whole life. What had that gotten her? A mother who told her what to do. Now, the sheriff was telling her what to think. Maybe it was time to break a few rules.

A text pinged and she pulled out her phone. Speak of the devil.

> **Mom:** How's it going? How bad is the house? Talk to a real estate agent yet?

It was like her mother had a second sense for knowing when Daphne harbored rebellious thoughts. She groaned, but looked around to ensure her mother wasn't hiding nearby.

Shaking her head, she reprimanded herself for the paranoia. Her mother was hundreds of miles away and knew nothing about her visit to the sheriff. It would stay that way, too.

> **Daphne:** House fine, gave it a clean. Took all my time. No agent yet.

> **Mom:** Plenty of time today.

Daphne silenced her phone. Suddenly, Maine didn't feel far enough away from Michigan. Maybe she would need to move to Alaska when her time here was done.

The phone vibrated, another message from her mom. *Leave me alone for once, Mother. I'm going to get myself a drink!*

Which she would do. After answering her mother's text.

Chapter Six

HOUSED IN A DARK brick building on Main Street, snuggled between the florist and The Taste of Italy restaurant, was The Sidecar—Cobb's local watering hole. As a child, The Sidecar beguiled her with its mysterious and forbidden status. The dark-tinted windows kept out prying eyes, much to ten-year-old Daphne's chagrin.

Today, all of its secrets would, at last, be revealed.

The dimness inside contrasted starkly with the bright outdoors. As the heavy wood door closed behind her, the room darkened further. A large horseshoe counter dominated the space. The wood was pockmarked but well-polished.

A sign hung on the wall nearest her, and read, "If you talk politics, you'll be asked to leave." A coordinating notice on the other side of the horseshoe read, "Booze & Politics don't mix. Save it for church." Message received.

A laugh escaped her as she hoisted herself into a chair. A tall woman approached with cropped black hair, a nose ring, and a bosom that Daphne found hard to ignore. A challenge made more difficult because of the message printed across her t-shirt. On a black background, written in white: "I'm a bartender, not a therapist." For the second time in several minutes, a laugh forced itself out of Daphne.

"Love your shirt." She pulled her gaze to the bartender's sparkling blue eyes.

The woman gave Daphne the quick once over. "Thanks. Whatcha having?"

"A Moscow mule. Please."

"No problem." The bartender drifted away to make the drink. The t-shirt was not a joke. She didn't seem the chatty kind.

A swinging door on the other side of the bar whipped open and a pint-size dark-haired woman bounced into the room. Her shoulder-length bob swished around her face, and she flitted about with grace. She could have been mistaken for a fairy. Daphne openly gawked, observing a mini dress designed in multicolored geometric patterns and a pair of leather biker boots.

"Violet, I put the boxes in the back. Thanks again for agreeing to promote me. I really appreciate it. I've put in a couple extra bottles just for you. You're a doll." The fairy threw a kiss at the bartender.

"Happy to do it, Betty. It's so cool knowing a celebrity. Don't forget us regular people and get all uppity like those Hollywood types." Violet, while still fixated on Betty, sliced up a lime, giving the air a fresh citrus smell before sliding the mule in front of Daphne. If Betty was a celebrity, she wasn't anyone Daphne recognized.

The stranger noticed Daphne and marched up to the chair next to her and plonked down. "Are you Flo's niece?"

Daphne seemed to have lost her voice, so she squeaked and nodded.

"Oh, it's so nice to meet you. Daphne, right? I'm Betty Bennet. I'm totally excited to have some fresh young blood in this town. We don't get too many new people, and even more rarely someone in my age bracket. Everyone's talking about it. Hey, Vi, can I have a gin fizz? Let's drink to you coming to town, Daph. Can I call you Daph? I give everyone nicknames." The petite, sweetheart-faced woman, at last, took a breath.

Everyone is talking about me? How? Why? Daphne's brain was in free fall. She couldn't remember Betty's questions in order. She gulped her mule and blurted out the first thing she could think of. "I've never been Daph before, but sure, okay. Nice to meet you, Betty. Is that a nickname?"

"Betty is totally a nickname. My real name is Elizabeth. Elizabeth Bennet. My mom was a classical literature fan. It's not as cool as it sounds, I promise you. With a name like that, you'd change it to Betty, too. And sure, everyone is talking about you. This is a small town, sweetie. You're front-page news. First, your aunt's death. Mega shocker. Sure, she was almost eighty, so not really out of the realm of possibilities that she'd die. But I don't know. You expect someone like Flo Winkler to live forever. Right? Then, her missing niece comes to town. Huge. This is like an earthquake for quiet Cobb."

"Missing niece?" She choked. Her neighbor Chet had also said she was "missing."

Betty paid no attention to Daphne's question and marched forward with her thoughts. "Besides, it's dull as dishwater here most of the time. I can't believe my luck. We're totally going to be friends. I can feel it. Did you know that your aunt and my aunt were best friends? I know I sound completely kindergarten right now. But I get these vibes, you understand. And the moment I saw you, vibe city. We are kindred spirits. Unless you are against friendship or something." The chipper face suddenly went serious as she peered at Daphne, looking for signs that something was wrong with her.

"Nope. No, I'm one hundred percent pro-friendship. But isn't this kind of fast for friends? Don't we have to be acquaintances or something first?"

"Those kinds of rules are made for lesser mortals. I used to be one of those people. Now I follow my gut and give everything one hundred percent."

"Wow, you have so much confidence. I'm impressed. Also, my life is rather shit at the moment. I can use all the friends I can get. Especially a kindred spirit." Daphne wanted to ask who was Anne and who was Diana in their relationship, but it was already obvious she was destined to be the sidekick.

"Oh, like your aunt dying? Yeah, that sucks. Damn. I totally should have handled that better. I'm sorry for your loss. I don't always think before I speak. Forgive me. Hey, Vi, can I get her a drink? Do you like a gin fizz? What about a gin rickey?"

"It's okay. I mean, yes, my Auntie Flo dying does suck. But you're fine. Don't feel bad. You don't have to get me a drink. I've got one." She looked down at her empty mug. "Well, I had one. I've never drunk a gin fizz or rickey."

"What? Then you are in for a treat, my friend. Vi, a gin fizz for my new gal pal Daph, and please use my gin." Her eyes gave a mischievous twinkle.

Vi gave her a nod and headed toward the swinging door.

"Did you say *your* gin?"

"I sure did. Bathtub Betty's Gin. Isn't that a scream?"

"That's pretty clever. How did you choose that?"

"It sort of chose me. I am a YouTuber. I started out doing these vintage clothing videos. I did okay. I had several thousand views. But nothing mega, you know? I thought I needed a better hook."

"Sure."

"I decided to mix food and drink with vintage dress. I wore my great grandma's 1920s white silk wedding dress and tried my hand at making some real Prohibition bathtub gin. I thought I would make it special and livestreamed the whole event. I had some great 1920s music playing. I thought I was super clever. Gave everything this *Great Gatsby* vibe."

"That sounds fabulous. Did you get a lot of views?"

"About that. I sampled too much of the gin and got a bit intoxicated."

"Oh no."

"It gets worse. Being a little pickled, I thought I would try dancing the Charleston, this big dance craze back at that time. Dancing and booze do not mix. Or at least they don't for me. I tripped and fell into the very full tub. I was wearing this white dress and nothing underneath. So, I'm standing up in the tub with a soaking white dress on. There wasn't much left to the imagination. And it was all streaming live for anyone to see." Betty raised her eyebrows.

Daphne snorted. Then she chuckled. Then her laughter built and built until it was out of control. She couldn't stop. Her sides ached from laughter. Tears streamed down her face. It felt glorious. "Oh, Betty. That is... awful..." She tried to speak in between her howling. "You must have... been... mortified..."

"Go on and laugh. It's funny. I was totally humiliated at first. But then that video went viral. I got a million views in a week. A freaking million views! You can't buy publicity like that. It changed everything. Since then, I've continued to upload videos of me doing retro recipes of food or cocktails wearing vintage outfits from the appropriate decades. My family has been squirreling away clothes and other crap for at least a hundred years."

"I promise to subscribe." Daphne wiped her eyes. "Your channel sounds great."

"I just worked out an agreement with a booze company, and we are launching my latest business venture: Bathtub Betty's Gin. I'm so excited. This has been totally a case of lemons into lemonade. And you can always spice up your lemonade with a little gin." She winked.

Violet returned with a bottle of gin in her hand. Putting it on the counter, she began to mix the fizzes. Daphne took a moment to check out the label. It read "Bathtub Betty's Gin" and had a logo of a girl in a tub with her legs sticking out. The girl in the tub had a passing resemblance to Betty, but it wasn't the best likeness.

"I know, it doesn't look much like me. But again, what do I care? If people buy it, I'll laugh all the way to the bank. Right?"

Violet set down two glasses in front of the ladies.

"Thanks, Vi."

The bartender nodded.

"Not very chatty, is she?" Daphne commented on the retreating Violet and took a hesitant sip.

"She's just shy. Gotta let her warm up to you. What do you think?"

I think Violet looks scary, not shy.

"This is great, I love it. I'm adding it to my list of drinks. I don't normally day drink. But I'm having a terrible day. No... I've been having a bad year, if I'm honest." She drank more of her fizz. "Seriously, this is good. Wow, I can hardly believe I am sitting next to a gal with her *own* gin."

"Thanks. I can hardly believe it myself." Her smile turned into a pensive look. "Bad year huh? This seems like a friendship test, and it's only my first day! You're hardcore, Daph. So, why is everything shit? I take it there is more to it than Flo dying." Turning her body sideways, Betty let Daphne know she had her full attention. "Lay it on me."

"Yeah, Auntie Flo died. And then she leaves me her house, which is sweet of her. But the whole situation has me feeling awfully guilty. When I was ten, I came to live with her for a summer. We had a great time after we got over that initial awkward phase, ya know?"

Betty nodded encouragingly. "I think that was the year I spent the summer at Girl Scout camp. I remember hearing about you when I got back."

"But I never saw her again. I thought we had this fun summer, but I don't know. We didn't keep in touch. I *just* found out she wanted to see me again, but my mom blocked it. Twice I've been referred to as her 'missing niece.' But I didn't know I was 'missing' until yesterday. How am I supposed to process that? Why didn't she tell me when I turned eighteen or something? I guess I could have called her, but I didn't. Now I feel like an ass. And on top of everything else, I'm worried that she might have been killed."

"What? I haven't heard anything like that." Betty's eyes bulged out of their sockets. "You're not serious."

"Totally." A vague awareness that she was not wholly sober anymore settled on Daphne. Not drunk, but she was relaxed enough to explain to Betty her possible murder theory and how Sheriff Allett had rejected the unfinished list as possible evidence of a crime.

"Whoa." Betty slouched into her chair. "That is major, girl. What are you going to do?"

"I don't know. Maybe the sheriff is right and Flo..." She remembered she was supposed to keep quite about the suicide. "That Flo just died of a heart attack. Part of me wants to leave it be. But how could I do that to Auntie Flo? Shouldn't I discover the truth about her death, for her sake? I guess I'm leaning towards starting my own investigation, as crazy as that sounds. I mean, I have lots of free time now."

"How come?"

"About three months ago, I lost my job. I worked for this great public library in the Chicago suburbs. I loved it. But there were cutbacks, and I was let go because I had been the most recent hire. They said it was nothing personal, but that didn't stop the fact that I was out of work. Did you know there isn't a high demand for librarians at the moment? I ran through my unemployment benefits and options pretty quickly. I finally called it quits and moved back home with my parents." She downed the rest of her drink.

"Oh." Betty patted her arm. "That's harsh."

"My mom keeps going on about me getting a job. Plus, she's on my back about my lack of a love life. Oh, I didn't mention that my fiancé and I broke up about a year ago. I found him banging the woman we paid to clean our place."

Vi rolled her eyes but kept quiet on the other side of the bar.

"Things were bad between us, even before the cheating."

"How so?"

"After three years of dating, I began signaling my desire to take our relationship to the next level and get engaged. I dropped a million not-very-subtle hints leading up to my birthday. So, on the big day, we're at his favorite steak house. He practically tosses a box to me and says, casual as you like, 'Here you go, babe.'"

"He did not!"

"The ring was fine. A .75-carat circle-cut diamond solitaire ring presented on a gold band. I'd left pictures of square-cut gems with platinum bands lying around, but most men don't know the difference, I guess."

"What did you say?"

Violet found something to do on their side of the bar.

"I told him that I loved it. That it was the perfect birthday present. I was happy at the time. I suggested we order a bottle of champagne to celebrate. Then he says, 'After what I just spent on that ring? Gotta watch the money now. You can have one glass if you want, I guess. I'll stick to beer.' Then he flagged down the waiter."

"Did you get the drink or not?"

"Not. I felt too guilty. Then he gives me this smug smile."

"Yuck. I hate smug."

"It was yuck. But I was young and stupid. I ate it all up. I convinced myself I didn't need a fancy proposal with him on his knee popping the question."

"But you didn't marry him."

"No. Month after month, he created new excuses for why we couldn't set a date. Too busy at work, family drama, or the old classic 'I'm too tired to talk about it tonight.' I didn't want to upset him, so I waited. And I kept on waiting. I waited until my twenties were almost gone. Then the cherry on top was finding him banging our cleaning lady. Now I'm the big three-o and single again."

Daphne glanced at her reflection in the large mirror behind the bar. She took in her shoulder-length blonde curls, pleasantly round face, and deep-brown eyes. While her figure wasn't slim like Betty's, it had some nice curves. Her legs were worth a look or two, for sure. "I'm as pretty as her."

"Who?" Betty looked around.

"The cleaning girl he cheated on me with. I'm as pretty as her. I don't get it."

"It isn't hard to figure out. He's a bastard. If this guy cheated on my new pal, then he is a bastard." They snickered.

"Yeah, a bastard. A rat bastard. The Rat Bastard King."

The two of them hooted like fools, the gin making its presence known.

Betty waved a finger. "You are totally better off without him. There are more fish in the sea."

"Auntie Flo loved fishing." Daphne released something between a laugh and a hiccup. "She would have said to throw Wallace back."

"Who's Wallace?"

"Rat Bastard. And that rat is already dating someone else. I saw his Instagram. He got over me super-fast. Am I that forgettable? And have I moved on? No. I still cry myself to sleep because it feels like no one will ever love me. I'm going to be all alone, just like Auntie Flo." Her laughter turned to sobs. She buried her head into her arms, crossed on the bar.

"Oh no. Don't cry. You aren't going to be alone. You'll see. Maybe you coming here will be a turning point in your life. You get to start over. Put all that bad stuff behind you and be who you want to be. If you want a man, then go out there and get one." Betty sounded like a coach talking to the batter in the ninth inning with the score tied.

"Yeah." Daphne lifted her head. "You're right. I'm going to live my dream life. This is my do-over. My chance to live the way I've always wanted. I'm miles away from my family. I own a house now. How many people get an opportunity like that?"

"Exactly." Betty smacked the bar. "I'll drink to that."

"I'm a librarian! I've read a million novels. I know what happens next. I ask a bunch of questions, and I'll find out the truth about Auntie Flo, become a local hero, and find love in the process. I can figure this out. I just need to find a tall, dark, and handsome fellow to make sure this story has a happy ending." Her mind drifted to her attractive next-door neighbor. He'd fit the bill nicely.

"That's right!" Betty cheered her on.

"This is what reading all those novels has been leading up to. This is the moment I've been training for. I'm going to have a storybook adventure. I'll make a new friend, live in an adorable small town, fall in love with a hot stranger, get a fancy new job, fix up a house, and uncover what happened to my aunt! The textbook reset for my life." She grabbed Betty's hand in excitement. "Oh, thank you, Betty Bennet. My guardian angel must have sent you. Wanna help me solve a possible murder?"

"Sounds like a blast." She bounced in her seat. "How do we start?"

"I don't know." She slumped back in her chair. "But I'm a librarian. I'll use books to figure it out!"

"A toast to uncovering Cobb's secrets." Betty raised her glass.

They missed each other's glass in their toasting attempt and started laughing all over again.

Violet stepped in front of them and held out her palms. "I'm gonna need your keys, ladies."

The two looked at each other and howled. Reaching into their purses, they placed the requested items in Violet's hands before ordering the next of many gin fizzes.

Chapter Seven

THE HOUSE IS TOO quiet. It's like it's waiting to hear Flo's booming voice again and I'm just trespassing here. It's unnerving. Get a grip and focus on the task at hand. Daphne's pen hovered over the pad of paper. She paused and considered her list, wondering whether anything else needed to be added. For the first time in Auntie Flo's house, the list-making was her responsibility. Instead of sitting at the kitchen table eating a bowl of cornflakes and reviewing her aunt's to-dos, she sipped her coffee and jotted on the paper herself. A bowl of cereal would have been nice. But there wasn't any in the cupboard, and she needed milk anyway. She added both items to her list. She needed enough food for at least a week. And ibuprofen, which she underlined.

Yesterday, she paid for throwing caution to the wind and guzzling the gin fizzes with Betty. That afternoon and the next day had passed in a bit of a haze. She'd hid indoors with curtains closed while she nursed a tremendous hangover. One of the drawbacks of being thirty was she couldn't drink like she was twenty-one anymore. In fairness, she doubted she'd ever drunk that much before. She felt awkward sharing her life story with a stranger, but it had been a relief to finally get everything off her chest.

A relative of Betty's had picked them up, and they'd dropped her off at home. She couldn't remember their name. Their age, gender, and any other identifying characteristics were mysteries as well. She couldn't have picked them out of a line-up.

Groaning, she gripped the pen tightly and added a second line under ibuprofen. "Never again, I swear."

A few hours later, after the worst of the hangover had passed, Daphne walked into town and retrieved her keys from The Sidecar. Vi gave her a mixed look of disapproval and pity. Muttering an apology, she turned beet red, grabbed the keys, and ran out of the bar.

Amid the confusion and mortification of her inebriation, some things remained clear: her vow to begin a new chapter, figure out what happened to Flo, and make a place for herself in this town. At least for now.

Fortified with coffee, and her pounding headache in retreat, she reaffirmed the plan. Her goal was to start her adventure somewhere else, a new her, in a fabulous new city. While not a hotbed of excitement, Cobb wasn't a bad place to begin her makeover. This could be a practice run.

What else was she doing with her time, anyway? Sure, she was supposed to be clearing out the house and putting it on the market, but when that was done, she'd have to go home and do the hard work of figuring out her next step. Not to mention how she was going to escape her mom for good. It wouldn't hurt to put that off for a few weeks, to give herself time to think.

She wondered what Flo had been up to for the last twenty years. Investigating her death seemed like a good way to learn more about her, since it would mean piecing her life back together. Maybe talking to her friends. Daphne had to admit, that sounded more interesting than emptying out the house. Besides, she had just made a new "kindred" friend. It would be bad form just to cut and run.

Jenn McKinlay's hero, Lindsey, from the *Library Lover's Mysteries* series, used her book smarts to solve crimes. In the process, she found romance and surrounded herself with a strong group of friends. As a fellow librarian, Daphne could identify with Lindsey.

She liked the idea of being the hero of her own thrilling, crime-solving mystery. She could do this. She would show the world, especially her mom, that she could achieve amazing things.

But one couldn't be expected to make all those changes on an empty stomach. That brought her back to her grocery list. She headed out the front door, locking it behind her.

⚜

Entering the "IN" door at the local grocery, Daphne selected a cart, threw her purse in, and pulled out her list.

She slowly worked her way up and down the mostly vacant aisles. Four bottles of in-case-of-emergency wine were an impulse buy. As she debated her coffee options, a woman in white slacks and a denim button-down shirt stopped next to her. Daphne sensed the woman still standing there, unmoved. Assuming she must be in the woman's way, she turned and pushed her cart to the side.

"You're Florence Winkler's young niece?" the woman queried politely.

"Umm, yeah." Daphne found herself at an information disadvantage.

"I'm Charlotte Watford. I'm one of your neighbors. I live about eight houses down the street. I heard Flo's niece was coming."

"Nice to meet you, Charlotte. I'm Daphne. Thank you for introducing yourself. Maybe we can have a proper chat when we aren't doing our shopping."

Charlotte looked into her full cart. "Oh goodness, this ice cream is going to melt. You're right, I should go. You must come over for coffee sometime and meet my husband, Tony, too." With a wave, she was gone.

Daphne waved back. A warm feeling spread in her chest. How friendly people were in Cobb. The charm of this quaint town was overtaking her.

Moving to the baking aisle, she fantasized about walking down the streets, greeting all her neighbors by name. Looking at the bags of chocolate chips, she could practically taste a fresh cookie. Her nose twitched at the idea of a house filled with the swirling scents of goods baking in the oven.

A mental lightbulb went on. She remembered in several of her favorite foodie mysteries that baked goods were often used as a cover to get information. The heroine (because a heroine almost always played the lead in her favorite novels) would make some sweet treats and then use the delivery to gain access to a neighbor's house. The food would be a bribe or distraction to get the unwitting suspect to spill the beans.

She would make a huge batch of chocolate chip cookies with black walnuts—her specialty—and deliver them to her neighbors, sort of a reverse welcome to the neighborhood. Once their guards were down, she would interrogate them about what they knew about Flo. Did they see anything the morning she died? Did they know of any enemies? It was pure genius. She gathered her required items and decided Neil Diamond would make good baking music. She found herself humming, "I am... I said."

Daphne sketched a neighborhood map on the back of an advert for Rossi's Hardware offering ten dollars off any plumbing supply. Squares representing the homes around Flo's house followed curvy roads toward the downtown. She planned to stick nearby, but filled out the paper as best she could, drawing the town hugging the Androscoggin River. She wrote down the businesses she could recall that lined the riverfront and on either side of The Green. The downtown was approximately a mile long, and then it turned into schools and homes—nothing worth noting on the map.

Putting the map in her pocket, she appraised the piles of plastic bags filled with stacked cookies. Carefully, she put them in a quilted tote and headed out to canvas the neighborhood. It felt like a reverse trick-or-treat.

Instead of asking for candy, she would be ringing doorbells and offering snacks to the locals. And unlike the cool fall weather that one could expect on Halloween, this was a sunny, warm, early June day.

The properties in the neighborhood had large yards. The houses were set back a little farther from the road, giving them privacy. This was different from the smaller, tidy, lawn-focused homes downtown. Here, trees, gardens, and space were the general aesthetic. While close enough to bike or walk to Main Street, this felt more like the country. When she was young, this neighborhood felt remote and wild compared to the gentrified suburbs of home.

Turning right at the end of the driveway, she marched past the Nolans' home. Deciding to start at the furthest point and work her way back, she continued past several other plots. Daphne doubted anyone further down would have been able to see or hear anything, so, before too long, she selected a house, stood up straight, and plastered on her friendliest Midwestern smile as she walked up the driveway.

Rhododendrons made a natural fence separating the house from the road. Lilac bushes were used as a barrier between the driveway and the lawn. Hydrangeas lined the front of the impressive structure. Daphne suspected it was an Italianate-style house from the 1800s. The three-story structure was white with a low-pitched black roof; wide, overhanging eaves; a cupola; bay windows; heavy trim around the doorway; and tall windows with black shutters. It was beautiful.

She pressed the bell. Quickly, the door opened, revealing a woman not much older than herself, with long, straight brown hair and dressed in pressed white linen pants and a black sleeveless sweater. Looking Daphne up and down, she asked, "Yes?"

"Hi, I'm your new neighbor. I wanted to introduce myself."

"Oh, yes. Flo's niece," she replied in a tone of indifference.

"That's me. I'm Daphne Patterson."

"I'm Marion Puddingstone." Her name came out like a sigh.

Daphne grabbed a package of cookies from her bag and thrust them toward the dismissive woman. "I thought I would introduce myself and bring a little gift for my neighbors."

Marion took the cookies, inspected them, shrugged, and opened the door wide. She turned on her heel and retreated into the recesses of the home, with Daphne hustling behind her. They walked on white Travertine tiles, past the stairway with a mahogany banister, and into a white and stainless-steel kitchen.

Marion dumped the baggie on the table in the nook and indicated her visitor should sit. "Would you like something to drink? I think I have some iced tea or sparkling water in the fridge."

Since the woman was already on her way to the double-door monstrosity, Daphne felt it rude to refuse a beverage. "Water would be great."

Two bottles clinked as Marion held them in one hand and carried glasses in the other. She placed them on the table and twisted the caps off. "I didn't know Flo very well, but I'm sorry for your loss. You didn't need to bring cookies over."

"It was no problem."

With carefully manicured hands, Marion opened the cookie bag and offered one to Daphne.

"Thanks," Daphne said as Marion sealed the bag up again. "You're not going to have one?"

"Trying to cut back on carbs."

Daphne felt the woman's eyes on her as she took a bite from her treat, and crumbs dropped onto the table. "You have a lovely home."

"Thanks. Historical properties are a good investment. So, where do you come from?"

"Michigan." Daphne took a swig from her glass. "Have you lived here long?"

"I think five years now." She played with the bottle cap before asking, "What do you plan to do with the house?"

"I'm not sure. I might stay for a while. It's such a wonderful town. So peaceful, don't you agree?"

"Peaceful? Sure, nothing remotely exciting happens here."

"Though I expect it was pretty noisy and crazy the day Auntie Flo passed."

"Yeah. Hard not to notice the noise coming from the police car and ambulance. Like one of those police dramas on TV." Marion belatedly twisted her face into a semi-sad look, as if remembering too late that the woman requiring the emergency vehicles was a relative of Daphne's.

"You didn't happen to notice anything early that morning? Or hear anything?"

"Uh, no." Marion stared at her guest.

"Do you know anyone who had a grudge against my aunt?"

"What? A grudge? Seriously?"

"Did you ever see someone engaged in a confrontation with Flo?"

"No, not that I can recall. Look, I have to get back to work. I have a meeting in a few minutes. Sorry to send you off, but I can't miss this."

Daphne allowed herself to be herded back outside, and the door slammed behind her. She doubted there really was a meeting.

The rest of the afternoon made for similar scenes. Most people were pleased to get the cookies and offered their condolences. In almost every case, she was invited in for a drink. Everyone wanted to know her plans for the house. Then, when she asked questions about the day Flo died or any possible conflicts her aunt may have had around town, they remembered something they had to do and scooted her onto the street.

Returning home, she collected all her information on her map, putting the homeowners' names and any details she'd collected in each square. After all the baking, walking, and drinking beverage after beverage, she had little to show for her efforts. She did learn that she had a coffee limit. Her limbs shook for two hours before the caffeine high wore off. She'd also ascertained that Charlotte Watford's husband, Tony, was allergic to nuts.

No one saw or heard anything on the morning in question. It was only after the cops arrived that everyone came out to see what was causing the commotion. As for whether anyone might wish Auntie Flo harm, no one wanted to comment. Most averted their eyes like kids accused of raiding the cookie jar, obviously guilty due to the crumbs covering their faces. Were they keeping some town secret?

In novels, the protagonists didn't have these problems. Heroines went to people, gave them baked goods, got a clue, and moved on. But Daphne's efforts had yielded nothing. It had been an utter waste of a day.

As the sun fell below the horizon, sending the sky into its magical blue hour after sunset, Daphne tried her best to drink it all in. Twilight was her favorite time of day. No color could compare to that mystical sapphire light in the sky. Popping two ibuprofen, she took a swig of whatever white wine was in the fridge to swallow them down. She'd already opened an emergency bottle of wine, and it hadn't even been twenty-four hours.

Maybe the reason she hadn't found any clues was because there were none to find. Flo's death was still a mystery. If she hadn't been killed, then why did she take her own life? Hopefully, her last card to play would bring her luck. She'd skipped her next-door neighbors, planning on inviting Chet and Phil over for dinner, with cookies for dessert. That would give her a better chance to ask them some questions. They would be the ones most likely to know something.

Heaving a sigh, she drained her wine glass. Darkness was falling. She headed inside to read one of her mystery books for inspiration. She would start fresh again in the morning.

Chapter Eight

The Next Morning - The Locals

Joe's Diner was located on the edge of Main Street. A red flashing neon sign welcomed individuals inside the worn but comfortable establishment. The floors were black-and-white checkered. A line of booths hugged the walls, and an old-fashioned counter with stools bolted to the floor filled the center. All the seats were covered in shiny red vinyl.

The diner decor was not a reproduction of the 1950s style. It simply had been around for decades, changing hands and names occasionally, but each owner had apparently seen no reason to renovate. In the sixties and seventies, the diner had started to look old and outdated, but around the eighties, it became vintage and remained that way.

The diner did not belong to Joe. The current owner was Parmelia King. Parmy—to those who knew her well enough—had, until a few years ago, been one Mrs. Joe King. During a bitter divorce, in a move of pure vitriol, Parmy went for the whole hog during the settlement stage and confiscated the diner from Joe. She kept the restaurant's name out of spite and to ensure Joe never forgot what he'd lost when he two-timed her.

The locals showed their appreciation for Parmy's steady hand over the menu and costs by making Joe's Diner the go-to place in Cobb. During breakfast, it overflowed with throngs of folks coming in for eggs, a cup of coffee, and the opportunity to get gossip from the regulars. Making it the most popular item in the restaurant.

That morning, the typical friendly atmosphere and banter were absent. Instead, heated voices and barking comments replaced them. As Parmy circled, filling coffee cups, it was clear that everyone was talking about one topic only. Daphne Patterson. And that woman had the town up in arms. Without her presence, the townsfolk were free to speak their minds.

"She brought cookies to the house," accused Marion Puddingstone, sitting across from her husband, Jackson. They were wearing matching white button-down shirts and navy slacks. They ran the insurance company a few doors down. A busy, dual-income couple, they often ate breakfast at the diner. Always the same poached eggs with dry wheat toast.

"Well, that was neighborly of her," Parmy pointed out as she refilled their brown ceramic mugs.

"Yes, that was. I don't know if we've ever had a neighbor bring us cookies. And they were delicious, too," Jackson admitted as he opened two creams to add to his coffee.

His wife rolled her eyes at him. Parmy wasn't sure if it was for the creamers or his comment.

"Okay, that was nice, sure. But then she asked all these impertinent questions. If I saw or heard anything the morning of Flo's death." Marion looked mortified.

"And did you?" Parmy leaned in, smelling gossip.

"Goodness, no, of course not. We were asleep. We only saw the emergency vehicles that came later. Then she started asking if Flo had any enemies. How am I supposed to answer that?" Looking indignant, she took a slug of her black coffee.

"That's a pickle." Parmy nodded and headed off with her coffee pot.

"What are we supposed to tell her?" The local hardware store owner Nino Rossi demanded loudly enough for the entire restaurant to hear him.

"That her aunt was not well-liked? A crotchety old broad who tended to get your backside up? Flo Winkler was not a nice lady."

The conversations were growing from small table ones to a full-blown town hall.

"I don't know about that, Rossi," countered Cemil Kaplan, the owner of the local bait and tackle shop. His wrinkled and weathered skin indicated a life often spent outdoors. "I never had any problems with that woman. She was always a good customer for me, and polite to boot." He shoveled in a large bite of his biscuits and gravy.

Angelica Vessels, ladies' hairdresser, waved her mug of coffee around as she joined the verbal melee. "She certainly liked her fish more than she liked people. Hardly had a nice thing to say about anyone when she was sitting in my chair." Her blonde hair was raised high on her head in a bump held in place with a sixties-style mod fabric headband.

Marion waited as the waitress placed her eggs and toast in front of her. "But what about her implications that something is amiss? Seriously, a murder, here in Cobb? What's she thinking? Is that normal where she comes from? I guess Detroit must be pretty dangerous, but this is Maine."

"I don't believe she is from Detroit, dear. But some town called Birmingham, wherever that is," interjected Jackson, but his comment only earned him a sneer from Marion. He silenced himself by putting a forkful of eggs into his mouth.

Rossi supported Marion. "Well, of course, it wasn't murder. That isn't how we handle things here."

"She really thinks Flo was killed?" Angelica asked incredulously.

Several heads nodded, and murmurs of yes floated through the space.

Angelica shook her own head in disbelief. "She's an outsider. She doesn't understand, does she? Well, we all know what happened, and it wasn't murder."

This had the effect of quieting the crowd. They all looked at each other. Faces were transformed to reveal discomfort, guilt, sadness, anger, or confusion. The actual cause of Flo's death was widely known. Sheriff Allett might have wanted to keep the suicide hidden for the sake of Flo's image in the town. However, secrets were hard to keep in Cobb, especially one so scandalous.

Most of the townsfolk found the truth difficult to discuss, so it was easier not to. They thought it best to get on with things and let Flo rest in peace. And yet, the question of why hung over the town. No one knew, and they didn't want to, in case they might be partly to blame.

"That may be. But someone needs to set this woman straight." Marion's voice was high-pitched with the righteousness of the wrongly accused. "Flo was not murdered, and her niece needs to stop this crazy investigation. I don't want to be interrogated like a criminal. I've done nothing wrong."

"*We have all* done wrong." Reverend Ambrose McDonald rose slowly but firmly from his booth in the corner. He paused to gaze around the restaurant. He wanted to make sure he had everyone's attention. "We have all sinned. Our sister Florence was in pain. So much so that she felt there was no way out."

Everyone winced. Several studied their placemats with great intensity.

"She needed her community to help lift her from her darkness. Were we there for her? No. Was she the kindest of people? She was not. She was gruff, sarcastic, and didn't suffer fools. But she knew her duty to her community. She served the sheriff for over thirty years. Whenever the church held a bake sale, she brought a plate of brownies. Did you know that?" He again searched out their eyes.

They shook their heads, guilt building up in their chests.

"Her neighbors and town let her down. Were we kind to her? I know she was always on the edge of our little community. Was that her choice or ours? Did any of you ever ask yourself that?"

Again, heads wobbled. Parmy blinked away a lone tear.

"Now her poor niece has come into town to deal with the death of her aunt and has just learned about the tragic circumstances. Can you blame her for struggling to come to terms with this? Is it such a stretch of the imagination to put yourself in her shoes? Maybe it is easier for her to believe that her beloved aunt was murdered than it is to accept she took her own life."

"Okay, Reverend. We do feel bad for her. But what can we do?" asked the practical Cemil.

"Thank you. This is what we're going to do. Everyone is going to go along with her so-called investigation."

Heads shot up, and eyes bulged wide. Murmurings of protest rumbled through the crowd. The reverend put his hand up to keep them silent.

"This is our atonement, ladies and gentlemen. We failed our sister Florence. Now, God has sent us another sister in pain and distress. It's time to show that we are the good people we believe ourselves to be. The loving neighbors we want to be. So, go along with her investigation. Show her all the kindness you can muster. She will find nothing. There is nothing to find. Eventually, she will give this up, and we can help her accept this painful loss."

A sizzling tension filled the space. Would they go along with his plan?

"Sometimes a dog gets a bone. They go crazy with that bone, and you just gotta let them have at it until they get tired. Then they will drop it and move on to something else." Cemil ran his hand over the stubble on his chin as he shared this pearl of wisdom.

"Daphne *is* in a lot of pain." Violet spun around on one of the stools at the counter. "At The Sidecar she was talking about how she lost her job a few months back. And then there was this fiancé. He cheated on her with their cleaning woman. She walked in on them."

"Men," growled Parmy as her eyes narrowed.

The tension in the room deflated.

"Can we do this?" Reverend McDonald gently asked, his chastising tone gone.

Heads nodded, and assurances were given.

"Excellent. I'm very proud of you all. Please spread the word." He felt safe knowing that the rumor mill would get the news to nearly everyone in town by lunchtime. He gave a silent prayer that he had done the right thing. "What harm will come from us answering a few silly questions?" he asked to no one in particular.

Chapter Nine

DAPHNE STRUGGLED TO ADD some form to the dining table's function. She found three tablecloths in a hall closet. She selected one with a white background covered with yellow, blue, and pink flowers. It was quite possibly the girliest thing in her aunt's home. Flo only owned an everyday set of white plates and plain glasses, which Daphne used to set the table for three. A few peonies from the yard drooped in a large mason jar in the middle of the table. It was the only vase-like thing she could find. Auntie Flo obviously didn't get many flowers. Giving a final glance over the room, she left to attend to herself.

Nature blessed her with curls. For years, she wasted hours and hours straightening them. Wallace preferred her in sleek locks. Since the cleaning lady incident, she hadn't flattened a single strand. Instead, she had started a more amicable relationship with her wild mane.

Eyeing her red "wow" dress, which she'd packed in rebellion after her mom left her bedroom, she ultimately rejected it. She would have zipped it up in a flash if her company was only handsome Phil. However, since both father and son would be at her table, the low-cut sweetheart neckline seemed a bit much. She'd just have to save it for a rainy day.

The thin-strapped sundress that fell above her knees seemed more appropriate. A fun lemon pattern covered the white dress, perfect for summer. Feeling a little daring, she decided to grab her red lipstick to enhance her already full mouth. It seemed silly not to take advantage of her time with her attractive neighbor, even if a chaperone was joining them. Maybe Phil would show up with flowers.

The gentlemen arrived at the door with a bottle of chardonnay as their contribution to the dinner. Daphne ushered them towards the kitchen, where a meal of roast beef and mixed vegetables waited. As platters of food were passed around, Daphne looked for a way to bring up the tricky questions she'd been dying to ask. She hoped an opening would come before too long and she wouldn't have to sledgehammer her way in.

After sipping the pleasant vintage in her glass, she began casually, "Phil, what do you do for a living?"

"Right now, I am teaching English remotely to several students in China and Japan. It's pretty rewarding and gives me the flexibility I need." He stole a quick look at his father.

Chet grimaced. "What he isn't telling you, which is kind of him, is that I had a heart attack a few months back."

Phil's eyes closed tightly.

Daphne looked over her guest for signs of fatigue and distress. "Oh, Chet, I'm so sorry."

"Thanks, dear. I'm doing better, but it was a little scary for a bit. The doctor didn't want me to be alone afterward. Phil here put his whole life on hold to move back home. I'm a lucky guy. Not every man has a son who would do that." He looked affectionately at his son.

Phil waved his hand. "Awww, Dad, it was nothing."

Daphne wondered if she would do the same for her mom. She liked to think she would.

"It was not nothing." Chet placed his hand flat on the table. "You put a lot on hold for me, and I appreciate that. I wouldn't be doing as well as I am without you." He looked back at Daphne. "With his teaching job moving online, he could move in with me and keep working." He shook his head in disapproval. "Though what hours? He is up at the crack of dawn to teach them."

"It's the time difference," Phil explained. "I'm online from about five until nine in the morning. It's the evening for them. Most of my students are adults who take classes after work. In the early morning, I talk with them, and then the rest of the day is flexible as to when I grade assignments and get to the other paperwork that has to be done. I won't lie. Getting up at 4:30 to be ready for my first student is a bit of a hassle."

"So that means you were up the morning that Auntie Flo died," Daphne interjected, seeing her opening. "Did you hear or see anything?"

The men exchanged meaningful glances.

"I'm sorry," began Phil. "I didn't see or hear a thing. I was up, yes. But when I have students, I use these noise-canceling headphones and focus on my laptop and students. Heck, sometimes I don't even notice my dad walking right behind me. He's scared the crap out of me a couple of times."

His father chuckled.

"I wish I could help you, but I didn't notice anything until later, when the ambulance arrived."

She gave a huff. "No one on the street seems to have seen or heard anything. How is that?"

"Look at the properties," Chet instructed. "The homes are set back, and everyone has plenty of trees and bushes. Privacy is sort of the point on the street. It's not like downtown, where everyone can see everybody's business." Changing the subject, he pointed to a framed award hanging on the wall. "That's for your aunt's service to the sheriffs, isn't it?"

Daphne got out of her chair and went to study the oak frame more closely. It was a merit award, thanking Florence Winkler for thirty-five years of service to the Androscoggin County Sheriff's Department. She turned around, confused.

"I thought Auntie Flo worked for the town of Cobb."

"She did, and she didn't. Cobb pooled resources with Hinckley and some other small towns for some public services as Androscoggin County. It's the same for firefighters and ambulances. Flo knew the police in all the local towns because she dispatched and worked with all the local areas."

"That makes sense." Daphne nodded her head. Working for a public library, she understood how some local governments had to share or combine resources to serve the people's needs. Hinckley, the nearest big town, was still about an hour's drive away. Cobb offered what you needed on a day-to-day basis, but for anything out of the ordinary, you had to go further afield. Given the drive, residents usually did several chores in one trip.

"I remember," Chet remarked wistfully. "She and Henry Clark were pretty good chums on the force together for a while. Too bad he isn't still around. He could probably tell you some great Flo stories."

"That is too bad." She frowned. "I would have loved to hear those stories. I feel like there's a great deal I don't know about her, but I wish I knew more." Lightly tapping her glass with her nail, she worried suddenly there might be things about her aunt she would not like.

"His widow could probably tell you a thing or two," Chet continued. "Penelope Clark. She and Flo were schoolmates and best friends. But I heard that she's having some troubles of her own. Her great-niece has moved in with her. Kind of keeping an eye on her. Seems to be a trend right now." He gave his son a glance that indicated that, while he appreciated his son's loyalty and love, he also missed his independence.

"Wait. Betty is keeping an eye on her aunt?" Phil laughed and slapped his thigh with his palm. "Isn't that like the patient running the asylum? What's her family thinking?"

"Do you mean Bathtub Gin Betty?" Daphne blurted out.

"You know Betty?" Phil's eyebrows shot up.

"We've met." She decided against expanding on the *how* of their meeting to her guests. "Well, maybe I can ask her about Flo. Speaking of my aunt, do you know anyone who had a grudge against her?"

Chet gave Phil a pointed look.

"No, sorry. Can't think of anyone," Chet said quickly, refusing to meet Phil's eye.

Phil nodded. "Me neither, though I didn't know your aunt that well. I did know that she liked fishing. I was wondering if you would like to go with me this weekend. I know a good spot your aunt showed me. She knew her way around a fishing rod. Thought it might be a nice way to honor her memory." He flashed her a dazzling smile. "What do you think?"

Her mind froze. Her vision narrowed on his dishy face and bright-white teeth.

He was asking her out! Someone besides Rat Bastard did want her! She felt as if she could float on air. A date was much better than showing up with flowers. But it was fishing. Yuck! She hated fishing. She quickly crashed back to earth.

Auntie Flo had tried to make a fisherwoman of her and failed. The worms were gross, the quiet boring, and cleaning the fish was more disgusting than the worms. She could hardly think of a worse way to spend an afternoon.

"I haven't held a rod in about twenty years. So don't expect much. But I'd be thrilled to spend some time with you."

After her guests left, Daphne phoned her new friend. She wanted to capitalize on the connection between Flo and Betty's family. When Betty was asked to make an introduction between Daphne and Penelope Clark, she squealed with delight and offered an invitation to come to their home the next morning.

Chapter Ten

Daphne stared at the stately manor and glanced sheepishly at her dirty brown truck. Her new vehicle required a wash, but even clean, she knew the truck would still look out of place here. The large Second Empire-style Victorian house reigned from the largest lot on the street. Tall oaks, pines, and walnut trees provided plenty of shade.

The house was painted gray-green, and the trim an elegant cream. An inviting porch welcomed visitors to the front of the house and then wrapped around the right corner. A mix of colorful plants that Daphne couldn't identify created a cheerful landscape surrounding the building.

The most dramatic element of the house was a square tower, rising to a third story above the pitched roofline. Windows poked out of the mansard roof on the third story, and chimney stacks rose even higher. The idea of Betty, in her sixties go-go dress, living inside the Victorian masterpiece felt oxymoronic.

Steeling herself, Daphne checked her attire. Her black slip dress and white t-shirt underneath shouldn't warrant automatic disapproval. Walking up to the porch, she felt even more intimidated by the large double doors with rounded curved tops. They opened before her hand formed into a fist to knock.

Betty stepped outside. "Great! You found the place." The same broad and chipper grin that Daphne had encountered at the bar greeted her. "I figured I would give you a quick heads up before we went inside."

"Sure..." Daphne nodded, but worry lines developed on her forehead.

"As I told you, I live with my Great-Aunt Pen. My mom and the whole family started to worry about her after my Great-Uncle Henry died."

Daphne nodded again, starting to feel like a bobblehead doll. Tugging down her dress, she replied, "Good to know."

"She's crafty. If you buy into the idea that she's losing her grip on reality, she will outmaneuver you. There's nothing wrong with her. I think she got to an age where she no longer cares what people think. So, her nieces and nephews mistakenly imagine she's senile, but she isn't. She just can't be bothered anymore with being nice to people she doesn't like. Let's hope she likes you."

Daphne's eyes opened wide.

Betty cackled as she slipped her hands into her dress's pockets. Her current outfit consisted of a white, short-sleeved, collared shirt and 1940s-style blue pinstripe pinafore.

"Oh, you are having a laugh at my expense," Daphne chastised her new friend.

"Not at all. Everything I said is true. But the look on your face is priceless. Come on, let's see how you do. The door on the left of the foyer is her bedroom. Don't go in there. She'll have a fit. We've moved her downstairs. Easier on the knees, ya know?" She opened the hefty door and signaled for Daphne to follow her.

Betty led her through a large foyer. The light-green walls were topped with white dental molding and reached twelve feet high. Across the room, a set of pocket doors opened to a lovely sitting area. A watchful, petite woman sat in a dark-green reclining rocker. The large size of the chair made her appear almost childlike. She wore a collared, cotton, flower-print dress and white canvas sneakers. Her belt emphasized her slim waist. *This was Flo's best friend? They seem so different.*

Betty pulled Daphne over to stand in front of the woman.

"Aunt Pen, this is Daphne," Betty began. "Please try to be nice to her. First, I like her. You know how hard it is to find a new friend in this town."

The gray-haired woman remained stoic.

"Second, she needs people to be nice to her. She's been having a hard time of it. And last, she is Flo Winkler's lost niece. So, she's part Cobb."

"Hmm." It seemed Penelope was not going to be persuaded so easily.

"It is very nice to meet you, Mrs. Clark. You have a beautiful home." Daphne barely resisted the urge to curtsy.

Mrs. Clark narrowed her eyes to examine the young woman more closely. "Well, you clearly don't get your manners from Flo."

Daphne smothered a laugh. While it was a mean comment, she could not deny the truth of the statement, and she doubted Auntie Flo would have been offended.

"Have a seat, both of you," Penelope directed.

The first hurdle had been cleared.

Daphne gingerly sat on the dark-green sofa. "Yes, I know what you mean. She was always a bit... bold in her manner."

"Bold, ha." Penelope slapped her knee. "That's a nice way of saying rude. She always spoke her mind. It was the best and worst thing about her. At least you always knew where you stood with Flo, though. Well, almost always. I hear you have inherited her old place." She gave her a hard stare. "Are you going to sell it and go back to Detroit?"

"It's Birmingham, not Detroit. Honestly, I am not sure what I want to do. I am at a bit of a loose end right now. I thought I would stay here for a while." She gave Betty a conspiratorial look.

"Don't you miss your family? Isn't there some young man waiting for you back in Michigan?" Penelope asked.

"No. I'm single at the moment." A blush warmed Daphne's face. "My family, I have my parents and my brother. My brother's a student at Notre Dame. And my mom and I... well, things have been a little tense between us."

"Yeah, Aunt Pen." Betty patted the victory rolls on her head to prevent an escape. "She just found out that her mom kept her away from Flo. Isn't that wild? Mega drama. It reminds me of one of your Lifetime movies."

"Flo was good to you that summer, but I suppose your mother must have had her reasons." Penelope's shoulders sagged a little. "But I know how frustrating it feels when family members start interfering with your life and making all kinds of choices for you."

"Oh, Aunt Pen. It hasn't been so bad having me here, has it? I think of it as an adult sorority. I'm no snitch." Betty held up three fingers, the Girl Scout salute.

Penelope chuckled. "I will admit. I've laughed a lot more with you here, Betty. You sure keep things exciting with all your internet stuff. And you introduced me to *Lucifer* on TV. What a handsome fellow he is. That man could tempt me to hell, for sure."

Daphne's eyebrows shot up. "You watch *Lucifer*?"

"Yep, we watch it together. Have you seen it? You won't even remember Wallace's name after you get a look at that hot devil." Betty giggled.

"I could look at Lucifer all day." A wicked grin spread across Penelope's oval face. "He gets my blood pumping. Speaking of blood pumping, you got any of that promotion gin about, girl? I'm in the mood for a G&T."

"It's only ten-thirty in the morning, Aunt Pen."

"I'm eighty years old, child. I could drop dead at any moment. I no longer have time for social conventions. You'll learn that when you get to my age. Besides, it's five o'clock somewhere." She cackled and threw herself back into her rocking chair.

"You're going to make me regret showing you how to use social media, aren't you? Fine, I'll be back in a few minutes. Daph, why don't you join me in the kitchen?"

"Sure." Daphne hopped up, feeling a twinge of regret for leaving; things were starting to get interesting. "Your aunt is a pistol," she admitted when they were alone in the kitchen.

"I can't believe my mom thought I could be a balancing influence on her," Betty said. "She's a force of nature. Don't get me wrong, I love her, even if she is going to make a barfly out of me." She pulled two glasses from a cupboard and held out a third toward Daphne. "Do you want one?"

Daphne felt unsure of how to proceed. She recalled her vow to cut back on alcohol. "You're going to have one?"

"Oh, yeah. Aunt Pen doesn't like to drink alone."

"Okay, then sure, why not?" Daphne shrugged her shoulders. "It's been that kind of month, as you know."

Betty collected the gin, tonic, and fresh lime. She deftly cut several slices of the fruit and squeezed plenty of juice into each glass. The ice made an enjoyable tinkle as it fell into the glasses. When she finished pouring the liquid, Daphne noticed that one glass had more gin than the others.

Seeing the look, Betty became bashful. "So, I haven't gone all the way over to her level of alcohol consumption yet. I use less booze. But this way, she doesn't have to drink solo."

"Why not make hers light as well?" Daphne took an offered glass.

"She'd know. She likes them as strong as a team of oxen."

"She's so small!"

"I told you not to underestimate her. But I guess she has a point. At her age, she should be able to do what she wants. I know I would want freedom when I turn eighty."

Grabbing the two glasses on the counter, Betty gestured back to the parlor. "We better get in there and see what kind of trouble she's getting up to."

Chapter Eleven

Upon their return, Daphne was surprised to find an unknown man in the sitting room, holding Penelope's attention. Something about him seemed familiar, but Daphne couldn't make the connection. He leaned on the fireplace, his arm resting on the carved cherrywood mantel.

"Hi, Betty," the newcomer said. He nodded, with a smile toward the frozen blonde. "Daphne."

Stiffly, she bent her head in return. Her stomach clenched. Like Han Solo, she was starting to have a bad feeling about this. Once more, she found herself the odd one out, like everyone else knew a secret she wasn't being told.

"Hey, Fitzy. Good timing," chirped Betty. "The internet is acting up again, and I need it fixed for my next upload. Here's your drink, Aunt Pen."

He settled himself into a leather chair as Betty asked, "You want one?"

"Uh, no, a little early for me. But you ladies enjoy yourselves. Since you moved in with Aunt Pen, this has become quite the party house."

"We're starting a sorority," Penelope quipped. "You can't join; no boys allowed."

Daphne tried to catch Betty's eye to signal that the man making himself at home was unknown to her. Finally, Betty looked at her. After some head nudging and eye twitching, the message was received.

"Do you want something *else* to drink, Goody Two-shoes?" Betty inquired.

"A glass of lemonade would be perfect."

"I can mix up a pitcher. Given that we are in the parlor and being all proper. I should make some old-fashioned introductions."

"Daph, this is Fitzy, my cousin. Fitzy, this is my new pal Daph." She pointed a finger at her cousin as she returned to the kitchen. "Try not to embarrass me," she warned him.

Daphne indulged in looking him over. He appeared close to her age and but about half-a-foot taller. He and his cousin shared the same dark hair color. While Betty's locks were fashionably styled, his were short and charitably described as pragmatic. A green polo and khaki pants covered his lean frame. She hated to stereotype, but he easily could be labeled a nerd.

"Nice to meet you, Fitzy. Is that another Betty nickname? She does love them."

"Yes. It is much preferred to the real one." He rolled his green eyes.

"Which is?"

"Byron."

Daphne tried not to react but apparently failed.

Fitzy nodded. "I know. It's awful. Betty's mom and mine, who are sisters, were both really into classical literature. Seriously, no one should be able to read that stuff until they are at least thirty. It's too dangerous. An old-fashioned name like Hercule wouldn't have been so bad, but Byron?" He shuddered.

"Hercule? Poirot?" Her eyes sparkled. "Are you an Agatha Christie fan?"

"Yeah. You like Christie too, huh? Cool. What do you think of the remake of the *Orient Express*?" He leaned toward her.

"I liked it a lot. I thought it was a well-done version. Though, of course, nothing compares to the David Suchet series." She'd watched every episode and movie several times. "Those are the best."

"Same. I watch those over and over. I have the collection on DVD." He beamed.

"You do? DVDs? How retro."

"I could bring them over sometime. I don't know if you've met many people in town yet. Making friends in a small town can be more difficult than most people think. Not everyone is super friendly."

"That would be great. I haven't made many friends yet." Daphne noticed Mrs. Clark staring at him with an inquisitive look. He seemed oblivious, and she decided not to bring attention to it. "I've got Betty and am getting to know my next-door neighbors, but it's slow going. I'm not exactly Miss Popular, with the whole trying to find out who killed Auntie Flo. Admittedly, I may have turned off a few neighbors." Should she have remained silent? What if he didn't want to hang out once he knew what she was up to?

"Betty told me about your suspicions." He frowned. "Murder does seem a little unlikely." Shrugging, he continued. "But trying to solve a real-life crime could make for interesting evenings. Maybe watching Poirot will inspire your investigation."

"Did you say Flo was murdered?" Penelope gawked at them.

Daphne and Fitzy shared a look of concern. Neither wanted to worry the older woman with anxiety that a killer was on the loose. Her mouth went dry. She hated lying, but freaking out her new friend's aunt seemed impolite.

"Oh, it's just a rumor going around," Fitzy reassured his great-aunt. "You know gossip is an Olympic sport in this town. People will talk about this until the next thing comes along. Don't worry about it. The sheriff doesn't think there was any foul play."

Penelope sipped at her cool drink. "Hmm. When Flo worked for the police, it might have made sense. But she's been retired for decades. Murders just don't happen in Cobb. I don't think Henry investigated even one the entire time he was on the force."

"Your husband worked for the Cobb police, didn't he?" Daphne's curiosity piqued.

"Yes, for thirty years. He gave a lot of service to this town. Then he retired, and fishing became his full-time job."

"I enjoyed many trout dinners over here. Aunt Pen, you sure could make magic in the kitchen with what those two caught," Betty said, referring, Daphne guessed, to Flo and Henry. Betty was holding Fitzy's lemonade, and she handed the glass to him. "Everything is ready for you upstairs."

"Okay." Fitzy took a quick sip of the lemonade and made a sour face. "Did you remember to put sugar in here?"

She grabbed the glass out of his hand and took a sip. "Yuck. I did, but not enough. I'll fix it and bring it up to you." She turned to Daphne. "My rooms are on the second floor. I have a bedroom and a separate work studio for video editing. I also have another room to record videos. I'm so lucky to have all this space." She winked at her aunt, who smiled.

Fitzy moved toward the stairs.

From her couch, Daphne called out to him, "It was nice to meet you."

"Oh, you met him already," Betty said. "He's the one who took us home from the bar."

His eyes danced before he quickly trod up the stairs.

Daphne's face turned hot as she hid it behind her hands. He was the mystery family member Betty had called to pick them up from the bar. The one she'd been too tipsy to remember anything about. That's why he seemed familiar earlier. *Can a human die of embarrassment? I'm about to find out.* She peeked through her fingers to find Penelope staring back, stifling a giggle.

"I think you're ready to join our sorority." Penelope's laugh was infectious, and before she knew it, Daphne smiled. For all the clumsiness of her entry, she was growing to like Cobb.

"Hey, Mrs. Clark. I'm going fishing with Phil Nolan this weekend. Do you have any tips or suggestions?" Daphne inquired. "I never took to it when I was young."

"Alas, I am no help to you, dear." Penelope started to rock. "I dislike the sport. That was Henry's hobby. I never took to it. Good luck, though."

"Oh, a fishing date with Phil Nolan. He is *sooo* cute." Betty made kissing noises.

"It's just a fishing trip." Daphne sat up, trying to act calm and relaxed. But then gave Betty a quick wink. "He *is* pretty cute."

Chapter Twelve

ANOTHER SATURDAY, AND DAPHNE wasn't getting any closer to who murdered her aunt. It had to be murder. The Flo she knew wasn't the kind to kill herself. But she hadn't seen Flo for twenty years. Who had she become since their summer together? The cookie plot yielded no information, and she lacked inspiration for how to move forward. She could still sell the house and head back to Michigan, like she'd originally planned. But the only thing waiting there were more unhelpful job applications from her mother and endless *suggestions* on how she should live her life. No thanks, she'd stick to her investigation. This was supposed to be her great reinvention, after all.

Today, however, she would have to pause her investigation. Fishing with Phil awaited her. She brimmed with excitement, while her stomach churned with nerves. She hadn't dated since Wallace. Finding him with another woman had shredded her self-esteem.

She'd tried downloading a matchmaking app, but all the guys looked shifty and likely to be players and cheaters. She hadn't been ready to wade into the dating pool. However, Phil did not seem like a player; he was a sweet guy who had moved back home to help care for his sick dad. He was a giver. She needed someone who would give as well as take.

What to wear on a fishing date continued to confound her. On the few attempts at fishing with Flo, Daphne remembered that she'd worn a t-shirt and shorts, maybe jeans, if the weather had been a little chilly. But she wanted Phil to see her as an attractive woman, not a scrappy kid. Her eyes closed as she cringed at the memory of the disastrous outings. Flo gave up after three tries and resigned herself to the fact that her niece was not a fisherwoman.

After her shower, Daphne went to work on her hair and makeup. She wanted this date to go perfectly. She imagined Phil holding her hand, helping her into the car, then using the excuse of showing her how to fish to put his arms around her as she held a fishing rod.

She looked over her limited outfit options and decided on the same black slip dress she had worn earlier to Betty's place. However, she opted not to put on a t-shirt underneath. Why not show a little more skin? Grabbing her shoes, she slipped into Flo's room. A tall stand-alone mirror allowed a final look at herself. Approving, she sat on the edge of the bed to put on her black sandals. Turning her head, she noticed a book on the nightstand titled *Fishing Guide to the Androscoggin*. She took it downstairs to check it out with a quick breakfast of cornflakes.

She skimmed the introduction and read about how the river started in New Hampshire, continued into Maine, and poured into the Kennebec River near the ocean. An angler could catch brook trout, salmon, or bass, depending on where along the river they found themselves. Daphne shivered at the thought. She didn't like fish. They were okay on a plate, but the way they wriggled around gave her the willies. She almost gagged on her cornflakes. She pushed the bowl away. Maybe she'd skip breakfast this morning.

She wasn't sure anything in the book would help her impress Phil. Closing the volume, she caught a glimpse of something that made her open it again. On the front page was an inscription.

It read, "For my favorite fishing partner. It doesn't matter if the weather is fair or foul. If we get a catch or break a line. The best part of the day is the short while that you are mine. Forever, yours."

Forever, yours, who? Daphne stared at the page, her mind racing with possibilities. No name magically appeared. She flipped through the book's pages, looking for further writing, but found none. According to the publication date, the book came out in 1980. Perhaps it was a used book that Flo picked up at a resale shop. Or did Flo have someone in her life after all? She sat in stunned silence as questions flooded her brain.

A loud knock snapped her out of her reverie.

She left the book on the oak dining table and rushed to the door. Phil was leaning against the frame casually. He had a chill vibe, from the still-damp hair to his faded green t-shirt and worn-out jeans and boots. He looked her over, and Daphne tried to read his face. It was either a smile or a smirk. She decided to go with a smile.

"Ready?"

"Yeah. Let me grab my purse." She turned away to collect her small, cross-strapped Kate Spade bag. Her mind spun between trying to process the new information about Flo and ensuring the date went smoothly. "I wish there was a coffee place in town. I would kill for a good latte."

"Oh, we can get a coffee at the bait and tackle store," he reassured her as they headed to his truck.

"Seriously?" She wrinkled her nose. "Who drinks coffee from a bait and tackle place?"

"Lots of people. Your aunt was a big fan. We'll be stopping to get worms and some other supplies. The guy who runs it is Cemil Kaplan. His family was from Turkey. They came here when he was a kid. Anyway, he opened the store. It sells hunting and fishing stuff and snacks, and then he started selling Turkish coffees at some point. You'll have to try it. It's an institution in these parts, and it's on the way."

He walked over to his door and left her to fend for herself, but she didn't let herself feel disappointed. While it would have been nice if he had held open the truck door, it wasn't necessary. She was a modern woman. She didn't need a man to cover puddles for her.

"How long have you and your dad lived in Cobb?" She hoped his father had lived in town during the 1980s and might know who had given her aunt the book.

"We moved in 2000. My parents wanted to leave Hinkley, feeling it was getting too big for them. They missed the small-town feel."

"Your mom..." She left it hanging as a question. He'd mentioned his parents, plural. That was the first mention of his mother.

He cleared his throat. "She passed away from cancer a few years back."

"I'm so sorry, Phil."

He kept his eyes on the road ahead. She got the hint. He was not in the mood to discuss it.

Daphne tried a less touchy subject. "Where were you living before you moved back home?"

"Manchester, New Hampshire, and worked as an adjunct professor at the community college there."

"Did you like it there?" His conversation wasn't giving her a lot to work with.

"Yeah, it's a nice town. The college was great. They even allowed me to take a year's sabbatical to come and stay with Dad. I'm hoping to convince him to move back there with me. I know he loves Cobb, and it's a great small town and everything, but..."

"Your life is back in Manchester?"

"Yes." He gave her a genuine smile. "Who would expect you to uproot your whole world and move to this small place? Like you said, they don't even have a decent coffee shop." He relaxed back into his seat.

She gave him a tight smile and slumped back. That had been exactly what she was considering. Not in a making-firm-plans kind of way, but in a dreaming-about-the-future sort of fashion. Sitting on Flo's couch and listening to her vinyl records, Daphne allowed some minor fantasies of morning coffee on the porch, painting over the oak-stained cabinets in the kitchen, having new friends over, chatting cozily in front of the fireplace, and warm summer romantic picnics on The Green with a new love. Upon reflection, she realized she'd been thinking about this idea frequently. Having distance between her and her parents sounded like freedom, not heartbreak, and the quiet life of Cobb appealed to her.

Yeah," she finally answered. "Tell me more about Manchester. I've never been there." Daphne allowed him to chatter on about New Hampshire and the town. She hardly listened to what he had to say. She was too busy trying to understand what she was learning about herself. She made little noises when he paused to encourage him. This continued until they arrived at a tidy-looking store with a sign that read "Kaplan's Sporting Emporium."

The bell rang as they entered the door. Along the wall were several refrigerated coolers holding ice, beverages, and ominous-looking plastic tubs. Her stomach flipped, fearing what was inside them. To the right was the checkout counter. A small coffee bar was set up behind. She observed a few copper cezve pots, white cups and saucers, a hot plate, a tiny bar sink, other odds and ends, and three bar stools.

Behind the counter stood an older man with salt-and-pepper hair, wearing a plaid flannel shirt. He nodded in recognition to Phil. Taking the initiative, she walked up to the counter and introduced herself. "Hello. I'm Daphne." She flashed him her white teeth. "My aunt was Flo Winkler. I understand she was a frequent patron here."

"Yes." He nodded but didn't return her smile. "I heard you were in town. My sympathies for your loss. Flo was one of my best customers. She knew her fish better than most. I will make you a coffee. She always had a coffee when she came through. We will drink in her name."

"Thank you, Mr. Kaplan, that's kind of you." She felt a little overwhelmed. Few in Cobb had shared words of kindness regarding her aunt. Her heart warmed, finding someone who seemed genuinely sad over Flo's passing.

The man went over to the little bar area. Daphne followed around the corner and sat on one of the bar stools to watch the process. As a former barista, she knew about Turkish coffee, but she'd never tasted it or seen it made. He measured a small amount of beans and put them in a grinder. The grounds, when finished, were very fine, and he placed them in the bottom of one of the copper cezve pots. He then added sugar and water and stirred. Finally, he put it on the small stove.

It wasn't long before foam began to rise to the surface. He poured a little of the foam into two small cups and returned the coffee to the heat. After it foamed again, he removed it and slowly poured the coffee, ensuring it did not disrupt the foam. Daphne reached out for one of the cups.

He shook his head. "No, this is not filtered, and it is hot. You must let it sit for a few minutes and let the grounds settle to the bottom while it cools."

Phil strolled up to the counter with his arms full. He carried a couple of water bottles and a plastic bucket. On it, someone had written "bait" in marker. Her stomach flipped again. To her relief, he placed his items over by the checkout area.

"You're trying the coffee. Awesome. Hey, have you had breakfast?" His voice was chipper and more excited than when he had picked her up.

"Not really." She thought of the mostly discarded bowl of cornflakes.

"Me neither. I'll grab some jerky." He left to go down an aisle.

Her stomach protested again. Jerky was not something she ate; she was not sure how it would agree with her.

When he returned with the jerky, he looked at his items, then her. "Oh, did you want some water? You probably should grab some. Want to stay hydrated."

She had thought one of those bottles of water was for her. Now she understood they were both for him. "Yes, that's a good idea. I will get one and be back to drink this coffee." She strode down the aisle, looked over her water selection, and grabbed a large bottle of her favorite brand.

A feeling of resentment began bubbling inside her. He didn't open her door; he wasn't even getting her a bottle of water. What kind of date was this? Was he trying to show her he wasn't an oppressive, old-fashioned guy? Maybe this was how they did things in Maine.

She returned and sat back down on her stool. Mr. Kaplan handed her a cup of dark coffee with a foamy top. After getting a nod from him, they both took a sip. She'd heard people talk about how bitter the coffee tasted, but it was sweeter and richer than she'd expected. It gave a nice punch. She'd be back for more.

"This is wonderful. I can see why Auntie Flo drank these so often. You make a delicious cup of joe. You are quite the artist, sir." She tipped the cup in his direction.

His eyes twinkled. "Teşekkür ederim. That means thank you in Turkish. I'm glad to meet someone who appreciates proper coffee. Your aunt understood that fish and coffee both take patience."

"To Auntie Flo." She held out her cup, and the man across from her raised his. They both took a sip. Phil shifted from foot to foot. She took pity on Phil and finished her drink. "Mr. Kaplan, how much for the water and the coffee?"

"Today, we remember Flo. They are on the house."

"You're a real gentleman, Mr. Kaplan. Thank you very much. You have a good day." Grabbing their items, they were out the door and back in the truck.

Once buckled up, Phil offered Daphne some jerky. The smell revolted her, but she didn't want to be rude. She took a stick from the bag and began chewing. He put on the radio and gnawed on a stick of his own. The ride passed quietly since their mouths were full and the radio was playing. This did not bother her much. She felt it was a sign of how well people got along. Could you spend time together comfortably, even though there was no talking? Did you feel you had to fill every moment of silence with them?

Thirty minutes later, Phil turned off the main road onto a bumpy dirt track. He parked the car at a gravel lot, immediately hopped out, and began organizing gear from the truck bed. Daphne stood around feeling useless.

Before they started down the gravel path to the shore, Phil doused them with bug spray.

Daphne almost gagged. "Do we need this?"

"Helps keep the no-see-ums away."

"Huh?"

"I think you call them midges."

They loaded themselves down with two camp chairs, a bucket of bait, two fishing rods, a tackle box, a net, and an ice cooler for their water, then headed out.

Her sandals caused all kinds of problems. She stopped and put down her share of the gear twice to remove a painful pebble that had lodged itself under her foot. She made a mental note never to fish wearing sandals again.

After what felt like hours, they reached the shore. There was a dock with a small boat tied to it.

Suddenly Daphne had visions of her falling ass over head into the water. "I'm not so sure about going into that."

"Oh, don't worry. Since you're a beginner, I figured I'd make it easier on you and fish from the dock."

Relief rushed through her but was replaced with disgust when he opened the bait bucket. Inside were wriggling worms. She could feel the coffee and jerky churning in her stomach. She swallowed hard.

"I... umm, Phil. Yeah, I don't think I can put a worm on a hook. Auntie Flo always did that. I mean. It's moving."

He laughed. "Squeamish, huh? Sure. I can bait it for you." He chuckled as he set both of their lines.

Her head spun, trying to follow his explanation of fishing how-tos and the equipment. Not once did he try to slide up to her to "show" her how to cast. Instead, he kept a prudish three feet from her.

The flurry of activity from when they arrived contrasted against the quiet as they sat, sipped their water, and waited for a fish to bite.

At first, Daphne was pleased again that they could hang out in silence, but then she drifted into boredom. Fishing was dull. She tried to converse, but Phil hushed her, telling her she would scare the fish away. Her boredom was turning to irritation.

After what seemed forever, her line tugged at her hands. He jumped up to get the net.

"Reel it in. You've got one!"

She did her best to follow his instructions. Controlling the rod, turning the reel, and battling the fish simultaneously was more difficult than she'd imagined. The fish broke above the waterline, wriggling and jerking. She saw the scaly beast and the hook caught in its mouth. Phil caught it in the net as it continued to dance for freedom. She could hear him talking. But he sounded far away. The smell of the fish and the bucket of bait suddenly overpowered her nostrils. The contents of her stomach started to lurch upward.

She dropped the rod and tried to get to the edge of the dock. But she was too late. The burn of coffee, jerky, and acid set fire to her throat as she vomited. It took her a moment to realize that, not only had she been sick, but it was like a scene out of a horror movie. She had thrown up with such force that she'd hurled on herself, Phil in front of her, and the fish still in the net. Puke was everywhere. The smell of it caused her to retch again. Feeling weak and shaky, she sat back in the chair and stared at him.

"I'm sorry," she whispered, knowing it was inadequate. She pressed her lips together hard to prevent blubbering like a toddler who'd noticed their sibling had two more marshmallows in their cup of hot chocolate.

Phil looked down at his vomit-covered chest and then at the fish in the net. "Well. Fuck."

He slowly pulled the shirt over his head, revealing his muscled torso. Daphne would have been more appreciative in different circumstances, even trying to find excuses to touch his tanned skin. Instead, she wanted to be as far from there and him as possible.

He unhooked the fish and threw it back in the water. "Don't think anyone will want to eat that now."

"No. I think I'll be off fish for a while." She snorted and looked at her messy dress. "Should I just jump in the river?"

"It's colder than it looks. I think I have a shirt in the truck." He looked her up and down. Puke and all. "It should be long enough to cover you. Mostly."

"*Mostly?*" She shied from his gaze. If there weren't so much vomit, this would be a classic romance trope.

He grabbed a few items to carry back to the truck and returned with a wrinkled, long-sleeved, flannel button-down shirt. He held it out to her.

Gingerly, she took it and looked for a place to change. She shuffled behind some trees, praying there wasn't poison ivy in these woods. That would be just her luck.

The revolting-smelling dress dropped to the grass, and she slipped the puke-free shirt over her head. Rolling up the sleeves that came well past her hands, she was grateful he was right. The shirt hung down to at least mid-thigh. A fraction of her dignity remained, though it was safe to say that their fishing excursion was over.

With the gear stowed in the back, Daphne snuggled into the seat. Sipping water, she could still taste the acid in her mouth. Her wounded soul wanted a shower, hot tea, and someone to rub her back and tell her it would all be okay. At least she could manage two out of three.

A shirtless Phil drove up the dirt path, onto the highway, and back toward Cobb. He spared her a pitiful smile. They both knew it wasn't her fault. She couldn't have known how strongly she'd react. After five minutes of embarrassing quiet, he put on the radio. The song *Cake by the Ocean* by DNCE came through the speakers.

"Cake by the ocean probably would have been safer than fish by the river, huh?" She quipped before she thought about what the title referred to.

He snorted and tried to cover his face with his hand.

A giggle escaped her. She looked at him.

He looked at her.

Laughter exploded and didn't abate until tears were wiped from their cheeks.

Between gasps, he asked, "Are you okay now?"

"Yeah. I'm feeling better, only dying of shame. I can't believe I did that. It's been like a nightmare. I won't blame you if you never want to talk to me again."

"It's okay. I mean, yeah, it was gross, and I won't be drinking any Turkish coffee for a while, but it's cool. I suggest no more fishing for you."

"Oh, I can promise I will never go fishing again. No fear of that. But it would be nice to hang out and spend some time with you doing something that doesn't involve worms."

"Sure. Okay."

Chapter Thirteen

THE TEMPERATURE DROPPED SEVERAL degrees as the sun dipped below the scarlet horizon. Leaving a few windows open, Daphne felt a cool breeze blow through the living room. She loved the crisp and scented air. After the worst first date in the history of first dates, the comfort of a crackling fire was required, so she'd lit one in the living room's oversized fireplace. Listening to the flames hiss and snap, she snuggled into her soft, cozy, off-the-shoulder cream sweater, clutching her hot chocolate like a life raft.

Betty, splayed on the other half of the couch, drank deeply from her own mug. Her lavender circle skirt poured down over the cushions. Her hair was pulled back in a high ponytail tied with a matching lavender ribbon. A collared, short-sleeved blouse completed the vintage look; she would have looked spot-on as an extra in *I Love Lucy*.

"Thanks again for coming over," Daphne said.

"No problem," Betty replied. "This room would be even better with a bunch of candles lit."

"I like that idea. I adore reading a book by candlelight. Something so romantic about it."

"Candles and a fire, and your first thought is to read a book?" Betty's eyebrow shot up. "You've got messed up priorities, my friend."

"You can tease me all you want. I just don't want to be alone. I'm trying not to fixate on my humiliation."

"Fixating is the worst. I remember in first grade, when I called Bobby Hershal a lobotomist. None of us knew what it meant, but it sounded bad.

He burst into tears and wouldn't talk to me for the rest of the year. I can't tell you how many showers I've taken hearing those sobs coming from the past. Made me feel like dirt."

"It was first grade. I'm sure he has forgotten all about it."

Betty blew on her mug and took a sip. "I'm glad you called. I love girl talk."

This kind of "girl talk" was unusual for Daphne, but she always felt comfortable talking to Betty. "I'm thrilled to have someone in my corner right now. You can tell me that the whole thing isn't as bad as I think."

"Yeah. Sorry, there's a problem with that. Your date might be even more embarrassing than my falling into the bathtub."

"At least it wasn't on video. I would die if millions of people were watching me upchuck in real time. I'm just hoping that Phil can look past this. He said he could, but we'll see. Do you think I should do something to try and make it up to him?" While the date hadn't been as planned, she held out hope for a better one. Phil had behaved a little standoffish, sometimes even rude, but she put that down to nerves. Perhaps all he needed was more encouragement.

"I'm not sure this is something you can make up for. How would you even start? I mean, what is the proper etiquette for this? What would Miss Manners say is the expected response for throwing up on your date?"

Speaking in a haughty accent, Daphne said, "A gift of carnations is the traditional form of apology when one tosses up their breakfast on their suitor."

"If you give your admirer a fever or the pox, red roses are an appropriate expression of regret," Betty mimicked.

"My mom made me apologize to my date to homecoming my freshman year." Daphne tried to snuggle deeper into her sweater.

"Are you serious?"

"Yep. My mom drilled me for an hour on the dos and don'ts of a first date. It was more don'ts than dos, of course. By the time the guy came to pick me up, I was a nervous wreck. His dad drove us to the high school. We had one dance, and then he tried to kiss me."

"That sounds promising. What happened?"

"I freaked out. I couldn't remember my mom's rules of dating. I ended up running to the girl's bathroom and hid until his dad picked us up. The ride home made for the longest ten minutes of my life."

"That's awful."

"They belonged to the same country club as my parents, and my mom ended up hearing what happened. She yelled at me for my rude behavior and made me write an apology to my date. I was so humiliated."

"I hope things went better at the next dance."

Daphne lowered her gaze. "I never went to another one after that. I didn't want to go through that again."

"Well, if I had known you back then, I would have been your friend date for every dance and made sure you went and had a great time." Betty jutted out her chin.

"You're the best," Daphne said over a stomach growl. "I'm getting hungry. How about you?"

"Yeah, I could go for a pizza. How does that sound?" Betty asked. Daphne's stomach made another loud noise. "I'll take that as a yes. I'll call it in. Do you want to pick it up or get delivery?"

"I didn't know they did delivery here. It's not on their flyer or website."

"They don't. You see, I order extra pizza and call Fitzy. He swings by, picks up the pizza, and comes over. Voilà: pizza delivery." Her eyes flashed with mischief.

"How often do you use Fitzy as a delivery service?" A manipulative streak in Betty was revealing itself. Daphne wasn't sure if it made her uncomfortable or envious.

"Not too often. Only when I really need something. Like food. I mean, what's he doing on a Saturday night? It's not like he has a girlfriend.

I'm doing him a favor. He gets to eat pizza and hang out with us. We're amazing. Besides, it's still close to a girls' night. It's only Fitzy!"

"He seems nice enough and is definitely harmless. Sure, call in the pizza and give him a ring. I can pick it up if he's busy or doesn't want to come."

"Trust me. He'll be free and ever so happy to join us."

Betty was right on both counts.

⚘

As soon as Fitzy came in with the food, he got comfortable in a living room chair and looked as if he was feeling right at home. There was minimal talking while the three of them devoured their dinner. Before long, a collection of greasy paper plates and a pizza box with one slice left covered the coffee table. Fitzy leaned back and patted his stomach.

Daphne mirrored his casual demeanor. Her hair was piled on her head in a messy knot, and her face had no trace of makeup. Instead of excusing herself to put on some lipstick or brush out her hair, which would have happened if Phil sat in the chair, she felt comfortable as she was. She enjoyed this new experience of hanging out with a man and not trying to impress him. Betty had been correct. He was just Fitzy. It felt like she'd known him for ages already.

"Betty, what food were you making in that outfit for your video today?" Daphne tucked her feet underneath her.

"Jell-O, of course. I made three different types and fed them to my niece and nephews."

"Jell-O?" Fitzy looked a bit concerned. "Isn't Jane all into this whole organic farm fresh food for the kids?"

"My sister needs to take a chill pill." Betty rolled her eyes. "We ate all kinds of crap as kids, and we turned out fine. She fusses too much over their diet. It's not as if they have food allergies or anything."

"Did she know you were going to give them Jell-O?" Daphne hoped the answer was yes.

"Of course not. She would have said no. The kid's reaction to the Jell-O was fantastic! Some they loved, some they hated, and one spit out a flavor they couldn't stand. I'll get so many views with that."

"What if Jane won't let you put it out there?" Fitzy pointed out the hole in her plan.

"Thought of that already. I made her sign the paperwork ahead of time," Betty crowed. "Too late anyway. I posted it right before I came over. Of course, she'll have a fit, but it's done, no big deal. The only consequence may be that Gabe starts requesting cherry Jell-O. He made a pig of himself. It was awesome."

"Wait a minute," Daphne interjected, as the significance of the names dawned on her. "Your sister is named Jane Bennet, and you're Elizabeth?"

"Yep, right from *Pride and Prejudice*. Our younger sister is Lydia."

"The one who runs away as a teenager to elope with the wicked soldier?"

"That's the one. The worst flirt and stupidest of all the Bennet girls."

"Your sister never ran off to elope, did she?" Daphne joked.

"No, but she's almost as boy crazy as her namesake. She is a terror on dating apps. I don't know that she will ever get married. I think she enjoys torturing men too much."

Fitzy opened his mouth as if he was going to argue that point, but Betty gave him a pointed look. He closed his mouth and glanced sideways at Daphne, letting her know that Betty was not exaggerating much. The talk of marriage and relationships brought Daphne back to the other topic that had recently taken up more room in her thoughts.

"Speaking of romance. Do you know if Auntie Flo ever had one? Not, like, right before she died, but earlier?" Daphne tried to slide the question in smoothly. But, given the shocked look on her guests' faces, she'd failed.

Fitzy let out a laugh. "Flo Winkler have a love affair?"

"I mean, maybe when she was much younger it could have happened." Betty frowned. "You'd think everyone falls in love at least once? But not Flo. I never heard even a whisper of a romance. Kind of sad when you think of it."

Daphne got up from the couch and went to the shelves that held her evidence. She pulled out the fishing book she had placed between two albums earlier. Opening the front page, she first handed it to Betty to inspect. Her friend sat back, shocked. Fitzy took the item and became absorbed in the brief inscription. He flipped through the pages.

"I looked already." Daphne interrupted his search. "It's only that one inscription."

"Well, Flo, you old dog." A wolfish grin spread across Betty's face. "I didn't think she had it in her. A secret love affair. But with who? What happened? Why hide it?"

"I have zero answers to your questions." Daphne sighed. "Any ideas who might have been Auntie Flo's... lover?" Fumbling over the last word, Daphne realized she needed to start accepting who Flo was, no matter if the real person aligned with the version of her aunt she'd imagined.

"I can't right now. But I will think on it," Fitzy promised

"Are you sure that inscription was intended for her?" Betty asked.

"No, but I think it's possible given how much she liked to fish."

"Don't worry, Daph. We might be able to figure this out if we put our heads together. What a dark horse your aunt was. It kind of makes me like her more. It's cool how people can surprise you, even after they are gone."

"I think I'm good with surprises for the night. How about we watch a movie? I can't believe how many DVDs she has." Daphne moved to the entertainment center that housed the TV, DVD player, and a couple of drawers full of DVDs.

"It's normal here," Fitzy explained as they looked through their options. "Cobb doesn't have a movie theater, and people don't always want to drive to Hinkley for the cinema. It wasn't until recently that everyone got reliable internet and could stream stuff. Besides, your aunt knew DVD technology, so she would have stuck with what was comfortable."

"Nerd," Betty teased him. "Wow, your aunt liked dramas and biopics. A lot of heavy stuff here. Oh, wait, look." She held out a copy of *Legally Blonde*.

Fitzy whined. "Oh, come on, a chick flick?"

"I love that movie." Daphne smiled. "I'm in."

"I see *The Perfect Storm* here," he suggested. "I mean, it isn't *The Finest Hours*. But still a solid New Englander sort of movie."

"Two against one, Fitzy." Betty handed the box over to him. "You're tech support. Put it in."

The girls returned to their perch on the couch. Fitzy groaned but did as he was told. And by the time the famous bend and snap scene came on, he was laughing as hard as the ladies.

Chapter Fourteen

DAPHNE FINALLY REMEMBERED THE point of her original visit to Betty and Penelope had been to learn more about her aunt. However, between her early-hour drink and embarrassment over forgetting Fitzy, she'd lost track of her purpose. Now, the need to gather further information was critical.

She was warmly welcomed back to the elegant home when she arrived for a visit that Wednesday. Betty got the hint that her bestie needed a little one-on-one time with Penelope. She served everyone's iced tea and departed under the pretext of getting some work finished.

Walking around the parlor, Daphne studied the art hung on the walls. Most were oil paintings of river and ocean landscapes displayed inside ornate, carved wooden frames. She wondered how long they had been in the family and hanging in this room. "These are lovely."

"Thank you. My grandmother painted the one over the fireplace."

The image depicted a large sailing vessel being tossed in the ocean. Didn't look like much fun to her. Clustered on the mantel were silver-framed pictures of various sizes. Most of the images contained a petite woman and a tall man. She guessed the couple to be a younger Penelope and Henry Clark. Other people filled the rest of the frames.

"Are these your family, Mrs. Clark? Betty never mentioned if you have children."

"No, dear. Henry and I were not destined for that. But we were blessed with plenty of nieces and nephews and grand versions to fill our lives."

"That sounds nice."

"You can call me Penelope, by the way. I did know your grandma and aunt, after all. Betty is right. You do have a bit of Cobb in you." She lifted her glass of iced tea at her as if giving a benediction.

Daphne took a seat. "How well did you know Auntie Flo and Grandma May?"

"Pretty well. I went to school with both of them. I was in the same grade as Flo, but being a small school, we often made friends outside our year. All three of us were in the 4-H Club together."

"Auntie Flo?"

"I know, it doesn't seem her thing. She didn't care for quilting or most of the things that May and I liked. But she had a real knack for canning and jams. I remember our senior year she won an award for both the best pickles and applesauce in the county. She would never tell me what her secret was either."

"Brown sugar. And she cooked it with orange peels," Daphne said. She hoped Auntie Flo wouldn't be angry. Penelope was her closest friend, not some stranger. Someone should keep on making that amazing applesauce.

"Brown sugar and orange peel, huh? I usually stick with lemons. Did she use lemon juice?"

"Oh yes, she used lemon juice, too, but cooked with orange peels and brown sugar. I remember that we went to an orchard in August and picked fresh apples. We made a huge batch. I'd forgotten all about that until today."

"Canning always made her happy."

"The house smelled heavenly." The warmth of those sunny summer days flooded back. "Oh, and the cinnamon. She put that in there, too."

"Hmm, well, maybe I will try that this August."

"She'd put on Motown hits, and we'd sing along with The Supremes as we cut the apples. She said that the right music for any activity enhanced the experience. I can't believe I remember all of that. It was so long ago."

Flo had given general instructions on cooking and then let Daphne figure the details out for herself. There was no hovering or commenting on every action, just a gentle nudge when help was needed. She played and learned in the kitchen at her own pace. She relished the peaceful feeling not found in her mother's kitchen. Her mom insisted on doing everything herself because Daphne's attempts fell short of her mother's standards.

"Your aunt had the best record collection." Penelope interrupted Daphne's trip to the past. "She loved music. While the rest of us girls were spending money on clothes, makeup, going to movies, and who knows what, she saved her pennies. Once a month, her dad would take her to the record store in Hinckley. She'd come back with the latest hits. It gave her a certain popularity. Everyone invited her to their parties."

"Sounds like you had a lot of fun hanging out together."

"You need to understand Flo wasn't like the other girls. Your great-grandparents had two children. Florence and May. Mr. Winkler, your great-grandpa, wanted a boy to do all those masculine-type things with him. When it became clear that God would only give them those two girls, he decided Flo was as close as he would get. He began treating her like the son he always wanted."

"That explains a few things."

"When she was young, he put her in pants and a flannel shirt, and they went hunting and fishing. He even had her help with the yardwork like any son would. She wasn't one for skirts or dresses anyway. She was a tomboy. I don't know if you gals still use that term. May was brought up more traditionally by her mother."

Penelope paused for a moment. Her eyes took on a distant expression, leaving Daphne to wonder what images from the past held the woman captive. She sipped her drink, causing the ice to shift. The noise brought Penelope back to the present.

"But I was talking about the records. Flo did get invited to the parties. However, I think it was for the music she brought and not for herself. Flo had a shy side. She didn't always know what to say. However, she could also be as bold as brass, in the right situation."

"I'm not sure I saw much of the shy part." Like, never, thought Daphne. "But I encountered the bold side."

Penelope chuckled. "I remember Sally Ferguson teasing your Grandma May back in high school. Goodness, I can't recall what for. There didn't have to be a reason. Sally was a mean thing. No one liked her. Anyway, as she passed by in the hallway, Flo saw Sally picking on her younger sister in a classroom. Flo marched in and picked up a stapler off the teacher's desk. The teacher was facing the blackboard, you see. She went up to Sally and stapled her skirt to the chair. Flo turned around, put the stapler back on the desk, and walked out of the room without a word."

Her law-and-order Auntie Flo had stapled a girl's skirt to a chair? Her jaw dropped. It seemed inconceivable. And yet, upon reflection, there were moments when she saw something like hardness mixed with humor in her aunt's eyes.

"Of course, she got into terrible trouble. But the students treated her like a hero for a week. Like I said, everyone hated Sally." Penelope gave a *harrumph* and followed it up with a good slug of her tea.

She wondered what her prim and proper Grandma May had thought of the incident. Was she grateful to her sister for being her savior or embarrassed by the rash and public act?

The picture Penelope was drawing for Flo started to become clearer. Daphne's heart lurched.

"So, you mean, she was kind of on the outside looking in?"

"I'm afraid so. While she was close to the group, she wasn't really part of it, if you understand me. Sadly, that never changed. Flo spent most of her life rather on the fringe of things."

"I never knew that. People seemed polite when I was here."

"Flo was plenty respected. Her job working for the police as a dispatcher secured that. And yet I was one of her few friends." Her face transformed into a piteous look. "The older she got, the grumpier she became. I don't think she was very satisfied in life."

"Flo must have been lonely." Daphne understood that feeling. A pounding sound filled her ears, and her stomach turned sour. "I could've helped with that."

"I know she was furious at your mom when Sarah wouldn't let you come back anymore. Your mother forbade any contact. I felt awful for Flo, being used like that. Just not Christian. And to do that to family to boot. Shameful."

Penelope shook her head and drained the rest of her drink. Shaking the glass, she motioned towards the kitchen. She went to the sink and returned the glass to its rightful place.

What had happened all those years ago? Daphne had been putting off the conversation with her mom, avoiding the inevitable nagging and disapproval. However, anger surged inside and crowded out her doubts. She wished she had a stapler to use on her mother. She'd fix her to a chair and ask her some hard questions.

Betty approached cautiously. "Oh, Lord. What did Aunt Pen do? I know she can be abrupt, but she has a good heart."

"What do you mean?"

"Your face. You look like you could go one-on-one with a grizzly bear, and I wouldn't put money on the bear."

"Sorry. I'm okay. It's my mom. I'm thinking about a conversation we are going to have."

"Ah, one of those. I get ya. Do you want to go out to dinner tonight? It might distract you a little before you call home." The pixie plonked down cross-legged on the floor.

"Sure, where do you want to go?"

"You pick. You're having the shit year. What's your favorite?"

Daphne opened her mouth to respond, but then she blanked. What was her favorite? Sure, she had a favorite... It was... "I can't believe it. I don't have a favorite anymore." Panic flared in her chest, and Betty looked at her as if she were possibly having a stroke.

"What do you mean you don't have a favorite? What kind of places would you go to with Rat Bastard?"

"After we moved in together, we would go to this steak restaurant on Friday nights. Wallace would order for both of us. He thought it was suave and sophisticated. I hated it. He would always order me a steak cooked medium rare." Her nose wrinkled in disgust.

"So?"

"I don't like it cooked that way. It's too bloody. I think it's gross. But he insisted that was the only way to eat a steak. You couldn't *taste* the flavor otherwise. He sounded so pretentious. I would only eat the edges. Then he would complain that I was wasting money and had no refinement."

"He said that to your face?"

"We would get the leftover steak to go home. Saturday morning, I would feel so guilty about wasting the food that I would cook him steak and eggs for breakfast." She looked hard at her hands.

"You are better off without that jerk."

"I just realized something." Daphne's face twisted with contempt. "I think Rat Bastard took me to that steak house deliberately. He knew I would only eat the edges. Then he would get steak for dinner on Friday and then again for breakfast on Saturday. He played me. He made me feel small because he wanted to eat a fancy meal twice."

The women exchanged looks of disgust.

"He is the King Rat Bastard, all right. What a scummy thing to do. Okay, no steak house for dinner. What do *you* want?"

"I've been eating what other people want for years. I ate where Wallace wanted. Going out with the women from work, I went along with the group. At home, Mom always decided on the restaurant. I can't remember the last time I really picked a meal unless I was alone."

"So, this is a big moment. What kind of food does Daphne want to eat? Know that in Cobb, your choices are Joe's Diner, the pizza place, and a Chinese joint. Anything else, we will run over to Hinckley. You pick."

She furrowed her brow. "Italian. I want some pasta!" she cried.

"Pasta it is!" Betty cheered back, shooting one arm into the air.

"We didn't get so excited about pasta back in my day," Penelope commented from the doorway. "Is this some new fad, like avocado toast?" She rolled her eyes and strolled toward her recliner.

The two women collapsed in a fit of giggles.

Even though she was laughing, Daphne still felt the coming conversation with her mother pressing down on her like a weight. But that would have to wait until after dinner.

Chapter Fifteen

Twenty Years Ago - Flo

FLO GLARED AT THE phone. Her sister, May, had called for another "chat." She had another name for them: interrogation. Was her granddaughter okay? What was Flo feeding her? What time did she go to bed? Did she check out any unsuitable books at the library? Had she made any friends? What families did they belong to? She tried to gently remind May that she was doing her family a favor, not the other way around.

Flo felt bad for Daphne. Sarah was a control freak at the best of times, but she had recently reached new levels of wanting to control the world. The kid asked if she could go outside and play before the sun went down. Asked? She and May had been raised to run out and be free once their chores were done. Never before had she seen a kid play so carefully.

Why had she agreed to let Daphne stay? Her father told her that family loyalty counted above all else. Even after his death, she still wanted to please him. Not that May and her descendants took the rule seriously. May got married and moved out to Michigan. Letters and phone calls became rarer with every passing year. Flo had traveled all the way out there to attend Sarah's graduation and wedding. Both times, she got a form thank you note from her niece and little else. It had been a pleasant surprise when the birth announcement for Daphne arrived, but since then, only a generic Christmas card had graced her mailbox.

The conversation with May left her grumpy, but sitting around moping wasn't her style. Best to grab the girl and head out. Maybe they'd try fishing again. The first time had not gone well. Calling Daphne, Flo hustled the girl outside.

Flo locked the door behind them on their way out.

"You always lock the door when we leave. I didn't expect that."

"Why? Don't you lock your doors in Michigan?"

"Oh, of course. But Daddy said that you lived in a..." Her forehead crinkled as she tried to remember. "Podunk backwater and that no one locked their doors. Mommy said that may be true, but there was a good chance you slept with a gun under your pillow. Do you sleep with a gun? Can I see it? What's a Podunk backwater? Sounds silly to me. Can we go to the library, please?"

"No," Flo said sternly as her face began to flush.

Daphne stopped abruptly to stare in surprise at her aunt's tone.

Keeping her voice firmly in control, Flo tried again. "I don't have a gun. Even if I did, I wouldn't very well keep it *under my pillow.*"

"I don't care if you've got a gun. I've just never seen a real one. Only on TV. You worked with the police, didn't you? I think it would be neat to see one in real life." Her eyes grew large like ocean waves on a windy day. "Have you ever shot a gun?"

Flo sighed. "Yes. I have fired a pistol under safe conditions. They are loud. Very loud. Imagine a firecracker. Now think of it going off right next to your head. It hurts."

She hoped this would discourage her niece from any further interest in firearms.

"Whoa." Daphne's mouth made an O shape. "That's so cool. You've lived a life of danger. You're not a hick at all. Daddy had it wrong. He works with numbers all day and plays golf. That's boring. I can't wait to tell the kids at school. I bet none of them have an aunt that's shot a gun."

"Let's go to the library. That seems pretty safe." A hick? So much for *family loyalty*.

"Cool." Daphne jumped high to get into the pickup truck. "I want to get the next book in the *Redwall* series. I even met this kid who's also reading them."

"That's nice." At least after Flo read May the riot act, she could tell May that Daphne had made a friend.

Chapter Sixteen

THE BLISS OF SHARING a tasty pasta meal with Betty an hour earlier had vanished. In an attempt to build up courage, Daphne circled the kitchen table, her hand hitting the top of the chairs as she passed each one. She'd lost count of the number of rotations she'd taken around the room. Feeling dizzy, she spun and restarted her orbit in the opposite direction. From her phone, resting on the table, set on repeat, sang Taylor Swift's "Look What You Made Me Do."

The conversation with her mother loomed over her. She didn't excel at confrontation, and her mother had a black belt in it. The Great Sarah Patterson had no problem telling people uncomfortable things and demanding that the world, including her husband and children, give her what she wanted.

Daphne pounded the next three chairs extra hard. *Thump, thump, thump.*

For thirty-five years, her father seemed content to let his wife control their lives. The arrangement saved him the bother of having to make too many pesky decisions. In general, the two of them got along well. Sarah supported his passion for golfing and always allowed a generous amount of time to accommodate his hobby.

Ethan, Daphne's younger brother, was no fonder of their controlling mother than Daphne was. But he had found a different way of managing her. First, he'd followed their dad onto the golf course and then, later, he'd left for Notre Dame to study accounting. Like father, like son. His plan was simple: get far enough out of their mother's grasp that she couldn't easily control him. He'd master the art of the dodge. Daphne envied his success. He never called home more than once a week, reducing their mother's influence.

It hadn't mattered when Daphne ran away to college. It never seemed far enough to escape her mother. The barrage of calls and texts assaulted her, bringing questions about where she was and with whom.

She felt dizzy. Was it the anger or the circular motion around the table? She turned around to continue her march.

Memories of posting photos on Facebook and the comments from her mom made her hands shake. She wore too much makeup or too little. Black made her look depressed, and pink gave the impression she was still a child. The implied warning of being unable to attract the right sort of man was always included.

All the cutting barbs wounded her self-esteem, even though they were wrapped in the bright pink bow of, "I just want you to be happy, honey." All the advice was for her mom's benefit, because Sarah didn't think her daughter was up to the task, no matter what the task was. Did her mom have a point about that? Daphne had to wonder. The last year was the most unhappy time of her life.

For the last three decades, almost all major decisions were made following the guidance of her mom. A new outcome demanded new behavior on her part. She'd take a page out of Ethan's playbook. Less communication and more independence. However, she needed to have it out with her mother before she could begin this plan. There were questions that required answers.

Her forward motion stopped as she scream-sang a verse along with Taylor.

She'd never been the aggressor in a conversation with her mother, so a support plan was called for. Step one: a glass and a half of wine at dinner—not enough to make her sloppy, but a little liquid courage couldn't hurt. Step two: a pep talk from Taylor, hence the song currently playing on repeat. Step three: write out her talking points on a notecard.

The header read, <u>Discussion with Mom</u>. Underneath, she'd scrawled:

-Why sent to Auntie Flo 20 years ago?

-Did Auntie Flo ask to see me again? (I already know, yes, I want to hear you say it.)

-Why refuse her? Why take that away from me? Why not let me choose?

-Want to say/Won't actually say – I'm tired of being told what to do by you. Why don't you think I can pick my own future? Wallace was bad for me! Why didn't you tell me to run away?

The fourth and final step was walking around the table. She wanted to build her energy, release some nerves, and sound cool and in control. Spiritually reaching out to one of her first female role models, she tried to channel her inner Jo March from Louisa May Alcott's *Little Women.* Jo spoke her mind and wouldn't let others tell her what to do. She wouldn't be scared of this confrontation. But Daphne wasn't Jo March.

Thankfully, the call was not a video chat; otherwise, her mother would observe her shaking hands. Taking several deep breaths, she felt as relaxed as she ever would. Pulling out a chair, she brought the phone and notecard closer. Turning off the music, she began the call.

Her mother answered on the second ring. "Hello, Daphne. I was starting to wonder if you had gotten lost in the woods. I haven't heard from you in ages."

It's been less than two weeks, but sure. "Ages."

"I've texted you." She cringed at the defensive sound in her voice. This was not getting off to a good start. She was supposed to be the aggressor here, not her mother.

"A text isn't the same as a phone call. You hardly said anything in those texts. Only that you'd arrived and that you were settling in. What does that mean, settling in? Aren't you clearing out the place so you can put it on the market? How is that going? Have you talked to some real estate agents?"

She bulldozed forward with solutions to problems that didn't exist. "Talk to more than one. They might lowball you on the value of the house. But they might be able to help you find one of those estate sale people. If there's anything worth selling."

"I have not talked to an estate agent, Mother," Daphne said firmly.

"Why not? Do you want me to come out and help you?" Code for come out and take over.

"No! I have it under control. I have not talked to anyone in real estate, Mom, because I don't know if I want to sell the house."

"You're not thinking of staying, are you?" Her mother sounded horrified.

"Mom, calm down. I don't know what I am going to do long term." *Sound tough, be firm.* "Right now, I am taking my time getting better acquainted with Auntie Flo and the town."

"Don't be ridiculous." The clipped, dismissive tone earned the phone a glare. "Aunt Florence is dead. You can't get *acquainted* with her now."

"Oh, but I can. This is a small town. People know each other a lot better than we do back home." The harsh edge in her voice surprised Daphne. She didn't think she had it in her. "I've been hearing lots about Auntie Flo from the locals. Also, about me."

"You? What could they have to say about you?" She tutted. "You haven't been in Maine in twenty years."

Did Daphne hear a hint of concern under the scornful words? "Correct, Mother. That's the point. Everyone talks about how I've been *missing* for twenty years. It seems that Auntie Flo told them she wished I had returned to see her again. They call me her 'missing niece.' I have a reputation for being hard to find, like Bigfoot." She paused to let it all sink in. "You never told me that Auntie Flo wanted me to come out to visit again."

A silence stretched out between them.

She continued. "You never asked me if I wanted to see her again." Still no response. "Because the answer would have been yes. I loved my time here. I never met anyone like her."

Finally, Sarah spoke. "She was unique." The last word dripped with sarcasm.

"Since I know she wanted me to return, and I would have wanted that, too, my question, Mom, is what was the problem? Why did you stop that from happening?"

"She... she wasn't suitable for a young girl to spend time with." Her voice was firm, with an "I am your mother" tone, indicating that the matter was concluded.

Daphne jumped to her aunt's defense. "If she was so unsuitable, why did you send me in the first place? And what made her unsuitable? I didn't see anything that was a problem. Maybe she was a little gruff, but she just wasn't used to kids."

"I didn't have a choice. I was desperate."

The confession stilled Daphne, and she decided to remain quiet. Hopefully, her mother would get uncomfortable with the silence and finally give in with an answer.

"It took several years to get pregnant with you. The pregnancy and birth were difficult. After years of trying for a second child, your father and I gave up on having any more kids. We thought you were it, which was fine. I could focus my motherly attention on you."

She rolled her eyes. Boy, her mom had focused on her like a laser beam. She earned the title of Most Helicoptery Helicopter Parent Ever.

"When I got pregnant with Ethan, I was not a young woman anymore. The doctor considered it a high-risk pregnancy." Her voice lost its strength. "I had several problems along the way."

"Mom, I never knew."

"Well, we kept that from you. You were only ten. The summer I was due, the doctor warned I was likely in for a difficult birth. Your father and I were concerned." She choked up. "We worried that something might happen to either the baby or me. Those things are not as common anymore, but we were prepared for the worst."

She cleared her throat before continuing. "We decided to ship you off for the summer. That way, we could deal with whatever came. Grandma May agreed to watch you. But just beforehand, she sprained her ankle very badly. She could hardly move around. There was no way she could take you on. There weren't many friends or family nearby to ask such a big favor."

"How did I end up in Maine?"

"Your grandma suggested we try her sister Florence. I was stressed, scared, and out of options. So, I reached out. She had just retired from the police force and agreed to watch you for three months. The birth wasn't the easiest. But by the time you got home, I was feeling better and ready to have my whole family together. No reason to ever ship you off to Florence again."

"But, Mom, she enjoyed me being there. I liked spending time with her. Why couldn't I go again?"

"I told you. She was unsuitable." The warmth and vulnerability present in her mom's voice just moments ago had vanished, sending a clear message: her mother did not want to discuss this further.

Daphne ignored the unspoken demand and plowed ahead. "Yes, you said. I want to know *why* you thought she was unsuitable."

"Her nontraditional lifestyle was not something I wanted my young, impressionable daughter to be exposed to. While you may not have understood at ten, if you continued to visit, who knows what would have happened?"

She tried to put the pieces of the puzzle together. A nontraditional lifestyle? Exposed? The lightbulb turned on, and her mouth dropped open in horror.

"Mother!" Bile rose in her throat. "Are you saying that, because you believed that Auntie Flo was a lesbian, she was unfit to spend time with me? And that if I had spent more time with her, I would become a lesbian, too? Are you kidding me?"

"You're not a mother. You don't understand our responsibilities to protect our children. She even had the audacity to question my parenting."

"I'm not a mother. I'm also not a bigot and a homophobe. I missed out on a great relationship with my aunt because of your hate? I don't even know what to say to that. Well, I'm certain now why she left everything to me, not you. I can't believe you. Your own family."

"You don't understand."

"You're right, I don't understand. I don't think I ever will. Do you know what you took from me because you worried your daughter might turn gay? Auntie Flo cared about me. Me, who I was, not who she wanted me to be. I don't think you can understand that. I knew you could be a cold person at times. But this... this takes the cake. I hope, one day, you know what it feels like to lose touch with a person you love. I can't even talk to you right now. Goodbye."

Daphne hung up the phone. She had just hung up on her mother. She'd never hung up on her mother. Ever. She dropped the phone as if this new knowledge somehow tainted it.

Warm and cozy were not words anyone would use to describe her mom. She knew her mother had high expectations of people. But a bigot? How had she missed what was lurking below? Yes, her mother had made snide comments about Auntie Flo being "butch." As a child, Daphne had not realized it was an anti-gay slur. She always thought it was her mother's expression for Flo's more masculine haircut and endless supply of flannel shirts.

The phone rang on the table. Her mother. She sent it to voice mail. She didn't welcome a continuation of their conversation. Taking a little time away from her mom sounded like a great idea.

Besides, she needed to focus on who was the killer. The passion to find justice for Flo busted open and crushed her usual timid thoughts. Significant action was required.

Chapter Seventeen

JUDGING BY HOW HER head throbbed, Daphne guessed the neighbor's lawn mower was the loudest in the world. An attempt to swallow left her tongue stuck to the roof of her mouth. With eyes still closed, Daphne began to check her body. Her back mimicked her head with pulsating pain.

She shivered. Why was she cold? Her quilt usually kept her toasty when the temperatures dipped during these early summer days. Her fingers tried to grasp the quilt and found only air. Her hands searched the mattress, which suddenly disappeared?

Opening one eye a fraction, she groaned. From her fetal position, she looked at the coffee table in front of her. An empty juice glass sat next to an equally empty bottle of wine—the second emergency bottle. She was on the couch.

Her phone vibrated on the coffee table. Now, she remembered why the emergency bottle of wine had been cracked open: her mother, the bigotry, the hang-up. She groaned again. "I can't handle this right now."

Slowly, she unfurled her body, stood up, and somehow stumbled around the table without smacking her shins. Upstairs, she filled a glass with water and chugged the whole thing while gulping down two ibuprofen. Waiting for the shower to begin running hot, she headed to the guest room.

She peeled off her clothes, which felt like a sticky second skin, and walked naked down the hall. The remote nature of Flo's house meant people couldn't easily sneak a peek at their neighbors, which was probably why Flo picked this place instead of something downtown.

Daphne stepped into the shower and the warm water heated her chilled body. If only the pressured blasts could clean out her murky mind. As she lathered the shampoo, she finally allowed herself to think about the conversation she'd had with her mother the night before. Her mother had kept her away from Auntie Flo because she was a homophobe. How had she not realized this? Were there signs she'd missed?

Her heart broke for how hurt Auntie Flo must have felt. Did she suspect that Daphne had the same prejudice as her mother? There had been years' worth of missed opportunities to get to know her crotchety but sassy aunt. What could she do about it now? Daphne grabbed her loofa and vigorously slathered peach gel over her.

The rising scent brought images of sunshine and picnics, and calm. She ceased scrubbing herself in Lady Macbeth style.

It's not too late. Aunt Flo is gone, but she seems to be everywhere. This was a small town, and its people knew Flo. With every turn, she found new pieces of her aunt. For heaven's sake, she was living in her house, ground zero of her life.

She'd been tiptoeing around, as if Auntie Flo would appear and scold her for making a mess. She must live among her aunt's things if she wanted to know her. Who knew what secret knowledge was waiting to be found? Without her looking, the mystery in the fish book had found Daphne. Imagine what was waiting for her to discover if she *intentionally* looked.

It was time to leave the guest room and move into Flo's room. Not only did she want to learn more, but she still had to find proof of foul play. An avid mystery reader, Daphne had learned that clues in solving crimes—small pieces of information about the victim, like whether they were allergic to peanuts or hated the color orange—were often critical in closing the case. Having no suspects or any line of inquiry, collecting information seemed the most logical way to proceed.

She hummed Taylor Swift's "Shake it Off" while towel-drying her hair and getting dressed. She made a beeline for the kitchen and forced herself to drink another glass of water. She needed hydration, but she wanted a fancy coffee, a cappuccino, or, given that it was summertime, an iced latte.

Cobb was a charming small town. However, it was missing a good coffee shop. Of course, someone could get a cup at Joe's Diner. The choices were regular and decaf. If a person needed to feed a caffeine addiction, Joe's did the trick. If Daphne wanted something a little more decadent, well, she was out of luck. Knowing she could make the same at home as she'd get at Joe's, she grabbed the well-used pot. As the machine started its process, the memories of her love affair with java filtered in from days gone by.

During college, she observed her freshman roommate, Cleo, at work behind the counter of a local coffee shop. With deft skill, she took orders, chatted with customers, worked the big, complicated machine, and even created the intricate latte art with a flair everyone admired. With unexpected generosity, Cleo accompanied Daphne to fill out her job application at the coffee shop. Before the ink was dry on the form, she had been hired, and introductions were made to the other employees.

Daphne felt like an idiot during her first week, as she bungled orders, avoided making eye contact with the scary customers, and was always just seconds away from blowing up the gurgling machine if Cleo wasn't there to step in. After the first week and two "discussions" with the manager, Daphne was in tears and ready to quit. She didn't need the hassle anyway.

Chill and mellow, Cleo put an arm around her roomie and consoled her, regaling Daphne with stories of her own newbie mistakes. Daphne finally started to laugh between the crying.

"Come on, Daphne, don't wimp out." Cleo gave her a playful slug on the shoulder. "Give it at least two more weeks."

"Okay, two more weeks. But what if I still hate it?"

"Then you quit. Not everyone is cut out to be a barista. But I know you can do this. I believe in you."

Such an unexpected and uncustomary expression left her dumbstruck. Her mother had dismissed this job as silly and a waste of time. Daphne didn't want to admit that she was so pathetic she couldn't even hack it at a silly job. Mom already pointed out all her faults, and the last thing she wanted to do was give her more ammunition.

Luckily, Daphne did improve. Two weeks later, only a few orders were coming out wrong. A month later, she was allowed back on the scary machine. With Cleo there, she was ready to face her fear and tame the beast. Over the Christmas holidays, even the criticism queen was impressed with the artistic foam heart on her latte. Her self-esteem soared, as did her love affair with coffee.

A different memory from that time crept in. The fuss her mother made when she told her Cleo was bisexual made more sense now. At the time, she'd responded to the concern with a blithe comment. "Neither of us is the other's type." She'd been so blind.

Daphne stayed at the coffee shop until she finished her master's. She asked for a high-end espresso machine with all the bells and whistles for her graduation present. When she moved for her librarian job, she carefully packed her most prized possession.

For a while, life had been full of weekend brunches at her new apartment with her new coworkers. Daphne loved making them her signature art-topped coffees. That faded once she and Wallace moved in together. He wanted it quiet on the weekends. Just the two of them. Wasn't he enough for her, he used to ask? Her confidence teetered, and she gave in.

After Rat Bastard left, she moved into her own miniature apartment her tight budget could afford, but she continued to avoid old friends. She was ashamed of how she'd abandoned them for a scumbag who cheated on her. She assumed everyone thought her an idiot. She certainly thought of herself that way.

Almost a year passed before she was ready to step out of her shell. To rebuild relationships, she invited her coworkers to lunch and brought homemade iced coffee. From then on, the ladies at work included her on nights out at the art film movie theater. As her life was getting back on track, the notice of her layoff arrived.

Her meager savings dwindled, and a replacement job didn't appear. Then came the offer from her parents. "Come home. Maybe you will have better luck finding a job here. At least you won't have to pay rent," her mother enticed.

Feeling like a dog with her tail between her legs, she whimpered back home in defeat. Home to endless conversations about how she didn't get it right and what she should have done, paired with nagging about finding a job and, more importantly, a man. None of which were helpful.

The recent talk with her mom caused her to rethink those barbs. Was her mom so obsessed with her being with a man, any man, just to make sure she wasn't a lesbian? Did her mom think, if she stayed single too long, she'd turn gay? She almost gagged.

Stealing a glance at her phone from the corner of her eye, she remembered the buzz it made when she woke up. Torn between wanting to know what it said and never wanting to hear from her mom again, she crept to the phone to check the message. Hitting the button, the screen lit up. The texts were from her father. That was rare. Usually, he left it up to his wife to communicate with Daphne.

> Dad: Talked with Mom. She is upset.

He had sent that text early in the morning while Daphne slept on the couch. After not getting a response for thirty minutes, he sent another one.

> Dad: I can see why you are upset too. Please talk with your mother.

After an hour passed, as Daphne continued to sleep, he sent his last message.

> Dad: I'm sorry about this. Do you need anything?

That was her dad. Not a talker by nature, he didn't offer to discuss the matter. Dad was a doer, a provider, an old-school man. Identify a problem, find the solution, and end the problem. Done. But he couldn't fix this and make it go away. Would anything make this better?

She turned away from the phone, distracted by the drip of the coffee maker. There was one thing he could do after all.

> Daphne: Go to my storage locker. Find box marked - coffee items. Ship here. ASAP.

She stared at the phone in her hands. She couldn't stop herself. While trying to change from the mousy woman who did everything she was told, some parts of her could not be altered. Manners were a reflection of a person. She added one more word before putting her phone away.

> Daphne: Please.

In the kitchen, she poured herself a giant mug of the caffeinated elixir. She drank in the fortitude. Today, she'd move her stuff into Auntie Flo's room. She didn't know what she'd find there. Maybe horrible secrets? Evidence of a silent saint? More likely something in between.

"Okay, Auntie Flo," she called out. "Your niece has returned. Show me what I missed."

She marched upstairs to the guest room, threw items into her suitcase, dragged it past the full bathroom, and opened the primary bedroom door. The exterior walls of the chamber slanted with the roof's pitch. The paint was light green, like when white pants got stained after brushing against the grass. It contrasted against the traditional dark cherrywood furniture.

The queen bed, adorned with a low headboard tucked against the slope of the ceiling, was covered in a quilt with a green circle wedding ring pattern on a white background. Furniture made of the same cherry stain dotted the room. The door divided the room in half at its highest point. Natural light poured in from the large window centered opposite. Underneath sat a delicately carved writing desk and chair.

Daphne spent the afternoon sorting Flo's clothes for donation. Given the different body types and that her aunt was a few inches taller, she couldn't keep much for herself. However, the plaid blue-and-white flannel padded jacket stayed. It was a little long in the sleeves for her, but she hadn't brought a practical warm coat from home. It seemed like something one should have while living in Maine. It might make her feel closer to Flo and possibly one step closer to finding Flo's killer.

Chapter Eighteen

Twenty Years Ago – Daphne

DAPHNE SILENTLY CAME DOWN the stairs to find the kitchen and living room empty, a moment of panic clutched at her young heart. But then she caught sight of the familiar short brown hair of Flo's head outside. She sat alone on the porch with her mug.

Clenching her fists, Daphne tried to get the courage to go outside. She failed. She repeated this ritual the next morning, and then again the morning after that. On day five, she finally conquered her shyness.

Opening the front door, Daphne found her aunt on the glider, sipping her coffee and staring out at the yard. Flo wore a mellow smile. This was a new expression to Daphne. Her aunt looked happy. What had brought this about?

Flo said, "Good, you're up. I'm just welcoming the day."

"Welcoming the day? How do you do that?"

"Oh, I just come out here. I have my first coffee. I watch the sun come up, and she looks down at me. Neither of us has to say anything. We kinda see each other, share a moment, welcome the day together, and then get on with things."

The long answer seemed to surprise both Daphne and her aunt.

"Anyway, you hungry? How about some breakfast?" Flo asked.

Daphne nodded, and they went inside for cornflakes.

It took until the last two weeks of her visit for Daphne to grab a mug from the cupboard, fill it with orange juice, and take it onto the porch. Flo turned toward her and got ready to go in for breakfast.

Daphne marched over to the glider, sat beside her, and said, "I thought I'd welcome the day, too."

Flo nodded. She cleared her throat, and they sat silently, emptying their mugs while looking at the trees, shrubs, and squirrels running about as the sun worked its way above the tree line.

Chapter Nineteen

THE FOLLOWING SUNDAY MORNING arrived like a fresh page being turned over. Shadows made by the light passing through the lace curtains of the bedroom windows told Daphne that dawn had passed hours ago. She probably should spend the day looking for clues and trying to solve the mystery of who killed Auntie Flo. Wasn't that why she moved into Flo's room? But she had no idea what to do next. She'd found nothing of importance when she went through her aunt's stuff. Her mystery books weren't as helpful as she thought they'd be.

The clue of the limes had found her. Logically, the next clue would probably do the same. Best not to worry about it too much, she decided.

Getting up, she looked out the window. The sunshine and blue skies promised a beautiful summer day. A person had to grab those when they came. The weather might not be nice tomorrow, and the murder case would wait for her. Perhaps a day in nature would help her see the next line of inquiry.

Spending time next to the river on the manicured lawn was a great way to begin the day. Who knew who she'd run into? Maybe the hunky Phil. She hadn't seen him in days. Sure, he lived next door, and she could pop over anytime. But she wanted him to come to her. After all she went through with Wallace, she deserved to be chased instead of doing the chasing. Didn't she?

She headed downtown to The Green. Others had the same idea. At the park, people were walking their dogs, a few teens were playing frisbee, and at least four blankets were spread out with occupants in various degrees of sloth. Spotting an empty bench near the river, Daphne ambled forward.

The maple, oak, and birch trees dotting the small park swayed slightly. A gentle breeze blew off the river—nothing like the brisk, forceful gales on the coast. While she knew she could be at the ocean within an hour's drive, here in the small river town, she felt almost as far away from the shore as she did back in Michigan. She made a mental note to take a day trip to the beach. It had been twenty years since she had been to the coastline here, and she wanted to see it through adult eyes.

Sitting on the bench, she closed her eyes and felt the late morning sun warm her cheeks. The water lapped against the rocks on the river's shore beyond her bench. The teens behind her laughed and shouted as they tossed around their Frisbees. The church bells began to chime from the Episcopal chapel, announcing the eleven o'clock hour. From a distance, she could hear the din of people being released from the building out into the sunshine.

"Welcome," she whispered to the day.

The scent of charcoal grills firing up for lunch drifted across the river. Finally, she opened her eyes and watched the dancing diamond patterns of the sun bouncing off the ripples of the water. Hypnotized by the display, she watched nature's show, feeling her body and mind slow down. It had been a long time since she felt so calm and still.

Opening her small Kate Spade Hayden bag, Daphne reached for her purse book. It was her habit to carry reading material with her. You never knew when you would find yourself on mass transit, at a doctor's office, or on a park bench and want something to read. Alas, her hand came out empty. She hadn't put her much-read and beloved copy of L.M. Montgomery's novel *The Blue Castle* into her bag when she'd rushed out the door that morning.

The noise level behind her had risen dramatically since the church services had ended. The Green was becoming crowded, and she didn't have a book. Slinging her bag over her shoulder, she ambled away from the water and took a left onto Main Street.

Several of the businesses were closed, it being Sunday. Puddingstone's Insurance, the jewelry store, the local Realtor, and the furniture store were all shuttered for the day. Past the funeral home was an old-fashioned ice cream shop and candy store. It was packed with kids getting bribes for being good during church services. Tucked next to it was the sign she had noticed with interest earlier in the week. In curly gold font on a maroon background was the title of the shop: "Your Books or Mine."

With relief, she found the door unlocked. The bell overhead tinkled as she entered the long rectangular space, glancing at the counter to her right. Wrinkled hands held up a newspaper, leaving the person behind it mostly hidden. A man lowered the paper, observed her, and raised it back up.

Taken aback, Daphne paused. She didn't know what to do. Should she walk past the man? But this was a small town. It seemed rude to ignore him, but he seemed to want to be ignored.

Swallowing hard, she awkwardly forced out of her mouth, "I love the name of your shop."

Lowering his paper to his lap, he finally looked at her. He glanced at her up and down. With a *harrumph*, he said, "My wife named it."

"She's very clever. What a great play on words." A smile plastered itself uncomfortably on her face. His face did not change its flat countenance.

"She died two years ago," he said with the same tight flatness as his face.

Her smile fell. "I'm... very sorry," she stammered and began to move away from him. Her stomach hurt, and her mouth was dry. She cursed her ability to always say the wrong thing.

As she slunk further into the store, she began to take in her surroundings. The room was dark. Too dark. The windows had heavy curtains that kept out much of the natural light. The air was thick with dust, and she coughed. She had a healthy appreciation for the smell that stacks of older books gave off. It comforted her. However, this was not that light smell;

this place was just unclean. She wondered about the last time anyone had used a dust cloth.

Circling, she took in the layout. Around the room's edges were shelves that went from floor to ceiling. Placed in the middle of the room were more shelves, but these were only four feet tall. Books were stuffed and crammed everywhere. Some of them were pushed in so tight she knew it was damaging the pages, making her wince.

She couldn't stop herself. She looked for labels or signs to explain the system of order in the shop. She finally found some faded, handwritten cards taped to the shelves. However, when she looked at the books, they did not always match the genre sign they were placed beneath.

Overall, the store was dirty, disorganized, and uninviting, which broke her heart. Books deserved a better home than this. They were her friends whenever she needed them. Right now, her friends needed help. The librarian in her wanted to remove everything from the shelves and reorganize them.

Her years of experience had taught her appealing ways to display books. She knew how to create a space that made people want to enter again and again. This place said, "Get out and stay out." The man behind the counter didn't seem to be enjoying himself either. Was he even making a profit?

No matter how cringe-worthy the environment, it was still a bookstore. She couldn't keep herself from meandering down the aisles. She found a paperback that piqued her interest. Agatha Christie's *Poirot Investigates* was waiting for her, and marked for an unbeatable two dollars. Even in her current state, she could afford that. A Christie novel could be just the inspiration she needed to help her in her investigation. She pulled it from the dusty shelves and let out a sneeze.

Returning to the counter, she passed a large table at the end of the counter area. Placed onto the long surface were crates and crates. Curious, she snuck a peek inside them. They were full of CDs and DVDs. And, of course, they were thrust inside with no order at all, just a big jumble. CDs were a dollar, and DVDs were five; even at those prices, she questioned if he sold any. She doubted it. Everything seemed to be covered in the same layer of dust.

Moving past the crates, she put her purchase on the counter and dug for her wallet.

"Just the one?" the man asked.

"Yes, please." The man raised an eyebrow as he rang up the purchase, and Daphne rambled on. "I am quite a fan of Agatha Christie. Well, murders, in general. Reading about murders, not actually killing someone. It's mostly cozy murders. Those grizzly hardcore mysteries are not my kind of thing."

"Hmm," he grunted again.

Daphne thought that was all she would get out of him as she handed over her money.

To her surprise, he said, "I don't mind the dark stuff myself. But I like that H. P. Lovecraft. He's handy with a phrase. Never comes directly at you with the scare."

"Oh, I know what you mean." She became animated, as she always did when talking books. "His work is so much about what he doesn't say, right? He gives you just enough to freak you out, but then lets your imagination do its worst. Not gory, but totally a good scare."

"You like Lovecraft?"

"Sure. I like Lovecraft and Poe and all those early dark writers. They have a real romantic flair, not like mushy romance, but more like a Beethoven kind of romance, bold and dramatic. I always read a little Lovecraft around Halloween. I find it's most enjoyable at that time of year."

"You should check out Salem, Massachusetts, at Halloween. That town does it up right. Did you know Lovecraft based the cemetery in *The Unnamable* on the Charter Street Burying Grounds in Salem? That's where I'm from. After I married Alice, we moved to Maine to be closer to her people." He stopped suddenly, as if he felt he'd said too much. "Well, at any rate, Salem inspired Lovecraft a little. Another claim to fame for the town. Of course, all anyone talks of is the witch trials." He slid the book into a paper bag and handed it to her.

"Can you blame them? I mean, the witch trials are pretty sensational stuff. But I'll make sure to read *The Unnamable* this Halloween. I'll also look up that burying ground beforehand to have a good picture of it in my mind when I'm reading. Thanks for that. I may consider traveling to Salem if I'm still in the area in October. Is it far from here?" She tried to keep things friendly, even though she could see he was attempting to crawl back into his shell.

"It's not too bad. About a two-hour drive, depending on the traffic." He looked at the counter. "If you go, I can recommend some other places to check out."

"Thank you, that's very kind. Two hours isn't that far. I'm Daphne, by the way. Flo Winkler's niece." She held out her hand.

He looked at it briefly before shaking it with a firm grip. "Flo's kin, huh?" He looked her over. "You don't look anything like her."

"No, I don't." She laughed. "She was taller than me and had dark hair. I take after my father's side. Though I think they broke the mold after they made Auntie Flo."

"Truer words." He chuckled.

"It's been nice meeting you..."

"Russell Abbot." He filled in the pause. "Thanks for stopping in."

They gave each other a nod, and she left. Daphne took a deep breath of the fresh air on the sidewalk. She felt guilty about her ability to get out while all those books were still stuck inside the unpleasant space. What could she do, though?

Chapter Twenty

AFTER LEAVING THE BOOKSTORE, her hunger for food and information drove her to Joe's Diner. She needed more intelligence on her aunt if she was ever going to get a list of suspects together and solve the murder. Betty had informed her that Joe's was the center of the rumor mill in Cobb. She pushed through the faded red door, noting that a new coat of paint wouldn't hurt the curb appeal.

A multitude of unfamiliar faces filled the room. Overwhelmed, Daphne shrank inward. Hoping to get precious details about Auntie Flo, she battled her nerves about again broaching the subject with a stranger.

Seated in a booth, Daphne hid behind her menu and repeated, "You're part Cobb. You've got this," several times in her head.

A woman with platinum blonde hair appeared, standing over her with an order pad. "What'll you have, hon?" Her pencil was poised and at the ready.

What do I say? How would Flo handle this?

"Hi. My name is Daphne Patterson. Did you know Flo Winkler?" Her mouth went dry, and her breath stopped as she waited for a reply.

"Flo? Sure, I knew her. Everyone did. You that niece from away that she left everything to?" The pencil tapped on the pad.

"Yep, that's me. I was surprised she left her house and stuff to me. I hadn't seen her in about twenty years. But we really bonded during that single summer," Daphne defended herself, though no one was attacking her.

"That's classic Flo. That woman marched to the beat of her own drum." The woman chuckled. "Whatcha you want to eat?"

"Umm." She glanced at the menu. "Pork chop special, please. Have you worked here long?" Daphne attempted to prolong the conversation.

"Very long. I'm the owner, Parmelia King. I'll put in your order now. Our dessert today is my world-famous key lime pie. Just something for you to think about while you wait." She walked away.

The first attempt at getting clues about Flo was a complete failure.

Daphne scolded herself for blathering and not asking what she wanted to know about her aunt. *Keep your eyes on the prize.* Quickly, she scripted out what she would say when Parmelia returned.

After an eternity, a brimming plate was set in front of her. Steam rose from the chops and mashed potatoes. She swallowed the saliva forming in her mouth. *Don't get distracted.*

Careful to make eye contact, she began, "I am trying to learn more about Flo. I stayed with her for a summer when I was ten, but that was long ago. Now that she has shocked me with this inheritance, I want to know more about her. But it is a challenge to get closer to a dead woman. I was wondering if you could tell me about her."

Yes! She'd gotten her speech out.

Parmelia put her pencil behind her ear and stroked her chin. "She was partial to my meatloaf special."

The pencil was back, and it looked like Daphne's quarry would leave again.

"That's good to know. I'll have to try that next time." *Try, try again.* Daphne gave her a wistful look. "I was hoping for maybe something more personal than that. Maybe a story or interaction."

Crossing her arms, Parmelia sighed. Her eyes shifted as she searched for the right words. Looking at the plate she had just set down, she turned up the corner of her mouth. "Your aunt once told me her applesauce was better than mine." Her posture was ramrod straight, and her lips tightened into a thin line. "I don't remember the exact words, but that was the effect of it. I sure remember that interaction."

"She was probably right," Daphne blurted out, cringing at Parmelia's raised eyebrows and the anger flashing in her eyes. She rushed to explain herself and head off the coming storm. "What I mean is, Auntie Flo was a first-rate canner. Really talented, like, she won awards for her applesauce. Did you ever get to taste it?"

The pinched face relaxed a fraction. "No, I can't say that I ever did."

"That's too bad. Since you work in food, you would appreciate it. I remember her making it with me. I've never tasted better applesauce in my life."

"Do you have her recipe?"

"I think I know where to find it," Daphne hesitantly said. She'd never hand over Auntie Flo's secret applesauce recipe to strangers.

"Make some, and I'll try it. I want to know if she insulted me or spoke her truth." A challenge had been laid down.

"But it's too early for apples. They won't start coming in until August," Daphne countered. *Was this how a lobster felt after being lured into a trap?*

"They sell apples at the grocery store all year. I will take into account they're not at peak freshness. If her sauce is as good as you say, it will shine regardless. I look forward to trying it." The woman nodded at Daphne and turned to attend to her other customers.

Without noticing the taste, Daphne chewed her food. *What if I can't find the recipe? What if it's a flop?* Sure, she and Flo churned out many batches that summer, enough to last Flo for the year. But that was twenty years ago. *What if I tarnish Flo's canning legacy?* Her stomach clenched. Leaving half her pork chop untouched, Daphne left in a panic.

She found the recipe, of course. Then, she watched about twenty YouTube videos about canning and applesauce until she could remember every step and stage of the experience with Flo. She probably could have given a TED Talk about canning applesauce—at least the theory of it. But now, she had to actually do it. Feeling nervous, she reached out to Betty.

That night, after listening to Daphne freak out for thirty minutes about making applesauce for Parmelia, Betty had a "brain wave."

"This is perfect for my YouTube channel, Daph. It is all me trying to do stuff in the kitchen while wearing cool vintage clothes. You'll join me, of course, because it's your aunt's recipe. This is going to be a blast!" Betty exclaimed.

Daphne threw out a couple of roadblocks. "I'm not sure. I don't have any skill at acting nor any vintage outfits." She couldn't come out and say no. No wasn't something she liked to say to people. Though if she had said no to Parmelia in the first place, she wouldn't be in her current predicament.

"Oh, that's not a problem. I'll ease you in. Two gal pals hanging out in the kitchen. How much fun is that? I'm thinking of 1930s outfits. I've got some pieces in mind. I'll bring them over, and we'll see what works."

"Sure, this could be fun." Daphne knew every word was a lie. But Betty had been a supportive friend since Daphne arrived in Cobb. She owed her.

Maybe it would be fun after all.

Two days later, Daphne glanced into Auntie Flo's large, curved, wooden mirror, staring at her strange reflection. Her blonde hair, parted in the middle, fell in sculpted waves. She poked the stiff style—quite different from her usual uncontrolled curls. Pouting her mouth, she studied the carefully applied red lipstick, admiring the perfect bow on her upper lip.

She might be standing in Flo's faded, cozy, earth-toned living room, but she felt out of place. Her outfit was a loan from Betty, the brains of this operation. Daphne fingered the borrowed blouse of pink-and-green plaid crepe fabric. She smoothed down the white crossover collar that looped across her throat, each end attached to the front of the blouse with a pink button. A quiet thought occurred to her—this was her living room now. A shiver ran through her body. To distract herself, she tugged at the short sleeves made of layers of fluttering material.

"Found it! I knew it was in here." Betty waved some cloth over her head. Putting a lid back on the plastic tub at her feet, she vigorously shook the fabric. Holding the apron out in front of her, she frowned. "I think I will run it in the dryer for a minute, Daph. I'll do the same for my apron, too. Where is the dryer?"

"Through the kitchen, on the way to the side door. Across from the half bath." Daphne gave directions for the familiar, and yet still foreign, home. Her stomach flipped as her hand skimmed over the front of the tulip-design skirt that fell to her calves. Glancing at the mirror again, she paused. *A stranger might mistake me for a young woman heading down to the nearest drugstore counter if the year was 1934.*

"That's right. I've seen it. I'll be back in a minute. Don't touch a thing. And stop fussing with the sleeves. You look fine. Oh, and keep an eye out for Fitzy," Betty said over her shoulder.

"*Fitzy* is coming?" Daphne's panic increased at the abrupt disclosure of Betty's cousin joining them. Furrowing her brow, she berated herself. *Why didn't I see this coming? They are crazy close.*

"He's helping with filming the YouTube video. He's a natural. But don't tell him that. It'll go to his head."

"But he'll see me," she whined, questioning the whole idea for the hundredth time.

"Oh, Daph. Thousands of people are going to see you." Betty waggled her eyebrows. "You should be seen. You look *sinsational*."

"Don't you mean sensational?"

Betty slowly looked Daphne up and down. "With my artistic efforts, definitely *sinsational*." With a giggle, she disappeared into the other room.

A light sweat broke out on Daphne's face and arms. *Relax. You don't want to ruin your makeup. How did I let Betty talk me into this?* That was easy. Daphne was a wuss. Attempting to become an ex-wuss was harder than she thought.

Daphne groaned. While the clothes were pretty, nothing had felt like fun yet. Flo would have told her that she'd made her bed, and now she had to lie in it. *Skip the grumbling, as well, kiddo.* Her eyes were drawn to the mirror again, but she forced her hands still at her sides this time.

"Sinsational?" she asked aloud. She hushed her inner critic and appraised the view objectively. She did look attractive. "I hope Rat Bastard is one of the thousands of people who see this."

"This is going all over TikTok. I'm sure your worthless ex will eat his heart out when he gets a look at you." Betty released an evil cackle.

Betty gave herself a quick look in the mirror. Her wide-legged, double-button sailor pants in a navy color swayed with her movements. A complementary navy, short-sleeved blouse, with a wide nautical collar and back flap, trimmed with three white stripes, emphasized her small size. Satisfied after mere seconds, she moved into the kitchen, last remodeled in the 1980s, to do her last-minute prep work.

A knock at the door pulled Daphne away from the mirror. Fitzy entered with a laptop bag, cords, and other pieces of technology she couldn't identify. Giving her a quick nod, he strolled to set up in the kitchen. Before Daphne knew it, Betty was tying the apron around her and discussing the order of the shoot. Necessary items had been listed on a grease board leaning against the counter, outside of camera view.

"Just relax, Daph," Betty instructed as she patted Daphne's back. "Be yourself and go with the flow. Pretend you've got a friend sitting at the table, and they've come over to learn how to make this special applesauce."

Fitzy yelled, "Action!"

Daphne stiffened and forced a tight smile on her face. Betty came across as her usual silly, charming self. Daphne froze for a second. Glancing at Fitzy, she knew her eyes were filled with terror. He gave her a thumbs up. It did not make her feel any better. Then he gave her a wink, and she snorted. She was so lucky to have made friends like Betty and Fitzy here in Cobb.

Betty rolled her eyes at the two of them. "Thank goodness, I have the power of editing. Fitzy, behave yourself. Don't worry, Daph, I won't humiliate you. You'll be amazing by the time I finish the episode."

Betty began asking leading questions about making applesauce. Daphne slipped into her old mode as a librarian, happy to explain things to people once again. This wasn't how to search for a book on the online card catalog, but the process of presenting information wasn't so different.

As they peeled and chopped endless apples, Daphne questioned if viewers wouldn't find it boring. Betty assured her that she'd speed it up and cut chunks out in the final product. Fitzy shut off the camera while Daphne added Flo's secret weapon, grated orange peels, into the sauce. The zesty smell hit her like a giant ocean wave. The orange and apple mixed together in a heavenly scent. For a moment, she was transported back to the moment she'd mastered how to peel with her small hands as her aunt nodded encouragingly. Flo only shared this recipe with a select few.

As Fitzy began filming again, Daphne's nerves failed to return. With a big smile, she looked at the camera and said, "Betty, maybe we should change our outfits."

Daphne observed Betty's quizzical look before continuing. "Well, we've been doing this for so long, I feel a decade has passed. I think we have left the 1930s behind and now should be wearing 1940s Rosie the Riveter outfits." Daphne laughed and gave her pal an eyebrow wiggle.

Betty's mouth hung open.

By the final shot, Betty and Daphne looked wilted but proud of the small stack of jars displayed on the table.

Betty put an arm around Daphne. "Thank you so much, Daphne, for joining me today. This was a memorable day for sure. Well, folks, that is how you make Flo's Famous Sauce—except for the secret ingredient, of course! I'll see you next time when we make history together." She ended by giving the camera a big wink.

Fitzy called, "Cut!" and they all collapsed into kitchen chairs.

"I make a motion for pizza," Betty moaned.

Daphne raised her hand. "I second that motion."

Fitzy laughed and added, "The vote is unanimous. Motion carried."

"Betty, you order." Daphne's voice was muffled since her face rested on crossed arms facing the table. "I'll pick it up."

"My car is blocking yours," groaned Fitzy. "I'll go pick it up."

Daphne wiped her brow. "When does the video go out?"

"In a couple of days. I will need to do post-production work on it," Betty said, while ordering the food on her phone. "When does Parmy taste this stuff?"

"I was thinking maybe tomorrow. Would you come with me, please? She scares me a little."

"Sure, but most of my time for the next couple of days will be spent editing."

While Fitzy was gone, the women put away the filming equipment and began cleaning the space. Upon his return, they lounged on the couch and chair in the living room, eating hot, cheesy pizza.

Fitzy picked up Daphne's recently purchased used copy of Christie's *Poirot Investigates*. "What's this?" He held it up for Daphne to see.

"A book, you fool." Betty laughed at her joke.

Fitzy rolled his eyes.

"Research. I thought it might help with the mystery of Flo's death." Daphne shrugged, feeling a little silly saying it out loud. "Might inspire me or something."

"Good idea. I'll get a copy myself. We can both read it. Maybe compare notes and see if we can come up with anything." Fitzy mustered a tired smile.

Daphne grinned back, grateful he didn't think her crazy.

The food was quickly devoured. Betty patted her full stomach. "Just what the doctor ordered. I want to start working on the video or go to bed. I'll figure out which when I get home."

"I can stay, Daphne," offered Fitzy. "We could brainstorm about the murder."

"You can't, Fitzy," interrupted Betty. "You're blocking my car in the driveway."

"I can move the car, let you out, then park again. No one is stopping you from leaving Betty."

"It's fine, Fitzy," Daphne stood up and yawned. "I'm worn out. I don't have enough little gray cells left to think about the murder now, anyway. But let's get together later and talk about the book, okay?"

"Sure." Fitzy gave his cousin an angry stare that a sleepy Daphne couldn't interpret.

"I feel bad about Aunt Pen. I'll be editing most of tomorrow and ignoring her."

"I'll come over," Daphne offered. "Then you can take a break, and we will go to Joe's Diner for the taste test."

With another yawn, Daphne ushered her friends out the door. She hoped her tired state would keep her from worrying about the upcoming taste test all night. Would she do Auntie Flo justice?

Chapter Twenty-One

THE NEXT MORNING BEGAN with the delivery of a package. Daphne almost cried with joy. It was her coffee supplies. She put the box in the truck and swung by the grocery store for ingredients on her way to Betty's. Once there, she prepped her espresso machine and impressed Betty and Aunt Pen with her latte skills, making each a cup with a foam heart.

Armed with a mug of caffeine, Betty marched upstairs to her office to begin editing. Daphne and Pen settled in the living room and chatted about the video and shared casual bits of gossip. The boost of energy from the beverage inspired Penelope to cook a roast for a late lunch. After writing a careful list, Daphne made a quick trip to the grocery store for the required items.

While the roast was cooking, Daphne and Betty decided it was time to deliver the applesauce. At Joe's Diner, the three women sat in a booth. Betty slid the container over to the waiting judge, Parmelia. Sitting beside her friend, Daphne hid her quivering hand underneath the table.

Parmelia popped open the lid and spooned out a large sample. She took a deep sniff. It passed the smell test, so Parmelia opened her mouth, took a bite, and closed her eyes. Sitting opposite, the two women watched her tongue move, exploring the taste and texture.

Several long seconds later, her lids popped open. A smile blossomed. "Well, dang. You both were right. This is the best sauce I've ever had. There is something in there. It's a flavor I can't quite name, but it seems so familiar. I wish I had known this years ago. I'm not going to lie. I felt hurt by what your aunt said to me. Now, I know she wasn't trying to be mean. With Flo, I should've known better." She helped herself to another spoonful.

"When it came to canning, she was a genius." Daphne frowned, wishing that Flo could hear the praise herself. "I wish everyone could know that about her. I'm gathering she could be a bit rough around the edges, but I get the feeling people didn't see Flo's kinder side."

"That's a great idea." Parmelia's grin grew wider.

"Idea?" Daphne had missed something.

"Yes, that is a good idea," Betty added. "You'd be interested in that, Parmy?"

"Absolutely."

"How much would you need? How much are you offering?" Betty began negotiating.

Daphne continued her befuddled stare at the two of them.

"She isn't going to do this for free, not even for Flo's memory."

"Hmmm, I always do a pork chop special on Sunday, and we go through a lot of sauce that day. I need about thirty jars, which would last me about three months, maybe less. People's tastes can be hard to predict. We will have to see. Be ready to supply more if it gets popular. I know this is better than grocery chain stuff. I'll give you five dollars for a medium size jar."

"Deal." Betty grinned at Daphne, who was finally catching up. "Oh, one more thing, though."

"Yeah?" Parmy raised an eyebrow.

"You need to tell people that it's Flo's applesauce." Under the table, Betty squeezed Daphne's hand.

Daphne could hardly speak for the lump in her throat.

"No problem. I always appreciated that she didn't take crap from no one." There were nods of understanding. "When can you get my sauce, Daphne?"

"I have a good-sized batch back at the house. I can bring it over later today."

"I can start serving them this Sunday with the pork chops. Nice doing business with you, Daphne." She held out her hand.

"Thank you, Parmelia." Daphne gave as vigorous a shake as she could manage.

"It's Parmy," she said in a warm tone.

⋘

Returning to Betty's place, they found Penelope and a guest putting dishes on the table.

Betty furrowed her brow as she looked at the two women. "Hi, Mom. I didn't know you were joining us for lunch. Daph, this is my mom, Vivan Bennet. Mom, this is my pal Daphne."

"I happened to be in the area and thought I would drop in," Vivan replied.

The look between Betty and Penelope informed Daphne that neither of them was buying that lame excuse. Vivan had come over for a spot inspection to see how her aunt and daughter were doing. Daphne got the impression that this was not the first time, either.

But Pen took it in stride and told Viv, "Now that you are here, you're welcome join us for lunch. Betty dear, I understand if you want to fill a plate and go up to work."

"You're sure?"

"Of course. Between your mother and Daphne, I will be well entertained."

The three other women sat down and filled their plates as Betty took her meal upstairs. Silence loomed as they ate several bites.

"This is a great pot roast, Penelope," said Daphne.

"Thank you. I have had much practice making it. Henry would have been happy eating roast beef every day. But, goodness, if a lima bean ended up on his plate, it was a federal crime."

The lima beans Daphne had bought at the store were in a serving bowl. Now that her husband had passed, Pen seemed to be making up for lost time. Vivan mutely raised an eyebrow.

"Do you play cards, Daphne?" asked Penelope.

"Not really."

"Your Aunt Florence enjoyed card games. She was a wizard with pinochle," added Vivan.

"Yes, there were countless nights that she would join Henry and me for a game. There is a three-person version."

"I remember her going over to the senior center in Hinckley when they had their pinochle tournaments." Vivan set down her fork. "She usually came home with a prize. Flo was a real card shark if you ask me."

After the meal, the ladies collected and carried the dishes into the kitchen. Vivan leaned over the dishwasher as she filled it. "Aunt Pen, I forgot to tell Betty she's invited to join us for church on Sunday. We'll have lunch at Joe's Diner afterward."

"Oh, goodie," exclaimed Daphne. "They will be serving Flo's applesauce then. I'm dropping off the first order after I leave here."

"Then I'll make sure to order it," declared Penelope. "I doubt Betty will come. When she is working on a video, it takes all her focus for days."

⊰⊱

The texts started rolling in at noon on Sunday. Daphne and Betty were both included in the chain.

> Parmy: This is Parmy. What did you do?

> Parmy: I've had a line out the door since eleven!

Daphne couldn't figure out how Parmy had gotten her number or what she and Betty had done. She knew she hadn't done anything. What had her new bestie been up to? Pulling up Betty's YouTube channel, she quickly found what she was looking for.

At the end of her most recent video, uploaded at ten the evening before, Betty added a clip of her talking to her fans. "Well, folks, that is how you make Flo's Famous Sauce except for the secret ingredient. Now, if you want to taste some of this amazing applesauce and find yourself near Cobb, Maine, you can head over to Joe's Diner for their Sunday pork chop special and get a side of this here sauce. I'll see you next time when we make history together."

Her phone chimed again.

> Parmy: Someone called for reservations, WTF?

> Parmy: Flo's Famous Applesauce is famous. Gonna need more. STAT!

Chapter Twenty-Two

Fitzy

THE NEXT EVENING, FITZY wiped his sweaty palms on his skinny jeans. But his nerves couldn't erase the grin on his face. He was finally spending some time with Daphne without Betty around. He carried the takeout to the front porch.

Daphne yanked open the door. "Thank goodness you're here. I'm starving. Here, I'll take the food. Come on in." She grabbed the bag and inhaled the smell of Joe's Diner's meatloaf.

Fitzy followed her inside, closing the door behind him. In the kitchen, a scene of chaos awaited them. Every inch of the counters and kitchen table was covered in applesauce paraphernalia. Filled jars were stacked neatly in several boxes. Daphne shoved items back, making a small space at the end of the table for them to eat. Fitzy pulled out plates and silverware.

Daphne attacked her takeout food box with a fork before she even sat down. She quickly shoved in another bite and gave a muffled, "Thank you."

He laughed as he moved the food from his box on his plate. "You're welcome. This is not quite what I expected when you said to come over for dinner and talk about solving the murder."

"Yeah, sorry about that. I have a rush order for Parmy. I've been saucing all day."

"Saucing?"

"My new term for canning applesauce. It's faster."

"I like it."

He played with the collar of his short-sleeved, blue plaid, button-down shirt. Did she even notice his change in clothes? The way she was attacking her food, he doubted she saw anything past the end of her fork. Did he really think a more attractive outfit would make a big difference?

Daphne finally paused in her eating, sat back and took a sip of water. She wore a sheepish grin. "Sorry about that. I was hungry. Okay, talk time now. I feel like we don't know much about each other, despite being together loads over the last few days. Betty said you spent some time living away from Cobb."

"Boston."

"Beantown! How exciting."

"It was. When I got there, the streets thrummed with energy. My coworkers and I loved the big city life."

"You? Living the big-time city life? I can't see it."

"Maybe someday I'll show you pictures. Yeah, I worked with this team. Lots of young guys not long out of college. It was the whole work hard, play hard kind of thing. Someone always seemed to get the guys a reservation at the hot restaurants or into the most select bars and clubs." Did it sound like he was bragging? He hoped not. He didn't feel proud of this time in his life.

"Wow. I would not have thought that of you. Did you meet any ladies at the bars and clubs?"

He blushed down to his roots. How to answer this? Not wanting to lie or sounding like a sleaze, he stayed silent.

"That is *so* a yes. Was it a lot of women then?" Daphne asked.

He looked down at his plate and shoved around a chunk of meatloaf.

"Byron Fitzgibbon, were you a *player*?"

"Okay, I will tell you. But you must promise not to tell my family—not even Betty. Especially not Betty. Can you do that?" Daphne had been open about her mistakes with Wallace. Shouldn't he be as transparent? Jeez, this was so embarrassing.

"This must be good. Yes, I will remain silent. Oh my gosh, do you have a secret family in Boston, and you are on the run from some ex-girlfriend??"

"Nothing like that," he laughed. "That group of guys I ran with attracted a certain kind of woman. I called them shiny women. You know the type—long legs, painted nails, fancy hair, plenty of makeup, and not much clothing. I was part of the group, and since the ladies liked going to expensive restaurants and clubs, they liked me."

"I know about those shiny women. My ex would always drool over them when we went out."

"Nothing ever turned into a real relationship. Every week or two, one girl left, and another filled her place. This went on for quite some time." He frowned. "I am not proud of any of this. I came home for a visit. My family bragged about how clever I was with my big job in the city. Like I was a real somebody. They would have been so disappointed if they knew the truth about how I was spending my time and money."

His gut still wrenched with shame. Now Daphne would think him the idiot he'd once been. But that wasn't him anymore. He had to make her understand.

"Your family would love you no matter what."

"Maybe. But I was disappointed in myself. What did I have to show for this high-flyer lifestyle? An empty bank account, no real relationships, no woman I would ever bring home, and I was tired. I realized that even my so-called friends weren't really friends at all. I don't care about going out to all those fancy places. I like more work-life balance. None of them even knew when hunting season began or spent their winters snowmobiling."

"I didn't know you were such a nature lover."

"I live in Maine. It's almost a requirement."

"Okay, so you are having this enlightenment. What happened next?"

"I started making some changes. I stayed friendly with the guys but stopped going out after work with them. This also removed the shiny women from my life. Which I found I didn't miss much."

"So what did you do with all this free time? Play video games all night?"

"No. Not every night. I checked out Boston. I'd lived there for a while but had never gone to a museum or any historical places. I discovered my local library. I joined their chess club. A bunch of us got season tickets to the Boston Theater."

"Check you out, Mr. Culture. Sounds amazing. But how did you end up back here?"

Yes, there is so much more to me. I'd like to get a chance to show you and maybe get out of the friend zone you've put me in.

"My quality of life vastly improved and was okay for a few years. Then, one day, I was looking out over the city from my condo. It was autumn."

"That sounds beautiful."

"Exactly. It should have been beautiful. But the city skyline felt like it got in the way. The trees had some nice color, but I wanted them to stretch out for miles. I missed home. I wanted nature. I wanted to hop on my sled whenever the mood struck me. I even missed my family and Cobb."

"You were lucky."

"How was that lucky? I felt miserable."

"You knew where you belonged."

"I suppose I did. An opportunity to work from home came up, and I jumped at it. My coworkers thought I was crazy and joked about me getting mugged by Bigfoot."

"Isn't Bigfoot found in the Pacific Northwest?"

"Actually, there was a sighting in the mid-1980s. Happened in Androscoggin County, as a matter of fact."

"Are you telling me I could be in the woods and a bigfoot might jump out at me?"

"It's possible, but not very probable. I'd worry more about bears," he teased.

"Yeah, that makes me feel better."

"Anyway, that's how I ended up back here."

"You surprise me, Fitzy. I didn't know you were an onion."

"An onion?"

"Layers."

Maybe she was finally starting to see the real him.

"Funny." He rolled his eyes. "Are we going to talk murder tonight or what?" He was ready to be done focusing on him. Time for a subject change.

He didn't seriously think Flo Winkler had been killed. But it made for a wonderful reason to spend time with Daphne. What harm could come out of humoring her for a while? Since the cookie failure, she'd hardly done anything to solve the crime. He doubted her interest in the topic would last long.

"Good point. Let's get comfy in the living room."

Chapter Twenty-Three

TIRED AND SORE FROM her all-day canning sprint, Daphne decided the kitchen mess could wait until the following morning. Finding the last of her strength, she opened the front door a bit, letting in some cool evening air, started a fire in the hearth, and lit an alarming number of candles around the sitting area. She collapsed on one end of the couch while Fitzy occupied the other.

"I've been following this Scandinavian lifestyle called hygge on Instagram," said Daphne. "It translates into cozy, calm living or something like that. People post lush photos of themselves in sweaters and blankets, sitting by a fireplace. The rooms are always full of all these pretty candles burning. This isn't worth posting, but I feel pretty comfy."

"It is pleasant. A+ for setting the mood."

She looked down at herself. Her wide-neck, pink t-shirt was slipping down one shoulder. Gray leggings tucked into thick white socks finished her sloppy ensemble. Was that a cinnamon smudge on the end of her nose? At least a quarter of her hair had escaped her bun and hung around her neck in tendrils. There was comfortable, and then there was just messy. She pulled the bun loose and shook out her hair. Fitzy stopped and stared.

Oh heavens, I must look a wreck. He is trying not to say anything. Look at him. He dressed nice and everything, while I look like every decent piece of clothes I have is in the laundry.

Taking a breath, she reminded herself that this was her pal. Betty won the award for best friend, and Fitzy received an honorable mention. Certain his stolen glances were likely due to the cinnamon, she regained her composure and returned to their conversation.

"Thanks," Daphne replied "I plan to visit the library this week and see if they have any hygge books. It's usually a winter thing, but I figure it can be used anytime if done right. I haven't been to the Cobb Library in ages. I wonder if it's changed much since I was there."

"Not that much. There are more computers and some new books, but I would say that most of it will seem very familiar." Fitzy's expression became wistful.

"How do you know that it will seem familiar?" She sat up a little higher.

"I remember you from the library." His eyes studied her reaction.

"Wait. Some random blonde girl walked into the library a million years ago, and you remember her?"

"You weren't some random girl." He smirked like he had something hidden in his pocket and had been waiting for the right time to pull it out. "You were reading a lot of *Redwall* books that summer."

"Wow, yeah. I loved those books. I haven't thought about them in years." She snuggled into the couch. "I was super addicted to them. Auntie Flo would take me to the library and let me check out a bunch at a time. She never rushed me or hovered to see what I was selecting. I lost count of how many books in that series I read that summer."

"And many times you came to the library, there was a boy who was also reading many books. *Redwall* books were his favorite as well. In fact, the two of you had several conversations about the series."

Her jaw dropped. "Wait. No! Seriously? You, were *Redwall* Boy? I wondered what happened to you. But then I returned to my normal life, and Maine faded away. Plus, my mom didn't approve of the books and encouraged me to find more traditional works to read." She slapped her thigh with her hand. "*Redwall* Boy. Sitting in my living room. Who would have thought it? Amazing."

"*Redwall* Boy. I like that nickname. So, discussing Agatha tonight won't be the first time we've talked books."

"I like that thought. I love thinking I have a childhood friend here in Cobb. Makes me feel like I belong."

Fitzy's smile didn't reach his eyes, and he seemed deflated compared to moments ago. Daphne tried to pinpoint what had changed but came up empty. Fitzy grabbed a backpack that he had brought in with him. He pulled out his copy of Agatha Christie's *Poirot Investigates*. Several pages had little colored flags sticking out. Next came his pens, highlighters, and notebook. Daphne gave an approving look as she pulled a similar-looking pile from the coffee table onto the empty cushion between them.

Fitzy opened up to a bookmarked page. "I suggest starting with chapter two, The Tragedy at Marsdon Manor. The story involves a murder dressed up to look like an accident or a possible suicide. Since that is sort of what you think happened here, I highlighted points in the story I thought we could discuss."

"Glad to know I wasn't the only one marking things in the book."

"One of the central points of the story was the insurance policy on Mr. Maltravers's life. Did Flo have one as well? I mean if it's okay to ask those kinds of questions. If they aren't too personal."

"It's fine. We need to look at every angle. Yes, she did. But I can't see how it helps us in any way. First, I was informed by Mr. Tippett, the lawyer, that normally, suicide will invalidate an insurance policy if it happens in the first year or two after a change has been made to the policy. Flo changed it at least a decade ago. And yes, I am the sole beneficiary. Since we know I didn't kill her, that looks like a dead end."

"You are handling this in a very logical manner, Daphne. I'm impressed. However, I have another tough question."

Daphne nodded to let him know he should go ahead.

"They also talked about a usual cause of suicide as financial trouble. How was Flo's money situation?"

"No money problems. I mean, she wasn't rich or anything, but she was comfortable. Flo seemed to be someone who only needed simple creature comforts to be happy. I thought we were supposed to be proving she was murdered, not that she took her own life."

"One of the best ways to show it was murder is to remove any likely reasons for the other option."

"I suppose. Okay, I want to point out this section, 'He had been out shooting rooks, a small rifle lay beside him.' The rifle is what killed him. The cops were right on the cause of death, well, once they did the autopsy. But they didn't get the motive right." Daphne bounced on the cushion. "He didn't kill himself with the rifle. The rifle was used to kill him and then planted near the victim to make it look like suicide." Daphne tilted her face up.

Fitzy leaned toward her. "Did the autopsy find the foxglove killed Flo?"

She had never noticed his eyes were a dark, chocolaty brown. Silence hung in the air for a moment until Daphne recentered herself. "The report just said heart attack on the form. But yes, it was the foxglove. Don't you see? She could have been poisoned by someone, and then that person left the foxglove out to make it look like she had done it herself."

"You make a solid point there. But there isn't any proof that anyone else was here that morning." They both slumped back at the same time. "There was another point I couldn't help but ponder over. While discussing the case with Poirot, the doctor said, 'It is fortunate for his wife, then, that there is this life insurance. A very beautiful and charming young creature, but terribly unstrung by this sad catastrophe.' What if there was a lover involved in this? You found that book!"

"Okay, let's imagine there is this lover. Man, that is too weird. Did the lover kill her? Why? She didn't leave the life insurance to them. Did they think that she had? Why would they think that?"

"And we must acknowledge that it could have been an *old* lover. That book was published in 1980. Even if the relationship began several years after the book was released, that was still long ago. I would think that people would hear about Flo having a partner. Yet, I've never heard any rumors, not from now or the past. If a relationship ever existed, the two of them kept it a closely guarded secret."

Daphne bit her lower lip. "Have you wondered if your Aunt Pen was the lover?"

"Aunt Pen!" He shook his head vigorously. "Come on, she was married to Uncle Henry for years. She was the picture of a devoted wife. No way."

Daphne wasn't ready to give up her theory yet. "You hear about people hiding that kind of secret for years. I mean, think of their age. Everyone says what friends my aunt and yours were. Their relationship goes back to high school. Maybe there was more to it than that."

"It doesn't add up. First, when Uncle Henry died, why didn't they get together, go public, or whatever? There was no longer a reason to keep quiet. There wasn't much time left, and let's face it, Flo wouldn't care what people said. Aunt Pen would care, but she would have gone along if Flo pushed her. That's been her nature until recently. Second, it's a fishing book. Aunt Pen likes fishing as much as you do." Fitzy sat back and crossed his arms.

Daphne grimaced at the thought of her fishing trip. "I will admit you have some good points. So, Pen is not a likely candidate for having a secret love affair with Auntie Flo. But who is? Why did it end? Did it have anything to do with her murder? Is all of this a figment of my imagination? This looks so much easier on tv. Poirot would have had this case solved by now." She covered her face with her hands.

"Hey, don't give up yet. We are just getting started. I think we've made some good progress. We've eliminated some ideas and have questions to work on further."

Daphne gave him a smile for his efforts. She gazed at his cheerful face, the outfit he must have spent time on, and remembered that while he looked presentable, she was disheveled. When starving, it hadn't seemed so important. Now, a burning embarrassment flamed on her cheeks. Her inner critic, which sounded a lot like her mother, began to whisper how terrible she looked. Allowing someone to see her in her current state was an embarrassment. Who'd want to be friends with such a slob? Her shirt and leggings began to take on the fashion styling of a bag lady.

"Umm, Fitzy. You know, I am going to run upstairs and freshen up. I feel a little grungy." Without waiting for a reply, she flew up the stairs.

In her room, she turned on the light and closed the door. In the mirror, she saw red eyes, threatening tears, and her smudged nose. Oh, what must he think of her?

A memory of Wallace came thundering in. She had carefully selected an attractive but modest dress in her favorite shade of pink for their usual Friday dinner. Giving herself a wink in the mirror, she left the bedroom. Waiting, Wallace looked her up and down and said, "Don't you have anything nice to wear? You should change. Oh, never mind. We will be late, let's just go."

Once again, she was tormented by a pit of her stomach. With shaking hands, she ripped a tissue out of the box on the dresser. She rubbed fiercely at the cinnamon spot on her nose. She grabbed one tissue after another, wiping her wet eyes and rubbing her nose until it felt raw. Her hand automatically reached out for another tissue but found nothing. They were gone. She picked up the box and was ready to toss it into the trash, but noticed it felt heavy for an empty vessel.

She shook it and felt something rattle on the bottom side of the box. She flipped it over and found the bottom had been cut open and retaped closed. The box had a false bottom. She ripped the cardboard apart. A slim red leather book dropped to the floor with a thud. She picked it up and began to leaf through the pages.

There was a knock at the door. "Are you okay?" Fitzy asked. Ignoring the question, she kept looking at the text. "Daphne, I'm coming in now."

The door opened. Daphne's nose was red enough to lead Santa on his Christmas Eve mission. Her eyes pried themselves away from the volume. "Fitzy, it's a journal. It's Auntie Flo's journal. There are entries in here from not long before she died."

"Where did you find it?"

"It was hidden in the bottom of a tissue box. Why would she go to such lengths to hide it?"

"To make sure no one found it. The real question is, who did she not want to see it? She lived alone. What does it say?"

Daphne closed the book and stood up. "Fitzy, I need to look at this. I want to do this right now."

"Sure, no problem, let's go downstairs."

"No, Fitzy. I want to look at it alone first. These are Flo's private thoughts. I need to see what is in them before I share them with anyone else. I'm sorry. You've been amazing tonight. I hope you can understand." She gave him a pleading look.

"Of course, I understand. That is personal and, I would imagine, very emotional. Call me tomorrow and let me know you are okay."

"Sure."

Daphne walked Fitzy downstairs. He gathered his items. Daphne opened the front door and gave him a quick hug. As his foot hit the bottom step of the porch, she called from behind. "Good night, *Redwall* Boy."

Chapter Twenty-Four

DAPHNE STARED AT HER phone as the alarm blared. Her tired first reaction was to throw it across the room. However, since it had an industrial-grade safety case, the phone would be unharmed and still yelling at her. It was time to get up. Fitzy would be expecting a call as soon as possible. Betty would want an update as well.

She texted both Fitzy and Betty. Betty knew nothing about the journal and was excited to come over. Daphne was stunned that Fitzy hadn't told her everything. Both cousins would arrive at 10:30 a.m. Looking around her mess of a kitchen, Daphne decided it was best to spend the next hour cleaning.

When they arrived, Daphne ushered them into lemon freshness and suggested lattes with her perfected heart art.

"That sounds fantastic. I need a pick-me-up." Betty slid into a kitchen chair and looked eagerly at the coffee maker. "I want to be good and caffeinated for this conversation."

Daphne took the hint and created a concoction using one of her largest mugs.

"This place looks amazing." Fitzy took in the spotless table. "I'm impressed. But I'll pass on the latte. I'm not really into fancy coffee drinks. Tea is more my thing."

"Tea over coffee?" Betty shook her head. "Were you switched at birth or something? How can we be related? And Daphne makes the best latte I've ever had. Weirdo."

"Auntie Flo's tea stuff is in the cupboard above the stove." Daphne didn't understand his anti-coffee stance any more than Betty, but she wouldn't pick on Fitzy for it. "You're taller than me. Would you get it? Help yourself to anything you want."

"Thanks." Fitzy rummaged through the cupboard and brought down a box of cinnamon tea packets. "This looks good. Have any sugar?"

"It's in the canister on the counter. Help yourself." Daphne nodded with her head. She finished a latte for herself and poured boiling water into a large mug for Fitzy.

"Just stop it." Betty bellowed and slurped her coffee. "I can't handle this much politeness. Why aren't you two grumpy like normal people in the morning?"

Daphne smiled at Fitzy. She liked his good manners.

"She just needs her caffeine to set in. Ignore her. You know, *Elizabeth*, in the real world, 10:30 means the morning is nearly through, not just starting." He tossed a barb to his cousin as he stirred sugar in his tea."

Betty's eyes drew into slits as she pointed a finger. "You can leave anytime you want, *Byron*. Isn't there work you have to do?"

"My day is pretty flexible. Perks of my IT job."

Daphne decided to put an end to the cousins' banter. She placed her mug at the head of the table, then retrieved from a drawer the journal, a notepad, and a pen. She sat down, and Fitzy sat across the table from Betty; the two were still eyeing each other with mistrust. Daphne needed to get them back on track.

"Okay, you two, enough teasing. We need to get down to business."

Both sobered up. Their focus switched to her and the red book.

Daphne continued. "I went through part of the journal last night. I was too tired to read the whole thing. I decided to start at the end, closest to her death, and work backward."

"A sound plan." Fitzy nodded encouragingly.

"But did you find anything of interest?" Betty asked. "Did she think anyone was trying to do her in?"

"I found some very interesting entries. Nothing so clear as she thought her life was in danger, but some suspicious stuff. It seems... I am not sure how to say this." Daphne paused, chewing on her lower lip.

"Oh, just say it! Get it out, girl!"

Lowering her voice, Daphne said, "Auntie Flo kept a watch on people."

Sitting back in her chair, Betty's mouth hung open. "Like she was a stalker? I can't believe that."

"No, nothing like that. She observed people around here, in Cobb. Then wrote about what she saw. There were also speculations about their behavior in her journal. It's rather clinical, like a report. She even used military time. I mean, isn't that weird?" Daphne's eyes darted between her two friends.

"Sort of. But Flo wasn't like other people, we know that," Betty offered.

"Maybe it's not so strange."

The two women stared at Fitzy.

"Think about it. She worked for the police for years, dispatching. Her work would have required her to log all her calls and what happened around here. Maybe when she left the force, she found she couldn't kick the habit. She continued to make observations and write them down. If you think about it that way, that doesn't seem so bizarre."

Betty raised her eyebrows, cocked her head, and shrugged.

Daphne chewed her lips more and nodded her head. "Okay, until we find information that disproves that theory, Fitzy, we will work under your assumption of why Auntie Flo undertook this journal."

"Good, we've got that settled. But what I really want to know is, what did she write?" Betty pleaded with her friend for the details. "What's in the red book?"

Pulling out her notepad, Daphne opened it and turned it so the other two could see. "I wrote down all the information from the journal that seemed important. I had to go through several entries to find the whole story. I created a sort of timeline."

Written was the following:

July 9th last summer – Jackson Puddingstone regularly leaves his house by himself overnight. This weekend, set out on Sat. 0612 hours, returned Sun. at 1150. At Joe's Diner, after a casual inquiry one day, he said he was going to insurance conferences. Who has heard of such things? And so often? I think I see a pattern. Seems to be gone every second weekend. Will confirm next month. Is he cheating on Marion? Is he caught up in drugs, smuggling, insurance fraud, or a second family? Will keep eye out and hopefully will gather more details. Need real evidence. Marion seems no more or less cranky than usual. She involved? Not know what is happening in own home?

Aug 13th – Prediction confirmed. Jackson Puddingstone leaves the second weekend of the month. Left Sat. at 0600 hours. Returned home Sun at 1300 hours, later than usual. Alone, same bag. Limped like he was injured. Bruises on left arm.

Mar 11th this year – Jackson Puddingstone leaves house Sat at 0630 hours (running late). Rushed to car. Returned home Sun. at 1015 hours. Alone, one small bag.

April 8th (last entry) – Jackson Puddingstone leaves house Sat. at 0600 hours. Returns home Sun. at 1000 hours. Again, solo, one small bag.

Daphne checked the calendar. The second weekend of July was less than two weeks away!

Fitzy and Betty took their time studying the sheet of paper. Betty turned her mug to show Daphne its empty status. She grabbed Betty's mug and made another latte, glad to be doing something with her hands. Sitting and watching her friends read her collected work had made her nervous and anxious. As the milk was heating, she turned to the table and asked them what they thought.

Fitzy responded. "I will admit this is some odd behavior, but Jackson Puddingstone? He's your neighbor and the most dull, boring, and stable guy in town."

"And if Fitzy calls a guy dull, he must be a fatal dose of boring."

Fitzy rolled his eyes at Betty's stab at him.

"I remember his wife when I gave cookies to people on the street. She didn't eat them. Didn't want the carbs," Daphne recalled.

"But this goes back like a year," Betty continued. "He leaves alone on the same weekend every month, around six in the morning. Where to? I mean, I agree with Flo. No one has monthly insurance conferences. Who is he kidding? The guy is so dull he can't even develop a decent lie. How is Marion buying this? Or maybe she is in on it."

"But in on what?" Daphne crafted a fern pattern for the top of Betty's drink and handed it to her friend. "Flo was great at recording his comings and goings. She found this strange pattern that does seem a little sus. But is he really up to something nefarious, and did he kill her for it? I mean, how would he know that she knew?"

"Well, Flo couldn't have seen any of this from her house," Fitzy stated. "Too many trees in the way. The logical assumption is that Flo was out having morning walks. That would be an excellent way for her to spy, I mean, check out her neighbors. People wouldn't ask a lot of questions. Were there other neighbors in the journal, or is Jackson the only one?"

"There were others," Daphne admitted, hanging her head. "But the most recent update on him was the last thing she wrote. Let's start with this one. If it doesn't pan out, we could look at the others. There are a few in there. Flo liked keeping tabs on what was happening with her neighbors. Probably more than was healthy."

"Flo Winkler, a certified busybody." Betty propped her head up with her hand and arm on the table. "Who would have thought it? She was the most private person in town, and here she was, keeping records of other people's secrets. That's so ironic. Is it wrong that it makes me like your aunt even more?"

"Jackson's next 'conference' is in two weeks," Daphne pointed out. "I think I will follow him and see where he goes."

"Whoa there. That doesn't sound safe," Fitzy protested. "You have no idea where you will end up. You don't know the area very well either. If he did notice your aunt checking on him and then killed her because he thought she was getting suspicious, then he might do the same to you."

"But Auntie Flo was right. We need real evidence," Daphne argued. "I'm not going to get anywhere sitting here. No one is taking my murder suspicion seriously. I need to get proof, and this is a solid clue."

"One of us could go with you," Betty offered. "Give you back up." She turned to Fitzy. "And if she goes to some dodgy place, we can split if it looks like it's going sideways."

"Look, we don't have to figure it all out today," Fitzy suggested. "We've got a couple of weeks, at any rate. But I think safety should be our number one priority. No one should be risking their lives for this."

Chapter Twenty-Five

WAITING FOR THE STAKEOUT was maddening. Even with everyone preparing for the big parade, the BBQ on The Green, and fun activities for the Fourth of July, Daphne still couldn't keep her mind off her sole murder suspect. She was so excited to finally have a lead. She attempted to distract herself until the second weekend of July with a long list of errands. Daphne had done all her laundry, tidied the house, grocery shopped, set up a card with the local library, read three books, and shook out all the rugs. She still had a week before the stakeout and three days to kill before the Fourth of July celebrations.

Salvation came in an invitation for tea from Betty's aunt. Sitting in the parlor, she should have known that a visit with Penelope would not be an everyday affair. The diminutive woman was working hard to balance a tray with two tall glasses filled with ice and a dark-colored liquid. Penelope informed her that they would not be drinking warm or standard iced tea, but Long Island iced tea instead. Taking a sip of her drink, Daphne's eyes bulged. Penelope did like her beverages strong.

"I like your kitten heels." Penelope settled into her chair, taking a small sip from her glass. "I used to wear sexy little things like that when I was younger. Now I get to dress for my comfort first and foremost." She wore white cotton stretchy pants and a white t-shirt with blue horizontal lines, giving her a nautical look.

"I like the heels. They aren't too uncomfortable to wear."

"Hmm. I used to say things like that. I wore all kinds of things to look pretty. I wanted to look attractive to men and fit society's standards. Back in the day, I stuffed myself into girdles, high heels, and clothes that were hot and restrictive. I would look at your aunt and be so jealous. She looked so comfortable in casual clothing, not trying to impress a soul." A gulp was consumed from her glass.

"I'm sure you were very glamorous." Daphne swallowed a small sip. She wanted to keep her head about her. "There's nothing wrong with wanting to look your best and be attractive to those around you. Though I have a hard time seeing you wearing something that didn't please you."

"I was a little glamorous once upon a time. But who was it for? See, that was the problem, Daphne. For years, I thought I was doing it for myself. It took the death of my husband to see that wasn't the case. When I no longer had him or half of our social circle to impress, the matching sweater sets, stiffly ironed blouses, and cumbersome skirts came off." Pen slapped the arm of her chair. "I hadn't been dressing for me at all. Because when I was given a choice and didn't have to worry about backlash, I chose another path. Now, it's all sneakers and soft linen for me. I can't be bothered with worrying about what is appropriate. Of course, my family was concerned I was losing my mind. What they don't understand is that I finally found myself."

"You seem to know what you want and don't hesitate to grab it now." Daphne chuckled.

"Exactly, my dear girl. But I spent most of my life trying to please other people. I didn't stop to ask myself, 'Penelope, what do you want?' It seemed like I was always following someone else's lead. Henry, the women's church circle, even my mother until she passed, and Flo had a strong personality."

Penelope stared into Daphne's eyes, causing the latter to shift in her seat. Sure, they had some parallels, but Daphne was trying to get more independent. She'd never let her deference to others consume her whole life.

Daphne studied the carpet's pattern as she said, "That sounds very frustrating and difficult. But I bet all those people loved you very much and didn't want to do anything to hurt you."

"I think they did love me. However, they loved me best when they could control me. Did any of them encourage me to think for myself? No one warned me that living to make others happy would leave me empty and lost."

"Oh, Penelope, how sad. You should have been happy along the way. At least you seem to be making yourself happy now."

"Things are much better now. After Henry died, I finally asked myself what I wanted and began making decisions based on my desires. I could be a free person at last." She pointed a finger at Daphne. "I think you can guess why I am telling you this. I wasted many years and have to live with those regrets. But you are young, child. You've got your whole life ahead of you."

"But, Penelope, that isn't happening to me. I'm living the life I want to live." As the words came out, Daphne knew they were hollow. Wanting them to be true didn't make it so.

"Bosh. That mother of yours has been controlling you for years. She kept you away from Flo. Betty told me about that Wallace fellow of yours, too. You should have turned on your kitten heels and walked out on him ages before he cheated on you. He was a selfish pig. You knew it, but you stayed with him. Coming to Cobb, running away from your former life, has given you an opportunity I never had. You have space to think, and a friend warning you of the consequences of going back to your old ways. Who do you want to be? Don't compromise your soul to placate other people. The cost is too great. Trust me, I know."

Penelope sat back in the chair, looking frail and spent. Admitting her failings had taken a lot out of her.

"Thank you. I appreciate you looking out for me. I promise you, I will think about it. Speaking of placating others. There is something I wanted to ask, but it is personal and kind of touchy."

"You've got my interest. Go ahead." Penelope stilled her chair and leaned forward.

"You and Flo. We're the two of you... um... ever more than friends?"

The small woman exploded with laughter. "I blame the news. It's getting crazier every year! All you youngsters think everyone has some sex secret. No, Flo was my best friend, but nothing more. What would her pillow talk have been? Fishing stories and canning tips?"

Daphne didn't know how to respond.

Penelope finally asked, "You going to the barbeque on The Green?"

"You bet." Daphne jumped on the new topic. "I'm looking forward to it. I've heard the Fourth of July celebrations are quite the event in Cobb."

"You heard correctly. The parade is nice, but the local high school band has never seemed to master marching and playing together. It's become a tradition to count how many times the students bump into each other."

"That's awful," Daphne admonished, but couldn't stop herself from grinning.

"Their worst was fifteen times. That was a very bad year. Usually, it's around five. One year, they managed to keep it down to three. The town burst with pride. Then there are games, for adults and kids alike. A sack race, egg relay, and like that. Of course, Fitzy will be there doing his usual thing."

"What usual thing? This is my first time going, remember."

"The grill. Fitzy brings in his big grill, and several other men will bring theirs. But Fitzy oversees it all. Today, he will be busy getting all those meats into their marinades and prepping the BBQ. He is the head griller."

"Fitzy is the head griller? I would have thought of him as a tech advisor or doing the fireworks. He is full of surprises."

"He makes the best burgers in the county. But I like his chicken best. I suggest you get in line early. His food goes fast. If you don't get there in the first hour, you'll be stuck with backup hot dogs. He's been doing it for years. Now, that's a boy who lives by his own code. I'm so proud of him." Penelope looked at her collection of family photos and smiled.

"You are lucky to have him in your family for sure. He loves you very much. I am so glad that I've become friends with him. He's helping me find my place here. I'll make sure to get in line right away."

Chapter Twenty-Six

TURNING SIDE TO SIDE, Daphne checked out her outfit. She'd taken Penelope's advice and selected something comfortable but cute, deciding that blue jean shorts, her Taylor Swift concert t-shirt, and white sneakers created a classic summer outfit. She held her hair back with a red headband.

It seemed like the whole town came out for the Fourth of July events, and there was every chance she would run into Phil Nolan. He'd waved at her when they were getting their mail at the same time a few days ago. But he didn't even stop to chat. Was he avoiding her? Was he still upset about the fishing date? Maybe she should show up with an "I'm sorry I barfed on you" bouquet after all.

Checking her phone, a squeak escaped her. It was 10:30 already. The parade started at 11:00, and then, as soon as it was over, she needed to hustle over to the grill line so she could snag a piece of Fitzy's chicken. Betty texted Daphne that she was welcome to join the family in their usual spot. All she needed was to get down there and find the group.

Daphne grabbed her keys and jumped into the pickup. Pulling out of the drive, she decided to head to the west end of town and park on the opposite side of The Green from where the parade was held. Parking was more likely to be found there. As she drove down the street, cars filled almost every slot. Finding a lucky opening, she whipped into the spot.

She paused with one hand holding her purse and the other on the car door. In her sights was one Jackson Puddingstone. What was he doing over here? His insurance business was on the other side of Main Street. Jackson huddled against the wall momentarily, stuffed something into his pocket, then quickly moved away. With him no longer blocking the view, she saw the ATM. She rolled her eyes at herself; there was nothing criminal about getting cash.

However, she reconsidered her original opinion as she watched Jackson cross the street. His walk was speedy, and his eyes darted back and forth. Alarm bells went off when Jackson did not turn and walk toward the parade. Instead, he got into his car and pulled away. He was heading out of town.

Without thinking, she pulled out of her spot, turned around, and followed his car at what she hoped was a discreet distance. After a few miles, the reality of her situation began to hit her. She was tailing a man she suspected of killing her aunt without backup or anyone knowing what she was doing. Then, there were the hurdles of having no skills in tailing a suspect or what to do when they arrived at their destination.

Her phone buzzed. Then it buzzed again. Probably Betty. The truck was old enough to be unequipped with Bluetooth, and not a fan of distracted driving, she left the phone on the passenger seat. She focused her attention on Jackson's car. For a moment, she thought about giving up. She could still turn around and go back to town. Sure, she would miss part or most of the parade, but she'd make it for the BBQ.

Shaking her head, she rejected the idea. This was too good an opportunity to miss. Fitzy had been pretty clear about him not wanting her to do this on her own. However, Penelope's words about not wasting time and living for yourself were ringing in her ears. Daphne's mother would never approve of her actions, so it seemed like a good thing to do. At her age, it seemed a little late to be going through a rebellious stage, but regardless, it was happening.

The heavy holiday traffic on the roads afforded Daphne cover. The downside was that keeping an eye on Jackson was more challenging, but she managed to stick with him on his way out of town. After forty minutes, on the outskirts of Hinckley, Jackson pulled off the main road and into the parking lot of a strip mall.

Following him, she found a spot not too close or far from her prey. Had she followed Jackson all this way, missed out on the parade and, now likely, the chicken as well, only to watch him do some shopping? She felt disappointed.

Jackson exited the car and turned his head back and forth, looking for something or someone. He made no move to enter any of the stores behind him. Excitement soared again. She leaned forward, keeping her eyes on him.

Several minutes passed before a beat-up black sedan pulled into the space beside him. A man got out of the car, though the word bear was more appropriate than man. He was tall, and had long, shaggy hair which matched his even shaggier beard. Tattoos ran up both arms. This beast of a man had on a white t-shirt, topped with a leather vest and battered jeans.

After being momentarily stunned, Daphne grabbed her phone and used the camera app to take pictures of the men talking. Jackson pulled cash from his pocket and handed it to the bear man. Daphne continued taking photos. She wished she could hear their conversation, but the men were too far away.

Jackson pointed toward the road, and the other man nodded. They exchanged a hug. Daphne could have sworn she could hear the thumping of the big man's fists on Jackson's back. Each man got into their car and left. This was definitely suspicious behavior. Jackson was up to something. Had Flo found out what it was? Did he kill her to protect his secret? Or maybe he was paying off this scary-looking guy because Jackson had hired him to kill Flo.

Daphne spent a moment checking her photos. They weren't bad. Several showed the money handover clearly. Then, she saw five texts from Betty, each getting more frantic. She replied, letting Betty know she was alive, okay, and on her way. She added a second message, promising she would explain everything. She also sent one of the photos of Jackson handing money to the bear man. Then, she put the car into gear and headed back to Cobb.

On The Green, she found Betty, her brow wrinkled with worry. Daphne rushed over. Betty grabbed her hands and began to check her body.

"Betty, quit it, I'm fine," Daphne laughed. "But, boy, I've got news for you. I think I cracked the case."

"You better start talking." Betty was not laughing; her face was tense and fearful. "You scared me half to death. You don't show up, you don't answer my texts. A whole hour later, you send a message that you are alive. How was I to know that you were sending it and not kidnappers? Aunt Pen also mentioned that the two of you had this pretty serious discussion yesterday. We all were getting concerned."

"Oh, Betty, I'm so sorry. I did not mean to worry anyone. I made a last-minute decision and had to run with it. I'm fine, I promise."

Betty smacked her friend's arm. "Don't ever do that again. I thought... I don't know what I thought, but I was thinking that maybe..."

Daphne hugged her friend. "I'm touched, Betty, I really am. I'm not used to people caring that much about me. It's been a long time. I guess I've gotten a little rusty on how it works. I will try to be more thoughtful of your feelings in the future. "

"Yeah, well, see that you do. Okay, now spill the dirt. Where have you been? What did you find out?"

Daphne recounted her morning's adventure to Betty. She explained why she couldn't respond to Betty's text. Then she pulled out her phone and showed Betty all the photos she had taken of Jackson and the bear man. Betty carefully looked through them.

"That looks like some shady stuff. But, Daphne, you were out there all alone. Anything could have happened to you. What if they had seen you? What if one of them had a gun? What if they'd kidnapped you? No one would have known where you were."

"Whoa. That is a lot of what ifs. I was out in public in the daytime. I stayed in my car the whole time. I'm not crazy. Besides, this is my first solid lead. Jackson has a motive. To hide whatever he's up to. He certainly had the means and opportunity. I just wish I knew what his big secret was."

"When you tail Jackson for his usual trip next weekend, please make sure either Fitzy or I am with you."

"Deal. Now, how about we get into the grill line? I'm starving. I haven't eaten a thing today."

Betty grabbed her friend by the hand, and they walked to the back of a long line in the middle of the grassy park. Betty regaled her with tales of how the marching band had done a superior job with only four collisions this year. Daphne lamented missing the parade with Betty and her family. This hit peak level when Betty shared how Fitzy's two-year-old niece Annabelle escaped from her grandma's lap, ran into the street, and climbed onto a float. When the family saw the little girl waving at them as she slowly crept by, they all dashed into the street to retrieve the child.

They were giggling over the girl's escapade when Daphne heard voices behind her she recognized. It was Jackson and Marion Puddingstone.

Chapter Twenty-Seven

"WHERE WERE YOU?" HUFFED Marion. "You left me sitting all alone."

"I'm sorry. I forgot something."

"What was so important?"

"I left some paperwork at the office that needed to get out immediately. I swung by and finished it but lost track of the time."

"I texted and called you. Why didn't you respond?"

"I told you, I forgot that my phone was turned off." His voice sounded tired. "I didn't see them until I was ready to leave the office. I got over here as fast as I could. I said I'm sorry."

"Well, I wasn't going to miss the food because of you." She pointed a finger. "I've already been through the grill line."

"I'm glad. I wouldn't have wanted you to miss out. I'll get whatever is left."

"I don't know what is with you, Jackson. Sometimes, you are so hopeless," she huffed, but the tirade seemed over.

Daphne got hot under the collar. He goes missing and that's it? He spins her some yarn about working in the office, and she buys it? Another woman duped by a man. He was up to something. Something bad. Something he didn't want his wife to know about.

Daphne thought about walking in on Wallace and the cleaning woman writhing together on the couch. An angry heat burned in her chest. Normally, she kept her emotions under control. Now, they boiled with rage. The man was a dirty, lying liar! She wished a million times that someone had warned her about Wallace. Although Marion seemed mean, she didn't deserve to be deceived in such a manner.

Jackson was clearly another Wallace, a cheater. And it looked like he could be a murderer as well. It was so clear to Daphne that Flo had been killed, and the only evidence she had was pointing directly to him. She'd show the sheriff how wrong he'd been when she unmasked the killer. Wouldn't the bold and brave Flo have confronted him? Even such a public setting would be nothing for her aunt. *Don't be such a mouse. Do it for Flo.*

Daphne left the grill line and marched to the Puddingstones. "Marion, he was not in the office."

"What?" Marion reared up into attack mode. "What do you know about any of this? Sticking your nose into things that are not your business again?"

Jackson shrank back from the two women.

"I know for a fact that Jackson was not in his office this morning." Daphne turned, put her hands on her hips, and looked at the man trying to disappear. "Isn't that the excuse he gave you for getting here late? But that is a lie, isn't it, Jackson?"

"Jackson, what is the busybody talking about?" Marion's hard eyes peered at him. "Were you or were you not in the office?"

"Umm... well... you see..."

"He was meeting some shady character over in Hinckley," Daphne blurted. She couldn't stop herself. "He paid him money. I don't know what for, but he clearly didn't want anyone, especially you, to find out. Maybe it's drugs or insurance fraud, or I don't know what. But it must be bad. The guy he met looked like a walking bear!"

"Is this true?" Marion yelled at Jackson. Then she turned and grilled Daphne, "How do you know this?"

"I happened to be there. They met in the parking lot of a strip mall. I thought Jackson was acting suspiciously. Here, I'll show you the pictures."

Daphne pulled out her phone and flipped through the incriminating photos of Jackson. "You can't deny photographic proof."

"What is the meaning of this, Jackson?" Marion shrieked. "What are you up to? Who is this man?"

Jackson groaned and put his head in his hands.

"I bet this has to do with your monthly getaways," Daphne continued. "Every second weekend of the month, you leave town alone. What are you doing when you go away, Jackson?"

Marion gasped. "You said those were insurance conferences for that stupid trade association you belong to."

"Oh, come on, Marion, how can you be so blind?" Daphne put a hand on her hip. "I know this isn't pleasant, but you need to wake up and see the ugly truth here."

"Oh, God. How could you, Jackson?"

People stopped and started to gather around them and watch the show. Daphne had gone this far; she might as well go all the way. It was time to show the community that her aunt had really been murdered. Almost no one believed her, but they might change their tune after this.

"My Auntie Flo walked around her neighborhood in the morning. She began to notice your monthly trips. She kept…" Daphne didn't want to give away the journal. "Some notes about it. She recorded that, every month on the second weekend, you left around six a.m. on Saturday and would return around ten a.m. on Sunday. She knew you were up to something wicked." Her eyes flashed with anger. "You finally noticed that she noticed, didn't you? That's why you killed her, isn't it?"

"Wait, what?" Jackson finally spoke.

"Killed?" Marion turned pale. "What have you been up to? What has been happening under my own roof? I had no idea about any of this. I'm not involved, I swear."

"Just stop!" he yelled. "I can explain all of it."

He had everyone's attention now. The audience had doubled in size. Everyone watched in stunned silence. He gave a very annoyed glance at Daphne before turning to Marion. He took a deep breath and met her confused gaze with his steady one.

"It's LARPing."

A confused Marion looked to Daphne, who just shrugged. Neither of them understood what he was talking about.

"That stands for live action role play. I belong to a group of people who get together once a month, and we go into the woods and have a good time. It is a great stress reliever."

"I still don't get what this LARPing thing is." Marion searched her husband's face.

"Everyone takes on a character. You create it over time." He blushed. "Your character belongs to a group, like a tribe or a clan. The goal of each weekend is different. Sometimes, it is for your group to capture a relic or just a big battle. The groups take turns arranging the goal."

"You play a character and belong to one of these groups?"

"Yes. My character is a Viking warrior. I belong to a Viking barbarian horde. I didn't tell you because I didn't think you would understand or approve. This is important to me. Frankly, I didn't want to hear you bitch and moan about it. Like you do about anything that doesn't meet your standards." He made air quotes around the last word. "So, I kept it a secret. The big guy I met today belongs to my horde. His name is Jeff. I gave him the money to pay for the weekend. I always give it ahead of time and in cash. I didn't want you to see a funny charge on the credit card and ask about it. Jeff agrees to store my stuff and brings it on the weekend. I've been doing this for over a year."

"A year?" Marion looked deflated. "You've been hiding this for a *year*?"

"Yes, I can see now that it was wrong of me. I should have shared this with you, good or bad. Next weekend is our monthly event. Would you like to come with me?" Jackson gave her a small smile. "You could see what it's like for yourself."

"Are you kidding me? No!" Marion turned her heel, pushed through the crowd, and walked away.

Jackson turned a despairing face on Daphne. "Just for the record, I had no idea Flo had noticed my comings and goings. She must have been the only one to care about what I was doing. I had no reason to kill her. I know the truth is hard to accept sometimes. But there just isn't a murderer here, Daphne. You've got to accept that." The throng parted for him. With his head hanging low, he shuffled towards the edge of The Green.

Daphne swallowed hard. That had not gone like she had thought it would. People looked at each other. Whispers fractured the silence.

Betty grabbed Daphne's hand and dragged her away. "Holy shit, Daphne. That was some hardcore, intense stuff. You sure know how to bring the drama."

"I was so wrong about Jackson," Daphne moaned.

"Jackson's into LARPing?" Betty asked. "I need to google that. He kept a secret life from Marion for over a year? Wow, that is a marriage on the rocks. I mean, when you accused him of being a murderer, Marion didn't jump to his defense. She babbled about how it wasn't her. Harsh. If I ever get married, I would want my partner to defend me from a murder charge."

"Betty, would you mind terribly if we didn't talk about this for a while? I need to process what just happened. I felt so certain Jackson was the killer. Now look at them. I feel terrible." Daphne's stomach growled. "I'm also still hungry. Let's get into the grill line. Okay?"

"Sure, pal, no problem."

They rejoined the line, which was much smaller now. When they finally reached the tables in front of four large grills, they saw Fitzy in an apron. He waved at them with his tongs. Daphne smiled. It was nice to see a familiar face, one that didn't know about the altercation with the Pud-dingstones. At least she wouldn't need to explain to him what happened.

Undoubtedly, Betty would enjoy recounting every last humiliating detail of the encounter to him later.

"Hi, you two. Glad you could make it. Sorry you missed the parade, Daphne; it was a good one this year. Betty texted me that you were okay, and something came up." Fitzy rotated some hotdogs while he talked.

"Yeah, I'm sorry I missed it, too. Betty will tell you about it later. I'm starving, chef. What do you have for me? Any chicken hiding back there?" she asked hopefully.

"Gosh, sorry, Daphne. That is long gone. All we have left are hotdogs. How many would you like?" He shrugged his shoulders.

"I'll take two. I could eat almost anything right now."

"Here you go. Enjoy. This looks like one of the most exciting Fourths we've ever had, between Annabelle's great escape and whatever was happening near the gazebo. I couldn't see it exactly—just a huge gathering. I've been hearing people say they've never seen anything like it. Did you guys see it? Do you know what the big scene was?" Fitzy wiggled his eyebrows and laughed.

Daphne and Betty looked at each other. Daphne sighed and looked at the ground for any sign that a hole might open and swallow her. "Yeah, we know all about it."

Stepping away with her hotdogs, she paused at the condiments table to pump out some mustard. Fitzy's shout of "What?" made her jump. Looking down, she saw the bright yellow stain on her beloved Taylor Swift t-shirt. All she wanted was to go home, hide in her bed, and not come out for about three weeks. But the day wasn't over yet.

Chapter Twenty-Eight

Betty: I told you there was a bonfire tonight.

Daphne: You did NOT tell me about a bonfire. Parade yes. Bonfire no.

Betty: It's a bunch of people our age hanging out. You gotta come.

Daphne: No, I don't. I don't know these people. They don't want me there.

Betty: I want you there.

Daphne: I made an ass of myself today.

Betty: Own it. Come.

Daphne: No.

Betty: Please.

Betty: I think Phil will be there.

Daphne: Tempting. But no.

Betty: Friend challenge. RU my friend?

Daphne: Send me the address and time.

⤴

Daphne sat in her truck. She couldn't do it. It was impossible to walk into the group of primarily strangers after her earlier humiliation. She stared at the cookies waiting on the passenger seat and looked down at her new, unstained outfit. Falling back on her new mantra, she asked herself what Flo would have done. Flo would have marched right into the party, head held high. If anyone thought badly of her, then screw them.

Transforming her face into a friendly smile and, hopefully, a confident air, Daphne got out of the truck. She adjusted the spaghetti straps of her lilac dress, which had a low-cut V neckline and an asymmetrical hem. Strappy, high-heeled, white sandals completed the look.

Grabbing the plate of oatmeal and raisin cookies, she closed the door and headed toward the backyard. The light of the flames could be seen from the street. Walking up the dirt drive, she quickly began questioning her shoe selection. The heels kept sinking down into the dirt and grass on her way towards the back. She resorted to a slow creep on her tippy toes to keep from toppling over.

Betty ran up to Daphne as she rounded the corner of the house. Betty was dressed in cut-off acid-washed jeans cinched with a bright-red belt. The row of jelly bracelets running up her arms and a neon-yellow tank were impossible to ignore. Looking down, Daphne sighed with envy at the very comfortable yet adorable black Converse high tops Betty was wearing.

"Have I time traveled to the 1980s?" Daphne chuckled.

"Totally rad, isn't it? But check you out." Betty let out a wolf whistle. "You are one hot lady. I don't think I've ever seen anyone look so fancy at a bonfire."

"Oh, Betty. I probably should have asked you what to wear. I've never been to a bonfire before. I think we had a few firepits at the country club for making s'mores as kids, you know, but nothing like this."

"Nope. I have no idea what that is like. Never been to a country club in my life. But I want to hear more about that later. You brought a snack? That is so sweet of you. I just brought some gin. Let's get you a fizz."

Betty took Daphne's elbow and wove them through the crowd. Their destination was a cement patio housing a picnic table and grill. Daphne was introduced to their host, Donovan.

"You brought cookies? That was nice of you. Just put those on the picnic table." He gestured behind him.

Daphne wobbled over to the table and set them down. Out of the corner of her eye, Fitzy caught her attention. Working the grill again, he waved in her direction. She waved back. Looking for an excuse to avoid a lecture on safety from him, she turned around and found Phil had joined Betty and Donovan.

"Don, my man." Phil cradled a can of beer in one hand. "How are things in the banking world?"

"Things are the same as usual at the bank. Which is good but sometimes dull." Donovan shrugged his shoulders.

Phil turned to Betty and said, "Betty, I love the '80s look you've got going on. You can't miss that tank top. I'm not sure which is brighter, the fire or that shirt."

"Thanks for the compliment, Phil. But wait until you check out Daphne. She's the best dressed lady here tonight."

Daphne wanted to hug Betty for the plug. She wobbled up towards Phil, allowing him to get an eyeful of her in that killer dress. "Hi, Phil, nice to see you. Donovan, you work at the bank? You're just down the street from the used bookstore."

"Yeah, Russell's place. He's had a hard time since his wife died."

"But it's got a lot of potential. Betty, did you want to come over tomorrow?" Daphne asked.

"Sorry, I'm editing. But maybe we could have dinner or something in a couple of days. I'm usually free by around seven?"

"Which means you will be there at eight," Phil teased.

"Hey, now!" Betty protested.

"You were an hour late for homecoming senior year when you were my date. I haven't forgotten the waiting and pacing. I'd thought you had stood me up."

"For pity's sake, that was like a million years ago." Betty swatted at Phil's arm. "I had issues with my hair and makeup. I was not as stylish then as I am now."

"You are very stylish now. But how is your punctuality?"

"A little better. She's usually only about half an hour late now." Fitzy walked up wearing an apron that said, "Kiss the Chef."

"Daphne, help a girl out. The boys are picking on me."

"Betty, you know that I adore you. I'm thankful every day that I met you. But..."

"Some friend you are." Betty gave a huff while still smiling. "I'm going to lick my wounds and make some drinks. You still want a gin fizz, Daph?"

Daphne tottered over and gave her pal a big hug. "I love you and your fizzes. I don't care if you run a few minutes late. You, Elizabeth Bennet, are worth the wait."

"I forgive you completely now." Betty gave her a peck on the cheek and went off to the bar.

"I'll help you carry them. You only have two hands," Phil said and disappeared behind her.

Daphne turned her attention to Fitzy and tried to hide her disappointment that Phil didn't want to keep hanging out with her. "You're grilling here after doing it all day at the parade?"

"Yeah. I love it. Food will be ready soon. I can't wait for you to taste my specialty finally. I'm making more chicken, just for you. Hey, there is a chair next to the grill. Why don't you have a seat? You look amazing, but those shoes look uncomfortable."

"They are killing my feet. I don't know what I was thinking. Thank you, Fitzy. You are such a nice guy. Lead the way." He offered hand and she took it for balance. "Betty and Phil will find us by the grill."

"Daphne." He placed her in the chair but did not let go of her hands. "I don't want to sound like some control freak or anything, but I want to say something about earlier."

"Oh." She gulped as his eyes bore into hers.

"Betty told me what happened. Daphne, you could have been hurt. If Jackson *was* up to something bad, he could have attacked you in the parking lot or the park. You got lucky that it turns out he is a good guy. No one knew where you were. I care about you—Betty and I both do—and we were worried. Don't go off like that again without letting one of us know. Please."

"I'm sorry." She looked down at the ground. "I didn't mean to scare you two. I had a hunch, and I ran with it. I'll try not to do that again. I got excited that I might have found Auntie Flo's killer."

"I'm trying to help. Maybe we just need to hang out more and see if we can't come up with other ideas."

"Sure. Okay, enough about that. Tell me about what you're doing on the grill."

Fitzy grabbed the spatula and pointed out the different meats sizzling. His face lit up as he explained his preparations. He reminded her of when she got to talk about books with people. His enthusiasm for the grilling arts was infectious. The smell wafting from the food made her mouth water.

A warm feeling spread through her body, like when she snuggled on the couch next to a fire with a good story.

At last, Fitzy handed her a plate piled high with chicken and sausages. While he procured utensils and a napkin, Daphne spotted Phil and Betty. Seated in two camping chairs they leaned toward each other, talking. The small table between them held four glasses.

Oh my gosh! I bet Phil is chatting up Betty about me. I knew he was interested in me. Betty really is my best friend. While I appreciate what she is doing, I'd rather spend my time with him myself than look on from afar. But I don't want to look desperate. I need an excuse to go over.

Fitzy presented her with the utensils and napkin.

"Thank you so much, Fitzy. I see Betty and Phil over there. I will give them this plate and get one of those fizzes that Betty promised."

Daphne saw Fitzy's smile fall as she walked away. But any thoughts about it were erased as she wobbled slowly over to the table. Drawing closer, they still had not noticed her.

Daphne called out, "Hey, Phil. Hey, Betty. I've got some BBQ for you. I'll trade you for a drink."

Her eyes went wide when her right foot tugged on something. Her heel plunged down into the grass. Off balance and partly stuck, her body's inertia pushed her forward, and Daphne tripped. The plate of BBQ flew out of her hands and landed with a smear on Phil's shirt.

From the ground, a horrified Daphne focused on the food falling from his shirt back onto the plate. Sauce dripped down his shirt. Near hysterical laughter penetrated the moment. She knew that sound, that mirthful chuckle, belonged to Fitzy. Was he laughing at her? Her stomach churned at the traitorous noise. Some friend he turned out to be.

"Phil, I am so sorry. I tripped. Oh heavens. I don't know what to say. Are you okay?" Daphne babbled, trying to keep tears at bay.

Betty tried to dab away the sauce with the napkin, but it was beyond help.

Phil stood up. "It's okay, Daphne. I saw you go down. It's just some food and sauce, nothing a washing machine can't fix. Is your ankle okay? That looked painful."

"Umm... I think it's okay." Daphne attempted to do a quick body check.

"Good. Well, this shirt is shot for the night. I can't wear this sticky thing. It's a good thing it's summer." Phil tossed the messy shirt over his head.

Daphne stared slack-jawed at Phil. His broad, muscular shoulders and chest were displayed for all to admire. What a body! It looked even better by firelight than it had during the day. Her eyes traveled from his defined pecs to his flat stomach. She prayed no drool dribbled from her lips. Fitzy's uncontrolled laughing stopped.

"That's one way to fix the problem," Betty smirked. "You should talk to Don and see if you can throw that in his washer. If you don't deal with that stain right away, it might not come out."

"Good point. If you will excuse me, ladies. I need to see a man about an appliance." Phil and his perfect torso sauntered off.

Betty helped Daphne to her feet and put her into Phil's empty chair. Daphne looked at the pile of destroyed food on the table between them. A moan escaped Daphne from deep inside. "Betty, I'm a disaster. I was hoping to make an impression on Phil. But not this impression. This, on top of the Jackson thing? He probably thinks I'm an idiot. Heck, even Fitzy laughed at me." Her lip wobbled.

"Daph, I'm sorry. It's not so bad, not really. Phil will clean his shirt, and everything will be fine. Hardly anyone noticed." Betty patted her friend's hand.

"Betty, everyone noticed. How could they not? If they didn't see me trip first, they couldn't have missed Phil's strip tease. Not that I'm complaining about the latter." Her lips turned up slightly at the memory.

"No kidding. Phil should go around topless more often." Betty cackled. "But seriously, everyone will laugh about it and move on to other topics."

"Maybe they will, and maybe they won't. I can't stay here, though. I feel so embarrassed. Plus, these stupid heels are killing me. I want to put some ice on this ankle." Daphne winced slightly.

"Are you hurt?"

"Not really. I'm just sore. Nothing some ibuprofen and ice won't fix. Too bad I can't ice my ego. I think I am done with my first bonfire. Next time, if I am invited to another one, I'll wear sneakers like you. I just feel like a first-class idiot. I want to go home and lick my wounds."

"I get it." Betty pulled Daphne out of her chair. "Let's get you home. We'll talk soon."

On the way to Daphne's car, Fitzy intercepted them. "You leaving already?" he asked.

Both women shot him with daggers from their eyes.

"What?" He stopped walking.

"I'll be back to deal with you," Betty growled.

Keeping an arm around Daphne, they continued to the front of the house. On the front porch, they could see Phil, still topless, with a hand outstretched on a pillar, leaning toward a giggling woman in a halter top.

"Perfect. I'm going home and never coming out again," Daphne moaned, heaving herself into the truck.

"Sorry, Daph," Betty said before her pal drove away.

Chapter Twenty-Nine

Twenty Years Ago – Flo

FLO LOOKED INSIDE THE kitchen trash can where broken pieces of glass sparkled. Her heart quickened. Was Daphne okay? Had the girl cut herself? May and Sarah would never let her live it down if her niece got hurt on her watch. They would refuse to let Daphne return for a visit, and she wanted her to return.

After a lifetime of living alone, the sudden appearance of a kid threw her world off its orbit. At first, everything felt foreign and strange. But now, she was enjoying playing host. Her niece had such a unique way of seeing things, and it allowed her to experience familiar Cobb with new eyes. Retiring from work had been a seismic shift in her life. If she wasn't taking care of Daphne, she didn't know what she would have been doing with her time.

Little creaks informed her that Daphne was coming down the stairs. As she crossed into the kitchen, Flo held up the bin. The girl's lip trembled, and she studied the floor.

"Do you care to explain this?"

"I'm sorry," she stuttered, cringed, and began shaking.

The child was terrified. What did Daphne think would happen to her? What was going on at home to illicit such a response? Did they beat the poor kid? How would Pen handle this? There wasn't anyone nicer than Pen.

"I'm not angry, Daphne." Flo's voice had a strange mix of firmness and caring.

"You're not?" She sniffled.

"I'm disappointed, Daphne. But I know you didn't do this on purpose."

Oh heavens, the kid looks like she's going to start bawling.

"I didn't." Daphne, now overcome, confessed her sins like she was standing before a priest. No sinner could have been more repentant. "I wanted some orange juice, and I didn't want to bother you. I was pouring the bottle, but I lost control, and a bunch spilled out, and it pushed the glass off the counter. It shattered on the floor. I'm so sorry. I feel really bad about breaking your glass and making a mess. I wanted to clean it up before you noticed. But there's no fooling you. There are also some soaking towels in the trash."

Flo sniffed the can. Based on the smell, half a gallon of juice must have been in there.

"You're sure you aren't mad?" Daphne asked.

Flo walked up to the girl and gave an awkward pat on her shoulder. "Honest, I'm not mad. I was worried. Daphne, you should have told me. What if you had cut yourself on the glass? Accidents happen. Things get broken. Sometimes, they can be fixed. Sometimes, they can't. But you should never try to hide them. That's not the Winkler way. We face the world, no matter what's been done. Though I do applaud your effort to fix the mess yourself. That is an admirable trait, but it can be overdone. Am I making sense?"

"Yes, Auntie Flo. I'm sorry I didn't tell you. I didn't think about getting hurt." Daphne paused, thinking something over. "I get to be a Winkler?"

"Your birth certificate may read Patterson, but you are fifty percent Winkler. You have Cobb blood in your veins. You're made of hardy stuff,

my girl. You can face unpleasant things because you are strong." Flo
thumped her on the back.

Daphne looked up at her aunt like she had saved her from a burning fire
and then given her a million dollars. The adoration was raw and genuine.
Flo felt unworthy of such love and, in the same breath, knew she'd do
anything to keep that in her life, even if it meant going to the library every
day or playing nice with Sarah. She'd known love in her life, but nothing
so pure as this.

Chapter Thirty

DAPHNE WANTED TO CRAWL into her bed and not come out until sometime around Halloween. That might be long enough for people to forget the scene she made yesterday on The Green and the following humiliation at the bonfire. However, living in Flo Winkler's house made that impossible. The more she tried to hide, the more she could hear and see Flo's disappointment.

Once, after seeing Daphne's unmade bed, Flo shook her head and said, "Maybe, in fancy Birmingham, someone else makes your bed, but not in Cobb, Maine. Here, you clean up your messes."

Daphne had no idea how to do that in her current situation.

Looking at herself in the bathroom mirror, she felt like a simpering Patterson who didn't know where she belonged. Narrowing her eyes, she peered hard at her reflection. "You are a Winkler! You're tough. You belong in Cobb!" she shouted at herself. Before her reflection could mount a counterargument, she decided to head into town—no more hiding.

Technically, she was not hiding; she was out in public. Her public place of choice happened to be a store where customers were as rare as an emotionally available man. The sole occupant of the used bookshop was its antisocial owner, Russell Abbot.

Books made her feel steady and at home. She nixed the idea of going to the library; even the patrons there would be talking about the incident. She was trying to be brave, but it seemed her bravery had limits. Baby steps.

Russell lowered his newspaper when she came in and gave her a nod, but gratefully said nothing and returned to his reading. Daphne was blissfully left to her own devices. The store remained every bit as dusty, dark, chaotic, and depressing as she remembered. But, at the moment, it felt like a haven. Not looking for anything in particular, she wandered from shelf to shelf.

Daphne couldn't say how long she had been "shelving." An automatic function from her years of work in the library, her hands moved on some sort of cruise control. She collected books misplaced based on genre or by alphabet and returned them to their proper sections. Her world was so out of control at the moment that her soul took any outlet to create order and peace. She was unaware of her actions until Russell shuffled up next to her.

"Hey, what are you doing over there? You messing up my books?" He pointed a finger in her direction.

"Messing up your books? Are you kidding me? You had an H. P. Lovecraft in the romance section, which I will be buying, by the way. I found a Rhys Bowen murder mystery in sci-fi. I won't even start on the random way these poor books are smashed into the shelves. Who puts these things in order?" she sternly shot back.

"I do." He jutted out his chin defiantly.

"How often do you check them over and re-sort?" Daphne crossed her arms.

"Probably did it only a few months back."

"A few months?" she sputtered, and he took a step back. "That's a weekly task, at least. And Russell, the way these books are crammed on the shelves... It is so bad for their bindings. Look at the poor things." She waved a hand at a shelf overstuffed with tomes.

"Well, you need to have them out so the customer can see what you have."

"The reader can't see what you have when they are distracted by the mess. Readers want order and pleasing displays."

"What makes you an expert?" he growled.

"My Master's in Library Science, several years of experience as a librarian, and being a lifelong book lover." She stretched tall, using all five feet five inches of her body and feeling one hundred percent Winkler.

"You working as a librarian right now?" Russell raised an eyebrow and stepped closer to her.

"Not at the moment. There was some downsizing at my library." She slumped just a fraction.

"Do you know anything about working a cash register and sales? Or is all your knowledge from a book?"

"I worked as a barista at a trendy coffee house for several years. I can make a cappuccino and change at the same time."

"Well, you seem qualified enough to me. I can pay a little above minimum wage, but not any big city wages, mind you." His hands were in his pockets, and he rocked back and forth slightly.

"Are you offering me a job?"

"Aren't you the sharp one, Professor?"

She corrected him, "I only have a master's, not a doctorate. So, I'm not really a professor."

"I won't hold it against you. I barely finished high school, but I never was afraid of hard work. This bookstore was Alice's dream. It was supposed to be our retirement gig. But then she went and died, leaving me this place to run. I feel I never get any time to myself." Russell scratched the back of his neck and headed back to the counter.

Daphne followed him. "It must be tough to do this yourself and be constantly reminded of her." Leaving Chicago helped her not think of Wallace each day. She couldn't imagine working in a place where she couldn't escape him.

"I don't mind the memories. But sitting all day is not good for me. I saw the doctor the other day, and he was getting worried about me. He suggested I sign up for this water aerobics class at the Hinkley Senior Center. Said it would be easy on the joints, and I like the water well enough."

Daphne struggled not to laugh. The idea of this single, retired man in a pool full of sixty-and-over women launched her imagination into overdrive. They would eat him alive. There would be plenty of divorced or widowed ladies. Did he have any idea that he was heading for shark-infested waters? She decided it wasn't her place to tell him.

"I've heard that is excellent exercise. I hope you enjoy it. How often would you need me to work here at the store?"

"How would working two p.m. to seven p.m. three days a week suit you? You strike me as someone who doesn't like mornings."

"Sales would be best in the afternoon and evening anyway." She avoided his accusation, even though he was correct. "Though I have a few conditions."

"Okay, let's hear them." Russell stood straight now, his game face on.

"You have to let me clean up in here. The dust is awful. I also will be sorting the books to get them into a proper order."

"Is that all?"

"No. The display window needs to be changed. It is not inviting and keeps out the natural light."

"Keeps the dust down."

She ran her finger along a shelf, and it came up dark with dust. "Clearly not."

"Point taken. Okay, you can make a few changes and tidy up a bit. It won't hurt the place, I guess. You can start this Friday."

"Anything else I need to know beforehand?"

"Yeah, if you could keep yourself from accusing anyone who walks in the store of murder, I think that would help sales." His eyes twinkled with mischief.

Daphne blushed. Even in this tiny corner of Cobb, she couldn't escape her growing infamy.

"I'll keep that in mind."

⋘

Leaving the bookstore, Daphne felt a burst of confidence. Someone found her abilities worthy. Getting to use work skills was more important than she realized. She gladly spent the time and energy required to earn her degrees. Landing the library job in Chicago had been a dream come true for her. Losing it a few years later became her nightmare. However, the painful memories felt more distant at that moment.

Riding a wave of fulfillment, she swung by the grocery store to gather the ingredients needed for a chicken roast recipe Betty had demonstrated on her channel while in a Victorian dress with puffed sleeves. With relief that no one accosted her about the park affair, she returned home as quickly as she could.

As she double-checked the recipe, her phone notified her of a new text. It was from her dad, who was still worried about her. She considered calling her mother but decided against it.

Instead, Daphne asked the potatoes as she cut them, "Why didn't he ask his wife to call his daughter and not the other way round?" The vegetables did not respond. Her mother's pride would not allow her to make the first move. Daphne had yelled at her, and thus, it fell to her to call her mother and patch things up.

"The problem," Daphne explained to the carrots, "is I'm not sure I'm ready to make nice." As the days of radio silence had flowed from one into the other, she'd enjoyed the peace. No constant critiques from her mother berating her—no attempts to pry and invade her space. Daphne'd relished the freedom. Now that she had tasted this new path, she didn't know if she could return to the old ways.

Daphne put her roast into the hot oven and began to fan herself. Maybe a long-cooking roast wasn't the best idea for July. The days were warm and sunny now. Summer had settled in at last. Pouring herself a cool glass of lemonade, Daphne took it and her phone out to the porch. The tart lemon refreshed her tongue, and the earthy smells from the flowers and trees of the yard delighted her nose.

Sitting there, memories of Flo hung close. Flo chiding her to face life's unpleasantries again flashed in her mind. With a sigh, she pushed the buttons on her contact list and rang her mother.

"Oh, hello, Daphne." Her mother's approach to the conversation was to adopt the haughty and righteous attitude of the victim. "This is a surprise."

"Dad sent a text. Made it sound like you wanted to talk." She sounded aggressive, unlike her usual submissiveness. This was *not* beginning well. Daphne grimaced.

Sarah Patterson paused. *Is Mom unsure how to respond?*

"He exaggerates. You know your father. But it has been a while since you called. Have you checked in with your brother lately? It seems he is gone for the rest of the summer. He got into a summer exchange program in Paris at the last minute. We won't see him again until the week before he returns to college," she huffed.

"No, I didn't know Ethan was in France. Well, good for him. He'll love it. I'll have to send him a text or email this week. I've been busy, lots going on here." A truthful statement, if also a bit misleading.

"Yes, I've heard." The haughty tone rose to a peak. "I thought I might get a call or text saying you were finally coming home after that event in the park."

"How did you hear about that?"

"My mother still has a few friends in Cobb. It seems one of them called her the day after and shared that you were accusing some man of murder. Then, it turned into a huge, unseemly fight between him and his wife. Anyway, it all sounded horrifying. And there you were, right smack in the middle of it. After fully embarrassing yourself, I figured you would want to come home."

Daphne would never admit to her mother that she had entertained that idea. Anyway, ultimately, she had rejected it. Daphne didn't know how long she'd be in Cobb, but it was still better than at home with her mom.

"It is more complicated than it sounds. I was wrong this time." Daphne gritted her teeth to keep from shouting into the phone. "But I am not giving up on finding Flo's murderer. I have no interest in coming home at this point. Thank you for your concern, but it is not needed."

"I don't understand this. You humiliate yourself on The Green in front of the whole town. Why you want to stay in that godforsaken place is beyond me."

Sarah had moved into ice queen territory and was throwing frozen barbs in Daphne's direction. In the past, if Daphne managed to withstand the passive-aggressive comments or the haughty snipes, this was when she would usually fold under the direct, full-on attack of her mother's spite.

"This doesn't surprise me, Mom. I think there are a lot of things you don't understand. Let me explain it to you. Why do I not want to leave here? Number one, I like Cobb. It is a cute town with good people, and my family comes from here. Number two, I've made friends. I didn't know how lonely I was until I started having friends again. Number three, I am trying to solve a murder. Maybe I am not doing the best at that, but I will keep trying. And lastly, number four, I am upset with you." She took in several deep breaths.

"You're upset with me?" Sarah growled.

"Upset? You know what? No, I'm not upset. I'm angry. No, wait, I'm furious! You took me away from Flo and Cobb. Flo understood me. She made me feel seen and heard. With her, I was a happier person. She accepted me for who I was. I didn't have to pretend with her. Do you know how rare that is?" Angry tears flowed down her hot cheeks. "Do you have any idea what it's like to have someone you care about be taken away from you, just gone from your life? No, of course not. The world bends to your will."

"Daphne Patterson, you watch your tone with me, young lady!"

"No problem. Don't expect another call from me for a while, Mother. You won't have to worry about my tone at all." Daphne hung up on her mother. As she pressed the button, she noticed her hands were shaking. A sheen of sweat covered her body. She felt like she'd run a marathon.

Having plenty of time before the roast would be finished, Daphne decided she needed a nice cool shower and a change of clothes.

Toweling off, the continued, intense feelings of anger surprised and overwhelmed her. How long had this hot ball of rage been hiding in her? How did she get rid of it? And how was she going to solve this blasted murder? She had no idea what she was doing.

Sitting down to her dinner, the chicken provided her no answers. Staring at the carefully prepared meal, she felt tired and numb. She no longer had the energy to care about the questions plaguing her. She wanted to be present without thinking about the past or future. A juicy chicken, cooked by her own hands, awaited. Putting a true crime podcast on her phone, she relaxed her shoulders and escaped into another world.

Chapter Thirty-One

The Second Saturday of July – Marion Puddingstone

MARION GROUND HER TEETH. Her jaw hurt with the workout she was giving it. Minutes after Jackson left, she rushed into her car to follow him. They drove for an hour until he turned down a long dirt road. Now, she searched for a spot in the packed, scrubby field that served as a parking lot. People in various levels of costume were heading towards a tent set up in an open clearing. Beyond the large open space were pine trees as far as she could see.

She forced herself to relax by slowly breathing in and out. A large banner in front of the tent read, "Welcome LARPers." At least Jackson had been truthful in what he told her on The Green. Her eyes rolled before she could stop them. Jackson said that her eyerolls grated on his nerves. She hadn't realized how often she rolled them until his protest. Once aware, she'd counted many infractions and was trying to be better.

Tense wasn't strong enough to describe the feeling in the Puddingstone house since the incident on The Green. Marion had yelled at Jackson that he was a liar, and his hobby was ridiculous. Her husband had countered by accusing her of being bossy. He continued that marriage should be a partnership, not one person making all the decisions. Her retort had been a mean comment about him being deceitful and too idiotic to make decisions for himself.

Marion knew, the minute it came out, that she had gone too far. Jackson gave a look of disgust she'd never seen before. Turning around, he'd walked out the door and driven off in his car. Petrified that he might actually leave her, Marion spent the afternoon crying, rage-cleaning all the bathrooms, and then finally stuffing her face with ice cream. Jackson returned after dinner, gave a brief nod in her direction, and headed upstairs. She heard him moving some of his things into the guest bedroom.

Since that argument, they'd shared only as many words as were necessary. Mostly, they spoke only about work or house matters. Marion wasn't sleeping well. Fear tormented her. Was their marriage heading towards divorce? Jackson's vanishing act caused her to realize how much she loved him. She didn't know how to explain that to him or to fix their problems. Old Marion would have ordered him back into their room and barked that he stop this nonsense. Those days were over.

Desperate, she'd followed him to this remote location. A struggle inside her raged on: Should she go after him or turn around and go home? An inner voice warned her, "If you leave now, you are giving up on him and your marriage. Is that what you want?" Marion shook her head, grabbed her purse, and headed toward the tents.

Under the banner sat a table manned by three people dressed in clothes that reminded her of the *Lord of the Rings* movies. The people gathered there were dressed similarly, wearing lots of neutral colors, leather vests, and overall, sporting a kind of grungy style. Everyone looked so bizarre. She saw men and women walk by in chain mail and armor and would have gaped if her jaw weren't clenched so tight.

"Are you registered already?" the genial man sitting at the center of the table inquired.

"Umm, no." She was distracted by a gaggle of women attired in colorful, flowing, brocade gowns behind him. They reminded her of a few Shakespeare plays she had seen. "Is that a problem?"

"Not at all. It is $15 for a walk-in day pass." He studied her doubtfully. "Have you been to one of our events before?"

"No, this is my first time. That obvious, huh?" She handed him a twenty-dollar bill and tried not to roll her eyes.

"Well... your outfit is rather modern. Some vendors sell items in the tents on the left, if you want something more fitting. Here is a pamphlet. It includes a map of the grounds and a schedule of events. Enjoy yourself."

"Sure." The eyeroll slipped out.

Marion headed over to the tents. Walking the short distance convinced her of the need for a disguise. She stood out, and everyone gawked at her. She wanted to observe Jackson without him noticing her, but it would be impossible without a wardrobe change.

Inside the nearest shop, a woman wearing a very low-cut peasant blouse asked if she could help. Marion insisted she was just looking. Wandering from rack to rack, she began to feel overwhelmed by the selections. Spread out before her were a variety of shirts, pants, skirts, and dresses. The clothes came in all kinds of materials and colors. Her head spun. A long rack full of cloaks caught her eye in the corner of the tent.

She fingered the materials. Several were rough wool or just cheap, uncomfortable fabrics. There were plenty of brown, black, and green to choose from, which did not appeal to her. A rich velvet cape in a deep blue hung at the bar's farther end. The clasp holding the two sides together was a fleur-de-lis pattern of rhinestones. It was stunning! She lightly stroked the black, satin-lined garment.

Looking at the price tag, her eyes bulged. That price for a silly cape? She could get a business suit for that same amount. She looked back over at the cheaper capes on the other end. No. If she were going to do this insane thing, she would do it with some style. Joyfully, the gypsy woman watched Marion walk up to the counter with the expensive item.

"Do you accept credit cards?"

"But of course, my lady." The bosomy gypsy spoke with a terrible English accent. "Doth thou require a carrying satchel?"

"A carrying satchel?"

"A bag. Do you need a bag?" The English accent disappeared.

"No, thank you. I will be wearing it out." Marion handed over her card.

"Very good, my lady."

The gypsy helped Marion get the cloak on and showed her how to open and close the clasp. The cloth fell to her ankles, and the hood did an excellent job of hiding her face. Marion hardly recognized herself in the mirror. It was as if, by magic, she had transformed into an elegant and mysterious woman. With a final thank you to the gypsy clerk, she left the tent and began to search for her husband.

Slowly, she worked her way through the various sections of the grounds. Next to the clothing tent were the food vendors, then screens hiding the portable toilets and hand-washing station. Nearby, a cluster of tents stood. Each one was different in size and color, but all had a banner hanging from the front. After looking at several, Marion finally remembered Jackson saying something about clans and tribes. The tents likely belonged to those different groups.

Her wanderings continued for half an hour before she finally found her husband. Hearing his name first caught her attention, which was helpful, because, without that, she might not have ever figured out the man standing next to the tent was, in fact, her husband. The structure was made from dirty white cloth. Some foreign symbols were written on the banner.

"Jackson, don't forget your weapon," a bear of a man shouted to her husband.

"It's Axel, Balder." He held up a double-sided axe to show the man, and even from a distance, Marion could tell was not a real weapon, but just a prop.

"Sorry, Axel. The battle starts soon. Let's get over there."

Gleefully, the two men hurried from their tent.

Marion carefully followed while trying to process the vision before her. Jackson was running around with more of him uncovered than covered. She couldn't reconcile the man who sold insurance with the one running around with a double-sided axe, half-naked. His torso was bare except for a scrap of furry fabric. Unlike a vest, it didn't come under his arms. Instead, it lay on his back and over his shoulders like a shaggy shawl.

A leather loincloth with several belts wrapped around his waist showed off his sinewy thighs. Leather boots came up to his knees, with a circle of fur around the top. She could understand why Jackson had kept this a secret from her. This is what he considered fun? Maybe watching the "battle" would help her understand him more.

A large open area had been set aside for the battle. Jackson and others dressed like him were at one end. They were joined by a group of *Lord of the Rings*-looking people. On the other side of the clearing gathered a group of chain mail and armor types mixed with pirates. Pirates? Marion shrugged her shoulders and settled in to watch the show. A man walked into the circle's center and spoke. Marion didn't pay attention. She couldn't take her eyes off Jackson.

His outfit was shocking, but she admitted he wore it well. No longer hidden by a suit, his lean, muscular body was on full display. It had been a while since she'd examined his body. Lines and curves of muscles were etched on his thighs and arms. The big furry thing on his shoulders and chest made his shoulders look broad. The belts focused her eye on his tapered waist. While Marion loved the velvet and satin of the cape, it started to feel warm.

Suddenly, came a shout and a flurry of activity. The battle had begun. Jackson let out a roar and charged a pirate with his axe. The pirate took out a sword, and the two began to pound each other. She gasped as the pirate started getting the upper hand and pushed Jackson to the ground. Then Jackson swung out one of his legs, catching the pirate by surprise and toppling him. The axe came swishing down. The "dead" pirate was removed, and Jackson went to work on a knight.

She watched for a half hour, and then a flash of red caught Marion's attention. A slash of crimson ran across Jackson's forearm. He'd been hurt. Marion's heart pounded with fear. The minute the fight was declared over, she ran to him.

"Jackson, your arm! Are you hurt badly?"

"It's Axel, it's but a scratch...." He replied to the woman in a blue cloak approaching him. Then he stopped and stared. "Marion, is that you?"

Throwing back the hood of the cape, the cool air rushed against her flushed cheeks. "Yes, it's me. That's not important. Give me your arm. I want to see your wound."

The big bear man strolled over. "Hey, Axel, got a nick, huh? You, okay? Who's the babe?"

"I'm fine. This is my wife, Marion." Jackson plastered on a fake smile. "Marion, this is Balder. His real name is Jeff. He's the guy who helps me out."

"Cool, the old lady came out." Jeff raised his eyebrows at Marion. "You didn't tell me she was such a hotty. Love the cape thing you got going on."

"Yeah, okay, Jeff. Enough drooling over *my* wife. Could you give us a minute, please?"

"Sure. Nice meeting you, wife." Jeff gave her a wink and swaggered away.

"Wow, he's..." Marion struggled for the right word.

"Yeah, he's totally that." Jackson chuckled.

"So... umm... I'm your wife?" Marion said, holding his arm and looking at the wound.

"Of course, you're my wife. What a question. Are you okay?"

"Well, since you moved into the other room, I wasn't sure if you still wanted me to be..." She couldn't finish the sentence. Tears began to well up.

Jackson's hand gently lifted her chin, so she looked into his eyes. "I know things have been rough lately. I've just needed some time to think. Why are you here, Marion?"

"I wanted to see if this was really what you were doing." Her voice trembled. "I needed to make sure there wasn't another woman."

"Oh, Marion, I don't want another woman. I just want you to be a little more considerate."

"Why didn't you just tell me that?"

"I should have. I guess I wasn't brave enough."

Beyond her control, her eyes gave a half roll. "Brave enough? Please. I just saw you wail on two pirates and someone in chain mail. You are plenty brave. That move you made on the pirate, knocking him over. Where did you learn to do that? That was amazing!"

"You thought that was amazing?"

"Yeah. I had no idea about this ass-kicker side of you. It... umm... well, I didn't hate watching it. I thought I would, but it turns out I don't."

"You like watching your husband in battle, huh? Well, I like this cape. You look like a beautiful queen."

He stepped closer to her, putting his free arm around her waist.

"I got it at the tent by the entrance. I needed something to help me blend in, but I like how the satin and velvet feel against my skin. Your outfit surprised me. It is very revealing. But you wear it well."

"Thank you." He moved a fraction closer and tightened his grip.

She could smell the salty sweat on his skin. "What is this whole Viking thing about?"

"We are barbarian Vikings. We are warriors. We invade a village and take whatever pleases our eye."

"And how does that work? The taking of whatever pleases your eye?"

"We just pick it up and carry it away with us." He growled and leaned his head towards her.

His lips descended upon hers. It was a fierce kiss. He stepped back. A giggle escaped her as he lifted her over his shoulder in a fireman's carry. It was hard to determine where they were going from her upside-down vantage point.

She heard plenty of chuckling as they weaved their way through the crowd. Jackson stopped in front of a tent. She recognized the dirty white fabric. He informed his clan that he needed to borrow the tent for a while. Laughing, they evacuated the structure and held open the flaps for him and his wife.

Marion heard Jeff on the other side of the fabric say, "This will make her a proper Viking bride."

Marion didn't care about Jeff's comment, the men's laughter, or the obvious indication of what she and her husband would get up to in the tent. As the fury of kissing and grabbing began, she knew that Jackson wouldn't be sleeping in the guest room anymore.

Chapter Thirty-Two

FLASHBACKS OF A PLATE of BBQ flying towards Phil replayed over and over in Daphne's mind that Thursday morning. She pressed the heels of her hands to her eyes. The part where he removed his shirt took center stage in slow motion. She stomped outside and down her porch stairs with a growl.

She checked that the tarp was securely fastened on the back of her truck. In the bed lay a pile of items for her bookstore window installation. While only her third day on the job, a determination to show off her skills encouraged her to spearhead this makeover.

Yesterday, thankfully, the plan consumed many hours of her mind's focus. She and Betty shared ideas back and forth and filled up a page with scribbled thoughts before landing on a summer theme. Her friend was coming around the store in the afternoon to help her with it.

A banner would be hung at the top of the display reading "Sail into Summer!" Cutout paper sailboats would hang down from the ceiling on fishing line. At the bottom of the display would sit a colorful lounge chair with a beach towel draped over its back. A sign on the seat would read, "Get Your Beach Read Here." In front of the chair, a cooler full of books would be placed on the side. To complete the look, beach balls, buckets with shovels, kites, and other summer toys would be artfully arranged.

With the theme selected, Betty and Daphne ran around town, visiting Betty's family and friends to gather items for the display. It had been a day filled with laughter, singing along to the radio, and chatter about nothing special. Betty briefly brought up the BBQ incident. She clarified that Fitzy had been laughing at Phil, and he felt awful that Daphne thought otherwise. The idea that Fitzy laughed at Phil didn't sit easily with her, either. However, knowing her new friend hadn't mocked her soothed her pain.

Focusing on her current task, Daphne gave the strap one last tug and headed back inside. She made herself a latte with a foam heart and grabbed Flo's journal. Time flew as she got lost in the pages. On her notepad, she kept a running list of notes of possible suspects and details from the journal.

Her phone alarm went off, letting her know it was time to get ready for work. If she moved it, she still had time to grab a proper lunch at Joe's Diner. Heaving a sigh, she looked at her pages of notes. There must have been six or seven suspects listed. How was she supposed to figure out who killed Auntie Flo? Rather than wallow in the hopeless feeling, she dashed out of the house in search of a good meal.

She waved to Parmy as she strolled into Joe's Diner.

"Hey, Daph. Help yourself to any seat. I'll be with you in a minute."

Looking around, Daphne was tempted to rush back out the door. Sitting in a booth, side by side, were Marion and Jackson Puddingstone. Her inner voice screamed at her to run. Then Auntie Flo barked at her to clean up her mess. If Anne Shirley of *Anne of Green Gables* could face stern Rachel Lynde and apologize for her transgressions, she could, too.

Straightening her spine, she marched over to the booth. "Hello, Mr. and Mrs. Puddingstone. I wanted..." She faltered. Then, she almost felt Auntie Flo's eyes burning into her back. "I wanted to apologize for what happened on the Fourth. While I am passionate about finding Flo's murderer, I did not handle that very well. I know I embarrassed you, as well as myself. Mr. Puddingstone, you must have felt violated, and I'm sorry."

The couple looked at her, then at each other.

"Thank you, Daphne. It is good that you see the error of your ways." Marion raised her nose to the heavens and somehow managed to look down at Daphne from her seated position.

Jackson reached over and grabbed his wife's hand firmly. He raised an eyebrow.

"Okay, okay. I do appreciate the apology, Daphne. But strangely, you kind of did us a favor." Marion's tone lost its frost. She and Jackson shared a knowing glance.

"I hadn't been honest with Marion. I should have told her what I was doing from the start." Jackson grinned at his wife. "If it hadn't been for you interfering, she never would have come to one of my LARPing events."

"You went to the event?" Daphne could not have been more surprised if the sky suddenly turned magenta.

"I wanted to see if that was what he was really doing." Marion blushed. "It wasn't as silly as I thought it would be."

"It's been the best thing for our marriage. We are planning a second honeymoon." Jackson nodded toward the travel brochures in front of them.

Daphne read the names. Most were in Norway, but one was for a place called Orkney. "I've never heard of this place," she said, pointing to the name.

"That is a Scottish island in the North Sea. It has many prehistoric sights. The northern islands of Scotland were very influenced by Vikings." Marion let out an uncharacteristic little giggle, and it was Jackson's turn to blush.

Intimate sparks flew between the couple, making Daphne uncomfortable.

"I didn't know that. Well, I am glad things turned out so well. I will leave you to enjoy the rest of your lunch then. It was nice to have this chat."

Daphne sat in the farthest booth from the couple she could get. Before she even put in her order, she sent Betty a rapid series of texts. This was too good to keep to herself. Daphne ordered a Cobb salad from Parmy, though on the menu it was called the "Our Town."

Fitzy strode in just as her salad was placed in front of her. After a quick scan of the restaurant, he found her, and without asking, he slipped into the seat across from her. Daphne froze with a fork inches from her open mouth.

He pointed at her plate. "That looks good. May I join you for lunch?"

She nodded her head, slowly chewing her greens. He flagged Parmy down and gave his order before continuing his conversation. "Betty told me about your plans for the display window. I think they are great. You are very creative."

"Thank you." She swallowed hard. An uneasy feeling swirled in her stomach at being around Fitzy since he had laughed at her fall.

"I wanted you to know I wasn't laughing at you at the BBQ. Daphne, I would never laugh at you. Phil normally is all Mr. I Could Be on the Cover of a Magazine Without Any Notice. In that barbeque-covered shirt, he looked so ridiculous, I couldn't stop myself."

"Betty told me as much. It's nice of you to say that. I was pretty confused. I couldn't understand why you would laugh at me. You are usually so nice."

"I am nice. I'm very nice. I doubt you could find a nicer guy in Cobb." The sparkle in his eye let her know that he was kidding.

Giggling, she signaled that all was forgiven. "I wanted to ask you a favor." She speared more salad.

"Anything."

"Do you have a fishing pole? I wanted to do this crossing fishing pole thing for the window. I found Flo's, but I need another. I thought you might have one."

"Dang, I wish I did. Sorry, that isn't my sport. Uncle Henry had this elegant rod. Though it broke somehow. I saw it in the trash at Aunt Pen's place this last year or so. But it was old, so not a big surprise. Too bad. It would have been great. Can you use just the one?"

"Sure, I'll change my design, no big deal."

"I had a question I wanted to ask you."

"Shoot," Daphne said through her mouthful of salad.

"I heard through the grapevine that you wanted to go to the coast." He drummed his fingers on the table. "I thought maybe we could go this Saturday. It's not a far drive over to Boothbay Harbor. Nearby are the Coastal Maine Botanical Gardens if you like flowers and green stuff. We could go for a boat cruise around the harbor. When was the last time you had a lobster roll?"

"Yes, yes, and not for years." She would have been happy to leave instantly if she didn't have work. "Count me in. As much as I love Cobb, I can't believe I haven't been to the ocean yet this summer."

"In case I wasn't clear, Daphne. I'm asking you on a date."

She narrowed her eyes. "A date?"

He nodded. "Is that a problem?" Fitzy kept silent as the wheels spun in her head.

Quickly, her mind fired off several thoughts. First, things could get awkward between her, him, and Betty if it went badly. Second, while she had never seen him as datable material, Phil was clearly a bust. Fitzy seemed more excited about spending a day with her than Phil. Third, Fitzy was nice. Given the lessons learned from King Rat Bastard, maybe she should try a *good* guy. She studied Fitzy. He was cute in an unassuming way. How had she never seen that before? Who knew? They might have a fantastic time.

"No. No problem. Not at all. It sounds like a lovely date."

They shared an awkward smile. Then she interjected, "Wait! We don't have to catch our own lobsters or anything. I don't think I would enjoy that."

"No, someone else will do all that for us. We just enjoy them."

"Good," she said, putting a hand over her heart. "I don't want another fishing debacle."

"It will be nothing but smooth sailing." He gently covered her free hand with his.

Chapter Thirty-Three

"I'm overwhelmed with possible suspects." Daphne moaned. "I've got pages of people with secrets. Are any worth murdering over? How will I know if one of these Cobb residents is the killer? Did you know that Angelica, at the hair salon, is having an affair with the guy who owns the barbershop? Is their pillow talk about the newest trends in hair fashion? Then, Nino Rossi, the guy from the hardware store. He's had trouble competing with those big box stores in Hinkley and had to borrow money to stay afloat."

"Gee, poor Mr. Rossi. I didn't know things were so tough for him. I'll make sure to buy more things from him," Fitzy said as he focused on finding the turn for the Coastal Maine Botanical Gardens.

"What if he's a murderer? Do you want to buy your leaf bags from a killer?"

He rolled his eyes. "I've known Mr. Rossi for my entire life. He is a great guy. He belongs to the Elks and coaches a team on the Little League circuit. He just isn't killer material."

"Then there is Noah Tippett, my lawyer. He lets his dog crap in his neighbors' yards without picking it up. Flo saw him stuffing trash into other people's bins and dumpsters. Apparently, he only tips ten percent at Joe's Diner."

"I didn't know all that. I'll grant you that's evidence of Tippett being cheap and not very community-oriented. But nothing points to him being a killer. He's just sort of a jerk."

"I was saving the worst for last." She crossed her arms. "It seems his sister went missing several years ago. She was never found. She is assumed dead. He could have killed her. Flo found out, and he had to silence her!"

"That is very sad for him and his family. But did Flo say she found evidence that Tippett had killed his sister? Or just that she had gone missing?"

"Just that the sister had gone missing." Daphne sighed.

"Then you only have circumstantial evidence—nothing to go to the sheriff with. I'm sorry, Daphne. But none of these people make good suspects."

"You're right. I know you're right. I do have others on the list, though. Maybe it's one of them?"

"This sounds more complicated than you first thought. No one will think less of you if you decide it's unsolvable. Let's talk about this later, all right? We are here. I want you to enjoy the flowers." Lowering his voice, he added, "Perhaps we should try to not think about murder on our date."

"Gosh, Fitzy. I'm sorry. This is a date, and I'm going on and on about the murder. Could I bring up a less romantic topic? I'm very excited to see this garden. Lead the way."

"Less romantic topics, huh? I could wax poetic about cleaning a grill, memorizing chess openings, and writing computer code. Or I could talk about how Betty and her sisters used to chase their poor dog, trying to dress him up in various outfits." Fitzy chuckled. "My aunt and uncle made them stop when the dog started to run away from home in protest."

"I can see Betty doing that. Okay, you've got my total focus on our date."

Fitzy let Daphne guide their wandering around the garden. The peonies, roses, lavender, and many other flowers she couldn't name were blooming. Making *oh* sounds, she stopped frequently to snap photos on her phone.

When her date lightly took her arm to help steer around workers fixing a bridge, tingles ran up her spine. She took it as a good sign.

They meandered on paths, pointing at sights that delighted or disappointed them.

"I adore daisies. They make me smile." Daphne touched the white petals.

"I can take or leave them. Never really did anything for me."

Fitzy stopped and took several photos of a flower with a purple sphere on top and a long, green stalk reaching up from the soil.

Daphne watched his camerawork and read a sign informing her they were called allium. "Of all the flowers here, for some reason, these are not the ones I would have thought you'd like so much."

"I like their geometric look. They are neat and tidy, which is rare in nature." Grinning, he took a picture of Daphne next to the flowers.

"Come on, I want to get a picture of us under that grass-roofed pavilion. I'll ask someone to take our picture." Daphne gripped his hand and didn't let go until they reached their destination.

After they'd had their fill of flowers, Fitzy drove them past a cute coastal village. They followed the road, hugging the coast, then turned into a grassy parking lot. Ahead lay row after row of picnic tables filled with people stuffing food into their mouths. Beyond the picnic tables sat a small white and blue shack with a cartoonish lobster painted on one wall.

"Looks really high-end. Do we need a reservation?" Daphne teased.

"Don't mock it until you've tried it. Heck, if they had reservations, I would have made one. This place is always packed. And for good reason. One of the best lobster rolls on the whole coast of Maine can be found here. Forget those fancy places in town. That's for the tourists. You want to come to where the locals go. Better food and costs a lot less. Let's join the line."

It took nearly half an hour of waiting before they each had a lobster roll, a cup of clam chowder, and a bottle of soda balanced on their tray. While Daphne felt confident in her practical sneakers, tan shorts, and pink tank top, she let Fitzy carry the tray in case she fell victim to another attack of klutziness.

She pointed a finger at the orange label on the soda bottle reading "Moxie" in white letters and asked, "What is that?"

"This?" He placed the tray on an empty picnic table. "It's Moxie. You've never had it?"

"Had it? I've never even heard of it."

"Goodness, Flo left a serious gap in your Maine education. This is the official soda of Maine."

"What's it taste like?" She gave the drink a dubious look.

Opening the bottle, he handed it over and she took a sniff. "Most describe it as having a root beer kind of taste. It's sweet but has a bitter kick to the end. You can order a Moxie float at Joe's Diner. The perfect summer treat. Go ahead, taste."

She tipped it back and took a small sip, letting it settle over her taste buds.

"Well?"

She swallowed. "Not bad. I see what you mean, it is sweet and bitter. I'll have to see if I can get some Vernors shipped out here for you to try."

"What is Vernors?"

"Michigan's unofficial *pop*. Think of it as a spicy ginger ale."

"Sounds interesting. I'd give it a whirl. Now, I think the *soda* goes best with a lobster roll. Dig in."

She took a large bite of her roll and chewed enthusiastically. Smiling, she helped herself to a spoonful of chowder. "I forgot how good the ocean tastes."

"Which are you enjoying more? The chowder or the lobster?"

"Can't choose one. Impossible."

"So you approve of the lobster shack after all?"

"You can bring me here anytime." She looked at Fitzy through her eyelashes.

They both turned a shade pinker and suddenly became very interested in their food.

Once full of the sea's bounty, they headed to Boothbay Harbor. The blue water sparkled under the afternoon sun. The harbor was filled with moored boats and lined with classic bright-white, clapboard buildings contrasting against the green trees behind them. The view lost some of its tranquility as throngs of tourists filled the sidewalks and crowded the businesses.

Slipping in and out of souvenir shops, Fitzy and Daphne started to keep track of all the items with a lobster on them. After reaching forty-seven, they gave up.

"Hey, you might want a hat or something to protect your face. The sun can get intense on the water," Fitzy warned.

She waved at a white visor with a giant red lobster and the word "Maine" printed across the band.

"Perfect," said Fitzy.

Wearing the hat as they left the shop, Daphne realized that she didn't mind looking a little silly around Fitzy. He didn't laugh at her, but with her. Glancing at her practical outfit, she was grateful. No urge to gain his approval by trying to look sexy hounded her. No more fishing-in-a-dress incidents for her. Only appropriate clothing from now on. She didn't think she'd ever had a romantic relationship that didn't involve her constantly trying to please her date.

A young man at the harbor in a navy-blue polo helped them climb on the boat. Daphne and Fitzy settled on a bench. After a safety speech, the boat pulled away from the dock.

"The water looks pretty calm," she noted.

"Do you get seasick?"

"Not that I know of, but better safe than sorry."

They took turns pointing out luxury yachts tied in the harbor and snapping photos of the postcard images found at every turn. She couldn't wait to send them to her brother in France in exchange for the batch of drool-worthy ones he was texting from Paris.

Chugging past Tumbler and Mouse Islands, she squealed as the boat glided past the Burnt Island Light. "I love lighthouses."

"Me too. Here, let me get a shot of you with the lighthouse in the back. Oh no, leave the visor on. Makes it even better."

"Michigan is home to tons of lighthouses. I always enjoyed going to visit them when I could. Going up to the top was the best part. However, not all let people up there. My mom thought they were old and dirty and didn't understand why I liked them."

"Her loss. I get it. They are a working building; they should be a little worn. The lights saved hundreds, maybe thousands of lives. People endured harsh conditions to keep the mariners safe. In Maine, we take that sacrifice very seriously. I think all old Maine families have someone involved in an ocean occupation, even if you have to go back a few generations."

"I wonder if any of my Winkler family in past generations made their living from the sea?"

"Very likely."

Daphne rubbed her arms.

"Cold?"

"A little. I forgot how chilly it can be on the water, even with the sun."

"Move closer to me."

She pushed her back into his chest and felt his arms wrap around hers. Her body stiffened as it pressed against his. It had been a long time since her body had made close physical contact with a man. His body felt rigid, as well, but his heat began to transfer. His warmth felt nice, as did being held. Heavens, she missed this. She forced her shoulders to relax and snuggle deeper. Fitzy's muscles loosened and allowed her to curve into him.

"Better?" he whispered in her ear.

Her eyelids closed for a moment. "Mm-hmm," she responded.

The sounds of water splashing against the boat and the motor's hum acted as a meditation mantra. She slipped into a tranquil state and drank in the beauty of Squirrel Island. The thought of living on an island appealed to the romantic in her.

She broke out of her reverie as they passed Ram Island Lighthouse. She stood up to grab some snapshots. Once complete, she returned to her snuggle position next to Fitzy. His arm snaked around her waist, pulling her an inch closer. She let her head rest on his chest.

On their return trip, he listed other local lighthouses they could visit. Preoccupied with the feeling of his arm wrapped around her and the increasing heart rate it created, she missed most of the names. Unwelcome, Wallace popped into her head. Every time they'd discussed doing something, it always ended up being what he wanted. Her opinion and desires had never mattered much. Gratefully, Fitzy's suggestions were based on shared interests.

Once they docked, Fitzy helped her out of the boat. Without words, they both walked in the direction of the car. Daphne would have liked to have held his hand again, but trying to weave through the crowded sidewalks made that impossible.

The drive back was filled with comfortable silences as they listened to music, which gave way to rehashing memories of the day. Once in her driveway, Fitzy got out of the car. He came around, opened her door, and walked her to the porch.

"Tomorrow, there is a fair going on to raise money for the sports teams at the high schools. The kids have to help put it on. It's pretty fun, usually. Would you like to go with me?"

Not only had the first date gone well, but he was already asking her for a second!

"Sounds great. What time should I expect you?" She took a step towards him.

"Six. We can go to the diner first, then walk over." He narrowed the gap between them.

"I'll see you at six." She swallowed hard. "Thanks for the wonderful date. You were right. It was all smooth sailing."

Fitzy stared at her lips.

She couldn't look away from his.

The hairs on the back of her neck rose as an electrical charge coiled around them.

Taking another step, a mere inch separated them. She tilted up her face. He bent towards her. Their lips barely touched. The light brush sent her pulse beating like a hummingbird's wings. He pulled back, and she moaned.

He slid his arm around her waist and tugged her closer, eliciting a ragged breath. This time, his mouth pressed to hers with urgency, sending shivers through her body. One hand pressed into his back while the other wove into his hair. Her mouth opened slightly, and he took her bottom lip between his. Her hands almost shook due to the adrenaline pumping in her veins.

Too soon for her liking, it ended. He leaned his forehead on hers, and they tried to control their breathing.

She felt she ought to say something, but anything meaningful escaped her. She was left with the first thought that entered her mind. "Byron Fitzgibbon, you not only have lips, but you know what they are for."

He chuckled. "Thank you?"

"I don't think those shiny women in Boston were hanging out with you for the fancy dinners. They were thinking about dessert."

He turned beet red. "You probably shouldn't mention that particular skill to my family."

"Are you kidding? It's the first thing I'm telling Betty. You know I am calling her the minute you leave, right?

"She's going to call me right after, you know."

"Say nice things."

Daphne called Betty as Fitzy pulled onto the street.

"I've been dying all day to know how it went. Well?"

"You never said anything about his kissing."

"Well, I wouldn't know, would I? Was it bad? He does know where to put his lips, right?"

"I felt it in my toes."

"It's weird knowing that about my cousin, but I'm happy for you. So, the poor fellow is finally out of the friend zone. I won't have to listen to him complain anymore."

"Wait, what? He talked to you about being in the friend zone?"

"Yep."

"Why didn't you tell me that he liked me?"

"No way I was getting in the middle of that. You two had to figure it out on your own. Does this mean you want to go on a second date?"

"He already asked me, and I said yes. It's tomorrow at the fair."

"He isn't letting any moss grow under his feet." Betty giggled. "You know, they have an old-fashioned tunnel of love ride at the fair."

Daphne could hardly wait.

Chapter Thirty-Four

UPON THEIR ARRIVAL AT the fair, Fitzy bought a fistful of tickets at the entrance booth. Folding them neatly, he tucked them into a pocket with one hand and took Daphne's with the other. Looking down, she saw their fingers intertwine. She squeezed his hand as they promenaded the main alley of the fairground. Fitzy pointed out the different games and people he knew along the arcade.

Daphne floated along. She was living in a real-life Hallmark movie. This was what she had wished for, even if it was a wish she'd made in a drunken stupor the day she'd met Betty in The Sidecar. Finding romance was included on her list of personal transformations. Fitzy wasn't the man she had imagined herself destined for, but she had never met anyone kinder. She didn't have to be wildly in love with him right now anyway. There would be plenty of time to see if those feelings developed.

Fitzy pointed to the bright-red sign that read, "Tunnel of Love." The O in love was replaced with a heart. The whole, hand-drawn entrance looked like a tacky Valentine's Day card. That did not stop them from giggling as they rushed forward to trade in some tickets.

Sitting close to Fitzy in the car covered with a large heart designed to give maximum privacy, Daphne admitted, "I've never been on this kind of ride before."

"Me neither. You don't have a fear of the dark, do you?"

Daphne shook her head as they disappeared into the tunnel. He turned his body towards her, and she followed suit. They swapped glances until they had each other's sole focus. Her heart was pounding in her chest. Mere inches separated their bodies. Was he going to kiss her or not? She imagined a kiss befitting a Jane Austen heroine. Nervously, she licked her lips. He tugged her to his side of the cart. No Mr. Darcy here.

Tingles shot from her chest, down her arms, and into her fingers. She ran her hand down his back. The polo shirt hid his lean muscles. He softly bit her bottom lip, drawing forth a whimper.

He tilted his head back and whispered in her ear, "You taste like honey."

Something about the hot air caressing her ear drove her to the edge. A mad desire to rip his shirt and touch his flesh rushed through her. Would his skin be as warm as hers? However, right at that moment the light pouring at the tunnel's end sent warning signals off.

She pulled back, and he looked confused.

"The ride. The ride is almost over."

"Oh."

Exiting the tunnel, both passengers flushed and smoothed down their hair for good measure.

"We could go back in the tunnel for another turn," she nervously teased.

"Definitely not. I can't be responsible for what will happen in there, and I have a reputation to protect." With a wink, Fitzy retook her hand and cleared his throat. "Why don't we find something a little safer to do."

Walking down the arcade, someone nodded, waved, or said hello to Fitzy every few feet.

"How do you know so many people here?"

"First, living in a small town makes it easy. You have no choice but to know everyone. Second, I'm friendly with some of the high school kids. I coach the chess team at the library. While it's mostly athletes here tonight, I pick up the high school chatter."

"Let's try a game," she suggested.

"Sure, anything look interesting to you?"

"Dunk tank. I've never done one." An evil grin spread across her face. "I want to dunk someone."

"You've got a wicked side, I see." He chuckled. "Come on, it's this way. The baseball kids put it on every year. Oh, I see Coach Fraser over there, too. Good, it's nice to know an adult is present. This event can get crazy."

The name tugged at Daphne's memory. Coach Fraser. It was familiar. Why or how did she know it?

Before she could solve the mystery, three baseballs were placed in her hands and a student in a baseball jersey was giving her instructions. If her ball hit the target, a player above the tank would be released into the water below.

Daphne put all her focus on the bullseye. It wasn't anything like tennis, but her hand-eye coordination was better than average, thanks to years at the country club. Her first throw went wide. With her second toss, the student in the tank laughed and pointed at her. His eyes bulged when he plummeted into the tank a few seconds later. The crowd around her clapped and cheered. The student who had given her the balls turned around to hand his buddy a towel. That was when Daphne saw the name Cunningham written on his jersey.

It all clicked into place. Cunningham and Coach Fraser were listed together in Flo's secret journal. She observed the coach standing apart from the students. His arms were crossed, his legs rigid and spread apart, all while barking orders at the teenagers working the booth.

"Get moving, Cunningham!" Fraser yelled. "Those balls aren't going to hand themselves out. Baxter, get your wet butt back in the tank."

Cunningham lowered his head and moved back to the table.

That Coach Fraser is a bully. I hate bullies. Look at the way he treats his athletes. I know what it feels like. Hasn't Mom treated me the same way at times? He's obviously horrible. Could he be evil?

In a hushed tone, she said, "Fitzy. That kid and the coach are in Flo's book."

His face paled. "Are you sure?"

"Yes, I remember now."

"What are you going to do, Daphne?"

Daphne took a moment to think. She didn't want to create another big scene like the one on the Fourth of July. But the investigation hadn't moved forward in ages, and the large group intimidated her. She would have to take a risk to find justice for Flo. Besides, that tyrant needed to be taken down a peg or two.

She marched to young Cunningham, leaned in, and spoke quietly. He nodded his head slowly. He called out to his coach that he would be back in a second. The two stepped away from the tank area. Fitzy trotted to Daphne's side.

Cunningham looked befuddled but smiled. "How can I help you, ma'am?"

"I am Flo Winkler's niece, Daphne."

"I've heard about you." He looked at the pair opposite him. "You said you needed my help. What with?"

"My aunt had a file on Coach Fraser. It seemed he was up to some questionable behavior."

"Well, you should talk to him then, not me, ma'am." He looked at the ground and then longingly at the tank area.

"Ah, but you were mentioned in there, as well." Both men stared at her. "She saw the two of you in a car. Where you shouldn't have been. Flo even noted that she approached you about this."

"Well... umm." Cunningham started to sweat and spared a nervous glance toward his coach.

Fraser noticed the look and walked over. "What's going on here?" His voice snapped, and he puffed out his chest. "Is there a problem with one of my players? Or are you bugging him?"

People around them stopped walking and stared.

Daphne sighed. She'd tried to avoid a public scene, but it now seemed impossible. "I was talking to young Cunningham here about something my aunt witnessed."

"Oh yeah?" Fraser spoke even louder and thrust his chest out further. "And what did that nosy Parker think she found out?"

Fitzy swallowed hard as the crowd thickened around them.

"She saw him in a car, about half a mile from the school, parked in a field partly hidden behind bushes and trees."

"So what? What's so criminal about that?"

"The problem is that it was after school hours, and he was in *your* car, Coach Fraser. Auntie Flo observed *you* in that same field on several occasions. Always in your car, but with various male students and after school hours." She stood as tall as her body could reach. "I was just asking young Mr. Cunningham here what happened in the car."

"Who do you think you are?" Fraser's face turned bright red. "What right do you have to come here and interrogate these fine young men? Get out of my face, you bi—"

"Now, now, Morris. That isn't the Christian way to behave," a man interrupted, breaking through the crowd. Everyone made way for the man dressed in a button-up, short-sleeved shirt with a white collar around his neck. "Hello, Daphne. I don't think we've formally met, though I've been meaning to make a house call. I am Reverend Ambrose McDonald."

Daphne shook his offered hand. "Nice to make your acquaintance, Reverend. I was hoping that Mr. Cunningham could answer a question for me. What took place between Cunningham and Coach Fraser in that car?" A great deal of murmuring spread through the crowd. "Seems several male students found themselves in the same situation."

"Seems like an easy question. I'm sure there is a perfectly reasonable explanation. Nothing unseemly about a coach and athlete spending time together." McDonald shared a knowing look with the crowd while his smile stayed. "It is better to clear the air than have rumor and speculation run amok. Gossip can ruin a good town."

"Thank you, Reverend. Now, Mr. Cunningham, could you please answer the question?"

He stuffed his hands in his pockets. He looked everywhere other than at Daphne. Fraser shifted his weight from foot to foot.

"It's okay, young man," McDonald reassured him. "Just tell the truth."

The boy shrugged. "A few of us on the team were in danger of failing our chemistry class. It's hard, and with all our time on practice and games, there wasn't a lot left to study. Well, Coach said he would take care of it."

Fraser shot him a stern look. The Reverend nodded for him to continue.

"He got the test questions from a couple of chem tests and gave them to us beforehand so we would pass the class. We wouldn't have gotten into the championship games otherwise. That's what was happening in the car. Miss Winkler did ask me about it once. But I told her nothing. Jeez, I didn't know she was keeping a file."

The coach looked like he was ready to throttle Daphne. He even made a few steps toward her. She knew if she was going to find out if he killed her aunt, it was now or never.

"You knew Flo was looking into your little scam," Daphne accused, pointing her finger at Fraser. "So you did her in! Didn't you?"

"No! The kid never told me. I didn't know Flo suspected anything. Even if I did, I wouldn't have killed her. I helped the kids pass school, but it was all for the big championship. There was a lot of pressure on us to make it." He pleaded with the crowd. "We'd never have made the playoffs without those kids eligible to play."

The light went out of Daphne's face. "Thank you for answering my question," she mumbled.

Observing the shocked look on McDonald's face, she saw it mirrored by their audience. Murmurs from the crowd grew. A few angry shouts were called out. She decided it was time to get out of there. Finding Fitzy's hand, she tugged him away and weaved through the mob.

"That did not go as I expected," Daphne admitted once they were safely away. "I tried not to make another public scene. It wasn't my fault. I only wanted a quiet, private word with the kid, but Fraser butted in. That plan failed, and I'm no closer to finding Flo's killer."

"You tried to be more subtle, I guess. I never suspected Fraser would cheat like that. And the irony is that we lost the championship in the end. He might lose his job and be blacklisted from coaching, all for nothing."

"People will do risky things when they feel desperate. Okay, he may not have been a murderer, but at least I uncovered a nefarious plot. I should get some credit for that. It's like the Puddingstones. Jackson wasn't the killer either, but it turns out my accusation made their marriage better. I am helping people in the end. Aren't I?"

"Yeah, though maybe next time you have a connection to the journal and want to question someone in town about the murder, you run it by me first? I don't know how many more exposed secrets the town can handle."

Chapter Thirty-Five

ON THEIR THIRD DATE, Fitzy admitted to being interested in Daphne from the night he drove her home from the bar.

"You were attracted to me when you took my drunk ass home from The Sidecar?" She raised one eyebrow.

"You're a cute drunk. When I got you inside, you said you had no money to pay your Uber driver, but you'd kiss me instead."

Her mouth made a perfect O shape. "That's like the start of a porn movie. Tell me I didn't drunk kiss you."

"You pulled me down to you. I didn't realize what was happening until your tongue was in my mouth."

"Oh, no! That was our first kiss, and I don't even remember it. At least it didn't go further than a kiss. Right?"

"After I pulled you off me and got you settled on the couch, you fell asleep immediately."

Daphne groaned and covered her face with her hands. His description of events made her sound desperate. She decided to be more cautious, especially about their physical relationship. Only restrained goodnight kisses from now on. That could be frustrating, since the first bolt of electricity from Fitzy's touch, her body suddenly remembered what it was like to be with a man.

During the seven days since their magical date by the ocean, Daphne felt like she was walking on air. Fitzy called or visited her daily.

Keeping with her new vow not to leap into things, she sat in a chair instead of next to Fitzy on the couch as they discussed plans for their next date.

"There is this bar in Hinkley that I go to for trivia nights. They do a great burger," he suggested.

"I'm not in a burger mood." Remembering Penelope's advice to focus on what she wanted, she countered, "I've been keen to try out that Mexican place."

"Okay, sure, fine. The latest superhero movie is out now. We could see it afterward. I've been looking forward to it for months now."

"I'm not in the mood for an action movie tonight. What about the one with the woman who leaves her old life behind and goes on a journey of self-discovery? It's based on a best-selling book."

"If that's what you want, sure."

As they closed the door behind them, a notification on Fitzy's phone went off.

"It's my sister, Georgie. They are having an IT emergency. She wants my help. Can we swing by before we go to Hinkley? It won't be more than half an hour."

"No problem."

Georgie opened the door before Fitzy could even knock. She waved them inside. "Thanks for coming over. The internet is down again, and kids can't watch their favorite shows. They are driving us nuts. By the way, watch out for low-flying toddlers. He's Martin and that is Annabelle." She pointed out as the two children raced around, laughing and squealing, bolting from the kitchen nook into the living room.

Georgie explained, "The house was built with some rooms connecting one another to make a circle. The kids like to run it like a race track most days." Two little bodies rushed by again. "It wears them out, so I allow it. Milo, come down here, please. Fitzy has arrived," she hollered.

"Hey, bro," said Milo as he joined them. "Thanks for helping out. Sorry to interrupt your date. Hi Daphne, I'm Milo."

Daphne smiled and nodded in his direction.

"No problem." Fitzy followed Milo down the hall.

"Come into the kitchen with me, Daphne," Georgie said. "I am keeping an eye on dinner."

"It smells great. What are you having?"

"Lasagna. I've just got to finish the asparagus."

Dishes filled the kitchen sink, the counters were littered with ingredients, and part of the table was covered in crayon artwork. Country music played from a speaker. Her mother would have found the clutter an affront to her clean standards. To her, it looked like a well-used, relaxed, happy place. It was a home she longed for, with room to be yourself, and know that version of you was enough.

"Could you grab the garlic bread from the freezer and put it on a baking sheet?" Georgie asked as she made space on the island to work on the vegetables. "It needs to go in when the lasagna is done."

"Sure." Daphne opened the bottom freezer and found the bread. Now, she needed to find a baking sheet, so she started opening cabinets.

"They are in the drawer at the bottom of the stove. So, you and Fitzy, huh?"

"Well, sort of. We have only been dating a week, so we're still figuring things out."

"I think Fitzy has things figured out. I've heard a lot about you from him. We all know how he feels about you. My brother wears his heart on his sleeve. I understand your last man had a scant relationship with honesty."

"You could say that. He had sneaky ways to control me. Then, of course, the cheating thing finished us off. He gets one out of five stars for honesty. Do not recommend."

"Fitzy is mostly an open book. Though he doesn't have an option. He's a terrible liar."

"Good to know. I'll put that in the plus column."

"What about you?"

"Me what?"

"Are you a good liar?"

The stove's timer went off, and Georgie pulled out a bubbling dish that smelled like heaven. The distraction gave Daphne a moment to think about how to respond to the question. Did she lie often? No, she generally told the truth. Lies made her uncomfortable.

"I don't like lying. Except to my mother. It makes things easier, if you know what I mean."

"I've heard a few things. I can understand. So, I heard you think your aunt might have been killed."

"I've got some evidence that points me in that direction. Did you ever see someone in a fight with Flo?"

"Hmm, a fight? Well, your aunt sometimes got people's backsides up from time to time, but that's not the same as a genuine fight."

"No arguments?"

"I remember being at the grocery and seeing Flo and Debbie talking with raised voices."

"Debbie, who? What did they say?"

"I don't remember much. But I did hear something about lottery tickets. Though, who cares about some cheap scratch-offs? Not exactly motive for murder, huh?"

"I guess not."

"Hey, do you two want to stay for dinner? We've got plenty."

"We should ask Fitzy."

"You'll find him in the office. Down the hall, last door on the left."

The modest home made it simple to find the room and Fitzy. He sat, staring at the laptop. She hated to startle him, so she knocked on the door frame.

"Hi there. Can I borrow Fitzy for a minute?"

Fitzy smiled as he walked toward her. Taking her hand, he pulled her into the hall and away from prying eyes. He drew her closer. With a hand firmly cradling her head, he tilted it up and crushed his lips against hers. Fireworks exploded.

Her body objected when he stepped back. The clandestine kiss was like giving only a few drops of water to someone after days in a desert. She needed more. A glassful wouldn't do either. She wanted to jump into the whole damn lake.

"What can I do for you?" he practically purred.

I have a long list of things you can do, and not one is appropriate to do at your sister's house. She cleared her head. *Get ahold of yourself, girl. Remember your vow to take it slow.*

"Your sister invited us for dinner. Do you want to eat lasagna here or go to Hinckley for Mexican?"

"Georgie makes a killer lasagna. But there's not much of a date atmosphere. What do you think?"

"I saw it come out of the oven. I vote here."

There was the added benefit of being around his family. Daphne would have to keep her hands to herself, and having observers would help her win the battle she was waging to maintain self-control.

"Lasagna it is. I'll be finished soon."

"I will tell Georgie that we're staying."

She took several deep breaths on her way back, hoping to recover her composure. When she returned, she saw six places set on the formerly messy table. She raised an eyebrow at Georgie.

"I took a chance. I've never had Fitzy say no to my lasagna."

They finished preparing the food. Georgie made a loud call to the household that dinner was ready. One by one, they arrived. Milo lifted Annabelle into her booster seat. Martin started banging his fork on the table. Plain noodles were deposited on his plate.

"He hasn't acquired the taste for sauce and cheese on his noodles yet," Fitzy clarified. "Until he does, more for me."

"If you two last until Christmas, Daphne, I'll show you how to make this yourself," Georgie offered.

Not knowing how to respond, Daphne stayed silent while her cheeks turned rosy.

"Georgie! Please don't embarrass me in front of my date."

"You've got some out-of-the-box thinking about dating," Milo teased. "Talk about an offbeat approach to romance. Is it still considered a date if you're eating lasagna at your sister's house?"

"Not you, too? I thought I could count on you to be a good influence on your wife. You know, the bro code and all that."

"Sorry, pal, your sister can't be tamed. I always liked that about her."

"Thanks, sweetie." Georgie gave her husband an air kiss.

Annabelle, taken with the action, began sending kisses to everyone.

"I love you, too, Anna," Georgie told her daughter. Then, she returned her focus to her brother. "If I want to embarrass you, Byron, I've got much better ammunition."

"This isn't happening. Please play nice, Georgie," begged Fitzy.

"Nice is boring. I've been waiting ages for you to bring home a girl so I could tell them your greatest hits. Now, with Daphne here, I've got some special ones to share. You see, this isn't the first time we've had to listen to Fitzy go on about a girl from Michigan."

Daphne looked from Georgie to Fitzy and back again. "You've got my attention."

"Well, two decades ago, we had to hear about this pretty and clever girl whenever he came home from the library. He went to the library a lot that summer. For a couple of months, it was nonstop. But then the girl left to go back home, and he moped around like a puppy who had been told they were a bad boy."

"I didn't know any of that. That's so sweet," Daphne elongated the last word.

Fitzy glared at his sister.

"So, you can imagine how excited he got when he found out she was coming back to town. He was like a kid who'd just won a year's worth of free ice cream."

"Ice cream!" shouted Martin.

"Okay, Marty, you can have some ice cream *after* dinner. Now, where was I?"

"You had just finished your story," Fitzy interrupted. "All done now. New topic."

"I'd like to hear more." Daphne's eyes twinkled with glee.

"Maybe you should give your brother a break, honey," Milo said gently. "You've said a lot already."

"Shush," Daphne exclaimed. "Go on, Georgie, I am all ears."

"He hadn't forgotten the girl he had his little crush on all those years ago. Everyone in the family became curious about what she'd be like after all that time. Then Betty, after a few too many drinks, decides to play Cupid and calls her cousin up to come and fetch her and the very woman he was desperate to see from the bar."

"Betty never said a thing! She's a crafty one."

"She is. But the story gets better. It was his big moment, the one he'd been waiting twenty years for. However, not only did she not recognize him from their youth, but she also forgot that he was the one driving." Georgie's shoulders shook with laughter.

Her husband smirked as he cut up bits of asparagus for his son.

"Oh no." Daphne turned to Fitzy, who shot daggers at his sister. "Fitzy, I'm so sorry. I had no idea you had a crush on me then or now. I feel like a stupid jerk not remembering who you were immediately."

"It's not your fault. You weren't supposed to know. I can understand if this makes us dating too weird for you."

"Weird? Are you kidding? This is like a fairytale. The boy who waits for his first love to come back to him. That is the sweetest thing. It's rather romantic."

"Really? You aren't saying all this to make me feel better?"

"Sure, I want you to feel better, but it's also all true."

Someone had had a crush on her for twenty years? She got engaged to a man who thought she wasn't enough, when all along, someone who would have been thrilled to be with her was here in Cobb. Not for the first time, she wondered how her life would have been different if she'd been able to continue her visits with Flo.

Milo changed topics to the computer problem. For the rest of dinner, Georgie refrained from telling more Fitzy stories. While eating, Daphne and Fitzy exchanged grins. She wondered if this was how Jane from *Pride and Prejudice* felt when Bingley returned from London and called on her family.

After the meal was finished and goodbyes were exchanged, Daphne and Fitzy sat in his car.

"You still want to try and make that movie?" Fitzy asked.

"No, I'm not in the mood to go to Hinckley now."

"Oh," he gloomily responded.

"Why don't you take me home?"

"Okay, if that's what you want." He looked directly ahead, his body stiff.

"It is. I want to finish the conversation we started in the hall."

Her vow of chastity was kicked off like flip-flops at the beach.

It was time to go jump in a lake.

Chapter Thirty-Six

WITH NOTHING BUT TWO public failures to show for her investigative work, Daphne was off the murder hunt. She wanted to solve the mystery, but her self-esteem could only handle so much. Besides, other things required her focus: her growing relationship with Fitzy and the launch of her vision for the bookstore.

Dragging a table from the back to the front of the store, she had transformed it into a display space. Zeroing in on the beach theme from the window, she piled it with summer reading suggestions and books about Maine. She promoted local authors on the ends of the bookshelves. Cobb didn't see a great deal of tourism compared to the seashore. However, camping and cabin rentals within easy distance of the river for fishing and boating afforded a cheaper option than staying on the expensive coastline, so there was a steady stream of travelers, especially in the summer months.

Between the eye-catching window and improved displays, the store saw an uptick in traffic and sales. Then she stumbled upon what would become a big seller for the store. Every day, a large travel mug full of her latte creations came in with her. Customers coming into the store would sniff the air and ask where to get coffee.

The disappointed frowns they gave when informed that it was her personal drink planted a seed in her brain. She brought in her professional-grade coffee maker and made small paper cup samples of her brew. As word of the upscale coffee treats spread, the store filled with people wanting a taste. Those people often left with a book.

Realizing the plan was unsustainable and a market opportunity was staring her in the face, she coaxed Russell into backing her latest scheme. Customers could purchase a travel mug for ten dollars and get their first coffee for free. Afterward, they could bring in the same mug and get a discounted refill. Russell balked at Daphne's suggested menu prices.

"Who would fork over that much? You can go to Joe's and get one for a third of what you're asking."

"No one would pay that for a *basic* cup of coffee, I agree. But this is fancy. I'll have a limited offering of high-end coffees for the customer. Lattes, cappuccinos, that sort of thing. Trust me, people will pay for outstanding java."

Russell *harrumphed* at the idea, but like with everything else, he let Daphne have her way. He couldn't argue that bringing Daphne on board had bumped up sales. Also, he enjoyed his free time and the new friends he made in his water aerobics class.

Daphne came in early on the day the box of travel coffee mugs bearing the store's logo was set to arrive. She and Russell set up an attractive display in place of the messy DVD crates.

A mere week later, Russell gruffly congratulated Daphne on her plan. It was a hit. Possibly because the coffee was only served when she and her coffee maker showed up, the scarcity resulted in a line throughout the store for her hot brew before she even arrived. As people waited for their drinks, they had time to browse the shelves, and most customers left with a latte and a new book.

Not resting on her laurels, she tackled the crates of old CDs and DVDs next. After brainstorming with Betty and Fitzy, it was decided to sell the items as a collection. Daphne put three DVDs in a brown paper bag. Written on the front in thick black letters, it read "Mystery Movie Pack." Listed below was the collection's theme, like thriller, summer blockbuster, rom-com, or military. Daphne placed the bags on the counter in a pretty wicker basket topped with a gingham bow—a perfect last-minute impulse buy.

Bags labeled "Book & Soundtrack" were placed in a matching wicker basket. Inside, the buyer would find two CDs that complemented the book. Fantasy novels were paired with classical or Celtic tunes. Romance got smooth jazz or love songs. Country music was matched with Westerns, and vintage CDs were combined with period cozy murders. No one was more surprised than Daphne at how popular the "mystery" options were. They flowed out of the store as quickly as the coffee.

Around the middle of August, Daphne began to notice the increased traffic of what she called the silver foxes. Some of these ladies came alone, others in a group, but all were between fifty and seventy. Daphne didn't recognize them as locals.

After overhearing a few conversations, she learned they lived near Hinckley and took water aerobics classes at the senior center. When she realized why they were coming, Daphne had to work hard to avoid bursting into laughter in front of two ladies in matching leisure suits.

Some wanted to see the store Russell owned; others hoped to catch his eye. Most wanted to spend some extra time with the handsome widower. Daphne delighted in his fan club. She didn't want him alone anymore. It didn't hurt that they never left the place empty-handed.

"Your entourage was here on Wednesday," she informed him, giggling.

"I don't have an entourage." His tone sounded gruff, but there was a twinkle in his eyes.

"Tell that to the women who come here. Have any of them asked you to come over for supper yet?"

"A few of them have, yes."

Was he blushing?

Daphne leaned over the counter and looked him directly in the eye. "How many of them have you said yes to?"

He broke eye contact and started organizing the till. "Four."

"Four? Russell, you are a player. No wonder we are doing such good business from your groupies."

"They are pleasant ladies and not groupies. Besides, it's only supper, it's not like we are going steady. Oh, and we've watched a few movies too. Some suggested we watch one of the movies they got from the store. Seemed impolite to say no." He shuffled around the counter.

"Russell, these are dates. They think you are a stud." Daphne bounced on the balls of her feet. "I'm happy for you. That explains the glow I've been seeing about you."

"Women glow, not men. I'm looking healthier because of this exercise I've been doing. The doc was right. This has been good for me."

"I'll say it's been good for you."

"Okay, that is enough out of you, missy. You come in here, turn my store upside down, and now I have to put up with this abuse as well."

"You're right. I'm sorry. I don't mean to tease." Daphne pitched herself onto the vacant stool behind the counter. "I just think this is wonderful. You do look great, by the way. I'd swear you are aging backward."

"That's nice of you to say. I do feel better than I have in a while. So, what is going on between you and that Fitzgibbon fellow?"

After asking him so many questions, she felt she owed him openness in return.

"He's the nicest guy out there. I've never dated someone so nice before. He asks me where *I* want to eat and what *I* want to do. He is so courteous. I knew my ex was a jerk, but comparing him to Fitzy, he's a plain old bum. Why did I stay with the jerk so long? I can't believe Fitzy and I have been dating for a month already. This summer sure has been flying."

"You got yourself a good one. Don't forget to ask him what *he* wants to do every once in a while, too. Consideration is a two-way street. But he should open your car door and walk you to the porch. A month already? Is it serious? Has he made his intentions clear?"

"Oh, Russell. We're not serious yet. No talks about intentions. We're just enjoying each other's company. On the days I work, he usually joins me for lunch at the diner beforehand. At least once a week, I'm at his place watching episodes of the Poirot TV series. We both love that show. He's taken me to see the Portland Lighthouse, as well as Cape Elizabeth, Nubble, and Pemaquid. He knows all the best local places for a lobster roll. See? All fun, nothing serious."

"You spent the night at his place or vice versa?" Russell crossed his arms.

"Perhaps. Hey, this isn't the Middle Ages. Our generation is more casual about that kind of thing. I didn't ask if you had any overnighters."

"Hmm, just consider that he might not be feeling as casual about this as you are. I don't remember seeing Fitzgibbon stepping out with a woman since he came home from the city. Something for you to think about." He tapped his nose. "I'm off. I got my water exercises, then supper at Widow Alice's place tonight." With a chuckle, he was out the door.

Daphne didn't laugh, however. Was Fitzy getting serious about her? She liked spending time with Fitzy and grew more fond of him daily. He made her feel special. She finally found a man who treated her with affection and respect. It was like in *Gone with the Wind*, when Rhett swept in after the Civil War and transformed Scarlett's life. Her poverty and hardship were in the past, replaced with joy, devotion, and whatever her heart desired.

While autumn was peeking around the corner, Daphne realized she hadn't thought past the end of August. Back in June, she figured she'd have Flo's murder solved by Labor Day, and then she could go home and get on with her real life.

Between Fitzy and her lack of progress on Flo's murder, she needed to reevaluate her plans. Daphne started up the coffee machine. But when customers came in to get a refill, share a little gossip, and stroll through the bookstore, she pushed any further thoughts about the future out of her head. Just like Scarlett, she'd worry about it tomorrow.

Chapter Thirty-Seven

DAPHNE SPRAWLED IN A languid, catlike fashion on her couch, her eyes closed. Fitzy droned on about the incredible amount and variety of falling stars they had seen.

"Darling, it was wonderful," she said. "I've never seen anything like it. But it was a month ago."

"More like three weeks."

Opening one eye, she rolled it at him. "Okay, three weeks. That was the beginning of August. It's Labor Day now." Her eyes closed again. "Maybe we can move past that topic."

"You're kind of grouchy today. Is something wrong?"

"It's just hot. We were out in the sun forever during the parade. I no longer have the energy to do anything or to talk about the Perseid meteor shower again."

He was right; she was grouchy. The heat made her sulky.

She considered sitting up but quickly discarded the thought.

"Do you want me to go?"

She sat up. "No, I don't. I'm sorry I'm being a pain."

"You want to go into Hinckley and do something?"

"I thank you for taking me to play Skee-Ball, the movies, bowling, and the country bar."

He made a sour face.

Daphne continued. "I know that wasn't your favorite date, but I had a blast learning line dancing and playing darts. I have a great time doing everything with you, but I want to read now. Since we've been spending time together, I've barely gotten a book finished."

"You want to read? But you want me to stay?"

Daphne nodded. "Maybe we could read together? Not the same book, of course. That's silly. But I could read my stuff, and you could read something, too. I've got several books around the place, or you could use my Kindle app."

"I've never hung out and read *with* anyone before."

"Neither have I. I hoped that, one day, I would date someone who wanted to do that with me."

"Give me your tablet. I'll find something to read."

He sat down close to her so that their legs touched. Her thoughts turned to activities other than reading. Did she want to pursue this invitation? Her sticky, hot, and gross body inspired her decision. "The tablet is upstairs. I'll run up and get it. Why don't you put on some reading music?"

"What do you want me to put on?"

"The ABBA album in the right-hand corner, the one where they're in a limo or something," she called behind her.

While upstairs, she made a quick stop in the bathroom. She ran cold water onto a washcloth and cleaned her body. It wasn't as good as a shower, but she felt less offensive and now more amenable if their reading time became more R-rated. Grinning, she dashed into her room, sloppily made the bed, grabbed the tablet, and returned to the living room.

Fitzy's gaze was firmly affixed to the album in his hand. He held up the paper cover. "Did you ever notice the dates on here?"

"The date it was released? Not really. I don't care so much about the details, just the music."

"No, look at the back cover where the songs are listed. Next to 'SOS,' 1992 is handwritten in black ink. That's side A. I don't know if that matters. On side B, next to the song 'I've Been Waiting for You,' 1972 is written with blue ink."

"What does it mean?"

"I'm not sure. There are two ink colors. So, Flo wrote them in different pens for a reason, or she wrote the years on here at different times and used different pens."

"That makes sense. 1972? I don't get it. The album came out in 1975. Look at the release year. Why would she write down a year before the album was released?"

How many times had she played that record and never noticed the writing? She had only been interested in the artwork on the front. This had been one of Flo's favorites, so she knew the album by heart. Daphne didn't need to look at the song list on the back.

"Let's start with the song with the earlier date written next to it. What is the song about?"

"The name says it all. This woman has been in love with the guy for a long time." She struggled to connect that song with Flo, even though the evidence of the fishing book suggesting her aunt had been romantic at least once in her life. "She's been waiting for him to notice her, fall in love with her, or something like that. Then he does, and she is over the moon about it. Life is wonderful and perfect because she is with the man she loves. "

"What about 'SOS'?"

"That is a breakup song. The woman is sad and melancholy because her romance is over. She doesn't understand why it has to end. She still carries a torch for her love. Oh, and she was not the one who wanted to break up. She goes on about how hurt, lonely, and confused she is."

"It isn't hard to guess what is happening with these dates. How grim."

"Yeah. Did she start her romance in 1972? Maybe she heard the song in 1975, felt this total connection to it, and wrote the year then. Whoever was her lover, they broke it off in 1992." She shook her head slowly, understanding the hurt Flo must have gone through. "Wait a minute! That would make this a twenty-year relationship. How did Auntie Flo have a relationship with someone for twenty years without anyone knowing?"

"And why hide it for two decades? It must have been scandalous or something. When it ended, did she have anyone to talk to?"

"Probably not. If she had kept that secret for twenty years, I doubt she would have started blabbing about it after it was over. All that pain and anger tormenting her, and no one to help through it. I feel so bad for her."

Fitzy slid his arm around her shoulders.

"I also am dying to know who this person was. Why did they do it? Did they regret breaking Flo's heart? Are they still alive now?"

"Unless there are more clues hidden amongst these records, I don't think we'll ever have an answer to those questions."

Without a word, they worked their way through Flo's sizable record collection. Fitzy and Daphne each started on opposite sides of the room. For an hour, the only sound came from the record player. Meeting in the middle, no other clues had surfaced from the shelves, and they accepted defeat. Flo's secret romance was still safely hidden.

"I'm sorry we didn't find anything more." Fitzy held out his hand.

Taking it, Daphne thought about Flo's broken heart. The end of her affair must have been awful. But she'd managed to have a relationship that lasted twenty years. That had to mean something, even if she spent her final decades alone. Had she been lonely afterward? Yes, Daphne felt sure she had.

Daphne was no stranger to the cruelty of loneliness. Even with Wallace, she had often felt alone. Since coming to Cobb, that ache had diminished. She didn't want to be lonely again.

Daphne rested her head on Fitzy's shoulder and hugged him tight. He wrapped his arms around her and stroked her hair. Her comfort was short-lived as an unwelcome thought whispered in her ear. "Your hair is frizzy. You'll never get a boyfriend looking like that."

"My hair must be a wild mess," she muttered.

Tears threatened. She tried to refocus herself.

However, the sinister inner critic raged, "You are a mess. What makes you think you are worthy of Fitzy?"

She stumbled in the darkness of her mind, unable to stop the catastrophizing spiral. The fear whispered to her, "He's nice and thoughtful. It can't last. He will see your weakness and reject you for it. It's mean men that you attract. Flo kept up a relationship for twenty years before ending up single and lonely, which is what will happen to you. She'd be so disappointed in you."

She shivered.

"Are you cold?" Fitzy held her closer.

Feeling his arms encircle her helped ground her and bring her back to the moment. She nuzzled harder into his body.

"Do you think I'm weak?"

"Weak? What are you talking about? Daphne, look at me." Putting his hand under her chin, he lifted her face and saw her lips tremble. "You moved hundreds of miles away to a place you hardly knew. You introduced yourself to strangers, which is my nightmare."

This admission elicited a weak smile from her.

"You are trying to solve a murder. And no matter how hopeless it gets, you keep going. I mean, you followed Jackson on the Fourth of July. Though please never do that again. You might put me in an early grave. You confronted Cunningham and Coach Fraser in front of a crowd. That required a Flo-level backbone."

"I got both of those wrong, though. Those guys had nothing to do with Flo's death."

"You've started a cottage industry of selling applesauce to the town's best restaurant, and nearly single-handedly, you've turned that dump of a used bookstore into something to be proud of. You astonish me with your strength and determination. How can you not see what I see?"

"I wish I saw the woman you saw. She isn't the person I see looking back in the mirror."

"Maybe you need to look in a different mirror." He kissed her forehead.

She fantasized about going through the house smashing up mirrors and her fears while singing along with Helen Reddy's "I Am Woman."

Chapter Thirty-Eight

Twenty Years Ago – Flo

Outside the window, snow fell in silence while, inside, a fire kept the chill away. A real pine Christmas tree with decorations tried to fill her home with holiday cheer. Flo felt nothing. Her body and heart were numb. Under the tree sat a gift addressed to Daphne. The message "Return to sender" had been written on the label.

Inside the box was a pair of moose socks, a jar of applesauce, one of the *Redwall* books Daphne liked so much, and a trout mug that matched hers.

At first, she thought it had been a mistake. She'd called Sarah to explain that her gift to Daphne would be late because of a post office mess. With unfeeling clarity, Flo was informed that the post office had not made a mistake.

"I appreciate the help you gave us this past summer," began Sarah. "It was very kind of you, and the gift was most thoughtful. But since I don't plan on burdening you again with a visit from my daughter, I think it would be best if we let Daphne get back to her old life as quickly as possible. If I had given her the gift, it might have left her conflicted and confused."

"Wait, are you saying I can't see or even contact her?" This couldn't be true.

"Correct. I realized it was such a huge favor to ask of a woman who's never had to deal with children, and I never want to put you out like that again. It's unfair to you."

Fair? None of this was fair. Was there a miscommunication? Had she done something wrong? Nothing came to mind.

"But I want to see Daphne again. I was thinking maybe one month a summer, like a summer camp kind of thing."

"With the new baby, our family just can't afford the cost of a plane ticket every year for her." Sarah's calm and insulting tone never varied.

"I'll pay for the plane ticket." Maybe there was still hope.

"I couldn't ask that of you. That's too generous."

"Coming here was so good for her." Flo switched tactics. "She makes her bed now. When she left, she was so happy."

An eerie pause stretched over the call.

"I'm glad it was a good experience for her. I am her mother, let's not forget, and I think I know what is best for my daughter."

I doubt that. She was a meek little mouse when she got off that plane on her first day here. When she left, she held her head high and never stopped smiling. You're going to take that from her. You'll grind her down again. You'll take her joy from me.

"Sarah, please, don't do this." Flo never begged. But Daphne was worth it.

"I don't know what you mean. I'm not doing anything." The fake politeness left Sarah's voice. The claws were out.

"You're going to kill her spirit. I know you want to protect her, but you hold her too tight."

"So you learned to be the perfect mother in three months? What could you possibly offer her that I can't?"

"I can let her be herself. I can let her live without needing to be perfect."

The sound of Sarah sucking in her breath was audible over the phone. "I don't know what you mean. But you can be sure that you'll never see or hear from Daphne again."

No, no, no. Everything was spinning out of control.

"You'll regret this. One day, this is going to come back and bite you in the ass. She's a Winkler, and you can't hold her down forever."

"The nerve. She is a Patterson. She'll never be anything like you. I know your dirty little secret. Do you think I want her to turn out like you? Goodbye, Aunt Florence."

The pain was starting to seep through the nothingness. Sarah knew. Did that mean May knew, too? She must. How else would Sarah know? Maybe she was right. She didn't want her great-niece to do some of the things she'd done. Did she even deserve Daphne's love? Was this the universe's way of paying her back for her treachery? No, it couldn't be. It was too unfair.

She'd spent the last few months thinking of things to do with Daphne next summer. She'd planned to ask Sarah about making the trip an annual event and then surprise Daphne with the news.

The disappointment was more than Flo could bear. She needed to vent her pain and anger. To have someone tell her it would be alright, even when it wouldn't. Only her best friend could provide comfort for something this horrible. She needed Pen. Through thick or thin, Pen always stood by her side.

Chapter Thirty-Nine

THE DAYS WERE GETTING cooler, and the tops of trees were changing color. But the late September sun shone bright and inspired Penelope to plan an outing. Betty grabbed Daphne's elbow and marched her into the community room at the Hinckley Senior Center. Mature women with bingo sheets in front of them filled table after table. Handsewn or crocheted bags to hold markers could be found on each.

On a riser at the front of the room, a man dropped a bag of balls into a machine with a hand crank. Plunking down into a seat next to Betty, Daphne accepted her bingo pad and marker. There were three cards on a pad to keep track of. Her stomach clenched at the thought of trying to manage three cards simultaneously. Turning to her left, she saw a woman with a marker in each hand and five pads in front of her. Daphne turned back to her companions with wide eyes.

"That's Mildred over there." Penelope pointed to the woman she had been gawking at. "She is a serious player. There are several like her. Don't bother trying to have a conversation with her. She isn't here for chit-chat. Winning is all she cares about. Personally, I enjoy playing and socializing."

Daphne nodded mutely. She remembered playing bingo games at the country club as a kid, but that didn't compare to this at all. This was cutthroat. Winning wasn't even on her radar. She just wanted to keep up. Behind her, she heard part of a conversation in progress.

"My granddaughter gave me a book to read for my birthday. It wasn't bad, but oh, the language. It was a bit upsetting to me," the high, squeaky voice huffed.

"At least your granddaughter remembered your birthday. I can hardly get my children to call me, let alone visit. I would gladly endure a few curse words to get some of their attention," grumbled her tablemate in a deep tone that hinted at years of smoking.

"It was not just a few curse words. They used the F-word. I've never used it in all my seventy years. Not even once," the first woman announced with pride.

"Hmm, I don't know. When I am really angry, a good curse word can help."

"Not me. I remember once, I was so angry at my husband, I could feel the rage rising from my stomach up my chest. I thought to myself, if I had a gun, I would shoot him right now. But I would never have used the F-word."

Betty and Daphne shared a look and clamped hands over their mouths. *This bingo is way more interesting than what I played as a kid.*

The man at the front started cranking the large wheel, and a hush fell over the crowd. Holding her marker firmly in her hand, Daphne focused on her card. Over the speaker system, a voice announced G-48. The game was afoot.

⤞

Halfway through their ten-page bingo packet, a break was called. A window opened in a wall, revealing a concessions stand. Ladies shuffled to go purchase drinks and snacks. Daphne used the opportunity to sit back and stretch out her shoulders and arms. Hovering over her packet with rapt attention had caused tension in her muscles. As of yet, none of their party had won.

"You having fun yet?" Penelope asked her.

"Yes, but it's more intense than I anticipated."

"Never mess with old ladies. We are tougher than we look."

"Oh, Aunt Pen, you are the nicest person I know," said Betty.

"You young people are easy to fool," Penelope smirked. "Don't have enough life experience yet."

As the conversation drifted to family gossip, Daphne let her mind wander. She returned to focus when the topic switched to neighbors they knew in the crowd.

The names were unfamiliar until she heard Penelope exclaim, "Goodness, there's Debbie Kirby."

She followed the outstretched finger to a young woman. The woman was notably young for the crowd, probably in her forties.

"I haven't seen her in a long time. She used to be a regular, but then she stopped coming. I wonder when she started coming back."

Daphne racked her brain. Debbie Kirby. Debbie Kirby. Why did she know this name? Had she come into the bookstore? No, her face was unfamiliar. *I got it! That name is one of the suspects from Auntie Flo's journal.* She tried to remember what Flo had written down about the woman. Nothing. It would have to wait until she got back home.

Over the speakers came the announcement that things were starting up again. On the ninth card, Penelope hooted in celebration. She had won.

With her prize money, she insisted on taking them to a Thai restaurant in town to celebrate. Daphne loved Thai food and hadn't had any since she came to Maine. She was happy to help Pen commemorate her victory. By the end of the meal, Daphne had cleaned her plate.

"Now that is a woman who knows how to enjoy her food. Betty, you should be more like your friend and eat up." Penelope's comment earned her an annoyed look from her niece.

"I'm full, Aunt Pen. I noticed you didn't finish all your food either. Let's get some doggy bags and the check."

"Thank you for taking me out tonight. I love hanging out with both of you. But I am ready to go as well. There are things I need to take care of," Daphne admitted.

They exchanged hugs in the parking lot, and Daphne climbed into her truck. As she turned over the ignition, she said to herself, "Third time's the charm."

Chapter Forty

TAPPING THE NOTEPAD WITH her finger, staring into space, did not inspire a solution. Daphne reread the remarks on the page. Debbie Kirby was Fisher Kirby's wife. Debbie struggled with a gambling addiction. The comment from Fitzy's sister about a woman named Debbie arguing with Flo over scratch-off lottery tickets flooded back. It had to be the same woman.

Flo had made a note to watch for signs that she had succumbed to her vices again. Fisher, Debbie's husband, needed to be alerted at once if evidence was found. The last part had been underlined in the journal. Bingo was technically a form of gambling, Daphne thought, but maybe the Kirbys didn't see that way. Daphne's instincts told her Debbie had given in to temptation again.

While she'd been off about Jackson Puddingstone's LARPing secret and her evidence on Coach Fraser had been pretty flimsy, this was different. Debbie was not only in the journal, but someone had seen her having a serious disagreement with Flo. This was the strongest motive yet.

Flo might have known Debbie and Fisher Kirby, but they were strangers to Daphne. Running to Fisher to rat on Debbie made her stomach lurch. No one liked being a snitch. She couldn't pretend that she didn't know about Debbie's transgression, though she wanted to. Flo had wanted Fisher told and as soon as possible. She must have had a reason.

Tap, tap, tap. *If you don't know enough about them, then get the information.*

Daphne went to Debbie's Facebook page using her phone and did a few quick searches. Amongst the funny cat memes and crockpot recipes were endless photos of Debbie and her kids. A daughter playing the flute at a middle school concert stared at Daphne from the screen. Another post showed an elementary-age boy in a dirty baseball uniform, ready to swing a bat. Listed below the image were supportive comments from Debbie and her friends. *Shit, she's got kids.* Releasing her evidence to Fisher might be like tossing a grenade into that family's home.

But what if Flo had been over at the senior center and happened to see her gambling by accident, just like Daphne? Maybe Flo had planned to tell Fisher, and Debbie got to her first. Was this woman a gambler and a killer? People who battle addictions sometimes did desperate things. Would a woman of two sweet-looking children take a life to play bingo on the down-low? That seemed a bit extreme.

Unable to make a choice, Daphne decided to sleep on it. As she got ready for bed, she prayed that the answer would reveal itself to her by the morning.

When Daphne slept between the fits of tossing and turning, it was full of stressful dreams, including one in which Flo chastised her for leaving her wet towels on the floor. "Clean up your mess, girl. This is a shared space. We both have to keep it tidy for each other."

Rising late, Daphne skipped a latte and went for a double espresso. Over a bowl of cornflakes, she searched for Fisher Kirby's contact information. His advertisement for house painting took mere minutes to find. She tapped the link for his cell number. Daphne knew a well-thought-out speech would be best, but she worried she might chicken out for good if she didn't strike now.

"Hello, Kirby here. How can I help you?" a deep, cheerful voice answered on the fourth ring.

"Hello, Mr. Kirby. My name is Daphne. I'm Flo Winkler's niece."

"Oh yeah. I heard you were in town. Sorry to hear about Flo. She had a good heart."

"Thank you." Few people had nice things to say about Flo, and Kirby's kind words made the conversation much harder. "That is kind of you to say."

"You doing some refreshing over at her place? I tried convincing her to slap a new coat on her house. She was sure it would last a few more years. Lord, she could be stubborn. I can get you a quote if you like."

"Umm. I need to speak with you, Mr. Kirby. It is rather important. How quickly do you think you'd be available?" She grimaced at her misdirection.

"Ah, it's that bad, is it? I can come over this afternoon. I'll see you around one. No, Jim, the blue is in the bedroom, and the gray is for the hall. Look, I'm sorry, Daphne, but I gotta run."

Daphne called Russell, warning him she'd be late but could work a few hours the next day to make up for it. She texted Fitzy next, asking him to move their lunch date to tomorrow. While happy to comply, he asked why. Fearing he might come over and try to stop her if she told him the truth, she typed that she had errands to run.

At ten after one, a dirty pickup truck parked in Daphne's driveway. A tall, slender man got out of the vehicle. A baseball cap covered most of his dark hair. Paint specks dotted his clothes and arms. He waved one hand at her while carrying a clipboard in another.

"Nice to meet you in person, Daphne. I'm Fisher Kirby." He smiled and then surveyed the house.

Standing up from the bench on the front porch, butterflies flew in an assault pattern in her stomach. "Nice to meet you, too, Mr. Kirby."

"Fisher, please. It's not as bad as I expected hearing you on the phone, but it sure could use a new coat. Do you want to keep the same yellow, or are you thinking of something new?"

"Fisher, please have a seat." She pointed to one half of the bench.

He seemed confused, but obliged.

"First, I must apologize. I wasn't clear on the phone. I didn't want you to come over to talk about paint. I didn't correct you when you mentioned it. I know that is a lie by omission, and I am sorry. But I do need to talk to you about something important."

Shifting uncomfortably on the bench, his smile fell. "I've changed up my schedule. I could be on a job site right now. I hope this is worth it. I don't like my time wasted."

"I promise you I am not wasting your time."

His arms crossed over the clipboard. "Okay, let's have it then."

"My Auntie Flo kept a journal. In it, she wrote comments about neighbors. I think she felt like a one-woman neighborhood watch. Anyway, you and your wife were in the book. Flo wrote about your wife Debbie's gambling addiction, and the need to warn you if it started again."

Daphne paused, letting the information sink in. Fisher nodded his head. His body became tight as if he was readying himself for a blow. Reading the disappointment in his eyes, Daphne knew he understood what was coming next. She did not want to hurt him or his family, but she still had to say the words.

"Yesterday, I was in Hinckley at the senior center. I went with some friends to play bingo. Your wife was there as a participant. A friend commented that she had been an active player once but stopped coming. It seems she is returning to old habits. Now, maybe you and her don't see bingo as gambling. But I felt I should tell you. I know it's what Flo would have wanted."

He removed his ballcap and ran his fingers through his hair a couple of times before replacing the hat. "Bingo *is* gambling. If she is doing that, she is probably doing other things, too. I don't want to hear this, but I need to." Fisher rose from the bench. "If you'll excuse me, I have some things to attend to." He marched to his truck. The door slammed behind him before he left.

Daphne shook as she stood up. Gathering her things, she locked the door, got into her vehicle, and headed into town for work. It was barely after her usual starting time.

As she entered the bookstore, the bell rang. Russell gave a quick hello, then rushed out to make it to water aerobics.

Feeling numb, Daphne took up her post on the stool behind the counter. Russell had left behind a short to-do list on a sticky note. Starting at the top of the list, she forced herself to complete the tasks, but she couldn't stop worrying about what she'd just done.

Chapter Forty-One

"YOU SURE YOU DON'T want a side of applesauce?" Parmy loomed over Daphne and Fitzy having their rescheduled date.

Daphne smiled. "I've been making so many jars. I need a break from the sauce, but I'll only be canning more as the month goes on. Ask me if I want some at Halloween."

After Parmy was out of earshot, Fitzy leaned across the booth and whispered to her, "You seem to have made a friend of Parmy. Remarkable. She does not impress easily."

"I have been making progress since I came to Cobb. Parmy's laughing at my jokes. I've made friends out of you, Betty, and Russell. Heck, even Violet doesn't give me the stink eye anymore. I might just fit in here yet."

Reaching across the table, Fitzy took her hand in his. "You fit in here already."

Her phone buzzed. She looked at the display. A text from her mother read, "Are you ever coming home?"

"Anything important?"

She shook her head and shoved the phone back in her pocket.

The red door to Joe's Diner swung wildly open. The chatter quieted as everyone gaped at the woman who'd entered the establishment. Her shoulder-length brown hair looked like a rat's nest. Wrinkles covered nearly every inch of her clothes, and her purse swayed back and forth like a weapon. It took Daphne a moment to realize the woman looking around the restaurant in a crazed fashion was Debbie Kirby. Their eyes locked, and Debbie swung the hand holding the purse toward Daphne.

"You! You homewrecker! How dare you!" With claws out, she charged towards Daphne.

Parmy grabbed Debbie around the waist, stopping the spitting woman a mere foot from her prey. "Whoa there. What is this about?"

"Fisher kicked me out. Said he was going to take custody of *my* children." She started crying. "Because of this bitch!"

Every eye in the restaurant focused on Debbie, then Daphne. Fitzy shrank to the back of the booth.

"I'm not a homewrecker." Daphne's voice rose as she defended herself. "I saw Debbie playing bingo in Hinckley. I simply informed Fisher that she was gambling again. That is the sum of my interaction with either of them."

"Is this true, Debbie?" Parmy did not release the woman who slumped in her arms. "You gambling again?"

Between sobs, Debbie focused on Daphne. "You didn't need to tell him. It's none of your business. Who do you think you are? He didn't need to know. It was fine. I had things under control, and you ruined everything. Why don't you just go back to where you came from, you meddling bitch?"

Turning into Parmy's shoulder, Debbie's body shuddered as she cried and wailed. Parmy enveloped her in a hug.

She frowned at Daphne. "I've got this. I think it would be best if you left."

Happy to comply, Daphne bolted for the door. Fitzy followed her a few beats later.

"I can't believe this." Daphne put her arms around herself. "Without Parmy stepping in, she would have attacked me. It's not my fault she is a gambler."

Fitzy's body was rigid as he asked, "Why did you tell Fisher Kirby his wife was gambling? How did you even know that was a problem for her? I doubt it's common knowledge, or I would have heard about it."

"Flo's journal. She was on my list of suspects. What if Flo saw her playing bingo or buying lotto tickets? Maybe she was going to tell Fisher, and Debbie got to her first."

They started walking away from the diner.

"That is a pretty wild assumption. Do you have proof that Flo knew she was gambling again?"

"Flo knew she had a gambling problem. She made a note to keep an eye out for any relapses. Her notes said she'd tell Fisher immediately if it did."

Fitzy stopped. "Sounds like your Aunt Flo was a busybody. What difference did it make to her what was going on in the Kirby household? It was none of her business."

Daphne stumbled backward as if his words physically punched her in the gut. "She was trying to keep an eye on her community. She wanted to help Cobb. She wanted to protect people."

"Maybe she was lonely, and her journal was a way to fill that loneliness. You've got Debbie all wrong. She isn't a killer."

"You don't know that."

"I think the real point is that *you* don't know. You went too far this time, Daphne. These are real people's lives you are playing with. Are you even sorry for what happened?"

"Of course, I'm sorry."

"I don't know what to think anymore."

She reached out for him. "Fitzy," she pleaded.

He moved away from her. "I need to get back to work."

"Can we talk later? Please."

Fitzy turned his back and stalked away.

She didn't run after him. Instead, she watched him march out of sight and maybe out of her life.

It was as if gravity had just stopped working, and she was floating away and didn't know how to get back down to the ground. Debbie being pissed at her was understandable, if not predictable. But Fitzy's response had come out of left field. He always supported her and could be depended upon. Her stomach flipped. He might not always agree with everything she said or did, but he'd been behind her one hundred percent until today. Just when she needed him most.

The lit neon sign for The Sidecar indicated it was open for business. A dark hole in which to hide sounded good. As the door closed behind her and she adjusted to the dim space, she sighed with relief that the only people in the joint were her and Violet. Daphne saddled up to the exact stool she occupied on her first visit.

Violet raised a curious eyebrow and crossed over to Daphne, clutching a damp rag. "Whatcha having?"

Daphne's first impulse was a Long Island iced tea. But she couldn't handle Violet's silent judging. She needed a drama-free environment. "Soda water with lime please."

Violet gave a short nod, which Daphne interpreted as a sign of approval. *I finally did something right.* Daphne watched Violet make her drink with practiced hands.

"No Betty or Fitzy?" Violet inquired as she wiped glasses, which looked spotless to Daphne.

"Betty is working. She is doing some hideous things with Jell-O while dressed like Audrey Hepburn. Given her petite figure, it is a good look for her."

Violet grinned in agreement.

Daphne forged ahead, knowing a purge of her hurt and anger would make her feel better. "Fitzy, however, was having lunch with me. Then, I had a dustup with Debbie Kirby. It was very upsetting. Instead of comforting me, Fitzy got angry and left me on the sidewalk. I mean, what the heck? I was nearly attacked. I am the victim here."

"Explain the Debbie Kirby dustup, please."

Violet lost interest in the glasses. Bracing her arms on the counter behind her, she listened as Daphne recapped the episode in the diner.

"Then my boyfriend just stomps off." She finally started working on her drink, happy to soothe her parched throat. "I don't understand what got Fitzy so mad."

Violet stood in front of her and leaned against the counter, leaving a foot between their faces. In a gruff voice, she replied, "That's because you don't see what is in front of you. You put your own feelings first."

Daphne sputtered. Soda water sprayed the bar. Glaring at the mess, Violet took a step backward.

"What are you talking about? You hardly know me."

"Oh, I've heard all the stories. People talk in here and I listen. Boy, have they been talking about you. I know you a lot better than you know me. Daphne Patterson, what is my last name?"

"Umm." Daphne blushed. Violet had her. "Okay, but just because I don't know your last name doesn't mean I am self-centered."

"Your world is all about you. Betty and Fitzy are your friends, not because you've put in much effort. You went on and on about your Rat Bastard. Have you ever asked Betty about her prior romances? Do you think she knows nothing about heartache? What was her life like before she moved back home?"

Daphne felt her defenses flare up. "My friendship skills might be a little rusty. I do care about Betty. And what do you mean I'm not seeing what is in front of me?"

"You walk around with your head in the clouds. How about *Phil Nolan*? Wow, you were both selfish and delusional. You only cared about how *you* felt. You had a crush on Phil. When he asked you to go fishing, you fantasized it was a date. He never said it was a date, did he?"

She slowly shook her head.

Violet proceeded. "He even tried to make it clear it wasn't a date. Did he pay for anything? Did he flirt or make a move on you?"

"No, he didn't," she whispered.

"You're not a bad person. Which makes this hard, but you need to see things for what they are. He told me he didn't want you to get the wrong idea. He tried to avoid you afterward, thinking you'd get the hint. But you were so focused on what you coveted, that you ignored anything that diverted from the narrative. A dreamy hot hunk next door to make your problems go away. You never stopped to think about his feelings. You disregarded the signs that were right in front of you."

Daphne moaned and put her head in her hands. She wanted Violet to stop; she couldn't hear anymore. But it wasn't over yet.

"You were in town for two seconds and caused a ruckus at the Fourth of July party. Next, at the fundraiser fair. Quite a show you put on. Now, you cause a confrontation at Joe's. All because you think you are on some holy crusade, never thinking how your actions are going to impact others. You got lucky with the Puddingstones. Their marriage *did* get better, but you had no idea it would go down that way. Yes, you exposed a cheating teacher, but what if he had been an innocent man, and your accusations ruined his career? You are like a wrecking ball going through Cobb. You need to stop and think before you act, Daphne. Real people are getting hurt."

"I don't want to hurt people, but what about finding Auntie Flo's killer? You want them to walk free? I can't do that."

"That's your biggest fantasy of all. Flo wasn't killed. You made her death into something it wasn't. Your theory is frankly ridiculous. You are not some sleuth from one of your books. This is the real world. If you were actually onto anything, Sheriff Allett would investigate. He isn't some country bumpkin, and he cared about Flo."

"You don't get it. You didn't know her like I did."

"It shook up a lot of us that Flo ended things like that. We wish we had acted differently. We didn't know how lonely and sad she was. I feel terrible about it. Most of us do. That is why people have been going along with your idiotic investigation and answering your dumb questions. We feel guilty, but that doesn't make you right."

"No, I'm sure it was murder."

"Stop, Daphne. The truth is hard to face. I know this started with good intentions. You love and miss your aunt. But you'll never grieve her loss until you end this wild investigation. Everyone has been tiptoeing around this because no one wants to hurt you. This absurd plan to lie to you has caused nothing but pain for everyone."

The pillars holding up Daphne's world were shaking. Grabbing some money from her purse, she threw it on the counter and ran out.

Chapter Forty-Two

WRAPPING HER ARMS AROUND herself, Daphne rocked back and forth on her couch. The soothing motion did nothing to calm her down or settle the thoughts storming through her mind. Had she gotten everything wrong? No, it couldn't be. Violet didn't know her, and she didn't have the same insight into Flo that Daphne did. Fitzy's response still felt unjustified. Okay, so she set in motion the dominos that resulted in Debbie's blowup, but it wasn't her fault the woman was gambling.

No one was listening to her side. She didn't make a public accusation to Debbie in the restaurant. She'd learned her lesson after the first two fiascos, hadn't she? Fisher came over and they had a private chat. No one needed to find out about the whole thing. She couldn't have been expected to know what he would do with the knowledge. If he kicked Debbie out, he probably had good reason.

Debbie was the one who'd fallen back into her old addiction. Daphne hadn't tempted her with a poker game or taken her to play the slots. She just happened to be in the right place at the right time to see the truth. But if she was right, a small voice asked her, then why did it all feel so wrong?

Usually, she would have reached out to Fitzy for reassurance. She had gotten used to his help figuring everything out. But he wasn't talking to her. Her stomach clenched with fear that he might never speak to her again.

Betty. Daphne would call her. They were best friends. Betty would take her side about Debbie. Betty would tell her that Violet was being mean, not honest. Her hands shook as the phone rang.

The voice that came out was flat and formal sounding. "Hi, Daphne."
Betty knew. Daphne's heart sank.

"Hey, Betty, have you spoken to Fitzy today?" She had to ask.

"Yes, he called me not long ago. I heard about Debbie Kirby and the diner. I've gotten several texts about it. Word is spreading through town like wildfire."

"Shit. I guess that Fitzy told you about our exchange afterward."

"He mentioned it. I've never heard him so upset."

"I didn't know that would happen after I told Fisher. I couldn't have known the actions he'd take. Debbie almost tore me apart. Flo wrote that Fisher needed to be told right away if Debbie started gambling again. I had to do it."

"No, you didn't." She sounded tired. "You made a choice, Daphne. There are ramifications to your actions. I understand you did not intend for this to happen. But many people are upset. I'm unsure how I feel about this."

"What did Fitzy say?"

"I'm not answering that. That's between you two. I am not going to reveal anything. If Fitzy wants to tell you, that's fine, but it's his story to tell, not mine."

Daphne swallowed a sob. "I understand. You're in an awkward position. At least you're not laying into me like Violet."

"Violet? What does she have to do with this?"

"I went into The Sidecar afterward. I needed a place to think for a minute. Then she started going after me, saying I live in a fantasy world and only care about my own feelings. She even had the nerve to tell me that I was wrong about Flo's death. That I couldn't accept the truth, so I continued my investigation. Can you believe her?"

Silence. Five torturous heartbeats thumped in Daphne's chest.

"Daphne, I think it is time for a reality check. When you told me the evidence of the limes, I thought there might be a chance. You were excited about the journal, and I figured we could have some fun. No harm would come from talking about possible suspects. But the more I thought about it, the weaker your theory felt. Then you started accosting people. Good people. You had no evidence, but that didn't stop you from making public accusations. You've ruined lives, Daphne.

"It was funny, when you went after Jackson and we learned about his LARPing. The coach wasn't innocent, but he wasn't guilty of murder. You stopped talking about it after you and Fitzy started dating. I figured you gave it up, but I guess that was wishful thinking. Enough, Daphne. People's goodwill can only stretch so far."

"Is that how Fitzy feels?" Daphne's head began to spin.

"I won't talk about his feelings, but I will talk about mine. I knew how he felt about you. Being a good cousin, I helped bring you two together. But you didn't notice him. You were all about Phil, which I understand. The heart wants what the heart wants. But after the fishing trip, I knew it was going nowhere. If Phil liked you, you'd know."

"Why didn't you say anything?"

"It wasn't my place. You're your own adult person. That was something you needed to figure out for yourself. I was happy for you both when you and Fitzy finally got together. In so many ways, you two are a great fit. However, in the last month, I've observed some troubling trends. You like him because he makes you feel good. He treats you well. But do you like Fitzy the person, or do you like how he worships you? Do you respect him?"

"Of course I respect him."

"I'm not sure you know who he is deep down. Can you tell me his favorite things? Who are his friends? What makes him happy? You have been in Cobb for three months. In all that time, I've never heard you commit to staying here for the long term. Is this thing between you and my cousin real to you or a summer fling? When things here become boring and difficult, will you cut and run?"

"Whoa. You never said any of this before. Why are you saying these things?"

"I didn't think I needed to, but things have changed. I don't want people hurt. Maybe, you should take a little time to be by yourself, look at your actions, and figure out what you want."

Chapter Forty-Three

UNABLE TO MOVE, DAPHNE stared at the quiet phone. Fitzy wasn't talking to her, and now neither was Betty. Everything felt out of control. Trying to quiet her mind, she decided to focus on one thing: Flo's murder. If she could solve it, she'd prove she was right, and they would forgive her earlier mistakes. Sure, she hadn't spent any time on the case for weeks. Enjoying life seemed more important. It was time to give Flo all her attention.

She had accused three suspects from the journal. All fell apart under examination. Maybe she should remove the journal from the equation. Perhaps Flo was simply keeping an eye on her neighbors, trying to keep them safe. Without it, what was Daphne's best lead?

Flo's mystery lover.

Every tiny clue ended in a dead end. How could she find out who this person was? Penelope no longer seemed like a candidate, and she hadn't even hinted that her best friend had a lover. Who else knew Flo, talked to her often, and liked her?

Then it hit her: Turkish coffee.

Flo had been a frequent visitor to Cemil Kaplan. He'd spoken fondly of her aunt. Had he been Flo's lover? Maybe, maybe not, though he might know who was. Adrenaline surged in her veins. There was no time like the present. She had to see a man about a mystery.

The gravel and leaves crunched underneath the truck's tires as Daphne parked at the bait and tackle shop. She'd considered possible conversation starters in her head during the drive. None hit the right tone. There was no way this wouldn't be awkward. Giving up on perfection, she decided to jump without a safety net. She grabbed the inscribed book from the passenger seat and marched into the building.

Behind the counter, Mr. Kaplan tended to a customer as the scent of coffee beans surrounded her. Attempting to look casual, Daphne ambled up and down several aisles. Luck was on her side. The man cashing out was the only person in the store. By the time she reached the front, the stranger had left.

A friendly smile blossomed on Mr. Kaplan's cheeks. He waved her over to his coffee bar and began his magical movements that would result in his rich, dark brew. "Haven't seen you in a while. Have you decided to give fishing another try?"

"Fishing? Never. Why would you think that?"

Mr. Kaplan nodded to the book in her hand.

Gripping hard on Flo's gift from the mystery lover, she shook her head. This was her opening. "But this is what I wanted to talk to you about. Here, please take it. It belonged to my aunt. I want you to look at what is written on the first page."

He glanced over the cover and back of the book. With care, he opened it to read the inscription. His eyebrows shot up, and he took a step back. "Goodness. This is a very sentimental item for Flo to have in her keeping."

He handed the book back.

"Have you seen this before?"

He shook his head.

"You're right about it being unexpected. I never knew this side of her. I have been trying to figure out the identity of this mystery person. They clearly meant a lot to her. She kept the book for a long time. I can't help but wonder if the person isn't somehow connected to her death."

"Do you suspect them of murder?"

"Maybe. They would be a logical choice. It's my last chance to discover who killed her. At least if I had a name and this book, the sheriff might reopen the investigation. I'll admit, I'm desperate."

"If certainty will give peace to your soul, I will tell you this. The person in that book did not kill Flo."

"What? How can you know?"

"Because I know. This book is old. Flo's romance ended decades ago. If violence had been their goal, it would have happened back then."

She watched him place the finished drinks in front of them.

"Do you know why they couldn't be together? Why she had to die alone?"

"The other person chose someone else in the end."

Daphne chewed her lip. Her last chance was slipping through her fingers. "Did Flo tell you about this person?"

"Yes."

"Can't you tell me more? Who were they?"

"No, I promised your aunt never to tell another person. I can reveal no more. I've already said more than I should have, though I think Flo would've made an exception to help you. She never gave up hope that you would come back one day."

"I wish I had. I could have known her more. Maybe things would have been different."

"I can tell you this about your aunt. She was strong, kind, and, yes, lonely at times, but she had a heart large enough to fit all of Cobb inside. Remember those things about Flo. Not her sad end."

The bell over the door rang. Someone was coming in. With a nod, Mr. Kaplan turned toward the customer. The two cooling cups of coffee sat on the counter, untouched.

She didn't know what to do next. She'd been wrong. Daphne stumbled towards the truck. She felt as if a bear had pounced on her, slashing until it reached her heart and ripped it apart.

Chapter Forty-Four

UPON RETURNING FROM KAPLAN'S, all the energy in Daphne's body evaporated. With heavy steps, she marched herself to bed. The next morning, even after twelve hours of sleep, she still felt sluggish. She cradled a half-empty coffee cup on her perch on the porch glider and yawned. The sun, glowing in an aquamarine sky, earned itself a glare.

How dare the weather give her a delightful September morning? A thunderstorm should be brewing, with cracks of lightning in the distance. She wanted a cold, wet, and brooding atmosphere, not a perfect day to head to the beach. It felt like Mother Nature was mocking her.

Then again, maybe a beach day was just what the doctor ordered. Sitting on the warm sand, listening to the waves crash, could help her find her center and figure out how to get out of her mess. Brushing her hair or taking any action to make herself more presentable required too much energy. Her purse and car keys were all she needed.

Everything in Cobb would only remind her of her problems. She roared out of her driveway. She passed the Puddingstone home. Her foot pressed harder on the gas pedal. She couldn't think in Cobb. She needed to escape.

On the highway, she tilted her head side to side, attempting to stretch out her tense neck muscles. A billboard advertised a hotel in the town she and Fitzy had visited. The beach there was as good as any other.

Betty's words replayed in her mind. They hurt, and Daphne wanted to scream aloud that none were true. But at least one thing Betty had said was still bothering her. In the last month, she'd been putting off making a final decision on where she wanted to live.

Her plan had never been to stay in Maine. She hadn't lied to Fitzy. She'd never said that she was moving there. But as the weeks went on and she had delayed choosing what she wanted to do, it made sense that Fitzy assumed she would stay. Being with Fitzy was incredible, and he made her feel treasured. She had been centered on those things. These past few months, her life had been lived one day at a time. Thinking about the future scared her.

This problem did belong to her. She thumped her hand on the steering wheel. Three months was plenty of time to decide. But what if she picked the wrong option? Her heart thumped with fear over making a bad choice. She didn't want to do this.

"Daphne, this isn't that hard. Figure out what you want and do that. What do you want?" she asked herself.

She didn't know.

Sure, she had her goal list. Get away from her mother, start a new job, find love, and live happily ever after. But her plan was thin on details. Where was this perfect place that would give her all she desired? Couldn't someone just tell her what to do?

Her exit appeared, and she left the highway. The first parking lot she found was for a chiropractor. She directed the truck into an empty spot. Her hands trembled as she shifted into Park.

Did she really want someone else to decide for her? No, that *couldn't* be. She hated her mom for doing that very thing. Maybe growing up under her mom's thumb made it simpler to say yes—a survival method. She had become the mouse. That excuse could have worked in her younger years, but not now that Daphne was an adult.

She got a job at college, pretending it was a sign of rebellion. However, many other students had them. Wanting to fit in, she followed the rest.

Her roommate encouraged her to work at the coffee shop and even made introductions. A typical interview hadn't even been required.

Looking at her life, she saw the pattern now. She followed the path of least resistance, avoiding any real challenges. An education in library management was a perfect career choice because it was connected to books and reading, with which she was already comfortable.

Wallace. He made her feel stupid, weak, and never enough. He made her cry. She hadn't liked like how he made her feel, so why hadn't she left him earlier? She let herself become a doormat, and he walked all over her.

Leaving him would have required her to take responsibility for her life. She always blamed him when things went sour. If anything went wrong, she'd blame him. When he was gone and she lost her job, resulting in a move back home, her mother became the reason her life sucked. Refusing to take control allowed her to be a victim of others. When was the last time she took responsibility for anything?

She'd blamed Fitzy for their argument and cast aside his feelings as ridiculous. She didn't allow him to have emotions or thoughts that disagreed with how she saw things. She treated him like Wallace had treated her. He adored her and lavished her with deferential treatment. Was that the only reason she dated him?

"No, no, no," she muttered to herself.

Shifting the truck into Drive, she eased back into the traffic.

The sand felt warm beneath her bare feet. The tide brought in big waves that crashed on the shore. None of it calmed her, another example of her running away from the real world. Violet's accusation of her living in denial burned. Examining every interaction with Phil left her feeling sick. He'd never said the word date. She came up with that one all on her own. In every example, he behaved kindly, but showed no signs of infatuation.

The embarrassment she felt over making a fool of herself with Phil couldn't compare to the shame engulfing her over her murder hunt. The most logical explanation for the limes being on the list but not in the house was that Flo either forgot to get the fruit or to throw out the list. She hadn't been young anymore, and a moment of forgetfulness could be expected.

The most logical conclusion was that her great-aunt had taken her own life.

Daphne gulped in breath after breath. It still didn't feel like enough. Her lungs burned. The edges of her vision became dark and fuzzy.

She felt a hand on her shoulder.

"Young lady, are you okay?" a woman who looked like a retiree inquired. Her eyes narrowed.

The surprise of the interruption worked to help pull Daphne out of herself. She slowed her breathing. "No," sobbed Daphne. "Though, I'm not injured or anything."

The older woman sat down. "What's wrong, dear?"

"My aunt killed herself."

"Oh goodness. That is horrible." The woman began to rub circles on Daphne's back. "Did this just happen?"

"No. Four months ago."

"Four months ago? Did you not know?"

"Yes. Well, no."

"I'm not following you."

"I was told then, but I didn't believe it. I convinced myself someone had murdered her. But now I don't think that anymore."

"I think I see. I'm sad for your loss. Whenever it happened."

Tears ran like a river down Daphne's cheeks.

"I'm Mary. What is your name, honey?"

"It's Daphne."

"Are you trying to figure out why she did it, Daphne?"

"How did you know?"

"That's the first question. The next will be if you could have done anything to prevent this. It is natural to wonder about both. You can't help but ask these questions. However, I will give you a warning. Trying to find the answers will only lead to madness. Even if they left a reason behind, you'll never understand everything that brought them to that point. In the end, the pain of living became too overwhelming."

"What am I supposed to do now?"

"Hurt. Then, wait until it doesn't hurt as badly. The rest of what you do is up to you. What does your heart want?"

"I want to love her. I don't want to let her go."

"Bless your heart. If you want to love her, then do that. Love her with everything you've got. She is more than that one decision. She won't leave you if you hold on to her. Make her a part of your life, and she'll never be gone."

"I've made such an unholy mess of things."

"Again, I'm not following."

"Don't worry about it, Mary. I don't know how I'm going to do it, but I know what I want."

"And what is that?"

"To fix the things I've broken."

Chapter Forty-Five

"Hey there, little brother." Daphne tried to sound upbeat as she wore a path around the kitchen table.

"Hi. I was surprised to get your text that you wanted to talk." Ethan's voice was tight.

"Is this a good time?"

"It's fine. What's happened? Do I need to come home?"

"First, let me say that everyone is fine. No one is sick or hurt." She heard the sigh leaving him. "I'm sorry. I should reach out more."

"The phone works both ways. I'm just as bad as you."

"Yes, but I'm your older sister. I should have set a better example." Daphne gave a chew to her bottom lip.

"I think I just heard Mom in that comment."

"You're right. That's part of the reason I'm calling."

"You want to talk about *Mom*?" Ethan asked.

"No. Yes. Sort of. I want to talk about me. Something has happened. I'm trying to figure something out. But I need someone who knows me and will be honest. Can you be honest?"

"Me? You want feedback from me?"

"Ethan!" exclaimed an annoyed Daphne.

"I'm just stunned. Désolé."

"Nice to know you are working on your French."

"Funny," came his sarcastic reply. "Yes, I can be honest. Are you in trouble?"

"No. Yes. I know I'm kind of mousy about things. No, I'm worse than a mouse. I'm a doormat, which is hard to take. And a woman in town told me I was self-centered. At first, I laughed because the queen of selfishness raised us. But then I began to wonder if she didn't have a point. Do you agree with either of these theories?"

"I have questions. However, to answer you. Yes, you are a doormat. Yes, you are self-centered."

Daphne covered her mouth with her hand. She used the words about herself, but hearing them, bold as you please, from her brother, felt different—harsher.

Grabbing a chair, she sat down, unable to continue her rotation around the table. "Wow."

"Don't feel too bad. It started with Mom. She isn't an easy person. All of us developed strategies to get by. Dad ran away and headed to the golf course, leaving us kids to fend for ourselves. He just took care of himself. Mom is completely self-centered. Our parents are not the best role models, Daphne. No one was teaching us compassion or how to make meaningful connections with others."

"Isn't that the truth? We did have a shitty childhood, didn't we?"

"Mom smothered me, and she barely had a nice word to say about you. In both cases, she was trying to control us. I was determined to be as independent as I could. To never need anyone. You? You just broke down under the weight. Hence, the doormat. No one cared for your wishes or needs, so focusing on your wants made sense. Who else was going to do it?"

"Holy crap, Ethan, how did you get so smart? I'm ten years older than you, and I'm just figuring this out."

She looked at her coffee maker, got up, and started making herself a cup on autopilot. Ethan must have tasted the best coffee in France—probably with crepes, too. A trip across the ocean sounded tempting.

She chastised herself. She was doing it again, avoiding her problems instead of facing them. Breaking this habit would be hard.

"Going away to college changed things for me," Ethan replied. "Joining my fraternity helped a lot. My brothers became like real family. Last year, this guy, Jim, had a bad breakup. He was low. I mean really low. The brothers had a meeting and talked about how to help him. His closest friends were sent to suggest he get some counseling. Then, we took turns keeping watch. Not that he knew we were doing it. We just hung out with him. Watched movies or played video games. We let him talk if he wanted to. Others went to his professors and let them know what was up. They got his assignments and copies of notes from other students. He would have flunked out otherwise. This year, Jim is focused on his classes, laughing, and cheering at the football games."

"Lucky Jim."

"Lucky me, too. I learned how one person supports another person. I'd never seen such compassion before. It felt weird not being so self-centered at the start. Now it's normal. I saw how much Jim improved after counseling, and I've gone myself. I didn't know how broken I was. That was one of the reasons I went to France this summer. I've been making progress, but I worry I'll regress if I go home. I can't chance that."

"Oh, Ethan. I had no idea. I will do whatever I can to help you stay on your path."

"Thanks, Daphne. I will probably need that help come Christmas. Will you be home by then?"

"I don't know where I will be living in December. But I promise I will come home for the holidays this year. I won't leave you hanging."

"Sweet. I know I said you were self-centered. But, Daphne, do you truly think that you *only* think of yourself? You just offered to run interference at Christmas, even though I'm sure spending the holidays at home isn't your ideal situation, either."

"I always blamed my doormat self for staying with Wallace for so long. What if part of it was my self-centered behavior? Would I have noticed quicker how he treated me like shit if I had paid a little more attention to what kind of person he was? When I went to college and first moved to Chicago, I sort of did what you did. I made friends and began to transform into a more complex person. Then, I found someone who treated me like Mom, and I returned to my old habits. I let myself and friends slip away. Sure, he encouraged it, but I didn't stand up for myself."

"Becoming a new you is hard to maintain. That is why I couldn't go back home this summer."

"I'm glad you stayed away. You sound happy. I feel like I am on the precipice of a new me."

"Are you happy in Maine?"

"I was, but then I did some stupid things. But I want to fix it."

"If you are asking yourself tough questions and working on solutions, it sounds like the place has been good for you. Do you think that's why Aunt Florence left you her house?"

"Possibly. It's a nice thought. I think mostly it was to piss off Mom. Auntie Flo could be sassy."

"What's next then?"

"I need to own my shit. Be a responsible adult, make decisions, and deal with what follows. I like the idea of being in control of my own destiny."

She banged the table loudly with her fist. It traveled through the phone, and Ethan laughed.

"Okay. How are you going to do that?"

"I think each problem requires a different answer. I need to start helping and caring about others to overcome the self-centered issue. There is someone I need to give a lot of focus to."

"Someone special?"

"Possibly. Hopefully. First, I have to figure out what I want and work towards getting it. I have to prove that, through my actions, I can achieve things."

"A sound plan."

"Agreed. I think this is our first adult talk."

"That is so sad."

"We could do this more often," he offered.

"I'd like that."

Chapter Forty-Six

Flo, a Few Months Before Her Death

FLO FINISHED HER ENTRY in her journal. Poor Kirby. She'd been having her usual Turkish coffee and chatting with Cemil when Fisher sat down at the counter. His head hung low, he mumbled out an order. She liked him. He was a good family man and ran an honest business. Though he'd been a bit rude in suggesting that her house needed a new coat of paint, he'd politely respected her refusal.

She and Cemil raised their eyebrows at each other. She nodded toward him and then Fisher. She wanted Cemil to ask Fisher what was wrong. Cemil shook his head and tilted it toward her. If anyone were going to ask, it would have to be her.

Flo had stood out in Cobb her whole life. She was tall, taller than many boys until high school. Girls shunned her because of her clothes and hobbies. Boys were confused about how to act with her because, after all, she was a female, even if she didn't behave like the other girls. May had been born with all the social skills and confidence. She made friends so easily.

Her shyness made overcoming her outsider status impossible. Over time, she built up a brassy, take-no-bull persona to compensate. While the community didn't love her and might even try to avoid her, they at least respected her. It was a lonely life, but people's regard, as well as her friendship with Pen and Cemil, made things easier.

Long ago, she'd hoped to have Daphne as part of her world. But that had passed. At least she knew she'd get the last word. A year earlier she'd made a will, giving everything to her great-niece. Wasn't that going to piss Sarah off? The only sad part was she wouldn't be alive to watch the fireworks herself.

The coffee was placed in front of Kirby, and Cemil gave her a pointed stare.

"How are things, Kirby? You look down at the mouth." She cringed. That was more direct than she wanted to sound, but she didn't know how to go about these problems in a gentle way.

"You could say that."

Should she continue or just shut up?

"Work problems?"

"Sort of. My workers complained that their last paychecks bounced. When I investigated it, the money in my account was gone. The bank informed me that Debbie had taken the money out. I have to pay them, but where will I get the cash? We have some set aside for the kids' college. I don't want to take it out of there. But I'm not going to have a choice." He twisted his cup around but never took a sip.

"What did she take the money for? It must have been important."

Kirby let out a harsh chuckle. "Important? She owed her bookie. My wife has a bookie. Seems she's been gambling in secret for a while. Only now, she can't hide it anymore. What am I going to do?"

"What do you want to do? This is a betrayal of trust, but do you still love her?"

"I shouldn't, but I do. If she wasn't gambling, I think I could get past this. Somehow."

"I think you have your answer. Let her know how you feel."

Kirby followed up a few days later. He and Debbie had a serious talk, and she agreed to get help. They would do couples counseling and work things out. But before he left, Kirby made her swear that, if she ever saw any kind of relapse, she'd tell him. She gave her word.

This led her to make his story an addition to her journal. After years of documenting the comings and goings with the police, Flo had felt at loose ends after her retirement. When Daphne left, she wasn't sure of her purpose. So, she began to observe her neighbors. While she might not be able to be close to them, she felt a duty to know and protect them regardless. They were her community.

She'd never expected to find such drama happening right under her nose. She knew that the Puddingstones had a difficult marriage. But when she noticed Jackson's weekend departures, she recorded them to see if she could find a pattern. Indeed, there was one. She could assume why he wanted to run away each month, but what he was doing, she didn't know. Poor Rossi was having issues at work. She saw more and more and began to log the little dramas of her neighbors' lives in a red notebook.

She didn't have an exact plan for all the things she saw. The big picture was that her town had many skeletons in the closet, and behind each door was something painful. She understood hiding secrets and the pain they caused. Hopefully, one day, she'd find a way to take her information and help all those people. By taking away their hurt, it might erase some of hers.

Chapter Forty-Seven

DAPHNE'S PHONE READ TEN o'clock in the morning as she stood before Penelope's home. There was a good chance everyone in the house would be awake. She prayed that Betty would allow her inside. It might have been better to text Betty to ask if they could talk. But being here, it was more likely Betty would listen.

Penelope opened the door upon hearing the knock. Her eyes widened in surprise. "Daphne, were we expecting you? Did Betty forget to tell me, or is this a sign of old age, and I just forgot?" The tiny older woman ushered her inside.

"Your memory is just fine, Penelope. I happened to be in the area and thought I would stop by." She clenched her hands. "It's not too early, is it?"

"Not at all, my dear. Better you as a surprise guest than a family member coming to check up on me. Though my guess is you came to visit my niece." Penelope went to the base of the stairs and called up to Betty, letting her know she had a visitor.

Arriving in the foyer, Betty crossed her arms. "Well, this is a surprise."

"Can we talk, please? Would you at least listen?"

"I don't know."

Daphne put a hand over her heart. "Does it make a difference that the first thing I want to say is I've been an idiot, and I'm truly sorry?"

"It might."

Penelope patted her niece's arm. "She said please, honey."

"Fine. Let's go up to my room."

Daphne nodded and followed her up the stairs. Betty had taken the largest room on the upper floor as her bedroom. Tall windows, draped with rich cream and floral curtains, flooded the room with light. A bay window overlooking the street invited people to sit in one of the high-back chairs and people-watch. Each took one of the seats.

"Okay, I'm listening," Betty said gruffly.

"Like I said downstairs, I've been an idiot. I can't believe I was so stupid and blind. I know I messed up, and I feel awful about it. I don't want to lose you as a friend. Since the day you came into my life, you've made me a better person. I like your humor, the eccentric way you see the world, and your kindness. I love you, Betty. You are my best friend. You are the best best friend I've ever had."

Betty's jaw began to unclench, but she remained mute.

"I know I wasn't as good of a friend to you. A relationship takes work and attention. I did a lot of taking and not so much giving. My priorities were about me and what I wanted. Before I came to Maine, I never fought to keep a friend. It was easier to let them go. Even gruff Auntie Flo had a best friend in your Aunt Pen. But look at what happened to her. It wasn't enough. What if I end up like Flo?"

Betty's face softened. "You are a long way from ending up like Flo. I wouldn't worry about that. I'm glad to hear that our friendship means as much to you as it does to me. I like you, Daphne. It's some of your behaviors I could do without."

"You're right, and I will try and work on them. I hope you'll give me another chance."

"Why? What's changed?"

"Everything's changed. You accused me of not committing to staying here or leaving. You weren't wrong. I thought about it, and the decision was so simple in the end. Cobb has everything I want. Flo's generosity gave me a chance to start my life over. I have a place to live, a new job I like, wonderful friends like you, and a chance at romance—if Fitzy will forgive me. I spent my life wishing for a place to call home. I don't want to leave now that I've found it."

Betty sat on the edge of her chair. "You're staying?"

"Yes. Though, I don't know if it will feel like home anymore if you hate me." Daphne leaned forward and played with the hem of her shirt.

"I don't hate you, Daphne. Are you sure you are committed to staying here and making a life for yourself?"

"I am. I know this will be a challenge, but I've already made a to-do list. Apologizing to you was first on my list."

"Taking a leap like this is tough. I know."

"You do? You are living a dream life and making it all seem so easy."

"Did I ever tell you how I got into YouTube?"

"You told me how you livestreamed yourself falling into a tub drunk," Daphne offered with a smile.

"That was how I went viral. I started on YouTube two years before that. My roommate and I lived in Augusta. We both worked boring, unfulfilling jobs. She suggested we each start a YouTube channel as a New Year's resolution. We thought it was the coolest idea, and both went to work on our channels.

"I have a degree in history and decided to lean in to that. After a month, my roommate abandoned her channel, but I loved it and spent more and more time on mine. I kept on doing it month after month. I realized that I wanted to be a creator full-time. But I would need the support of my family. I was sure they would all think I was a joke."

"So, how did you fix that? I mean, you made it. What happened?"

"Flo. I came home and stopped by to see Aunt Pen and Uncle Henry. Your aunt happened to be here, too. At one point, I went to sit on the porch and drown in my self-pity. Flo joined me and asked why I was unhappy. I told her my problem. My dream of making YouTube content full-time. I knew my family would have an opinion and smother me with what they thought was best."

"I know all about that problem." Daphne's mom came to mind.

"Exactly. Too much outside input can ruin things. Flo told me that, in the end, you go to bed with yourself every night. You need to make sure that you like the person you share your bed with."

Daphne felt a little jealous that Betty had that moment with Flo. "She sure understood life."

"I know. Your aunt was amazing. I always admired the way she marched to her own drum. I decided that I would take after her and stand up for myself. During that trip, I called a family pow-wow and outlined the plan I made for myself. I told them how I needed support, and what that looked like. My family stunned me. They were supportive of my dream. Thanks to Fitzy's cheerleading, many of them were already fans of my content."

"What happened next?"

"I packed up and moved in with Fitzy for a few months. He has more than enough room at his place. Then Uncle Henry died, and I moved in with Aunt Pen." Betty raised her arms to gesture at the room.

"You were brave to take such a risk. I can only imagine what it's like to have such a supportive family."

"You have family support, too. Your aunt left you a house, and because of her, you can live your life how you want. Now, you just have to figure out what you want and go for it."

"I do know. I'm staying. Which means I need a full-time job. I'm going to ask Russell for more hours at the bookstore. Now that business has picked up, he can afford to give me forty hours a week. Next, I need to work on the self-centered problem. I want to help make others happy."

"Do you have an idea how?"

"Yes. I thought about you and Penelope. Both of you have been wonderful to me. I want to return the favor. I know doing your work and spending time with your aunt can stretch you thin, and you feel guilty about not being there for her."

"I wish I could do more to keep her active and not spend so much time alone."

"Exactly. I can help both of you at the same time. What if I took Penelope out regularly? We could go into Hinckley, and she could do some shopping or run errands. Or perhaps lunch and a movie. She'd have a nice day out, and you get an afternoon you don't have to worry about her."

"That would be nice. It would be a treat for her. She is fond of you. I wouldn't feel like I'm neglecting her so much."

"I want to be there for you both. Isn't that what friends do for each other?"

"Yes, and I'm glad you figured this out. I didn't want to lose my best friend either."

Chapter Forty-Eight

THE NEXT MORNING, SHE parked her truck in Fitzy's winding driveway. In her nervous excitement, she'd left early; now she had a few minutes to kill. Taking the extra time, she observed his house and yard. The white, wood-planked home had been built in 1790, with additions made throughout the years. Multiple chimneys rose from the black roofline. A spacious lawn surrounded the home and was bordered by a small wilderness of trees and bushes.

She missed Fitzy. Their radio silence had lasted less than a week, and she already missed him like crazy. Every day, she glared at her phone, willing it to show a text from him, a message saying he wanted to work things out. In the end, she'd texted him and asked to talk. Thankfully, he'd agreed.

The same old argument repeated itself in her head. Yes, in their relationship thus far, he had been putting in more effort than her. She enjoyed him planning outings with her interests in mind, how he listened to her, and how he let her have the final word.

Yikes, that is self-centered. Is that the only reason I like him?

Of course not. They shared common interests, like a passion for Agatha Christie, lighthouses, and learning new things. His kisses left her weak in the knees, and they knew how to make each other laugh.

Betty's accusation that she didn't know the real him hurt, because she worried it could be true. However, she had a plan to make things better, if he would let her.

Daphne marched up to the blue door and lifted the knocker. It was yanked from her hands as the door flew open. Fitzy stood at the entrance with a nervous expression. Had he been watching her the whole time?

"Hi. Thanks for seeing me so early." Daphne studied his face carefully. "I didn't know if you had plans for today."

"Come in." He moved back to let her through. "It's Saturday, no special plans today. I saw you sitting in your truck for a while. I wondered if you'd changed your mind."

"Oh no. I just got here early. I didn't want to impose by knocking too soon."

She followed him to the kitchen. In the nook, she sat on the window seat, and he took a chair on the opposite side of the table.

"I've been pacing the floor for the last thirty minutes, looking out the windows for your truck," Fitzy admitted.

"If I'd known you were ready a half hour ago, I would have come sooner. I was making my usual circles around the table."

They let out matching half-laughs. *It's a start. Now it's time to talk about why you're here.*

"I'm sorry. There are so many ways I've messed this up. Where do I even start? First, I was a jerk after we left the diner. You were upset, and I dismissed your feelings. I didn't listen. That was wrong. Secondly, after talking with Betty, I'm concerned that I like you because of how you make me feel and not for who you are."

"Is that true?" Fitzy held his breath.

"Half-true. That's *something* I like about you, but not the *only* thing. I also like that we have things in common and we can be ourselves around each other. I do enjoy how you make me feel cherished more than I should, but I spent too much time focused on how I felt. I need to make an effort to get to know you better, too."

"I think I had a part in creating that problem, too. I also talked with Betty. It seems she was as direct with me as you."

"You? I screwed up. You haven't done anything wrong."

"She told me I needed to figure things out before I talked to you. She also said to wait for you to make the first move. I was starting to fear you wouldn't."

"I know my faults, but what do you need to make sense of?"

He ran his finger over a nick in the table. "Apparently, I have a goddess complex."

Her brow wrinkled in confusion.

Fitzy continued. "When Debbie came into the diner and said all those foul things, I didn't say or do anything. My brain shut down. I could only think about her anger, words, and how everyone stared at you. These strange feelings were rushing inside, but I didn't understand them. I only knew that they were uncomfortable. I got angry."

"You had a right to be mad."

"Later, I felt like a worm. You were under physical attack, and I did nothing to protect you. I never saw myself as that kind of man."

She wanted to reach across the table, hold his hand, and comfort him. He looked sad and defeated. As much as she longed to touch him, she knew Fitzy would reject her overture. They weren't there yet.

"After I left and talked to Betty, I understood better. I was frustrated about your continual interference with other people's lives. I never liked it. Then I got angry with myself for yelling instead of protecting you."

"Your frustration is valid. But still, there is no reason to be angry with yourself. I don't blame you for anything." She wisely left out that, in the beginning, she'd been happy to blame him.

"Betty also pointed out that being angry with myself was stupid. This next part is so hard to say."

"Then don't. There's no reason to make yourself unhappy."

Fitzy ran his hands through his hair and placed them flat on the table. "I need to say this. Just let me get it out."

Daphne nodded.

"You see, Daphne, I've had a crush on you since we were kids. As we talked in the library that summer, you blew me away. The other girls I knew were nothing like you. You were smart, funny, and very pretty. When you returned to Cobb and I saw you again, I felt like that awkward kid again, pining for this girl.

"I wanted you to see me as this amazing guy, the kind of man you would want to date. I became so focused on winning the affection of my dream girl that I turned you into some goddess figure. I placed you on a pedestal of perfection. You could do no wrong. Whenever you said or did something I didn't agree with, I shoved it away. You were a fantasy, incapable of having flaws."

"Until the diner."

"Exactly. I couldn't sweep that under the rug. I couldn't hide from your humanity any longer. The pedestal broke, and I got mad that you weren't perfect anymore. I didn't know how to reconcile the two versions of you, so I just left."

"Where does that leave us?"

"I'm not sure. I don't want to end this. I know I care about you. But is it the real you or a fantasy that I'm attracted to? How do we get past this?"

"I've got the answer for that one. Given that I also need to learn more about who you are, I came up with an idea."

"I always knew you were smart. Whatcha got?"

"Spend more time together."

"I like this plan so far. Continue."

"We each need to get to know more about the other person. This means fewer date activities and more time spent simply hanging out and showing our true selves."

"So, what's an acceptable outing?"

"Grab a piece of paper. A list will help. We'll make it together."

Chapter Forty-Nine

FITZY SET DOWN THE large cooler on Penelope's kitchen floor with a thud. Daphne gently placed her paper bag on the counter. She was relieved that, since her talk with Betty three weeks ago, she was again welcomed into the house with open arms.

"Okay, let's see what you brought me." Penelope urged Fitzy to open the cooler.

"Everything on your list is here." He popped open the lid. "Lobster meat, cooked and cut clams, scallops, and a huge hunk of cod."

"I love seafood chowder for Sunday lunch," Betty said from the kitchen table. She was peeling a pile of potatoes. "Doing the prep is also a great excuse for missing out on church."

"You better shake a leg with your peeling." Penelope pointed a knife at her niece while arranging the scallops on a cutting board. "Or the family will be here before you're finished."

Daphne took the cartons of cream out of the paper bag and put them into the fridge. On her second trip, she carried bottles of Bath Pale Ale.

"Oh, you got some fancy brews." Betty smiled. "This is more of a gin house, but I won't say no to one of those."

"And maybe, if you're lucky, I will let you have one," Fitzy smirked. "Daphne got those for me."

"It's true. We were at the bar for trivia night. I got Fitzy a draft beer because I know he likes them. But then I learned that he is picky and prefers to drink certain local varieties."

"I didn't realize I'd become such a beer snob. But a man wants what he wants."

"I blame your picky palate on all that time you spent in Boston." Betty finished peeling and started cutting the potatoes into chunks.

"I think it's kind of cute." Daphne gave him a wink. "I got to meet all his teacher friends, too. They sure are smart. The first time I went, our group won a free appetizer."

"My nephew is a clever boy." Penelope patted his arm. "Now, Fitzy, you can be helpful by going outside and cutting some chives from the herb garden for the chowder."

"Yes, ma'am," he replied as he headed out.

Betty paused until he was out of earshot. "Good job, Aunt Pen, getting him out of the way. Okay, Daph, spill it. How are things really going between you two?"

"Honestly? Things are great." Daphne glanced at two doubtful faces. "Seriously. Since the talk, we've been spending lots of time together. I'm letting him teach me chess. Yesterday, he showed me how to use the riding lawnmower at his place. I might want to get one for my place. And it's been nice spending Sundays at church with him and your family and then having a meal afterward."

Daphne thought to herself about the reverend's homily about forgiveness. He'd said, "Christ instructs us to forgive those who trespass against us, as we surely have trespassed against others. I want to remember someone else who needs our forgiveness. This person is often overlooked. We need to forgive ourselves. To sin is in our nature. With God's grace, we can find strength to resist temptation, but God knows we will stumble. God still loves us, imperfections included. We should follow God's example and love ourselves despite our imperfections. Forgive your trespasses, as does God."

It had never occurred to her that she should forgive herself. If she wanted Cobb to absolve her trespasses, she needed to do the same. She was grateful that her friends had accepted her into the fold once more.

"Church fun?" Betty asked.

"Maybe not fun, fun. But enjoyable. I like all this bonding time. My family never had any of these weekly traditions. We occasionally did a Sunday brunch at the country club, but it wasn't the same. Everyone had to look and act perfectly, because if we did anything wrong, someone would comment about it later to my mom, and then she would act as if the world was ending. I also didn't have much extended family nearby, so we didn't hang out with cousins and stuff. I love this."

"And we love having you, too," Penelope said. "I wanted to let you know, Daphne, that the family has noticed that you've been making an effort to connect with us. We all appreciate it and think you are the sweetest thing. I'm so happy you came back to Cobb. I've been having such a good time."

"What's everyone talking about?" Fitzy asked as he set the chives on the counter near Penelope. "I bet it's about me."

"We were talking about church, Mr. Smarty Pants," Betty answered.

"Oh, did Daphne tell you she signed up to bring refreshments for the fellowship period?" inquired Fitzy.

"You need to be careful with that," warned Penelope.

"Why would I need to be careful?"

"Keep it simple," Penelope advised. "A while back, Kendra Wilson made this fancy spinach and artichoke dip with bread. She got stuck bringing that dish everywhere for years. Plain cookies and muffins should be safe enough."

Daphne laughed. She wondered if her mother knew what she had been missing out on each time she pushed one of her children out of the kitchen because they were *ruining* a meal. Preparing dinner with her whole family like this would have been nice. Could that happen one day? She doubted it.

"Thanks for the advice. I will take it under consideration," Daphne assured them. Hey, Penelope, hand me your phone. I will take some pictures of you prepping the food. It will look great on your Instagram."

"Wait, what?" Fitzy stood, still halfway to the stove, with a large pot in his hands.

"Yes, Daphne showed me how to start an Instagram account. For the last couple of weeks, we've been posting pictures of my garden. This week, I learned how to film videos and share those."

"Aunt Pen, what kind of videos are you taking?" Betty asked.

"Mostly squirrels in the yard, trying to get into the bird feeder. They are sly things."

"Penelope has more followers than me," Daphne said. "Those squirrels are popular."

"I don't know what all these likes and follows mean," admitted Penelope. "But Daphne says it's a good thing, and I'm a hit. So, I'm happy. Betty, now that you are done with the potatoes, the onions need to be chopped."

"Oh, Aunt Pen," Betty whined. "I hate cutting them. They always make me cry."

"Don't worry, pal. I'll do it," offered Daphne. "You've done plenty. I'll take a turn."

Chapter Fifty

Happiness radiated from Daphne like the sun's rays. It was the following Saturday, and she was spending it with two of her favorite people.

In the bookstore window, Fitzy carefully arranged the skeleton in a chair, legs crossed, and a book in its lap. He'd taken out Uncle Henry's old fishing hat and placed it on the head. "Ta-da. He looks pretty good."

"It could be a she. Don't be shoving your patriarchy on us," Betty remarked.

Fitzy pointed out the hat.

"Okay, it is Uncle Henry's hat. But a woman could be wearing it."

"I don't like that hat." Daphne put her hands on her hips.

"What's wrong with the hat? It's a great hat," Fitzy maintained.

"I am sure it is the king of fishing hats. I've just had enough fishing for a lifetime."

Fitzy removed the hat.

"I've got a sou'wester hat at home. It will take me ten minutes tops to collect it," Betty offered.

"I love that idea!" Daphne exclaimed. "If only we had a couple of stuffed lobsters to add among the leaves. Only in Maine would you find a display window like that."

"As a matter of fact, I do."

The other two stared at Betty.

"Don't give me that look. I need all kinds of props and accessories for my videos. Okay, I'm leaving."

Fitzy sauntered over and put his arms around Daphne's waist. "Alone at last." He kissed her. She let out a little moan. He began to pull her closer.

She took a step back. "Fitzy, we are in front of the store's display window. Anyone could see us."

"It's early. I left a nice warm bed at dawn to finish your October window before customers arrived," he argued.

"I need to paint the sign. It'll read, 'Are You Dying for a Book?' Isn't that so cute? You can refocus your energy by putting more leaves on the floor."

"Then will we be finished?" He threatened to kiss her again.

"No, the table display is last. I think you can make it until then." She tossed some leaves in his direction.

"Oh no, you don't!" He grabbed two handfuls and hurled them in her direction.

It was on!

"What the hell?!" Betty roared, walking into the shop. "I leave for a minute and come back to chaos."

Daphne and Fitzy looked around them. Leaves were everywhere: in the window area, amongst the bookcases, and down each other's shirts.

"We're sorry," Daphne struggled to get out between gasping laughter.

"You should be. How could you leave me out?" Betty stuffed the yellow hat on her head and grabbed a handful of leaves, running towards Daphne.

Daphne wondered if things could get any sweeter than this. A week later, Daphne found that it could.

A brook bubbled cheerfully as she crossed the uneven path of rocks, attempting to keep her new boots dry.

Fitzy held out a hand to pull her onto the opposing bank. "I told you. You can get the boots wet and your toes stay dry."

He'd presented her with a box over lunch on Monday and explained that it was for a hike he had planned that weekend.

"I know what you said. I'm fighting a lifelong habit over here. Give a girl a break." She gave him a playful shove. A swirl of leaves fell from above. "You were correct about autumn hikes in Maine. The colors are stunning. Almost as good as Michigan's. The bright orange is my favorite. Which is yours?"

Following the trail ahead of them, Fitzy looked left and right. "The deep red is mine. I don't think I told you that it was Aunt Pen who got me into hiking. She didn't like fishing with Uncle Henry. Instead, she'd go for nature walks. When I was old enough, she started taking me."

"How sweet. This brisk air is like breathing in extra-charged oxygen. I feel super pumped." Daphne thumped her chest.

"I don't think it's the air. More likely, it's the Turkish coffee you made us stop for at Kaplan's place. I still don't know why you insisted on going there. You make amazing coffee."

"You don't know if I make amazing coffee or not. You drink tea. Blah. I wanted some Turkish brew, which is a different thing altogether. Also, I hadn't seen Cemil in a while and wanted to stop by and say hi."

"I didn't know you two were so close."

"We're not super close. However, I would like to fix that. He and Flo were friends, and he tells me stories about her. I think he misses her, too."

"I know you said you were sure you wanted to stay in Cobb." He looked away. "I worry that you might miss your old friends and favorite places."

"I don't have a lot of ties in Michigan. My mom always tried to control who my friends would be and pushed me toward a certain set of girls. They were mostly mean, spoiled brats. Nope, I won't be pining for folks back there. Though, I will miss the Great Lakes. Huge bodies of water, kind of like the ocean, but no salt or fear of sharks."

"Sounds like you had a difficult time growing up. Do you have any good memories from childhood?"

"Books." Daphne didn't hesitate. "There was a library not far from our home. At least once a week, I would lie to my parents and tell them I had to get help from a teacher. I would swing by the library and swap out my books. A kind librarian took me under her wing. We'd briefly discuss what I read each week, and she'd hand me a new selection. She turned me on to the *Redwall* series. I got hooked right before I came to stay with Auntie Flo. Who knows, we might have never met all those years ago if wasn't for that librarian."

"Remind me to send her a thank you note."

Daphne pulled out her phone to check the time. No need to rush.

"I promised you'd be back in time," Fitzy assured her. "What are you up to?"

"Betty, Aunt Pen, and I are having dinner and drinks at the Thai place. Then we are going to check out a movie. Pen suggested the latest superhero film. I worry it will be too violent for her. I suggested maybe a comedy. She informed me that most movies today don't make her laugh. She prefers violence to dumb jokes. Superheroes are also easy on the eyes, apparently."

"I could join you ladies."

"No boys allowed. I'll see you at church tomorrow."

"You've got your offering ready?"

"Yes. I grabbed boxes of blueberry muffin mix at the grocery store. Nothing fancy. Plain paper wrapping, too."

"The student has become the master."

Chapter Fifty-One

DAPHNE DRUMMED HER NAILS on the counter of the empty bookshop. When summer ended, so did most of the tourist foot traffic. It made sense that the numbers would drop off. But they were dealing with a free-fall plunge instead of a slight reduction. Even coffee sales were down. The locals who did come in no longer engaged in chit-chat but got their beverages and left.

It happened outside the store as well. At the IGA, people drove their carts around her or rushed to another aisle altogether when they saw her coming. When at Joe's, the weight of angry stares pressed hard on her shoulders. When Parmy reduced her order of applesauce, that was the last straw. Daphne paid her a visit to find out if Parmy was still mad at her.

"I never was mad at you," Parmy assured Daphne. "It's just tragic. The Kirbys are friends of mine. I love Debbie, and it breaks my heart that she is gambling again. She is getting help, but Fisher isn't letting her come back home. He doesn't want her to take him and the kids down with her. I can't blame him. The town is hurting for all of them."

"I probably should have stayed out of it. But I only wanted to help the Kirbys. Flo made it sound vital that Fisher be warned. Why did you reduce your order if you're not mad at me?"

"People aren't eating it as much. Some customers are requesting not to be served Flo's applesauce."

Daphne gasped. "I didn't realize how seriously the town was taking this. How do I fix it? I can try to make it up to one individual at a time, but how do you get an entire town to forgive you?"

"I wish I knew the answer to that. Some people are already past it. Your attendance and participation at church has been noticed. Others are just angry at life in general, and you're an easy target. Keep doing what you're doing. Things will get better."

But how long will that take? Book sales were down, and the empty store meant money lost. Russell had supported her and given her the extra hours she'd requested. Would he have to put her back on part-time, or worse, let her go? She didn't have rent or a mortgage to worry about, but she had food, utilities, and gas to pay for.

She wanted to stay in Cobb. Auntie Flo's house had become her home. She was in love with Fitzy and couldn't imagine life without him. No matter how strong her love was, however, she needed a job. Fitzy probably would offer to help, but she couldn't accept that. She earned her own way now.

If the town didn't forgive her, she realized, her future looked bleak. She'd have to leave. Fitzy might offer to come with her, but she wouldn't ask that of him. Fitzy loved Cobb. It was in his blood. He left the sparkling world of Boston to return to his roots. The guilt of him giving up everything that mattered to him would crush her and pollute her love for him.

She'd finally gotten Betty back, discovered the real Fitzy, and created the life she dreamed of. Now, all of it was threatened.

She got out a piece of paper to make a new to-do list. The page remained blank. The task overwhelmed her. She didn't know how to apologize to the town.

Her phone buzzed.

Fitzy: Are we still on for tonight? My costume is ready. Superman is waiting for his Lois Lane.

Daphne: Sorry, have to cancel.

Fitzy: What's wrong?

Daphne: Headache. Want a quiet night alone.

Fitzy: Okay.

She switched the store's sign to Closed before slumping on the floor behind the counter. She was still there as darkness fell and kids ran down the sidewalk screaming, "Trick-or-Treat."

Chapter Fifty-Two

DAPHNE, FITZY, AND HIS family attended church services the morning after Halloween. Daphne struggled to stay focused. The night before, she'd laid in bed staring at the ceiling, feeling hopeless. Halloween and All Saints' Day, also known as the Day of the Dead, brought Auntie Flo front and center in her thoughts. If the town made Daphne leave, she would lose Flo as well. In her house, among her things, even listening to her records, she felt Flo's presence. If she lost that, she'd lose her aunt again. Her throat tightened.

Reverend McDonald stepped into his pulpit and began his sermon. "A child asked me recently what made saints so special. I told them that saints are holy. The child then asked what holy means. I thought today was a perfect time for all of us to reflect on this. How do you explain holiness so that a child can understand? I explained that holy means set apart, something special, and remembered on important occasions like today."

The congregation nodded.

"Flo was holy," Daphne blurted out, surprising herself.

The church went silent as if everyone held their breath. Most had heard her declaration and turned toward her. Even the reverend stared. Something compelled her to stand up.

"I'm sorry to interrupt the services. But, Reverend McDonald, you said holy means set apart. Flo felt set apart. She loved Cobb, but couldn't find a way to fit in. People kept her at a distance. You said holy meant special. My aunt was special. She was amazing, and few people knew that. And that loneliness must have pressed down on her like an unbearable weight."

Tears streamed down her face. Fitzy tried to tug her back down, but she brushed his hand away. She needed to see this through.

"Everyone knows I've been trying to find out who killed my aunt. I recently discovered that you, Reverend, were behind the campaign to encourage people to go along with me. You're a very compassionate man. Thank you. I want to thank everyone else for putting up with me while I work through my grief."

Fitzy and his family looked at each other, checking to see if anyone knew what was happening. A rash of whispers spread across the congregation.

"You are wonderful people, and I'm sorry I ran through this town like a bulldozer. But Auntie Flo was special and important. She was holy to me. I couldn't accept that she could take her own life or that she had that much pain in her heart. However, I now know it to be true. I guess my point is... I wanted to let all of you know that I am giving up my investigation. The questioning will stop. And I hope you can forgive my foolishness. I never wanted to hurt anyone."

Fighting the sobs, she ran down the aisle. She heard the reverend try to regain control as the congregation burst into excited chatter. Daphne dashed into the cloakroom and cried her heart out. The weight of the words and the truth they held flattened her. She wanted to sink to the floor. Fitzy soon opened the door. He came in and held her while she wept.

They hid in the small room through the rest of the service. The sound of chatter started right outside the door. The fellowship phase had begun. At last, Daphne felt steadier.

Betty pushed her way through the door. "Holy shit, Daphne. That was amazing. I'm so glad I came to church. This town is going to talk about this day for years to come. You two need to come to the fellowship hall."

Daphne shook her head. "I can't face everyone."

"Yes, you can. If you were brave enough to stand up and say all that, you can handle their kindness."

"Kindness?"

"By the time you finished talking, half the parish was in tears. Me included. Everyone wants to say how sorry they are about Flo and to smother you with love. Everyone feels awful about how they ignored Flo and then made you feel like you were unwelcome. With your public apology and acceptance of Flo's death, everyone is now ready to forgive and forget. There isn't a bad word being said about you or Flo."

"Seriously?" Fitzy's eyes opened wide.

"Completely. Let's go, you two." Betty grabbed them by the arms and pulled them from the cloakroom towards the fellowship hall.

Crowds of people surrounded Daphne. She lost track of the number of hugs she received. There were offers of get-to-know-you lunches and dinners. Some shared their memories of Flo, others admitted how Daphne's churchwide confession had touched them. Most offered words of sympathy.

After thirty minutes, Fitzy stepped in. He thanked everyone for their compassion but explained they needed to depart. Daphne sighed with relief and wordlessly let him lead her away. She felt hollowed out and exhausted. He helped her into his car. She closed her eyes and breathed.

Fitzy got in, and Daphne turned toward him. "I love you, Byron Fitzgibbon."

"I love you, too, Daphne Patterson. It was my lucky day when Flo's missing niece returned."

"I'm not lost anymore."

Chapter Fifty-Three

AFTER FINISHING WORK, DAPHNE stopped by a local farm and picked up cornstalks. She'd create a cozy fall vibe by tying them to her front porch posts. Everyone warned the snow would descend at any moment now, but she wanted them for Thanksgiving. A white, mid-sized sedan blocked half of Daphne's driveway. Peeking at the license plate, she saw the car was a rental. She opened the truck's tailgate and carried the stalks onto the porch.

Who did the car belong to? She'd fired off a text to her father a few days earlier, saying that she needed her winter clothes shipped out to her. It was impossible to imagine him flying all the way to Maine to drop off some clothes. The front door opened, and Daphne's jaw dropped.

"I was beginning to wonder if you would ever get here." Sarah Patterson tapped her toe on the wood momentarily, then returned inside.

Daphne collected herself and followed. "Hello, Mom. I had to work. I don't remember getting a call or text saying you were coming." She removed her jacket and hung it on a peg near the door.

"I see you haven't made many changes to the place." Her mother didn't respond to Daphne's comment, but Daphne didn't notice. She was too busy studying three large suitcases sitting just beyond the entrance.

"You don't pack light, I see."

"Your father said you needed warm clothes. Two of those bags are for you. One is mine." Sarah strode to the living room and sat on the couch.

"Thank you." Daphne tried to make herself sound genuinely grateful. *Be compassionate to others. Even if they don't deserve it.* She slid into one of the chairs across from her mother. "I need warmer clothes. But you didn't need to bring them out yourself. Dad could have sent them in the post."

"I found myself with some free time and thought I would come out and see what has bewitched my daughter into staying here for so long."

"How long are you planning on staying, Mom?"

"I think the better question is, how long are you planning on staying here?"

"I had planned to tell you and Dad both on my visit at Christmas. I wanted to do it face-to-face with both of you."

"I'll make sure to update your father."

"Mom, I'm not visiting. Cobb is my home now. I love it here, and I've decided to stay."

"What about your family?" she protested.

"As you demonstrated, we can visit each other easily. It wasn't an issue when I lived in Chicago. I don't see the difference now. I'm even in the same time zone."

"Chicago. *Humph*. Look how that turned out. That failed even with your family only five hours away. Cobb is over a thirteen-hour drive." She shuddered. "How are you going to make yourself a success of it here? Alone?"

Daphne's urge to defend herself roared from within. She tamped it down. Old habits and ways of communicating would not fix their problem. "This is not going to work, Mom. Not anymore."

"What are you talking about?" Red bloomed across Sarah's cheeks.

"I'm sorry if this hurts. That's not my intention. But I can't do this anymore. I'm not going to let you control my life. I'm thirty now. I won't let you bully me any longer. This isn't healthy for either of us."

Her mother flinched as if she'd been struck. A stab of pain pulsed in Daphne's stomach.

"*What*? I don't know what you are talking about. Bully? What an accusation. After everything I've done for you. I've given you the best, every opportunity, and this is how you repay me?" she growled. "I've only wanted to see you succeed."

"You wanted me to succeed based on what success looks like to *you*. You never even asked my opinion. You just bulldozed over me, time after time. All your actions come down to you wanting control. You've tried to control both Ethan and me our entire lives. I don't think it's worked out like you planned."

Her mother leaped up from the couch and began to pace. Her hands clenched open and closed. She looked like a caged animal. A sob broke from her mother. Tears rolled down her perfectly made-up cheeks.

Daphne hurried over. She berated herself. Her words had been too harsh. Impulsively, she wrapped her arms tight around her mother. She expected to be pushed away. Instead, she was allowed to hold her while her mother wept for several minutes.

When the tears began to slow down, Daphne led her mother into the kitchen and seated her in a chair.

"I'm going to make us some hot chocolate." Daphne went to warm up the water.

"Do you have tea?"

"Yes. Is Earl Gray okay?" She held out a box from a cupboard.

"That's fine. I'm surprised you have any. You always hated tea."

"I still do. It's for Fitzy. He adores the stuff. To me, it's vile, but the things we do for love, right?" Daphne smiled as she thought about him.

"Love? You love this boy?"

"Yes. And I think we can call him a man. He's over thirty. We'll come back to this later. Right now, I'd like to talk about what just happened." She sat down near her mom while waiting for the water to boil.

"I've made a mess of things. I only wanted you and Ethan to be safe and well taken care of. I felt that, if I was around, I could make that happen. You're right. I try to control everything. But I do it because I love you two so much. I will admit to being a control freak, but I protest the bully charge." She sniffled.

Daphne understood doing the wrong thing for the right reasons. She felt things would progress if she could meet her mother halfway. "Okay, I rescind the bullying charge."

"Thank you. When I was out of my mind with worry about Ethan's birth, I had to send you to live with a relative I barely knew and had been taught to mistrust. When you returned, I hardly recognized you. I suddenly had a new child in my house. I didn't know what Florence had done to my darling girl. I blamed her for many things that I probably shouldn't have."

"She did nothing wrong. She took good care of me and was there for us when you needed her."

"I know that now. Looking back, I thought I felt angry, but my true feelings were jealousy. In just three months, she connected with you in a way I never could. You talked about her nonstop after your return. I hated her for that."

"Our problems weren't Auntie Flo's fault."

"No, they were mine. When you came along, I had you to love and you to love me. But we didn't connect as I had hoped. I've always wanted to be a part of your and Ethan's lives. But the more I tried, the more I seemed to lose you. Ethan dove into golf and sports, spending hours with your father. Who, in case you didn't notice, spends precious little time with me."

"I'm sorry you felt like that. I wish we could have done things differently." She rose to pour the hot water into a pot for the tea.

"Me too. I messed things up with you first, then again with Ethan. Now he's run away from home as well. In our conversation, you said you hoped I would feel what it was like to lose those you love."

Daphne squeezed her eyes shut.

"I do know what it is like. I've lost you and your brother. I can't remember when I last had your father's love. I'm alone. Worse than that, I'm lonely."

She walked over and laid her hand on top of her mother's. "I'm sorry. I never should have said those awful things to you. I had no idea what you were going through."

"No, you didn't. But I kept all of this from you. We could have fixed our problems ages ago if I hadn't been so proud. I didn't listen to you enough. Now I've lost you." She sniffled.

"Mom, you haven't lost me. You know right where I'm going to be. We can visit and talk on the phone. There is a lot of repair work to be done between us. Maybe we can even start having normal mother-daughter conversations. Doesn't that sound nice?"

She wiped her eyes. "It does."

"I'd like us one day to be friends. That's what Auntie Flo would have wanted."

"I doubt that."

"Since moving here, I have learned a lot about her. She was a decent and generous person. She was just a bit of an outsider. I'd like you to get to know her, just like I've been able to. And if you are interested, I'd like to introduce you to Fitzy and my new friends." Daphne bounced in her seat. "Oh, and you can see the bookstore, and we'll eat at Joe's Diner. You'll love Parmy. I'll take you for Cemil's bait and tackle for a Turkish coffee. We can play bingo with Aunt Pen and her cronies if there is time. They are so much fun."

"That sounds nice, dear. Let's make plans tomorrow. Right now, I need that tea. You can tell me all about this man of yours. I want to see if he is good enough for my daughter."

"Mom." Daphne groaned.

"Sorry, dear. Old habits and all that."

"I'm glad you came." There were a lot of old wounds to heal. She hoped this was the start of better times.

She returned with their drinks and began regaling her mother with all the wonders of Fitzy.

Chapter Fifty-Four

SARAH SURPRISED EVERYONE, INCLUDING herself, by staying a week. Practicing their new skills of honesty and compassion, Daphne and her mother were pleased to find they didn't argue nearly as much. Since the town had forgiven her, Daphne proudly dragged her mom around Cobb.

Sarah found the food at Joe's Diner more palatable than expected. She and Parmy shared stiff hellos during their introduction. But Parmy and Sarah laughed together when Parmy shared the origin story of the establishment's name and how she'd wrangled ownership from her ex-husband.

Fitzy invited the ladies to his place for dinner, grilling steaks to perfection. He made sure Daphne's was well done.

"Are you a fan of theater?" Fitzy directed the question to his guest.

"I love theater. You have plays here?"

"There is a community theater in Hinckley, but if something special comes to Portland, I make a weekend of it."

"I didn't know that." Daphne pointed a fork at him.

"They haven't shown anything I'm interested in recently. We can look together if you'd like."

"Yes, please."

On the car ride home, her mother admitted that Fitzy was intelligent, nice, and very much in love with her daughter. She added that he was a vast improvement over Wallace and that Daphne had finally learned to pick better quality men.

Daphne arrived for her shift at the bookstore with her mother in tow. As Sarah wandered around the shop, Daphne attended to the waiting line of coffee customers. She chatted casually with her clients, asked about their lives, and remembered people's names and favorite drink orders. Her movements seemed effortless as she managed several tasks simultaneously.

"I'm Russell Abbot, the owner. It is a pleasure to meet you, Mrs. Patterson."

"Sarah, please." She shook his hand gently. "My daughter says nothing but wonderful things about you and your store. I've never seen her at work before. She seems quite in her element."

Daphne smiled as she overheard the compliment.

"You can say that again. She was born to work with books. Let me take you around and tell you about what she's done to this tired old store."

Daphne kept an eye on them as they walked between the shelves and circled the entire premises. Russell pointed out all the improvements Daphne had implemented since her arrival. As they inspected the turkey-inspired front window display, she caught Russell saying the store even smelled better.

"Her arrival was a godsend to me." His deep voice carried through the space. "I needed free time to improve my health. I'm feeling the best I have in years, and this place has never looked better. Plus, profits are up. I'm lucky to have Daphne."

"Yes, her work here seems most impressive. I'm sure both of you will be sorry when she leaves." Sarah tossed out a verbal grenade.

Russell looked horrified. "What? Daphne didn't say anything about leaving. I thought she'd decided to stay in Cobb."

Daphne longed to run over and stop their exchange. But a line of customers meant she was stuck at the counter. She had no intention of leaving her post, but she had to wonder what her mother was talking about.

"Oh, she's staying. She's taken with Cobb and can't seem to part with it. However, since she will be moving here permanently, she will need a proper job. She has a master's degree, after all. I know she loves working here, but as a salesperson? I don't think so."

With the last customer leaving the counter, Daphne ran over to join her mother and Russell. "Mom, I can't believe you said that. There's nothing wrong with selling things for a living."

"But all that education, darling. I thought you wanted a job that put it to good use."

"I am. It's because of my experience and knowledge that I've improved the store. More changes are coming, too. I'm planning an online business, a seating area, a book club, and am even going to get this place its own coffee maker."

"She's a powerhouse." Russell grinned at Daphne.

"Then, for all that effort, I think you need to be paid more than a sales associate," her mother argued.

"Oh, Mom. I planned this as a surprise, but you need to hear this now." Daphne and Russell shared a look.

"I don't like surprises."

"I think you'll like this. Russell and I have been talking about me and my future."

"And you're right," he added. "Daphne is much more than a sales associate."

"I've been promoted to manager. I'm getting more responsibility and a raise. That's just for now. After six months of being a manager, we've agreed that I can buy part ownership of the store if I want to."

"Some of that money will go back into the business to help cover the cost of the changes your daughter has planned," Russell said.

"Do you have the money for this?" her mother questioned. "I know you got some from Aunt Florence, but I didn't think it was a great deal. Besides, any money you have could buy security for the future."

"I am not using anything from Auntie Flo. I will cash in my ring."

"What ring?"

"When Rat Bastard—I mean Wallace—and I got engaged, he gave me a ring. He didn't want to get married, but he used the ring as a prop to show off to his friends and coworkers. When I caught him cheating on me, I kept the ring. He bugged me for a few months to get it back. But I wouldn't return it. At first, I was angry, but then I thought maybe we would work things out. Man, I was stupid. Even once I realized that I never wanted to see him again, and I felt I deserved the ring for personal damages incurred."

"Remind me, dear, what sort of ring is it?"

"A circle-cut, 2.5-carat solitaire diamond on a platinum band. Its rating is F color and VVS2 clarity."

"Wait a moment. I remember getting a call when he proposed and not being impressed by the too-small ring with a gold band."

"That's true. But after we got engaged, he told his buddies at the office. The other men began bragging about the gigantic, expensive rings they had gotten their fiancées. They asked Wallace what he'd given me. He realized the budget-friendly ring he picked for me wouldn't work for his image. Without asking my opinion, he took my ring and traded it in. The knuckle-dragger I ended up with got caught on everything. I've got it with me at the house."

Her mother nodded approvingly. "I'll take it back to Michigan with me. I know some people in the jewelry business. I'll get you top dollar for that ring. I agree. It was the least Rat Bastard owed you. I hope Fitzy does a better job when he proposes."

"Mom!" She blushed. While Sarah was too blunt for Daphne's taste, she trusted her mom to get a fair price for the ring. Turning shy, she asked, "What do you think of my plan?"

"I think you've thought this through. It's a sound plan, and I'm proud of you. I like the idea of you being a business owner. I can't wait to tell the women at the country club."

Chapter Fifty-Five

Penelope Clark

BRIGHT SUN AND BLUE skies reminded Penelope of September rather than the beginning of November. Not foolish enough to waste the glorious weather, she moved onto the porch of her home. The heat from the sun allowed her to wear a light jacket. Sitting in her rocker, she observed the objects on the small table beside her. A glass of ice, gin, tonic water, and fresh lime shone in the sunlight. The other items were a frame, a loose photo, and a lighter. By her feet was a small metal bucket. Penelope decided to do some out-of-season spring cleaning.

She sipped a bit of her drink and smiled. Betty had left hours ago. She'd return around supper time, allowing Penelope a quiet afternoon all to herself. Lifting the picture frame, she opened the back and slid out the photo. From the print, a much younger Penelope, Henry, and Flo smiled at her—a familiar card night at their house. Rocking back and forth on her chair, she let her mind slip back several years.

Penelope had let her best friend into the house. "Thank goodness you are here," she'd said, nearly sobbing with relief.

"Pen, oh my. What's wrong? Can I get you anything?" Flo marched her friend into the kitchen—Pen's territory.

"Yeah, a G&T. Don't forget the lime." Penelope plunked down into a chair at the small circular table.

"How could I forget the lime? You've been drinking these for decades. I know your drink and how you like it." Flo won a gentle smile from the sad woman.

"Thanks. I need a real friend right now. I can't believe this is happening to me," she wailed.

Flo took the chair next to her friend. "Here's your drink, start talking. You pregnant?"

"For heaven's sake, we're fifty. I've gone through the change, same as you." She took a slug of her drink. "No, I'm dealing with a midlife problem. Henry has been cheating on me."

"Damn." Flo sat back in her chair. "Are you sure? What proof do you have?"

"Proof. You and your police people are always going on about proof," Penelope growled.

"Sorry, force of habit."

"I have proof. I went to bed two days ago, but I wanted a glass of water. I came down here to get one. I overheard Henry talking on the phone. And don't ask if it could have been work or a friend. Don't insult my intelligence. He could only have been talking to a lover. I remember that kind of talk, though he hasn't used it on me in a while."

"I'm sorry you overheard that, Pen," Flo whispered.

"Don't be sorry. I've seen signs for months now. So, yesterday, I had it out with him. Told him I knew, and this could not go on. I'm his wife, dammit. How could he do this to *me*? Maybe he doesn't love me like when we first married, but I'm owed some respect."

"This is awful. What did he say?"

"We had a raging fight. Henry gave me his word he would end it. But he admitted he'd been unfaithful for years. Years! I feel like a fool."

"You could divorce him. It's not the scandal it once was."

"Scandalous enough, thank you very much. Besides, what would I do? I've been a professional homemaker for thirty years. I don't know anything else. I'm not a modern woman. You have a career to support yourself. You were smart, Flo. You never depended on a man. No, I've made my bed, and I'm going to lie in it. But I'm going to make sure Henry does, too."

"If he swore he would, then he will."

"Thank you, Flo. I needed you to help calm me down and see reason. I know I'm doing the right thing. It's going to be okay in the end. I know it." Penelope kicked back the rest of her drink.

Penelope took the photo in her hands and vertically ripped through the right third. She gripped the torn image of Henry, giving it a crunch, and tossed it into the trash. Taking another drink, she continued rocking. Another memory came forward. This one was from about a year ago, not long after Henry had passed.

When Henry had died, Penelope had nearly collapsed from heartbreak and shock. Her life partner was no longer around. She struggled with what to do with herself. Many of her patterns revolved around him, and with Henry gone, she felt lost. Sharing her grief with Flo was the only thing helping her process the loss. Several weeks after Henry's death, Noah Tippett dropped by with some estate paperwork still requiring attention. Henry had made several bequests to their family members and such. She promised him she would look it over.

Sitting at the kitchen table, she'd spread out the papers. Line by line, she went over the items and made a list on a pad of paper of the tasks she needed to attend to in the coming weeks. The last item stunned her. Henry requested that his fishing pole be given to his "fishing partner" Florence Winkler.

Henry loved that fishing pole. She often wondered if he cherished it more than her. He'd left it to Flo? Tilting back in the chair, she swore she heard the other shoe drop. She'd always wondered who his mistress had been. She'd scanned the church at Henry's funeral, wondering if the hussy would have the nerve to show. Now she had her answer. Yes, the hussy had attended the funeral. She'd sat on Pen's right side.

Henry's betrayal and the discovery of Flo's treachery hit her like a bus. Was her best friend, the woman she went to for comfort about the affair, her husband's lover? She felt sick and hurried to the bathroom to empty her stomach's contents. When Henry had said that he ended his affair, she believed him. She didn't question his promise now. However, giving Flo that fishing pole meant one thing. He wanted Flo to know that, not only had he loved her once, but even though their secret relationship had ended, he loved her still.

Cleaning herself up, she decided to stop playing the fool. Henry was out of her reach; however, Flo could be dealt with. Ending their friendship was not going to be enough. She wanted justice for her pain. The only way to find that now was revenge. She'd make sure Flo felt the same level of betrayal as she did.

After Henry's death, the family installed her great-niece in her home. She loved Betty and enjoyed her company. However, it did nothing to stop her need for vengeance. Thankfully, Betty spent much time on her YouTube business, leaving Penelope time to plan. She decided to go to the master for advice. After reading several Agatha Christie novels, Penelope realized the perfect weapon waited in the flower beds around her porch. However, it was now winter, and the required foxglove would not bloom until spring.

She worked on her strategy and tweaked it over the months. Everyone commented on how well she seemed to be doing. A spark had returned to her eyes. Then, talk began about how her character had changed. She spoke her mind and did what she wanted when she wanted. The word sassy was bandied about. She thought it odd that planning someone's death brought her to life.

May arrived, and the foxglove bloomed. At last, her plans could be put into action. She called Flo, requesting a chat. She insisted it was important, but she wanted it face-to-face. She suggested she meet Flo for her morning ritual of welcoming the new day. Flo could have her usual coffee, and she could have a gin and tonic.

While limes were a staple in Penelope's house, Flo didn't keep them in the house. Knowing that Flo would have to make a trip to get them and thus increase the likelihood someone would learn about the visit, she called her friend the day before, informing her she had picked up limes and would bring them over herself. One less thing to worry about.

On Flo's last day on earth, Penelope awoke early. Upstairs, Betty slept, unlikely to surface before noon. Penelope'd spent years hiking and indulging in nature walks. While her age may have advanced, her walking skills had not abandoned her. Carrying a bag, she trooped the twenty minutes to Flo's house. No car noise indicated her arrival. Between the early hour and abundant tree growth on the street, she had little fear of being noticed.

Flo waved from the front porch, and she returned the salute. They each took a seat on the bench.

"Morning."

"Hey, there, Pen. Looks like it's going to be a beautiful sunrise." Flo pointed to the light beginning to creep above the tree line.

"I'm glad to hear it. Flo, you have been there for me so much these past months, in fact, over the years. You sit and enjoy the sunrise. I don't want you to miss any of it. I'll go in and make our drinks. Let me take care of you." As she turned to walk inside, she could hear Flo thanking her.

Yes, she was about to kill her former best friend. And murder was wrong. But at their age, she reasoned, was she really taking much time away? There was no other way to make Flo feel the same horror and betrayal she had.

From her bag, she pulled out the foxglove powder, already crushed. Putting it in the bottom of Flo's favorite mug, she added coffee from the pot. Worried the taste might be too bitter, she stirred a little sugar into the cup. Then, with practiced hands, she prepared her own favorite drink. With a spring in her step, she returned to the porch. As she sat down, she handed the mug to Flo.

Flo took a sip and made a face. "Hmm, tastes off."

A lie already planned, Penelope answered calmly, "I added some sugar. Live a little, be reckless. We aren't getting any younger." She sealed the deal with a wink.

They watched the sun work its way above the horizon.

"So, what is all this about? You're not a big morning person, Pen."

"True." Penelope noticed that Flo's mug was more than half empty. "I got some paperwork from the lawyer. Noah Tippett, you know him?"

"Yes, Pen, I know your lawyer. He's mine, too. Not a lot of choice in Cobb. What happened with Noah?" Flo downed the rest of her mug, paying full attention to Penelope.

"He had these papers of bequests from Henry I didn't know about. Henry wanted certain things to go to people. The last one surprised me. It had to do with his prized fishing pole."

"His fishing pole?"

"Yes, he left it to you. I couldn't help but wonder why he would give it to you." Penelope observed Flo struggling to keep her eyes open. Her breathing had turned raspy.

"The pole? Did you bring Henry's pole?" Flo coughed.

"I don't have it. It's broken."

"Broken? How?"

"Oh, that was me. I snapped it in half and threw it in the trash. Henry didn't need it anymore and neither will you. You see, Flo, I figured it out. I know you were Henry's lover. How the two of you must have laughed over my stupidity. Now, it is my turn to laugh. You've just drunk poisoned coffee. It's going to look like you didn't want to go on anymore and gave yourself a heart attack. Such a tragedy." She stood up as Flo clutched her chest.

"I'm sorry, Pen," she rasped.

"Don't be sorry now. You should have been sorry then," Penelope hissed.

There it was, on Flo's face, the look of revelation when your best friend stabs you in the back. Here was her justice.

"I was sorry then. I love you, Pen. So much." She sputtered her words. "I just couldn't stop myself from loving Henry, too. Forgive me."

Penelope stood over her former best friend, and part of her felt pity for Flo. No! This woman betrayed her. She needed to learn her lesson. Where was this remorse years ago? No mercy.

"I can't do that, Flo. Goodbye."

She left Flo, clutching her throat and chest.

Returning to the house, she began to erase any signs of her visit. She washed her glass and put it away. She wiped down the counter, then staged the foxglove and other items to make it look like Flo had done this to herself.

She had considered a suicide note but went against it. Too often, a killer was caught with a poorly done note. Best to let the scene speak for itself. Flo wasn't a note sort of person anyway. She put the lime, gin, and tonic she'd brought into her bag and checked the fridge to ensure no green fruits could be found inside. Turning around, however, she missed the to-do list stuck with a magnet on the appliance. The only clue as to who had visited Florence Winkler the morning of her death.

With a nod, she started walking back home. Flo's dead body lay crumpled on the bench. Penelope passed her without a second look.

Penelope ripped the photo in half, crushing Flo's face, before dropping it into the bucket. The last part of the picture joined the others. Using her lighter, Penelope set fire to the corners of the shreds and watched them burn in the metal bucket. She rocked in her chair. A satisfied chuckle emitted from her. What a careful plan she'd devised. But she'd missed the blasted list. That Daphne was a clever girl. Gratefully, the sheriff had thought it was unimportant.

She set down her drink and picked up the loose photo on the table. Flipping over the frame, she slid the image inside and clicked it into place. Turning it to face up, she admired her handy work. Her face, Betty's, and Daphne's were grinning back at her. The waiter had snapped the photo at the Thai restaurant on their girl's night out. Betty then arranged to have a print made for her aunt.

Thankfully, Daphne would never know any of this. Things had gotten a little tense while the investigation was going on. The girl had good instincts, but she was unlikely to figure out the truth without training and proper support. Influencing Betty and Fitzy about the ridiculousness of the claims, Penelope used them to help sway Daphne's point of view. Daphne's budding romance with Fitzy was a godsend. She had been totally distracted.

Pen didn't want to tarnish the beloved image that Daphne had of Flo. Spending the summer and recent months in Flo's home had been good for her. Penelope hoped, one day, that Daphne would join her family through marriage. It would cause such stress for her and the family if they found out the truth. What good would come of it? And with the big mea culpa at the church, Daphne was finally accepted by the town.

Now, Penelope could finish grieving and work on forgiving Flo and Henry.

She made sure the fire was out. The ashes were dumped in the trash, and the bucket was placed in the garage. She removed all evidence of her little project. The porch looked normal once more. A cloud drifted overhead and hid the sun's rays. The air grew colder. Back inside, she placed the picture on the mantel. She looked forward to sharing it with the girls.

"Friends and family are so important."

Chapter Fifty-Six

"DID YOUR MOM GET off okay?" Fitzy asked as he hefted another box from Daphne's porch into the foyer.

"Yes, she was smiling and reminded me to send her love to Russell." Her back protested under the weight of the box she had lifted.

"She and Russell seemed pretty chummy the last few days."

"No comment."

"How many more boxes do we have to bring in?" He dug his hand into his lower back.

"I haven't counted. It would probably freak me out. The box you just brought in has all my Jane Austen novels."

Fitzy shuddered. "Just don't start calling me Darcy. Where are you going to put all of them?"

"You're way more of a Mr. Knightley in my opinion." She looked around at the boxes piled throughout the living room. "I don't know. I'll figure it out later. I might need to get some more bookcases."

"I have room at my place. The place is so old that it has a home library. There are loads of shelves and most are empty."

Fitzy and Daphne stopped in place and looked at each other. Was he offering her storage or was he asking her to move in with him? Did she want to? She loved him, and maybe one day it might progress to living together or something more official. But not yet. She wasn't ready to give up spending time in Flo's house. She needed to grow a little more personally.

"Thank you for offering, but I want my books here. That way, I can get one anytime I need it."

"Okay. Just know that the offer stands. I won't be filling the shelves anytime soon."

"Good, it will save me time pulling everything off to put books in their proper order someday."

"Wait a minute. Are you telling me, in your home library…"

"That I use the Dewey Decimal System? Yes, I do. Does that scare you?"

He gathered her in his arms and whispered, "It makes me love you even more."

Acknowledgments

First to my readers, thank you for picking up this novel. It means so much to me to know that the people and places I created are out in the world. I hope that you took Daphne and the town of Cobb, Maine, into your heart. Please consider writing a review on social media, Goodreads, or with book retailers if you loved the book. In case you are wanting to experience Cobb for yourself, I'm sorry to say it is a fictional small town. However, as a traveler to Maine, I encourage you to visit and delight in the beauty it has to offer.

This book was a group project. Being a writer is something that I couldn't do without my village. I am grateful to the skilled individuals who brought Daphne to life: my editor, Cassidy Sachs; my proofreader, Shannon Cave; my cover designer, Ashley Santoro; and Rachel Agusti for my author photo. Suzanne and Yvonne, your words of wisdom pointed me in the right direction and walked me back from the ledge of insanity.

The constant support and encouragement of my family and friends kept me going. None of this would have been possible without my husband. I love you, Sweetie! Nikki, you are the best of all sisters. You put up with a lot from me, and that's one of the reasons you are the "nice" sister.

It is impossible to mention everyone who assisted me in some way along this journey, but here are a few. Thank you to the Shelby Township Writers' Group and my alpha and beta readers: Kevin, Melissa, Shirley, Francine, Allie, Sonia, and Kara. Your wonderful questions and suggestions helped me create the story I wanted to tell. Lou, I owe you for your brilliant suggestion of the name Cobb.

Questions for Discussion

1. How did the book make you feel? Did it evoke any emotions? Make you laugh, cry, or cringe?

2. Would you have wanted to spend a summer with Flo when you were ten years old?

3. Who was your favorite character and why?

4. Which of the characters' responses were you most sympathetic with and why? Which were you most unsympathetic with and why?

5. Which character did you dislike or disagree with the most and why?

6. How did you feel about Phil after the fishing date? Why do you think Daphne continued to pursue him?

7. Were you wanting Fitzy and Daphne to get together? If so, when did you start to feel that way in the book and why?

8. While very clever, why did Daphne not solve the crime? Is it better or worse for Daphne not to know the truth?

9. How did you feel about Penelope through the novel, and did it change at the end?

10. What do you think happens to the characters after the novel concludes?

About the Author

Jacqui Lents was born and raised in her beloved Michigan, where her life has meandered more like a lazy river than a high-speed expressway. Prior to focusing on her writing and hosting her award-winning podcast, *Jacqui Just Chatters*, she was a high school social studies teacher. Before being Queen of the Classroom, she dabbled in at least fifteen different jobs. She has worked as an apartment leasing consultant, a night receptionist at her Michigan State University dorm, and even a janitor (where she mastered the fine art of cleaning windows).

When she's not reinventing herself, Jacqui can be found throwing axes (responsibly), attempting to conquer her TBR pile, swimming in her loch, or spending time with her husband, who has yet to flee despite her ever-evolving hobbies.

Connect with Jacqui on social media IG @JacquiLents and FB Jacqui Lents Author or by signing up for her newsletter at www.JacquiLents.com

www.ingramcontent.com/pod-product-compliance
Lightning Source LLC
Chambersburg PA
CBHW050013120726
47903CB00006B/1746